Mario 5

Afire

Mario 5
Afire

by

George Hatcher

Warning
Adult matter

This book is intended for adults. Violence and sexual antics are not intended for minors or sensitive readers. Mario is a work of fiction. Fortunately, all the people in the book lived and died only in my imagination. Any resemblance to actual people should be apparent in your imagination too, when you read the book. The story is purely a product of long, boring plane flights leading to flights of fantasy, the wild goose-chasing of a caffeine-fueled imagination, and a dull foundation of years of experience in wrongful death cases. Like Mario, I am no lawyer. Unlike Mario, I do not employ nubile sex groupies, or toss people out of high rise buildings when they get on my nerves.

This is a work of fiction. All of the characters, organizations and events portrayed in this novel are either products of the author's imagination or used fictitiously. Any resemblance to actual events, to persons living or dead, is purely coincidental.

CasaHatcherPress is an imprint of
Pretty Face, Inc.
225 South Lake Avenue Suite 300
Pasadena, CA 91101

For details, contact:
CasaHatcherPress.
http://casahatcherpress.com
(818) 519-2976
Mario5: Afire

Mario 5: Afire by George J. Hatcher
First Edition January 1 2016
Library of Congress Cataloguing-In-Publication data on file
ISBN: 978-0-9983762-26 (hardback)
ISBN: 978-0-9983762-33 (paperback)
ISBN:978-0-9983762-4-0 (ebook)
R:180301
10 9 8 7 6 5 4 3 2 1

George and Molly 1968

My one and only Molly
It's all for you and only you.

Acknowledgements

Jody Clinker, as always thanks for keeping your eagle eye sharp.

Jorge Bouza, good audio production, good voice.

Jason, thanks for the edits. We'll get that next cliffhanger to you ASAP.

If it were up to my collaborator and editor, Allie Bates, this book would still be in edits. Once again, I had to pry it out of her grip. This time she was still marking up the epilogue. We see into the life of things. Now if only you would move a little faster...

Works by George Hatcher

One Wilshire

Fiction by George Hatcher

Ambulance Chaser Series
Mario 1: Woman in Jeopardy
Mario 2: Coming of Age
Mario 3: Risky Business
Mario 4: Free Fall (2017)
Mario 5: Afire (2018)
Mario 6: Flyboy (2018)

Independent Titles
Arabe (2018)
Pretty Face (2018)

CasaHatcherPress Pasadena California

June 1980

Something had jolted me awake. I waited a breath, and there it was. A shrill, strange ring. Phone. Midnight phone calls are never good. They're always news you don't want to hear. Death is only a phone call away. I reached blindly and clicked on the bedside lamp, revealing the redecorated guest room in Sami's London flat. It took a moment to orient my head. At Jason's invitation, we were in London on an unplanned getaway to Sami's London penthouse. When Sami had been alive, Jason and she had had an 'open' relationship, and though her loss had struck me hard, it had been even harder for him. Twenty-one months had passed since Sami died, but I feel her presence here, and take strength from it.

Pixie sat up in bed holding her clenched hand over her mouth as I answered the phone.

"Mario Luna speaking."

"Thank God I got you, Mario. I'm at the end of my rope. I tried your other numbers but they go to—"

"What's up, Tom?"

Tom was breathless as if he'd been running, and his voice was ragged.

"Two masked men got to him when he was on the way to his car. His man got two shots out, killed both motherfuckers. One shot each right in the face, right through their fucking masks."

"Who is he, Tom? Who got shot?"

"It's Oscar. He's hanging on, but he's not conscious."

My heart stopped for a second, a painful jolt. I looked toward Pixie. Her face had gone white. She mouthed the word, 'who?'

I told Tom, "We'll get the first flight home."

I hung up and looked over at Pixie.

"Oscar's been shot."

I said the words, but the reality hadn't really hit. So much has happened since Sami died, and now this. Sometimes I wonder just how I got here, but without a crystal ball to see the future in, what could I have done to make things different? All I could do now is hope and pray for Oscar to pull through.

My name is Mario Luna, but most of the people who matter just call me Boss. I'm not a lawyer. If I were, my job description would be as easy as one word. I am an entrepreneur assisted in various enterprises by my team, Jo, Pixie, Niley, and Letty. I live in Pasadena, alone in Casa Luna, my behemoth of a house. I own a mixed bag of apartments and duplexes which are currently being handled by a management group. I have an open relationship with Melina Marron, my lawyer and girlfriend who lives across the street from me and who owns and runs Marron's Supermarkets. My journey to becoming a master in karate and judo began when I was ten, so it's fair to say I'm pretty good in the martial arts department. Some people say I am an ambulance chaser, but if they say it to my face, they're going to end up with a fat lip or an earful. A chick can get away with calling me that, but I'll kick a guy's ass. I hate that handle. I started hustling new business for lawyers at fourteen, and not once have I chased an ambulance. A lawyer named Jake used to call me that. He claimed it was a compliment, and said nobody generates as much new business as I do. I used to handle client development for Jake. He was number one in my book, and it really threw my life off-kilter when he was found murdered.

My bread and butter was my contact list, the accumulated sources who sent me auto accident case leads. Back in 1975, the attorney Oscar Cooke bought that list. I took off on a world tour, found and—two short months ago—lost a lovely woman named Sami. Considering the impact she'd had on my life, I could hardly believe I'd known her for less than three years. 1975 had also been the year I established an understanding with Oscar, AKA Oz, the lawyer I've worked with ever since. Jake used to introduce me as his client development guru. Oscar introduces me as his international case strategist. He says I work like a man on fire.

The first time someone tried to kill me, I flipped the shooter off the balcony before his bullet took me down. The second time someone tried to kill me, I was in my own bed, and I tossed my midnight attacker out of my high-rise apartment before he could brain me with a baseball bat. The third time, well, I got shot again, but still managed to toss that fucker out a window of my high-rise apartment. The IRA terrorist blast in London just this September that eventually killed Sami is the same one that put me in a coma. I've only been home a couple of weeks. It's been a tough decade getting through my twenties.

What I do for a living, wrangling new clients for lawyers, can be a cut-throat business. While I was working an aviation case in Venezuela, I got kidnapped by competitors, and though I obviously survived that experience, that whole Venezuela situation has been following me like a bad dream. A couple of crazy Venezuelan lawyers are pissed off at me because they are in prison after kidnapping me and dumping me in a coffee warehouse in the middle of fucking nowhere. Even though they have a history of ransoming and killing off the victims of their kidnappings, and they should have been locked up for a hundred years for kidnapping, no one thought those charges would stick. My rescuers planted drugs so the pair of lawyers would at least go down for possession with intent to sell. If they didn't want to go to prison, they should have left me the hell alone. These are rich, vindictive guys who will be plotting revenge, whether or not they are behind bars. The one good thing out of that experience was meeting Pepe Camacho, the guy Oscar asked to rescue me from the Venezuelan jungle. Pepe is Colombian, about as rich and powerful as it is possible for a man to be, and he has decided to be my friend. His sister Camila has become even closer.

Carson, a childhood buddy who followed me into the 'ambulance chasing' business, is now handling my resources for Oscar. I moved on to aviation cases.

Chapter 1
November 1978
Recuperation

"I guess no turkey at your house this year, *ese?*" Carson asked me on the phone. He has called regularly since my return from London.

In September in London, I'd been in a coma. My recovery is what it is. I am underwhelmed at the thought of a holiday and decided to gaff off hosting Thanksgiving this year.

"I can't handle it," I said. "I'm fucking worn out. I feel like I was hit with a hurricane, three forest fires, and the Santa Ana winds. I'm not anti-social, but no way do I want company right now."

"Hey, if you get a case and can't do it, call me. I can do it. I can go with your team."

"I'll keep that in mind," I lied. My team could handle everything just fine. "So far, it's only small stuff. Routine."

"Help me out, Mario. Let me make some of that big green."

"You got all my old contacts," I reminded him. "I was sitting pretty when all I had was income from those sources, the same income you should be making now if you are taking care of business."

"Alright, *ese*, I hear you."

He just didn't get it. I was trying to be nice and not just cut him off. He branched off into reminiscences from our childhood when we were growing up across from Hollenbeck Park. Now he was going on about Señor Chapo, my dog-owning next-door neighbor who had adored Aunt Carmen.

This wasn't the first time Carson had tried to get in on aviation. I'd rather lose a case than involve him in my business. We were cool as far as it went, but it didn't go far. I'd learned my lesson about Carson a long time ago. As a kid, Carson had been a snake. Once a snake, always a snake. A friend, but a snake.

"Hey, you know I prayed for you when I heard about that explosion in London, when you were in a coma and all that."

"The prayers were heard. Thank you."

"No thanks needed, *ese*. You and I ar*e carnales*."[1]

---

[1] Brothers

Chapter 2
November 1978
Return to Normal

Melina kept a tight schedule, so I knew something was up when she wanted to head out for breakfast. It wasn't even Sunday, our regular hang out day.After she buttered me up with breakfast, Melina was at the wheel on the way home. She slowed to five miles an hour—quite unlike her—to rubberneck at a structure that could only be described as four stories of ugly. Two mph. One mph. Next thing I knew, we had pulled over in front of the ugliest building in Bunker Hills. It was the way she looked at me that told me something was up. She had a challenge in her eyes, in the set of her shoulders, in the lift of her chin.

"Let's buy this building," she said.

"No way in hell. Why could you possibly want to buy this monstrosity except to put it out of its misery?" I looked from her to the building. It was even uglier than it had been five minutes ago.

"You must be kidding."

She explained the deal, a fast turnaround investment. The seller had not yet listed the property, and would sell only on condition that the sale would have no contingencies, and escrow would close in thirty days. A deposit of a hundred thousand dollars [2] would be forfeited to the seller in the event that

____

[2] $100,000.00 in 1979 had the same buying power as $356,620.38 in 2017

anything went wrong with closing the escrow on time. He wanted one million dollars for a building that needed two million put into it to make it a useable property. It was a tear down.

"The group who owns the land on either side is planning to develop."

"They own A and C, and you want to hold B hostage," I mused aloud. "B for butt ugly. Diabolical."

It didn't sound like a bad investment. During my last rendezvous with Pepe's sister, Camila Camacho on her plane at Van Nuys Airport, she had indicated that if I ever had an investment, apartments, or anything else in mind, she would be interested. I was already holding four million dollars of Camacho cash in my home safe, money I was holding for her because she intended to buy a house in Pasadena. Every so often, she sent me more cash to add to the pile. Camila wanted more than sex with me, and a house in the Los Angeles area. She was hungry for investments.

The Camachos have money to burn, but Melina is dead set against them. The Camachos were behind the biggest blow-up our friendship ever suffered. This is what happened: Easter of this year when I was in Rome, Melina received some of my insurance papers, and, quite properly, came over to put them in my safe. The problem is, she found the stash of Camacho money. Millions of cash piled in my safe. She has a valid concern that the money is dirty and dangerous. She worries about me bringing disaster on myself. She may be right, but there are two things I cannot ignore. One is that I can never fully repay that debt to Pepe for saving my life; the other is that unlimited money can be made working for Pepe. I'm talking easy millions here. It's so much that I really don't care if the money is, as Melina puts it, smelly.

I approached Melina with the idea of inviting Camila in, and she violently shook her head. "No way, José. Wherever it comes from, that money stinks. I'm staying away from it. Remember the coffee plantation where the kidnappers were holding you? The Venezuelan soldiers who got you out 'discovered' sacks filled with cocaine. Valita said the drugs must have been planted.

Those soldiers and their cocaine were linked to Pepe."

I'd met General Maldonado when I'd gone to get Valita out of Venezuelan custody. The general was a good friend of Pepe's. I didn't doubt the possibility of a drug connection between them, but I sure wasn't going to tell that to Melina.

"I wouldn't be breathing if it wasn't for Pepe. And it was his plane that provided you a free round-trip to London when I was in a coma. He didn't have to send a jet for everyone who cared to come."

Melina looked balky. "I met him. He was so cool, so smooth in person, butter wouldn't melt in his mouth. Keep it friendship. No business. If you lie down with dogs, you get up with fleas."

 I shrugged. "Fuck it. Lead the way to the deal."

Melina's friendly banker, Martin Keating, gave us a signature loan for a million dollars, due in one hundred eighty days. Having as many apartment buildings as I did, I was familiar with financing. Our financial statements were solid, but to get a signature loan, that easily, that fast, it was highly probable that Melina had knocked boots with him to get what she wanted. I didn't ask.

"If something happens, I can pay it off from my stores' credit line."

"If something happens, I'll have to sell something to come up with that much cash," I said. If the worst happened, I could always ask Camila to bail me out from my end of the bank loan in exchange for a piece of the action.

"Trust me, Cuz. This is a good deal. Six months is tight, but I think we can swing it in that time frame."

"Oh, so we're back to Cuz?" I swatted her ass.

"Been Cuz since we met. Why stop now?"

We closed escrow in November before the month was over, in record time, long before the thirty-day seller requirement.

Following the close of escrow, Melina and I headed for the Occidental Tower. We spent a few moments on the observation deck on the thirtieth floor, then moved up two floors to a have a cozy dinner at the Tower restaurant on the thirty-second floor. We shared a number of toasts. One of them celebrated our ownership of the ugliest building in downtown Los Angeles. One of them was for Sami. As I mentioned her name, and we touched glasses, I realized that in the excitement of closing the deal, I had not thought about Sami in the past twenty-four hours. I felt a little guilty, but then, looking at Melina, I wondered if she had concocted this business deal to distract me from the grief haunting me.

I wasn't even close to being over the bombing that killed Sami and kicked my ass. I had good days and bad days. I was still waking up in the middle of the night experiencing random moments from my coma where I was aware and unable to move. I dreamed of the bombing, getting lost in the smoke, searching but being unable to find the injured girl, or finding her and not finding the way out. I'd wake, find myself in my own bed, only recall fragments of the dream, but I would be as shaken as if it had just happened. Sometimes during the day, I still cough, and taste smoke.

As Thanksgiving approached, I wondered if the blast had done something to my brain. Most of the time, I was in a foul mood. My team suffered through it. I don't know how they endured me, or why they didn't leave. I was always growling and snapping at one or all of them. My temper was so short that I couldn't even stand myself. Everyone got a piece of me, except maybe Melina, and she only escaped because she was never around. She got home after midnight, got her massage from Betty our masseuse, and hit the bed only to get up early and start over. As we resumed our old routine, Sunday remained the main day we saw each other. I approached Sunday with the mindset that I could sort of behave for a couple hours one day a week. In spite of my best efforts, the mask slipped and the chip on my shoulder escaped my control, but only briefly, like when Melina nagged me about fulfilling my yearly obligation.

"Fuck, I don't even feel like going to my aunt's house for Thanksgiving," I told Melina.

"Visiting will be easier than hosting. The girls say you haven't been in the car very much. That the last time you left the house was for our dinner at Occidental Towers."

"Don't feel like going anywhere."

A doctor in Pasadena had my charts from the London fiasco, but I had only seen him twice. I didn't want any of the prescriptions he offered me for pain and anxiety. He suggested that I consult a shrink, but I wasn't going to do that.

My team was concerned. Letty didn't have kids, Pixie has her daughter Lainey, Jo is a widow with kids, and Niley is raising not only her kids, but her sister's kids. Seems like they'd have enough to do without keeping an eagle eye on me. The girls were upset about my lack of interest in them, but only Pixie had the balls to mention it.

"Boss, we don't turn you on anymore?" she asked.

"I stay turned on."

"Letty says you haven't even touched her. She's here when we leave, in case you want her."

"Letty doesn't stay just in case I want her," I snapped. "She lives here, not at her apartment. She's not just waiting around to see if I want to fuck."

Pixie's eyes widened. "Wow. Fuck. Boss, defensive much? What's all that?"

We ended up in a hug, me bending slightly, her arms roped around my neck in an anxious stranglehold. Pixie has always been very physical.

"I have to get over something. Not sure what the fuck it is. Maybe my brain is fried."

"Your brain is not fried."

"I was in a coma two months ago, out to the world. Sometimes I don't feel like all of me is here. I left part of me in that hospital bed in London."

Pixie hugged me tighter. "I remember. I'll never forget how you looked in that hospital bed."

Her lip quivered, then she started to cry. I immediately got pissed at myself for what I said. I wasn't looking for sympathy, just an excuse to justify how cold I had become. Not cold, precisely, but my sex drive had vanished. For a guy as sexually active as I usually am, I guess that translates into a whole lot of unreleased tension.

I would have been okay just to wallow at home. On Thanksgiving Day, it was a team effort to get me out of the house. Melina, Letty and Johnson maneuvered me into the car, and Johnson drove us to my aunt's house. Pixie and Lainey, who had been involved in the preparations, had been there for hours by the time we got there. It turned out to be a good day except that my aunt worried me silly with all the attention. I would have felt healthier and happier if she hadn't constantly been reminding me to take it easy. As far as my aunt was concerned, my waking up from that coma was a gift from God, and I needed to start attending church like I used to do as a child.

Pixie and Letty were on the edges of their seats the whole time my aunt scolded me, waiting for me to blow my top. I managed to hold my tongue. Since coming back from London, they were familiar with the angry me. Melina had a pretty good idea how much anger I was holding back. She told me it was probably a combination of losing Sami, plus all the trauma, and that one of these days, I would be back to normal. In the meantime, she said I could yell at her all I wanted to. For some reason, because she said that I could, I couldn't take my temper out on her. Or maybe I was getting over London. I was happy to leave the Thanksgiving table and go home where I could brood uninterrupted, or yell at the walls after the help had gone to their quarters on the far side of the property from the main house.

Camila and Pepe stayed in touch, but not jointly. They called frequently during December but never were they were actually together. Their adopted sister Olga called me at least twice a week while she was flying solo doing Camacho errands. Errands meant depositing money in various countries across Europe and South America.

"Amor, are you well enough to enjoy the holidays?"

"I'm fine. I'm debating getting a tree and decorating the house."

"I'm going to be in Rio for Christmas. You said you loved it there. Come join us."

It was just the beginning of December. I was no more excited about the prospect of traveling to Rio for Christmas than I had been about Thanksgiving, or about December in general. I had an excuse in my pocket, and fired it off. "I'll ask the doctor. If it's okay, I'll let you know. Thank you, Baby, for thinking of me." The thought of visiting for the holiday made me as grouchy as the thought of buying a tree, and stringing tinsel that would just have to be taken down and thrown out.

"All I do, Amor, is think of you."

As it turned out, I didn't need to get a Christmas tree or mess with house decorations. Life snapped back to normal with a plane crash in Portugal. Jason called. A Boeing 727 overran the runway, landed in the ocean and exploded, taking with it more than a hundred and thirty passengers.

It was thanks to Jason that I had moved from automotive accidents to aviation. It was thanks to Sami that I met Jason. He always called to give me heads up on an international case I might be interested in. He used to have the kind of open relationship with Sami that I had with Melina. Though he was still shaken from losing her, and still on leave from his work as an insurance lawyer representing insurance companies headquartered in London, he called me regularly, and insisted that I call him if I needed any help on a case. Sami's death had taken a tremendous toll on him. Most of our interactions were on the phone with the ocean between us.

"Are you okay?"

"I'm getting there. How about you?"

"I'm getting there."

"I'll get you the manifest in a day or so and send it to you."

When Jason gave me a manifest, it wasn't like the list of passengers published in a newspaper. His was the real deal. A manifest included addresses, phone numbers, a great deal of personal information that helped me hit the ground running when we arrived to meet families of victims.

I assured Oscar and Tom that I was fit and on board. Tom promised to have the retainers and firm brochure in two days. Everything was bilingual, English and Portuguese. [3]

Oscar insisted that I take the plane to Portugal. "No point in it just sitting in the hangar. I'm too busy with clients to take off and fly for fun. You know the crew. Why fool around with the bother of airport lines and commercial flights?"

"It seems costly."

When I'd been in a coma, Pepe's DC9 took everyone round trip to London to see me. Must have cost him a bundle. Oscar's plane was an egg beater next to Pepe's jet, but it still cost a bunch to operate.

"Take the plane. Don't worry about the cost. Consider it a business deduction. Sign up as many as you can. Don't worry about the cost of using the Lear. I'll make it up."

"You're lucky, my boy," Tom said. "I wish I could go."

"First class is cheaper," I said.

"Mario, take the plane already," Oscar said.

The girls were excited about the prospect of flying to Portugal in the Lear, but given the nature of what we do, they had misgivings, too.

"What if we run out of fuel over the Atlantic?" Pixie asked. "Camila takes a big jet if she's crossing the ocean. She doesn't use her Lear."

"No problem. The pilots are good. They've been trained to land on the ocean."

"Boss, don't say that," Jo said.

---

[3] A retainer agreement is filled out with client present, but Tom liked to have all the particulars about the crash typed in. The firm book was a nicely bound brochure showing all aviation cases handled by the firm with a brief explanation of each. The book with a photograph of Oscar on the cover is often a door opener, especially to a family of a victim and/or a local lawyer that asks about the firm's experience.

"We aren't going to run out of gas," Niley said, managing to sound like she was saying the opposite.

"I hope not." Letty chewed on her lip.

On the day of departure, no one spoke of crashing or running out of fuel. The hang-up on the Lear was that we were limited on luggage. I took seven suits, shirts and ties, and four pair of shoes. I tried never to wear the same suit twice to a family meeting. Jo supervised so the girls were able to keep the load low, without sacrificing the clothes needed to look elegant and professional. Many will say that clothes do not make the man, but we had to look the part. We were representing a highly respected United States law firm that had the means to fight it out with the giant insurance carriers on behalf of the victims. We couldn't walk in looking like a bunch of hippies, freaks, or California dreamers.

We'd flown enough with the flight attendant, Chastity, that she was our buddy. She had seen the girls bare-ass naked and probably knew what my dick looked like. She wasn't a participant but didn't seem to mind the activity. I finally got around to asking Chastity why we need a flight attendant on a small jet like this. Seemed like an additional expense that Oscar didn't need.

Chastity explained, "While I do take care of passengers' needs, I also take care of the pilots' needs so they can focus on flying. I perform certain protocols at the captain's request, like closing the hatch, and handling and checking out emergency equipment. Also, I'm cleared on emergency first aid."

"What about while we're in Portugal? What are you doing then?"

"It depends. On this trip, we're supposed to be on call till you need us to fly back."

"We're going to stay overnight in Miami," Captain Ron explained. "We can only fly so many hours."

I told the girls, "We'll do the tourist thing in Miami while Ron and Steve sleep."

"After we get to Spain, we need another break," said Steve.

"Cool." I looked over the flight plan.

I closed my eyes as the plane roared down the runway. Small planes like the Lear are noisy and fast. I love the physical thrill. The girls did a grito.[4] Chastity would have been startled out of her seat had she not been belted in.

"I'm coming," screamed Pixie. The girls clapped for Pixie.

Pixie was a comedian with a dirty mouth. I've known her practically all of my life. No matter how bad I felt, she could always make me laugh, though sometimes it wasn't on purpose.

This time around, we didn't provide any sexual activity for Chastity to witness, but we enjoyed the plane. Why fly commercial with a bunch of strangers when there was a jet like this for us to fly in? It takes longer to get to Santa Cruz, Portugal on a Lear than if we had flown commercial. As difficult as it is to get good sleep on a plane, we managed to do it. No one complained about not having cabins and beds, though Niley griped that it would have been nice if we could have had some sex. After we landed, the pilots made certain the Lear was secure at the private airport where it would remain until we left for home. When we landed, we hit the ground running.

Juan, a private eye who is part of my team, was aboard the big SUV that picked us up. He lives in Puerto Rico, and had been here for three days, preparing. I had the hots for Juan's girl Valita, though I'd been the one who introduced them. She had been employed as a housekeeper by the jerk lawyers who had me kidnapped, though her job had been more like slave labor. How she got arrested, how I got her out, and how Juan met her, that's a long story.

"Where is Valita?" I asked.

"She working. Next time if you want me to bring her I will."

"You and she were a good team during the fire case," Jo said.

"You bet," Niley said.

"I bring next time," Juan said. "I got two interpreters. You going to like them. They translate fast."

---

[4] Grito is a howl/scream at the top of your lungs

"Interpreters?" Letty asked, looking out the window.

I was sandwiched between Letty and Jo.

"The language here is Portuguese. Most of the passengers on the plane are from Portugal."

"I thought Portuguese is like Spanish," Pixie said.

"No way," Jo said. "You'll see. It's like Spanish and French had a baby."

"The retainers are in English on the left side, translated on the right side to Portuguese."

"I haven't looked at the retainers," Pixie said.

For clients, we would handle it one situation at a time with a translator/interpreter, when necessary. Like other cases we'd been on, the families of victims were at a hotel. For us, the good thing was that they were in one hotel. It was full, but I wouldn't have wanted to stay there anyway. Our accommodations were two blocks away at the much nicer Hilton where I rented a suite with four attached singles. When I got the keys, the first thing Pixie did is run through all the bedrooms, checking them out. They all had televisions, phones, decent views, identical queen-sized beds, attached bathrooms, and a chocolate on the pillow. The only variation was color scheme, and even those didn't vary by much. They connected in a straight line to the master suite.

"Boss, you could have saved a shitload of money. All we need is one bedroom."

"Pixie, we're here to work."

"It's not like you want us, anyway."

"I haven't been in the mood," I growled. Since the coma, except for Sundays with Melina, my sexual activity had been nonexistent. I didn't like the reminder. The desire was there, but the phantom of Sami and the bombing kept appearing like an emotional cold shower. It totally fucked me up.

"I was joking around, Boss. I just have such a big mouth."

"Pixie, we know. Button it," Jo said.

The master suite wasn't bad. The bed was a king, and the attached living room had a sleeper sofa and a grand piano.

"What a waste," Letty said.

"I didn't ask for the piano. The suite comes this way," Jo said.

Juan had arranged an appointment with a law firm that Jason had recommended although, as in the past, I could not use Jason's name. I already knew that José Bozi was an experienced aviation attorney. He was a slim man, thin, silver-haired, deeply tanned, and favored linen suits and hats. My presentation to Bozi was the same as with other local lawyers I had associated Oscar's firm with in other countries.

"It's a Boeing. We may have product liability, and if so, that gives us a shot in a US court."

"And what if we just have a case against the operator of the airline?"

"In that case, our firm will probably get the case settled without a trial with the insurance carriers in London. We have had a lot of cases there in the past."

"So have I," Bozi said.

"I'm sure you have, José."

"What if we put on our presentations to the families together, and for every family we sign together, I will get our firm to advance you two thousand dollars against your split of the fees?"

Bozi was paging through the impressive firm brochure I'd handed him. His expression changed to one of interest.

"Make that three thousand American, and we'll make this a joint venture. I will handle everything that needs to be handled in Portugal, and your firm handles the case with the insurance companies. If the case goes to trial, it's also on you."

"If the case goes to trial in the US, we handle. If it has to be tried here, you handle."

"Of course, Mario. That's what I meant."

"Meet me halfway," I said. "Twenty-five hundred, but only for adults.

Minors under 10, no advance on fees."

"Make it three thousand[5] for adults only. Minors under twenty-one years I get no advance unless the decedent is married and has dependents."

The negotiation showed me that Bozi knew the business. Getting compensation for minors is difficult.

"Deal," I said.

We shook hands. Once a retainer was counted, Oscar would immediately wire Bozi's bank account.

"Mario, I must mention I've never had a deal with a foreign attorney before. If we get lucky, we could sign many cases."

I smiled. "We will sign a whole bunch of cases."

"I like you, but other than this book you gave me about the law firm, I don't know this Oscar. I don't know you, but you are here and we just shook hands."

I wasn't sure where he was going, but my smile was fixed.

"I don't want anything to happen to my attorney fees."

"Nothing will happen to your attorney fees."

"You will be responsible for my fees?"

Without hesitation, I replied, "Absolutely. Oscar is a straight up attorney, and there is no way he would cheat you or anyone."

Bozi extended his hand. We shook again.

"Don't let him disappoint me, Mario."

He had been recommended by Jason, so I let it pass, but he was becoming creepy. His insecurity reminded me of the *pendejos* in Venezuela who ordered my kidnapping. They were lawyers too.

José Bozi called a press conference the next day. He introduced me as the representative of a very powerful American law firm with years of aviation experience. For the first meeting, Jo, Pixie, and Niley arranged catering at the hotel where we were staying. Twenty families showed for the meetings. Two

---

[5] $3,000.00 in 1979 had the same buying power as $10,698.61 in 2017

days later, the girls arranged for the meeting to be held at the families' hotel. We didn't hear anything from the airline operator, but Bozi heard in the wind they were furious that we were gathering the families and soliciting them.

"We are not soliciting," I said.

"Don't worry about it. We're in Portugal, not America. I will handle this."

After a week, I realized we were in for a long stay. I called the office.

"Oscar, the pilots and Chastity are just using up dollars at their hotel. It's a waste. And I don't want to feel pressured or rushed."

Oscar ordered the plane and crew to return to Los Angeles.

I won't say the job isn't stressful. After the recent loss of Sami, I had a renewed sympathy for what the families were going through, and sympathy hurts. Sometimes the girls mentioned something that made the families ask about my health. It wasn't that the bombing or the coma became part of the spiel, but it was just something I was having to live with. I've been successful because I had always connected easily with the victims' families, but on this trip, I felt a tighter bond. Maybe it was my imagination, but I feel it was because they had their ghosts, and I had mine. It wasn't always smooth, but with this kind of volume, kinks are expected. A family we had signed that had lost two loved ones met with me in a conference room at my hotel. There were three family members. The decedents' father explained that a lawyer from Chicago had offered them an advance of five thousand dollars to sign with him.

"If you are sure you prefer to change attorneys, there is no problem," I said. "It's like I told you before you signed the retainer, you can discharge us. I just want to be sure you feel you are doing the right thing."

"Mario, we're so sorry but we need the advance. Your lawyer can't give it to us?"

"I can help you with a little, but it would be from my own pocket. Lawyers are not supposed to advance money to their clients. It gives the appearance that we are getting you to sign with us for the money. I'm sorry."

Jo handed me the retainer they had signed.

"Are you sure?" I asked once more.

They left with the original retainer.

Bozi caught up to me. He was not happy. His wrinkled, too-tanned mouth was pursed in a rigid grimace that showed exactly how unhappy he was. Being mad made him look ten years older and not so hip. His silver hair was perfect though.

"In Portugal, when a client signs a contract, they can't just come back and say they changed their mind."

I smiled at Bozi. While working with him, it felt like he had become my friend.

"In America, we don't force clients to stay with us. If they want to split, we give them a big hug, give them back their retainer, and wish them luck. It pays well in karma. You'd be surprised how often they come back."

"This cost me six thousand dollars,"[6] he said, referring to our advance agreement.

"We have cases being signed every day. We're going to get the rest of the plane."

The next day, another family walked. An Illinois lawyer, Robert Lewis, was torching us with the five-thousand dollar advance, way too much money to advance a client from the get-go. In case of a complaint to the bar association back home, it would not look good. From a business point of view, the client could take the money and fire us somewhere down the line and there would be little we could do about getting the advance back.

"You are too soft," Bozi complained.

"I'm not soft. Here, touch my biceps." I put one arm up for him.

Bozi pulled his hand away, and walked off growling.

Our former client had told me that Robert Lewis was staying at my hotel. I dialed the front desk to connect to his room.

---

[6] $6,000.00 in 1978 had the same buying power as $23,326.76 in 2017

"Robert Lewis is not here, Mr. Luna," the hotel operator said.

"When did he leave?"

"I don't have that information," she said. "Let me transfer you to the front desk."

"Robert Lewis is not a guest here," the desk attendant said.

"Can you double-check? I was told that Robert Lewis is here."

"I see that the Lewis Law Firm reserved a room, but the man in the room isn't Mr. Lewis. He is a representative of the firm, a Mark Adams. Would you like to be connected?"

"Please."

Adams's voice came on the line. I introduced myself, and dived right in, believing we would easily come to a meeting of the minds. After all, we did the same thing for a living. We should be able to understand each other.

"Mark, do us both a favor. Stop offering our clients five thousand dollars to fire us. A whole lot of families do not have lawyers yet. Why mess with our clients?"

"From my end, it looks like you already have the whole plane."

I took a couple of deep breaths before I responded. "We don't have the whole plane."

"Like I said, looks that way from my end."

I heard the sneer in his voice, and a click as he hung up on me. I had to do something about this situation before it escalated. Bozi was giving me a hard time. I could not let this asshole get away with doing this.

I went down to the front desk. Five dollars to the pretty receptionist got me Mark's fifth floor room number. Ahead of me, a couple of travel-worn families were waiting for the elevators to open, but the lights above the elevators showed them both lingering on the tenth floor. I looked at my watch, and waited a minute or two.

Fuck this. I plowed through a glass door to a showcase of a stairwell. The landings were brightly lit with comfortable chairs, in a setting like a greenhouse with a mass of potted rubber trees, and ferns growing toward big windows. The stairs were fully carpeted except for a mosaic on each landing with the floor's number. Grass cloth covered the walls, and gold art deco sconces cast warm light. I saw all this at a run, while taking the stairs two at a time, getting a little angrier with each bound. Mark ought to understand that the whole plane was an even playing field up until the families signed their names. From that point, it was hands off. I turned on to his floor and would have taken the hall at a run, except there was a couple in front of me going into their room. I jerked to a stop. We nodded politely at each other, and I walked sedately past them, waiting until they were inside before I knocked. I'm glad they were there, because it gave me a second or two to put the brakes on.

I knocked.

Mark Adams answered the door.

I saw his room at a glance. Not a suite. His suitcase was out, and he hadn't bothered to put his things away, though I could see the closet had suits hanging in it. He was wearing a white undershirt and what looked like pajama bottoms. His hair was sandy, his features soft, like he was made of wax that someone had heated and slightly melted. His lips were wet, repellent, and his tongue appeared too big for his mouth.

He looked a little startled. I waited for him to invite me inside. He didn't, but I walked in anyway without introducing myself.

"Mario Luna," he said. "I just talked to you on the phone."

I was a little surprised that he knew my name. I'd never seen him before.

"Right. I came here to finish the conversation we were having until you hung up on me. Stop messing with clients who have signed retainers with our firm. Stop bribing poor families with money. Just stop. I seriously doubt Robert Lewis knows what you are doing, but I don't care if he does or not. Stop this shit."

"I don't tell you how to get your clients. You're wasting your time telling me what I can't do."

He shrugged, swigged the last of his beer, and crushed the can. I got a nose-full when he waved the crushed can in my face. He smelled like a one-man keg party, stale beer, cheap cologne, body odor, and cigarettes.

I batted his hand aside.

Color rose in his face. I actually saw the color rise up his throat till his whole face turned bright red, and his mouth contorted into a strange, big-lipped frown. He was a large guy, almost eye to eye with me, and heavyset. He was very out of shape, but I could see he was accustomed to bullying to get his way. I was not here to be bullied. I was here to make a point.

"Stop fucking with our clients."

"Fuck you, man," he said, stupidly. He took a step toward me, got practically nose to nose.

My patience was wearing thin.

He batted at me again with the hand holding the crushed can. He had to be stupid. He would break his hand if he kept holding his fingers that way. I poked him with what Cosmo used to call a knife hand, directly in his sternum. It wasn't a hard blow, but it doesn't take much in that spot. He wheezed, dropped the can, and his left arm rose up to protect the vulnerable area. He gasped for breath, flailed his right arm at me. I dodged it, easily.

"I'm not afraid of you, man. Fuck you," he gasped.

He didn't seem worthy of a punch. I slapped him.

"Motherfucking punk. Stop bribing our clients, or else."

"Or else what?" he sneered. He took another swing at me, but didn't come close to a hit.

I punched, a short jab aimed at his chin, an uppercut. His jaw snapped shut, and he squealed. His mouth filled with blood, not so much from my blow, but because his mouth had snapped closed, and he bit his tongue. Okay, well, maybe the way I hit him had something to do with it.

I wrapped the collar of his undershirt in my hand, winding it a couple of times till his air was close to being cut off, and his feet barely on the ground.

"You come around one of my clients again, and I will ship you back to the states in a wheelchair. Got it?"

His arms went up in resignation, and his words followed suit. "I'm sorry, man. Sorry. I give up."

I dropped his collar.

He fell backward at least a foot, and he waved his hands like he was carrying the white flag of surrender, or maybe he was just trying to get his balance.

"I don't want to come back here, and believe me, you don't want me back."

He mumbled something, a mouthful of apologies. He seemed to have trouble standing on his feet, either because of me or the beer. Probably a combination of both.

I took the stairs to our suite on the tenth floor, walking them two at a time, with no problem. I had been taking it pretty easy since the coma, but I guess I was in better shape than I thought. I wasn't even out of breath. I felt better than I had in months, ready to take on the world.

Christmas snuck up on me while I wasn't looking. It was my team who made it real. There was no Christmas tree, no decorating, if you didn't count a couple of glass ornaments the girls had hung in random spots in the hotel room. Glass Christmas trees made out of prisms that were suction-cupped to the window. A paper-maché Santa Claus on top of the tiny refrigerator. I don't know where they got tinsel, but it was on everything. I gave room service a bundle of bills to leave it alone until December twenty-sixth. I think the mistletoe on the showerhead was Pixie's doing. Even without a tree, the girls made it special. The girls and I celebrated in my suite. We had room service go all out. *Bacalhau da Consoada* was on the menu, a Portuguese tradition, a fancied up preparation of cod. The girls ordered a lot of seafood, and one of everything on the dessert menu. Room service delivery was performed by a guy dressed up as Pai Natal, the Portuguese Santa, who must be a twin of the American Santa, and he was accompanied by three elves who did all the heavy lifting and smelled like they'd been celebrating early in the kitchen. Then the girls called home and talked to their families, and listened to me as I called my aunt and Melina. Several bottles of champagne later, we hit our own beds. In the morning we exchanged gifts we had gotten at the local market. I had bought a local craftsman's entire inventory of handmade gold jewelry. (To be fair, it was a good price, there wasn't too much of it, and it was beautifully made.) I parceled it out in six leather pouches I'd bought from another local. I put all the cuff links and oversized rings in a pouch for Juan, and made sure that Valita had a share too. I'd also picked out a little personal thing for each of them: guitar strings and a fancy pick for Pixie, a little glass animal for Letty's collection of little glass creatures, a charm for Niley's gold charm bracelet, and a big purse for Jo. The girls had picked out stuff too, so I had things to open. Mostly gag gifts, but I loved them. There was no sex, and no one complained. I don't know if that meant they were content, being polite for the holiday, or they were still worried about my health. I knew better than to bring it up though, because if I had, they'd have wanted to talk about it.

We spent Christmas day hitting tourist spots in Lisbon. The whole city glittered with the season, and I think we all got drunk on it. We sat on a park bench in the night, and watched the locals sing Christmas songs. The park and church looked so holy, I felt like I'd been to church. When we got back to the hotel, I called my aunt and told her about it. She told me she'd been thinking of me. I don't show it to her often enough, but I do love my aunt. She's been mother and father to me my whole life, and sometimes I wish she had an idea of how much she matters to me. I was glad the girls had gone to bed, because I didn't want them to see me crying. I do feel things more deeply this past year. I think most of the time my team wants me to be a rock, but now I have to work the facade, since the coma.

I was so busy meeting with clients that all thought of Adams and his

Chicago lawyer boss got shoved to the back of my mind. I didn't mention anything to Bozi, but every day, he asked me if we had lost anyone else. As the days passed, it became a joke. I didn't think of Mark again until seven days later. Bozi made his joke, and I realized we'd lost no retainers for a week.

I never said anything to the team or Bozi or anyone about my visit to Mark's room. But maybe it had done me some good to let off some steam.

"Boss, you don't seem as stressed," Jo said. "You laugh more. You found your smile."

"The grumps is gone," Letty said.

"Maybe the next good thing will be that we can all start fucking again," Pixie suggested.

"Oh, your mouth," Niley said.

"Fuck you, bitch."

Instead of telling them to stop like I always did, I let them rattle on. It was after hours, and we were drinking wine in the suite. I was still in mourning for Sami, but I was feeling better. I don't think I'll ever come to terms with her loss. At least now I felt that I could learn to live with it, as I had learned to live with losing Harry, Jake, and Tanis. My fluctuating mood was getting some notice from the home team.

Camila showed up with no warning. I got a phone call from the airport after she landed. Two hours later we were in bed in another suite.

We fucked for hours.

"Christmas in Rio was nice. I wish you could have made it."

"Me too. I've been buried in this case."

"Of course, you have. There's always next year."

Our bodies were sliding on steaming sweat. "You are amazing, Amor," she said in Spanish, out of breath.

"I missed you. It's been so long."

"Too long. I flew here to see you, to be with you like this. Do you think

I missed you?"

I didn't respond in words, but our bodies grinding together had no problem communicating just how much we missed each other. I felt a hint of guilt that I'd been so cold to my team.

I find myself especially attracted to strong, independent women. Women like Camila, Melina, Olga and Sami—may she rest in peace—they are rich, but the attraction has nothing to do with their money. To steal a line from a John Wayne movie, they have true grit. They have backbone.

Sami, a woman who didn't have to work, put herself in a profession in service of children. I had never talked with her about her specialty, but I know she chose pediatric oncology to give her life meaning.

Camila, two years older than I, independent, flying all over the world at a whim, involved in mysterious businesses. Olga, one year older, bouncing all over the globe carrying millions of dollars in currency and diamonds and who knows what else.

Melina, when I first met her, was just starting out. She had the property she'd inherited from her parents, and her seed stake from her father's life insurance. Her business had been nothing but an idea in her head. She made it real. Melina was driven, even before her first place of business had been fully constructed. When we first met, she'd been determined not merely to follow in her father's footsteps, but to reinvent the family market to a huge supermarket, much like a Safeway and other chains. Now she is a commanding force in her field, always looking to expand, involved in all aspects of the business from the ground up, managing a small gold mine, a big fish in the not-so-small pond of Los Angeles County. Like Pygmalion to her own Galatea, she had created herself. Except for one thing, our relationship would be perfect. She hates that she's older than I am. I don't care about age at all. As far as I am concerned, her being ten years my senior is nothing. She looks like a twenty-one year old.

The lure of these women is more than their power. The attraction is also mystery. It is like they are the opposite of my team. I love my team, but I know them well. Coming home to my team is coming home because I know what to expect. They are familiar, domestic, trusted like well-worn jeans, comfy socks, or the safety and congenial welcome of one's own bed.

A week later, when Camila returned to Portugal, I had been fore-warned. I'd been expecting her arrival. I was happy. The girls, not so much.

Pixie saw me leaving, and snarled, "I hope she's on her period, Boss."

"Not called for," Jo said. Letty and Niley had just looked shocked.

"Oh, you don't bleed, bitches?"

"Seems to me all of you should be grateful to Camila and Olga for the trip to Hawaii. They hosted you and treated you like fucking royalty." I re-minded them.

"We are grateful, Boss. Pixie is just nuts."

"I'm sorry, Boss," Pixie said. "I can't help it. I don't want to share you with an outsider."

"No strings," Jo said, her voice light. "We're all free agents. You know this."

"No problem," I said, stealing the last word. I usually avoid it, but I can be mean when the situation calls for it. "If Camila has her period, there's always Olga."

I met Camila at the airport. Thirty minutes after she landed, we took off for Paris. When we checked in at the Hotel Ritz, we got a two-bedroom suite. Olga was a beauty for my eyes to feast on, and with her around, I walked around with a hard-on. I was beginning to think I was physically well, or almost there. When we were alone, I told Camila about the ugly building investment.

"Amor, let me in on something you buy. Be nice."

"I may have to. If I don't make the deadline, you can be my safety net."

"Amor, we have many types of business in many countries."

"Compared to what you're used to, this deal is tiny."

"If you are involved, there is nothing too small or too big."

"No shit, Baby." I didn't know what to think of this blanket proclamation. "Thanks for that."

She narrowed her eyes, and looked at me considering something in her head. "We are not counterfeiters if that's what's behind that look you just gave me. We have a lot of cash looking to be placed. Real cash."

I was sure of that. The one thing I knew for certain is that they had a lot of money, however it was being earned. "Can I ask you something straight-forward?"

She nodded.

"Personally, I couldn't care less where money comes from, yours or anyone else's, but not everyone is like me. I'm not an expert, and have no experience with other countries. In the States, there is scrutiny over where investment money comes from." Melina had told me there was a lot of scrutiny in the US.

"Amor, our money can pass any test."

I didn't ask what she meant by test. I smiled as if her reply were sufficient for me. "Baby, don't get upset about my question. If the money wasn't clean, I wouldn't expect you to tell me it was. It's not like I know the difference between clean and dirty money anyway."

She put both of her hands on mine and squeezed reassuringly. "Amor, come to me when you need a partner in any business investment, no matter the size."

"Baby, I don't care if you're a mobster like in the movies. You, Pepe, and Olga are my friends. I treasure your friendship."

Her brown eyes were warm on me, but too serious for my mood.

"Plus you're a hot chick."

That never failed to make her smile. The wattage on her smile doubled.

"We treasure your friendship, too."

We weren't in bed, but I reached around her back and undid her bra. She laughed and slid it through the armholes of her shirt. The room was a little chilly. Behind the red silk shirt, her nipples stood at attention, but she still wanted to talk about money.

"Amor, just before Christmas I bought diamonds in Budapest in exchange for cash. Now I will use the diamonds to buy something else that will get that money in to our bank accounts."

"You don't need to tell me this," I said, kissing her. Olga had already made the money-laundering clear, but had not called it by name. I tried to think about the kiss, and not that money exchange Camila had just described. My mind skittered around what Melina would say if told her about this. I doubled my efforts to get Camila thinking more about sex and less about finance.

Camila kissed me back, but she wasn't done talking. "I don't want you to be afraid to bring me an investment. This is not a Godfather movie."

"I loved that movie. Saw it twice."

"I did too."

"Right now, I am more afraid of your ignoring certain pressing matters."

She flexed against me.

"Very pressing matters."

 "Amor, you are so special to me."

She dropped the money talk. Finally.

My body was busy appreciating her moves, but my brain was still churning. There are those that say my client development work is soliciting business for an attorney and is, therefore, dirty, and because of it, my apartments, house and proceeds are dirty as a consequence. But it's not true. It's just name calling. Sticks and stones don't hurt me. Find me laughing all the way to the bank.

"What did the girls say when you left them in Portugal?" Camila asked.

"They're so busy, they probably won't notice me gone."

That was a lie, of course, but there was no reason to bother Camila about it.

The break with Camila one weekend and Camila and Olga the week-end after was like an oasis to me in a desert of work. After forty-two days on the Portugal case, we flew back by commercial airline.

We arrived at Casa Luna and the girls went straight for their cars. I made Jo promise to get some rest before delivering a hundred and six retainers to Oscar and Tom. We had a partner, so all the fees would not belong entirely to Oscar, but the split to José was only twenty percent of the attorney fees. That gave Oscar eighty percent to play with. So far, José had done very well with the deal I made to give him $3,000 for each person over 21 years old.[7] It was a lot of money for Oscar to front, though Oscar would recover that money by deducting it from Jose's split of the attorney fees. As for what that much money meant in LA? An experienced, high-priced legal secretary made between two hundred and two hundred fifty a week. [8] Three thousand dollars was a whole lot of money.

The housekeepers welcomed us home. Miguel appeared in his whites and greeted his cousin Letty like she'd been gone a year. Eventually, he shook hands with me.

"Boss, what would you like to have for dinner?"

"Surprise me," I said. "No, surprise Letty and me." I looked at my watch. "Bet she'd kill for a hamburger right now. She hasn't had a burger since we left LA. Let's do dinner in two hours. Letty and I are going to spa the trip out of us."

Miguel smiled. Letty had used the spa before, but I'd never announced it like an event.

We did the sauna, the steam, the ice spa and the hot spa. There were three showers, but we used one. I lathered that pretty body of hers and she did me in kind. I guess the Portugal trip fixed what had been broken in me in re-

---

[7] $3,000.00 in 1979 had the same buying power as $10,698.61 in 2017
[8] $250.00 in 1979 had the same buying power as $891.55 in 2017

gard to sex. Maybe seeing Camila and Olga had stimulated my senses. Being with them had kicked me out of the dumps I had been in. The passage of time had something to do with it, too, though it really hadn't been long since we lost Sami. Letty being there with me for the entire night and waking up to her in the morning was a treat. I enjoyed every minute. I used to feel lonely at the apartment when everyone left, but I knew Melina was just down the hall. Rattling around in this huge house, how can one person not feel lonely? I knew I could always hop in my Rolls and go clubbing, pick up chicks, bring them back for a night of fun. I had not done it since Sami died, though. Mostly, I liked being in my house. Letty stayed when the team left every afternoon. I was fine.

"Are you a morning person?" I asked. We'd moved from the spa to the couch in my workout room. Still hadn't made it to the bedroom.

"You mean morning person like waking up, or liking morning sex?"

"It's morning somewhere," I said.

"I like it like this in the morning." She turned, and gave me her back. I spooned her, cupped her breasts and pressed my body against hers. The couch cradled my back, and surrounded us in the scent of suede and soap.

"Kiss the back of my neck, please," she whispered.

I moved slowly inside her. Our bodies moved, but the friction where we were joined was fierce.

One good thing about having my own cook was breakfast at any hour. It was still dark out when I ordered breakfast. Letty spent the night in my bed, woke up there too, and then I asked her to join me in a room Melina called the oriel, a beautiful oval room with ceiling to floor French windows, and a round wrought iron table with a very thick glass top. By the time we took our seats, the sky was starting to lighten.

"When are the girls coming back?" Letty took a seat at the table. She was wearing a pony tail, and smelled like lemons and cinnamon. I think when

I showered, she snuck into the kitchen and started baking with Miguel again. She smelled delicious and vibrated with energy.

"I told them to take a week off. They need time to be with their kids. We were gone forty-two days. The week off goes for you too."

"I wouldn't know what to do with a week off, Boss. I'm here for you."

"I feel bad the girls didn't take me up on coming back for Christmas to be with their families. Last year they flew home, then back to Puerto Rico after Christmas."

"We had fun in Portugal. Christmas and New Year were a blast."

Miguel set an omelet on my place mat, a heaping serving platter in the middle of the table, and a hamburger in front of Letty. She gave him a huge smile. I laughed at the hamburger for breakfast, but understood how much she'd been craving them.

"Nothing in the world I missed more than a good burger, except for one other thing. Not having sex. I'm so glad the dry spell is over. Boss, thank you for last night and this morning. So good."

"You're thanking me because we had sex? Come on."

Letty always cleared out of my room before the girls arrived. The sex was not a secret. Sleeping in was.

"If bedroom walls snitched, the team would bitch, and they'd be justified."

I served myself two sausages, and a slice of fried ham. Letty buttered a slice of wheat toast, and put it on my plate atop a heaping pile of potatoes. No doubt she had picked that up from Pixie. Niley buttered my toast too.

"You need to do one of two things."

"What?"

"You can't live back there with the housekeepers and Miguel. You are not a domestic anymore. I should have moved you. You can move to an apartment, one of mine or something you find here in Pasadena or wherever."

"You're kicking me out." Letty frowned, and sipped her coffee. "That's option one. I make enough to afford an apartment. I can do that, sure. You said there were two options."

"You officially move all of your things to the guest room you use. But you have to understand, it's not a commitment."

"What will the girls say if I do that? And what would Melina say?" Letty's brow furrowed.

"It doesn't matter what the team says or what Melina says."

Letty stirred her coffee. "What do you prefer?" She didn't seem to have an opinion of her own.

I thought about it. I loved her availability. I called her on the intercom, and she'd be there in minutes. If she lived in a guest room, she would be even more convenient. But while I loved her availability, I didn't love her like a full-time commitment. I did not want to be around her all of the time. When she was around, I was glad I was not alone, but I wasn't celebrating that it was her.

"I prefer you get your own place. You can stay over anytime you want. I just want you to have an address of your own."

"Done, Boss."

We returned to my bedroom. It was early, still daylight. The bed was made. Letty pulled off the comforter and extra pillows while I sat in a chair and watched.

"What is it, Boss?" She looked at me coquettishly over her shoulder. She'd already shed her clothes, and used the pose to her best advantage. She was slim in the right places, and padded in the right places, and didn't mind showing off her body. She got off on it.

"You're a hot chick, Letty."

She gave me that sidelong look, and pulled the curtains closed. I'd taken Sami's cue, and had blackout curtains installed. The room went pitch black.

We slept for hours. The door to the bedroom opened, and I instantly woke up. Letty stirred a little.

"Hey Cuz, you brat. You didn't even call to let me know you're back."

There was just enough light for me to make out Melina moving through darkness towards the bed. I had no idea of the time. She stopped. I extended my arms to her, and beckoned her to come to me. Melina placed her body on mine and kissed me. She was fully clothed, sprawled on top of me, her lips on mine. I pulled the sheet away so there was nothing between us except what she was wearing.

"I missed you," she said.

Letty sat up. "Oh, I'm sorry. I'll leave," she said softly.

Melina said, "Go back to sleep. It's just me."

I pulled her hard against me, and laughed.

"What did you do with your panties?"

She moved like she was going to get up.

"Oh, I'll go get them if you—"

"Don't you dare," I said, pulling her down on me. "I missed you so much."

I lost track of everything as Melina kissed me again, deeply.

It was five in the morning when my body clock kicked in and woke me. Melina had already slipped away. I really didn't know if she'd just left or if it had been five hours ago. Letty was still asleep. I'd erased the jet lag. I hadn't been working out the way I used to, but my body clock didn't seem to know that. In September of last year, after waking from a month-long coma, I'd been warned to take it easy. I had scheduled a checkup with the local doctor I had only seen twice. I wanted his go-ahead to work out, but once I decide something, it is hard to wait. I went down to the gym and exercised for more than an hour, lightweight stuff. It was irritating that a couple of months not working out made me feel out of shape. The gym work tired me out more than it should have, and I was going to hurt tomorrow. I sat in the hot steam, then showered, shaved, and put on a robe. I walked to the kitchen for coffee. Miguel was already there.

"What time you want to eat, Boss?"

"Not for a while, but I'm going to be starved. I could eat a horse."

Letty was not in my bedroom. I walked around the guest rooms, but she wasn't there either. I called her on the intercom.

"Where did you go?"

"I came to my place to shower," she said through the intercom.

"Take your time. We'll eat breakfast when you get back."

"Are we taking the day off?"

"Fuckin-A," I replied.

"Awesome."

Two hours later, I got a call from Jo.

"Boss, I'm going over to see Tom Jones to deliver the retainers. Everything is organized. They should be able to pick up, and run with it."

"I'm sure it's perfect. Go back home when you're done."

"Are you sure?"

"I said a week off, and I meant it. I'm sure. Pass the word on to Pixie and Niley to stay home. Rest and enjoy your families. I can only guess how much they missed you."

"Thanks, Boss. Call if you need me for anything." She hesitated, then asked, "Is Letty looking after you?"

"Letty is around. When you get back, I want you to help her get an apartment. One of mine or whatever she wants."

"Is she paying?"

"She's making good money now, and that's what she'd expect. If it's one of ours, make sure the management company gives her a deal. Deposit not necessary. I'm friends with her Boss."

Jo laughed. "Sure Boss. I'll handle it."

It was time to hang up, but I didn't, and neither did Jo. I just sat on the line.

"I'm not a mind reader, but there's something on your mind," Jo said.

"Tell me."

"I came close today to sticking Letty in a guest room. But it would be like she's shacking up with me, and using the guest room like an excuse. I wish I could have all of you here with me. I get fucking lonely when you all go home. Letty runs over here when I want her. It's convenient. Sometimes I think it is fucking wrong of me to use all of you, and more recently, Letty."

"Who is using who, Boss? Since when are you so parochial? It's a new world, free love, and all that. Swinging is in. I think sometimes we're the ones keeping you from tying the knot with Melina. Maybe Letty shouldn't get her own apartment. Just let her stay. No one cares." Then she added, "Melina might care but only you would know that. We're all open about it, and we want you too. Honey, I know we joke about it, but we all love you. It may be a joke to you, but we're your office wives."

I had to laugh. "I'm sorry I've been a prick lately. I—"

"Stop it, Boss," Jo interrupted. "No need."

"I like the office wife thing. I forget who told me that before. I think it was Letty when she asked me if the office wives approved of her."

"If Pixie, Niley or me, want to get laid, we're free agents, as free as you are, right?"

"Of course."

"Well then, don't feel so obligated. When you hear us bitch about not having sex, blow it off. If we want it so bad, we get a vibrator out or we get a Sancho[9] somewhere."

She laughed again.

By the next week, Letty's stuff was installed in an apartment in Alhambra in one of my buildings. It took a single morning for the girls to buy apartment essentials. Jo, Pixie, and Niley helped Letty pack her clothes, move, and unpack. I didn't go, but Miguel went along for the heavy lifting. They were all

---

[9] a man who steals another man's girlfriend is often referred to as "Sancho"

so competitive, each one with her own ideas, that I knew it would be a madhouse helping Letty arrange her new pad. Since I was the one putting distance between us, it seemed strange to go over there. I hoped she continued to spend her time with me and not at the apartment, but at least I would know if she was with me, it would be her choice, and not like she had nowhere else to go.

I caught Miguel rushing back from doing his part in the move, on the way to his room to change into a clean chef coat, though I knew there were at least half a dozen of them hanging in the chef's pantry closet. He must have showered at Letty's new place. His longish hair was tied back in a ponytail, but it was still wet, the furrows of his comb evident. He was wearing an undershirt that emphasized his body-builder physique, and he didn't seem at all tired. Everything Letty owned had been contained in a sadly small supply of boxes, though there'd been more clothes than I'd have expected.

"Miguel, what do you think about Letty having her own apartment?"

"It is good for my little cousin to have a place of her own."

"Are you comfortable here? Do you want your own place? But I confess, I'd hate to lose the convenience of your being here."

Miguel chuckled. "I love my place back there, and being rent free is a dream, not just to me, but to everyone living back there, too. We're all putting money away just from the savings of not having to pay rent, utilities, and food."

"You're a good man, Miguel. I'm very fortunate to have you."

"On the contrary. I consider myself a lucky man to be working for you. At your service, always, Boss."

Chapter 3
February 1979
Acapulco

A week after we returned from Portugal, the girls were back at my house searching newspapers for small aircraft crashes. I passed out their bonus checks for Portugal, then led the way to the master bedroom where we partied the rest of the afternoon and night.

"Boss, your dick is shorter. That's what you get for not using it," Pixie said.

"Pixie, that's mean!" Letty said.

"Who says I haven't been using it?"

"In that case, it's shorter because you're wearing it out."

"Pixie!" Letty took a sip of her wine, and replaced it on the end table.

Niley said nothing, but she rarely did. Jo said nothing, too busy laughing at Pixie and Letty.

I wanted to pinch myself to make sure I wasn't dreaming. It had been a long time since my team and I had gotten together like this. I wanted them more than ever. I wondered at myself, at how I could have been working all day every day with eager sex goddesses, and me, impervious to them. My libido had returned with a vengeance. I couldn't help noticing how the results of the karate workouts and hard calisthenics they'd been practicing showed up on their bodies. Their asses were rounded but hard. Their abs were ribbed with muscle, their stomachs taut, their legs shapely. Even their faces had taken on a leaner quality, making them look more determined. I'd noticed the changes in their faces last Wednesday.

Wednesday was when the girls met regularly at Melina's in her basement shooting gallery. I wasn't sure they'd even be in this Wednesday since I'd given them time off, but I heard the gunshots as I approached. I made a mental note to tell Melina she could use some more soundproofing. Their shooting coach was a physically square man, retired cop, former military sniper. He'd already set up targets by the time I arrived, and the team was already at work training with firearms. The coach had offered me a gun, but I refused it. Because of my conviction years before, I was not permitted to have a gun or be around firearms unless or until I had a pardon for my conviction. Since my conviction was federal, that meant I needed the President of the United States to sign my pardon. A joke. The girls were so savvy with the weapons it made me proud. Their coach drilled them like they were in the military. I was just as proud as when they practiced karate with me and showed off their chops. I slipped out while they were concentrating on their targets, and I doubt they'd even noticed me there.

After a couple of days off, we were all back in my office.

"Hey Babies. I missed you. No question the workouts are showing. You are all looking delicious."

Pixie turned to face me and struck a couple of model's poses in quick succession, a move Niley called 'playing Farrah.'

"Jo, make her stop," Niley said. "She's doing it again. This is not *Mario's Angels*."

"Boss, my body was always delicious. What you mean?" Pixie asked, shaking her head so that her latest "Farrah" hair framed her face to best advantage.

"Only that your body looks more delicious, Baby."

The conversation led everyone to my bedroom where I kissed every inch of their bodies. It was a memorable night.

I woke up exactly the way I like to wake up, my team around me on my huge bed. Not having them like this for so long had been like fasting. That was clear only now, after a night of bingeing on them.

"I've been snubbing my team something terrible," I told Melina later, on the phone.

"So, do something about it. It's winter. Buy them what I want," Melina suggested. "Buy them some sunshine."

It was perfect. "You're brilliant. I'm taking them to Acapulco. It's eighty degrees there. Imagine that. Join us?"

"I wish I could go, but I can't. You should see the doctor first."

"I'm only going for a few days."

"Even so, the doctor."

As much as I did not want to see a doctor, I did go. Not because I wanted to, not because Melina made the appointment, and not because she shared that information with Jo, and not because I found the appointment pinned on my schedule by my office wives, plus Melina. I found their involvement annoying and presumptuous. The only reason I visited the doctor was to get the go-ahead on a real work-out. For too long, I'd been limiting myself to mild calisthenics and jogging. Karate gives me an edge, and I did not want to lose it.

The general practitioner I'd been referred to after London was a rounded gentleman with an Italian last name, graying hair like an Elizabethan monk, tufts of chest hair poking through his shirt which was unbuttoned down to the fourth button, and more gold jewelry than I'd ever seen another doctor wear. After I got back from seeing him and told Melina about it, she kept breaking into laughter.

"What's so funny?"

She got in control of herself, then said calmly, "I think it was the part you described about hearing him clinking down the hall twenty yards away." She started laughing again, and gasped out, "Yep. That's the part that hit me."

I borrowed Oscar's plane and offered to pay, but he would hear nothing of it. He said there was only one condition. "Don't get kidnapped."

"I promise. Not going to happen."

From the get-go, the flight had a different ambiance from our usual work flights. Normally the girls dressed for work when aboard a plane. This time, they were wearing shorts and summer tops beneath their winter sweaters and long pants. Before Van Nuys was out of sight, the girls had stripped off their winter clothes, revealing summer stuff underneath. I guess the clothes change was something they had planned together.

"That's jumping the gun, isn't it? We're still over California."

"We left winter behind in LA," Pixie said, in her brave short shorts and halter top covering goose-pimpled winter skin. I could see the girls' bikini straps under their summer clothes. They were prepared to take Acapulco by storm.

"Yeah, but it's January in the clouds." I pulled my sweater tighter. I'm not lying. I was cold, and looking forward to sun on the beach.

Since none of us had been to Acapulco, it was only when the plane was making its final approach that we realized what a paradise we were coming to. We were arriving in daylight. The pilots gave us plenty of notice so we were all watching the windows.

The dwellings below looked like crushed shells against the green foliage and blue water. As we drew closer and came out of the clouds, the buildings took shape. We could easily make out the hotels on the beach. The colors were clear and amazing: azure sky, aquamarine water, luscious green vegetation, white beach, sparkling sand. No LA smog. The water was an amazing collection of clear blues that I don't think any artist could capture accurately, and I could in no way adequately describe. As the plane turned, the line of the horizon changed color like a kaleidoscope, and on the opposite side of the plane, the sun poured light into the cabin.

"Looks almost like Hawaii. I hear this is a party town," Pixie said.

"We're in the tropics, now, Babies," I said.

The bright green of the tops of the palm trees were evident everywhere, sprinkled around the fringes of land curling around the bay. As we descended, I could see the froth atop the water as the waves broke white and rolled out to dissolve on the beach.

"Look at all the hotels." Niley's face was pressed to the window like a kid at a candy store.

"Which one is ours?" Letty asked.

"Your guess is as good as mine about which one is the Hilton."

"I've never seen water so blue," Pixie said, with her face plastered against the glass like Niley. "You can see the waves crash on the beach." She waved furiously out the window as if she could be seen, then looked over her shoulder at me. "Someone was water-skiing."

"Hawaii has totally blue water too," Letty said.

"Fuck Hawaii. We're in Acapulco now," Niley said.

I held on to the armrests, and hoped they wouldn't do a grito later when I was carrying luggage and couldn't cover my ears.

When the pilots turned the plane away from the beach to approach the runway, the girls moaned in disappointment, but not for long. The airport was minutes from the beach.

I had taken Oscar's recommendation of the Hilton, a place where the famous gathered, at least, according to Oscar's secretary, Junie. The girls had promised Junie that they'd try to get some autographs. I got the presidential suite with three bedrooms adjoining it, but our plan was to squeeze together in the master. We dumped our things in my suite, and went straight to the beach.

"I want to suck up every drop of sun," Pixie said.

"She's speaking for all of us," Letty said.

We played in the water like kids, though the surf was high and wild. Even if we never needed their help, I was glad the hotel had three lifeguards on the beach. We watched people water skiing.

"We all want to do that," Pixie said. There was no time for it on the first day. The days were short. It was already getting dark.

We showered on a sidewalk outside before walking barefoot to our suite and showering again. We dressed in shorts and ate downstairs, without ceremony.

A mariachi group of eight moved from table to table, singing familiar ballads. If I'd been alone, I'd have paid them to leave, but the girls loved it. Pixie talked one of them out of his guitar and stunned them all when she played and sang. The whole restaurant got so quiet there was no sound but her husky voice and the guitar she was strumming. When she stopped, the whole restaurant burst into applause, and stood up. The mariachi group was dumbfounded. I stood up with everyone else during the standing ovation, and the girls and I were clapping our heads off. I could have swelled up and popped, I was so proud of her. As the whole restaurant gave her a standing ovation (including the band), she blushed and beamed, but I know how she loved the attention. Hands down she was better than the group. Jo and Letty and Niley and I had a time getting her back to the table. It was great to see her so happy. She loved the limelight.

Our table was covered in seafood, and the girls were munching away. They were all rosy from the sun already, and as bubbly as the champagne they were drinking with dinner. We toasted frequently. We'd already toasted Oscar, the band, the pilots, the maître d', the people at the table sitting next to us, and our formally dressed waiter.

"I'd be doing a good job if I was working alone," I said. I had their attention, but raised my glass and stood. "But with you, and thanks to all of you, I'm doing so great I can't fucking believe it. The Portugal case is perfect proof of how well we work together." Over a hundred families signed.

"Hear, hear."

We downed a single bottle of champagne that night, because we had an early morning. We were up with the sun, or at least awake with the sun. And a wonderful morning it was, too, with all of us in bed till noon, experimenting in a way we had not done in a long time. We had iced fruit delivered by room service while looking at our 180-degree view of the beach. We could also see the cliffs where movie stars had houses. A huge yacht named Denny's was parked out in front of one of the houses. We found out later it belonged to the owner of the restaurant chain. Then we did the tourist thing in our very own hotel SUV with a driver and guide. The saltiest thing we did on the second night is to have cocktails at a hilltop mansion that had different shows going on stage, couples fucking and doing it all. No orgies for the public, but there was one big room with a stage where an orgy was going on to watch, with hot chicks and guys that a person could select then retire with to a room if they felt accommodating. We weren't looking for that kind of entertainment, but we checked out the rooms, drank some mediocre wine, laughed a lot, and got extremely horny in preparation for our own private party back at the hotel. The scenes we had witnessed brought up some memories.

On our drive back to the hotel, I felt a little maudlin. I felt my eyes getting wet as I told the girls about the orgy Sami had taken me to in London. I felt a flurry of emotions: sadness that Sami was gone, fondness for the experiences she had gifted me with, thankfulness for the girls now with me, and even some pride that I was strong enough that the memories did not overwhelm me as they had during the first months of my recovery. That night was really not as wild as the orgy with Sami, but it was tender and meaningful, and would have been one for the record books if we'd been keeping any.

The third day, we went to see the seventeenth century fort, and watched some cliff divers. Jo signed us up so we took a tour bus to visit el Zócalo, and listened to a tour guide tell us about Acapulco's old town square. It looked like a dull little park to me, but the girls wandered around, sat on the stone benches, threw some coins in the fountains, and we took each others pictures posing in the gazebo before we returned to the sand outside of our hotel, and played in the surf. The water was warm, choppy, but bearable. It was crazy to think of it being February-cold back home. The water had calmed enough that I didn't feel the need to herd the girls close under the eye of the lifeguards. I hired five boats, five motor boat captains, one teacher for each of us, and we took water-skiing lessons, laughing equally when we were able to stand up as when we crashed on the water. The trainers were hands on. They hold on to your ankles to steady you as you move. They ride on the skis with you. By the next morning, I was on the water before the girls, already showing off my water-skiing skills. I'd had a good teacher. We were together most of the time, but the girls did spend a while every day getting autographs. I teased them about it, since more stars live at home than in Acapulco.

"We promised Junie," Pixie protested.

I didn't try and stop them. They were having a blast. Plus, they looked stunning. We ate a couple of meals at cliffside restaurants with amazing views, rode around in taxis that were Volkswagen beetles driven by guys who spoke with what Pixie called a dreamy accent, visited all the tourist spots, and spent every free minute at the beach.

On our last day there, I called Camila.

"Baby, I miss you. What part of the world are you in?"

"I'm in Bogota. Amor, I would have gone to Acapulco to meet you. Why didn't you call me?"

"It was a last-minute trip. A gift for my team. They kicked ass in Portugal."

"Bravo, Amor. Que Bueno."

I was waiting for the team to pack when Pepe called.

"Camila said you were in Acapulco."

"About to fly home now. When are you going to let me pay you back for flying everybody to and from London?"

"You worry too much about the little things." He laughed.

Not unexpectedly, the rest of his call followed along the same line as Camila's. The girls still hadn't finished packing, so I called Jason. He was back to work, and sounded a little better.

"The penthouse is just sitting there. Sami wanted to give it to you. Wish she had."

"She gave me more than enough. I expect her father will put it up for sale."

"Sami named me executor of her estate years ago. Her father wants nothing to do with the affairs of the estate. Funny part of it, if it's funny at all, is he's practically the sole beneficiary."

"You are so smart, Jason. Not sure how you are handling the estate and everything else you have going, including your own personal affairs."

"You're the smart one, Mario."

"What about Ginger and Crispin?" Ginger and Crispin were Sami's staff. I remembered them with fondness. Especially Ginger, who had kept me company when Sami and Jason were busy together.

"They still live on the third floor. They own their flats now, part of what Sami gave them for their service."

"Good to hear."

"They are still taking care of the penthouse, and still get paid for it. No one to cook for, but they spend their regular hours there as if everything was back to normal. The hospital stuff is gone."

Jason's voice was infused with sadness, and it was rubbing off on me. The ache of losing Sami was pushing aside the warmth of Acapulco. The five months that had passed were not nearly enough time to get over losing Sami. I wondered if there is a set amount of time when there comes an end to grief.

When I hung up, I made another call. I located Olga through the same assistant that I called to get Camila. Most times, the assistant cross connected us, no matter where they were.

"Hey you, you haven't checked in," I said.

"Hey you back. I'm sorry, but I've been running like crazy. I hear you're in Acapulco."

"Just leaving."

"I'm jealous. You probably spent the entire time playing in bed with your team."

"We spent about the half the time on the beach."

"Amor, I want to see you. I call you at home tomorrow."

"Deal. I want to see you, too."

"So what is it with you, Boss?" Pixie had been in the process of checking the hotel room to make sure we hadn't left anything behind. She always heard everything said anywhere in the perimeter of her presence, and she always had to get to the root of it, whether or not it was any of her business. In fact, the farther it was from being her business, the more likely she was to be interested.

"What is what?"

"You have this hard-on for Camila and Olga?"

"Wrong. I have this hard-on for Jo, Pixie, Niley, Letty, Melina, Camila, and Olga."

My reply shut her up for a good thirty seconds. Then she nodded abruptly, and patted me on the back. "That's more like the Mario I know." I knew I wasn't hearing from the member of my team, but the girl who had been my sweetheart when I was all of fourteen years old.

I looked at our room one last time, walked out on the balcony, and felt the Acapulco breeze soft on my skin, smelled the salt sea air.

"It was good here," I said.

Pixie, for once, said nothing. I'd seen her shake out the sheets, finding someone's lost panties, and one sock. She found a pair of flip flops that belonged to Niley, and packed all of the hotel's unopened toiletries, the unopened packet of Hilton coffee, and the hotel stationary in my suitcase. I decided to put the spoils on the conference table in the office when I got home so the girls could decide who got to keep what. I'd already grabbed a dozen gift shop hula girls for their car dashboards or rear-view windows.

"You did a good job finding shit," I told her.

I was tired, but it was a good kind of tired. The trip had been a breath of fresh air. Even more than we'd needed the playtime, we'd needed to reconnect with each other. The girls boarded in summer gear, but when I got back to the plane, I was already dressed for the Los Angeles winter. None of us had a problem falling asleep. We all slept every minute of the four-hour trip back to Van Nuys Airport.

Chapter 4
March 1979
Payday

In March 1979, the six-month note to the bank was due and our friendly banker wanted his million. Luckily, in my business, when it's payday, it's payday with a capital $. Portugal was big. I wrote a check for my share of the loan. Melina did the same.

"I was ready to ask Camila to take a piece of my share," I confessed to Melina. "However, I'm flush with the Portugal money."

"You wouldn't have."

"Trust me, I would. I'm not afraid of her money. I want her money."

"You're too smart to be so trusting."

"Baby, please. It's old news. It turns out we didn't need her money, but I would have been happy to use it."

"It's old news but with this deal of ours, I know it's on your mind."

"It's on my mind, all right."

"You are being silly. Take her money and do what with it? Do you have investments right now that just need funding?"

"You're right, Babies. I have nothing right now, but...I have a knack for finding niches that others have trouble finding."

"I would advise not to," Melina said. "Don't take offense. Don't be mad. We don't agree on everything, and if we did, I'd be useless to you."

"I'm not mad, Baby, but stop thinking bad things about Camila or Olga for that matter."

"Do you still have that two million in your safe?"

It was the first time she had brought this up in a good while. It was a good time to bring her up to date.

"Actually, it's four million."

"What! She doesn't need four million to buy a house in Pasadena. She's just using you. Or I should say, the two of them are using you. Three of them if you count Pepe. Something's up."

"Baby, leave it."

"It's your funeral. Don't let them blindside you," she said.

"Oh come on. It might be jail, but not a funeral," I forced a laugh.

"Asshole. You're supposed to be smarter than that."

"I got the money in my safe. Who is the smart one?"

"Aren't you curious where it came from?"

"I know where it came from. It came from Camila and Olga."

"Asshole. *Pendejo!*"

"Four million is a lot, but I'm not sure I'd sell my house for four million."

"You would."

"I don't know about that. Four million is a lot of money, but not that much when you are buying a house like yours or mine or some of the houses in our neighborhood."

"I don't understand why you need to be the person holding cash for her."

"She trusts me. It's a sign of trust."

"Oh, please. Give me a break. There's a reason we have banks. They're scheming. I just don't know at what."

"Can we change the subject now?" My voice was still level, and I was still in good spirits.

Melina had been walking around impatiently, but she returned to her chair, and sat across from me at my desk. She picked up the check I had written and put it in an envelope with hers.

"I will messenger this over to the bank."

"Thanks, Baby. Are you in a hurry?"

"Why do you ask?"

I smiled. I glanced at the conference table. I loosened the tie I had put on that morning, and slipped it off. She followed my look. There was a certain way we look at each other after a disagreement. A fresh look, like, we've said enough. Let's start over.

She caught on. Her elbows were on my desk, her hands on either side of her face, chin set between them. She licked her lips. She was dressed for the office in one of her designer suits. Slipped off the jacket. Unbuttoned her top few buttons. Tugged her panties off, and dropped them in the seat of the chair where she'd been sitting. I glanced at the panties. A scrap of black lace.

"On the conference table?"

My cock was in full agreement. A moment later, my head rested on some books like a pillow, my back on the table where the team did their newspaper searches for crashes.

"You better not call me Olga or Camila, asshole."

Melina was upright and fully clothed except for the missing panties. I rucked the skirt up over her hips as she mounted me, and cupped the curve of her ass. I pulled her down on me so that our lips locked. She came immediately as I entered her, then she did most of the work. No awkwardness, no fumbling. Our bodies were so used to each other. Our bodies knew every nuance, every dip and sway and grind of this dance we'd shared so many times. The table creaked beneath us, bumping softly. She did something, changed her angle or something, changed the rhythm. Heat flared between us, but the frenzy was all inside, explosive, my first climax, her second. I wished she had not mentioned Olga and Camila at a time like this.

Chapter 5
April 1979
Easter

"What are you doing on April fifteenth?" Olga asked.

I rested the phone between my ear and my shoulder, scratched my head and glanced down at the worn black leather calendar book on my desk, but did not open it. Nothing was written on that date. I hated calendars. My team was my calendar. Especially Jo.

"How should I know? That's two whole weeks away."

"Camila can't make it to Rome this year, but she has front row seats for mass."

"Can't get much better than that." I recalled the whirlwind trip I'd taken to Rome last year. "We were second row last year." The Pope, so very close to where we were sitting.

"So, do you want to?"

For a second or two I was confused about what she was asking me. "To what?"

"I haven't seen you in so long. The phone calls are no substitute for seeing you in person. When we captured you in Portugal and took you to Paris, it was such fun. And now, I'll have you all to myself. Seems like you are totally over that terrible incident in London?"

"I'm good Baby. I've been out doing cases. My life is back to normal."

"So are you game for Rome?"

Then I caught on. "Without Camila? You and me? On the front row?"

"Right!"

"Camila suggested this?"

"Right, she did."

"Do we have permission to fuck?"

"Don't need permission to fuck. We can fuck. We can do anything we want."

"I'm in," I said, not thinking of mass. The thought of going to Rome locked in a flying bedroom with Olga gave me an instant hard-on.

"I can hardly wait," she said.

"Me too." I was in my office alone behind my desk with a stack of papers in front of me, all ready to go at the prospect of again making it with Olga.

"Are we flying commercial?" I asked, though I knew better.

I heard a laugh. "I don't fly commercial, and neither do you, Amor."

"Hey, Camila calls me that."

"I know."

"I'm hard," I admitted.

"I know. I feel it through the phone."

"What about you?"

"I'm getting so wet."

In a couple months, it would be a year that I had been sitting on four million of Camacho money. I never mentioned it, and neither did they. Four million just sitting there. I got up and walked over to it, but left the safe unopened, inevitably thinking of the cost of the plane we would take to Rome and back. I returned to my desk and tried focusing on work, but before long Camila called.

I grabbed my phone and started pacing.

"Que Bueno Amor, que vas a Roma!" [10]

---

[10] How good, Love, that you are going to Rome

"Thank you for the invitation."

"I have business in Lima. I want you to have a good time with Olga."

"I'll miss you," I said. "We always have such a blast."

Her reply was a good-humored laugh. "You won't have time.

I didn't laugh. "I will," I promised.

"Amor, you and I will get together. Maybe next month if you aren't on a case. If you're on a case, you have to tell me where."

"Sounds promising. I'll let you know where I am." Camila's surprise visits when I was out on a case were hardly a surprise.

I was glad I didn't have to choose between Camila and Olga. I wondered what it would be like waking every day to either of them. They were filled with secrets, and this fact about them intrigued me to no end. Melina guarded her privacy, and I used to consider her secretive, but not like the Colombians. Distance helped add to their mystique. Would I ever know their secrets? Did I really want to? Melina was right. They were scheming and I knew it. I just didn't care.

I was in my room with a suitcase open on my bed. I had picked out clothes that Letty had packed for me, neatly and methodically. It was the night before my departure, and I was feeling bad for Letty. The rest of my team had families to celebrate the holiday with. Though she had an apartment, her home was my house, and she was directly responsible for keeping me from getting lonely after the others left. She had all the benefits of a wife without the obligations.

"Here I am flying off to Rome, and leaving you alone. I feel bad," I said.

"Boss, I'm going to be fine. You said I could stay here. You know how I love it here. Besides, it's just Easter."

"If you had kids, you could do an Easter egg hunt."

She looked at me like I'd grown a second head. "I don't have any kids, and I'm not likely to suddenly have some between now and Easter."

I hugged her. "You're way too good for me."

"Other way around, Boss."

She slept in my arms that night, but was gone in the morning. I only knew she'd been there because of Melina's call.

"Hey asshole, I came over last night. You and Letty were dead to the world. I didn't have the heart to wake you."

I felt a jolt of conscience. "You should have gotten me up. Always wake me."

I worried over what Melina had just told me. I am alive now because my sleeping self had been aware of danger. After all the years of karate and judo, I should never sleep so deeply that danger doesn't wake me. Light sleeping had saved my life when an intruder came in my apartment with a baseball bat and a gun.

"I don't know who you are getting closer to, Letty, Camila or Olga."

Melina sounded preoccupied, maybe even jealous. I did not ask her if she was jealous though her tone was different from normal. I don't know what she was feeling. The only thing normal was that she called me asshole. She always said that when she wanted to get my attention. I realized that she, too, had no one to share Easter with, and felt like shit. I wondered if I should tell her to go to my aunt's. Even if she went elsewhere, Melina always prepared a huge meal on Easter Sunday that we shared, eventually. This year, she did not mention it to me. I didn't know how she'd feel about my being gone. The last Easter I was away, she had worked. Her markets were open on Easter Sunday. I guessed that with me gone, she'd be working.

"Letty has the number at the house in Rome if you need me for anything."

She sighed. I felt it all the way down my spine.

"Safe travels, Cuz."

"I'll miss you," I said.

"Asshole. I hope when you stick it in her, you call her by my name."

"You're so mean, Baby. You almost sound jealous."

"Don't get your hopes up, Cuz."

"No good wishes?"

"Safe travels, Cuz. Come back safe."

When I got off the phone, I had a realistic moment. If I was married, I wouldn't be on my way to Rome for Easter Sunday with a fox like Olga. If I was married to Olga would the fun cease? Or Camila? Or Letty? If I married anyone, it would be an open marriage, for sure. But who? Trying to figure out an answer was stressing me out.

Olga called to let me know she was landing at Ontario Airport, and not Van Nuys. Letty drove me there, about twenty miles from Pasadena.

"I knew there was an airport in Ontario but never been there," I told Letty, as she drove sedately through traffic. Pixie would have been twisted around in the seat, but Letty only glanced sideways in my direction for an instant, and only at a traffic stop. No one else was with us, so I was in the front seat, passenger side.

"That makes two of us, Boss. I had to map this thing before we left the house."

"What would we do without our Thomas Guides?"

"No map books?" Letty snorted. "We'd be fucking lost, Boss. I'd still be going in circles on the freeway."

She was driving, but wearing shorts, not her chauffeur outfit. When we pulled into the airport lot, I got out of the car, and walked over to the driver's side. I leaned in, took her in my arms behind the steering wheel, and gave her a hearty hug and kiss through her open window. It was on the awkward side since there wasn't really room, but I never let that stop me. I sent her on her way, watching the Rolls disappear from view before I headed inside.

One of the Camacho pilots met me near the United Airlines ticket counter. I recognized his LAI livery, blue, yellow, and red like the flag of Bogata, with a crowned eagle embroidered on one pocket, and LAI embroidered on the other. Carrying my suitcase and a garment bag, I followed him through a couple of doors to an open jeep. Outside, the noise was deafening, as big planes were continuously landing and taking off. If my hands had been free, I'd have covered my ears. The pilot handed me ear cups and put on his own. The mind-blowing noise on the tarmac was tempered slightly with ear protection, but still booming, thundering, ear-piercing. Everything vibrated in sympathy with the planes. The jeep took us about a mile to where Olga waited. I went up the air stairs ahead of the pilot and when I reached the top, I turned and shook his hand.

"Thank you, Chuck."

"My pleasure, Mr. Mario."

"Mario is good enough."

The cockpit door was open, revealing three pilots, plus Chuck. Seeing them, all I could do is think of the expense. Two flight attendants introduced themselves as Ray and Martin. They were young, trim and clean-shaven. If I hadn't seen four pilots already, I might have thought they were pilots. Martin took my suitcase to the bedroom cabin.

Olga came flying into my arms. I pushed her to arm's length to get a good look at her beaming face. It was good to see her. Olga is taller than my team members, but I picked her up and gave her an enthusiastic greeting. She was in Camacho black silk pajamas already, her hair in a ponytail.

"Thanks for having me," I said, looking around.

"Do you want a tour before we take off?"

I nodded. She showed me through the plane, a Boeing 727 with a configuration different from what I'd seen before, with a single bedroom cabin. Eight passenger seats were just outside the cockpit next to the galley. Wide seats with plenty of room to recline, no doubt for the pilots and flight attendants to rest in. In the center of the plane, two built-in modern sofas faced each other with a long table between them like in a living room. A few single seats were next to windows. Olga and I sat side by side on a sofa. Martin appeared with a choice of champagne or red wine.

"I'll take a Coke," I said.

"Me too," Olga said. "No booze yet. It's a long flight."

Martin returned with our drinks and Ray brought out a platter of cheese, crackers, dry fruits and three different jams.

"This looks catered," I said, reaching for some cheese.

"We can get nice catering when we land here. In Van Nuys, it's more difficult."

"Why did you choose to land at this airport?"

"No choice, really. Van Nuys couldn't accommodate us."

The attendants left. The pilot came on the PA and asked Martin to close the hatches, check emergency exits, and report back.

"Why do you have flight attendants when it is just us?" I recalled what Chastity had said,

"The four pilots have to eat and be taken care of. I could handle it, but I wanted you to have all my attention. Martin and Ray work for Pepe full-time."

"And the pilots?"

"Them too." These were pilots I had never seen before.

We felt the big plane roar sleekly down the runway and become airborne.

"We're off, Amor."

"Baby," I said, wrapping my arm around her, tucking my feet under the coffee table. We kissed as though we had known each other forever. She touched my face and held me for a minute or so with her hands on each side of my face. I did the same thing to her. We probably looked pretty silly. I could see every mascaraed eyelash, the smooth tan of her skin, the dark eyes, the slanted eyebrows, her dramatic cheekbones that reminded me a little of Valita.

"You're you again. You don't look at all like that person I saw lying in a coma."

"You told me that in Paris already." When we'd gotten together in Paris with Camila, she'd also said that we were going to be close friends for a lifetime. It wasn't the first time that I wondered what I had that made me so special. It wasn't my dick. I'd heard that Colombians have monster dicks, probably bigger than mine. It wasn't my looks. So, what was it?

"Olga, why me?"

"I don't understand."

"Out of all the strangers in the world to befriend, why did Camila and Pepe pick me? How did it happen? Why did it happen?"

Olga looked at me blankly.

"I don't know what you mean," Olga said.

"I know how lucky I am to have you, Pepe, and Camila as friends. So, I ask, why me?"

"You are special, Amor. We are the lucky ones to know you."

"You are special."

"You are too. Are we arguing over how special we are?" She giggled.

My questions and her non-answers weren't getting me anywhere. I still wondered why Pepe had pursued the friendship. Maybe I'd been a little infected by Melina's caution. I only saw them sporadically, and only on vacation. I knew how sneaky Carson was, or the how open the girls were because I'd spent so much time with them. I knew how they operated, how they lived day-to-day, and what their goals and motivations were. All I knew of Camila, Pepe, and Olga is what they told me. In spite of the carnal knowledge, Camila and Olga were mysteries I would enjoy unraveling. Tall, beautiful Olga, with the gorgeous cheekbones and straight, silky hair. With Olga in reach, why was I wasting my time exchanging words?

One of the attendants closed the partition separating us from the rest of the plane, giving us total privacy where we were seated. The pilots made an announcement. Just the usual, leaving the airport kind of message. All of them got a word in, and introduced themselves. I couldn't think of a time when I'd heard from four pilots in the same message.

"Four pilots," I said, laughing. Really, it was excessive. Still, given what I'd seen of the Camachos, it could have been six.

Olga thought I didn't understand.

"Amor, pilots have to rest. Four pilots mean getting there faster. In a few minutes, two pilots will come out and sleep for at least four to six hours then relieve the other two."

Of course, I knew it didn't take four pilots to pilot the big plane. "On Oscar's plane, we make refueling stops, rest stops, stop stops. All the stops we have to do to get to someplace like Portugal are so the pilots don't fall asleep at the wheel. I get it. That was why I was laughing. Two sets of pilots."

"Pepe just took over another small airline. He has thirty planes now with daily routes to and from Colombia, Bogota, Venezuela, Peru, and Chile."

"Wow. The jets like this, are they part of that fleet?"

"No, he has two Lear Jets, three DC9 and two 727s for business and personal use but not for paying passengers. Do you like this plane?"

"I love it, but I like you more."

I sipped my Coke, and my ears popped. I shook my head. Olga handed me some chewing gum for my ear pressure. "Camila said she had to be in Lima."

"Yes, she's making a big marble and granite purchase for two construction sites in Chicago."

I took a sip of my Coke. "She's amazing."

"She is. She buys the marble and granite from the quarries, pays cash, sells the granite and marble and gets paid by wire or check. The stone arrives by ship."

"Sweet," I said. Camila had mentioned purchasing stone before, but had never gone into detail. I am always curious about Camacho business. Melina would say I am more curious than what is healthy. I hoped she'd tell me more so I gave her a little encouragement.

"And then?"

"When she closes the deal, I will fly to Lima to pay."

"I remember you telling me you are the banker."

"Not a banker, but I pay anything that has to be paid. Especially Camila's deals."

I kissed her. When I said, "You are amazing," I wasn't referring to her banking skills.

In Rome, the customs officer came aboard. He paid us a brief visit that was more like a social call, stamped our passports, and then we disembarked.

Three days later, on Easter Sunday, Camila called.

"You didn't go to Easter Sunday mass?" Camila's voice was loud but maybe it was the speakerphone. "You know what we go through to get those tickets?"

"Camila, I know. I'm the one that gets the tickets," Olga said. She was lying naked in her bed, and I was next to her, feeling overdressed in shorts.

"Should I ask why?"

I sat up and stretched. "It was my fault," I chipped in.

"It was me." Olga jumped in with a smile that only I could see. "I wanted to do something daring."

"And what did you do instead?"

"We overslept," I lied.

"We fucked," Olga said, truthfully, at the same time.

"What?"

Olga repeated herself. This time, I kept my mouth shut.

Camila actually laughed. It was a real laugh. I didn't laugh, but Olga laughed, too.

"I love you, Camila," Olga said.

"*Yo Tambien te amo, hermanita,*"[11] replied Camila.

"I'm sorry about the tickets," I said.

"Next year the three of us will go to mass together. Olga, you'll need

---

[11] I love you too, little sister

to get three tickets and they better be first row." Camila's voice was still loud, but she didn't sound angry.

"I promise. I will get them."

Olga met with the chef about what to provide for lunch or dinner. The staff was up for everything and anything. If we wanted a massage, Olga would ring. Several times, four showed up: two females for me and two males for her. It wasn't sexual, just four-hand massages. The service was better than any hotel I had ever been to. I couldn't help comparing this to Sami's London flat. Sure, Ginger and Crispin were fabulous, but this Roman house had an excess of help eager to be tapped for whatever service was needed. The luxury was out of this world. I was in Rome for six days. We never left the house until the helicopter took us to the airport.

"Is this what a honeymoon is like?" I asked Olga.

"It was so much fun. I never had a honeymoon, so I don't know."

"One thing for sure. Your servants here will celebrate that we're finally leaving."

Olga laughed. "We did keep them hopping, didn't we?"

I kissed her as the helicopter went airborne.

Later, we were in the bedroom cabin, at 30,000 feet. Olga was on top, moving ferociously.

"Amor," she said, without slackening her pace, "do you have a problem holding another three million?"

I stopped. She followed my lead, and gave me a sidelong look that made her look sly, mischievous, conniving. I was being handled again. I couldn't help noticing, and I couldn't help wishing she would be straightforward, and not use sex to manipulate me. I wasn't so driven by testosterone that I was unaware of what was going on. I played along. The sex was great. Unreasonable as it was, with Olga proving Melina's point, it was Melina I was irritated with for infecting me with her suspicions.

"Should I ask why?"

"Camila wants to buy a house. You know that. You have such a big house. Just put the money anywhere. Don't worry about it."

We were staring at each other. I didn't know how to answer, but wanted to break the tension.   "Can I keep the suitcases? I already have two."

"Of course, Amor. And keep one hundred thousand for yourself. There's so much money right now, we can't put it to work fast enough."

"A hundred thousand just for storing the money?" I chuckled.

"No, Amor, for your services."

"I owe Pepe too much to take anything from him. He gives and gives. Look where I am right now." I looked down where we were still joined. She adjusted her position just enough for me to realize that as little as I wanted to talk, the conversation had not interrupted my eager dick.

"We trust you. We don't just leave money with anyone."

"I get it," I said. I didn't get it, but I wanted to shut down the talk.

"Thank you, Amor."

She finally stopped the business talk and started to move with intention, sending waves of excitement through me. Afterwards, we put on our pajamas and adjourned to the main cabin to be served a meal that had been catered in Rome. It began a tart with something like cream cheese and a green vegetable I did not recognize.

"No worries," Olga said, "It is Swiss chard and ricotta cheese."

It wasn't bad, but I don't think I'd have chosen it at a restaurant.

"So tell me more about Camacho," I said.

"LAI is the name of the main company of Camacho. It stands for Latin American Investments."

"And what is the name of the airline?"

The next thing the steward brought out was a vegetable stew that Olga called vignarola. For me, the lemony lamb was the best part of the meal. Olga liked the strawberries in cream and wine that was the dessert.

"Aerolineas Colombia. The airline operator he just took over will have that same name."

"Good name," I said. I don't know what I was expecting. Camacho Airlines. No. They'd never have a name so obvious. If it was my airlines, I'd want my name on it. I wonder why Pepe didn't use his family name.

"Would you consider working in acquisitions?"

"What?"

"Only during your down time when you are waiting for the next case to happen."

I'd had three glasses of wine with dinner. I hoped my head was clear.

"Baby, I can't work for anyone. I never have."

"No, Amor, not working for LAI or Camacho. Not working for anyone. All you do is hunt out income properties, businesses, anything that you believe is a good investment that will give LAI a good return. You negotiate with sellers, brokers or whatever. Get the listing broker to convince the seller to accept part or all of the sales price in cash."

"And...?"

"When the sale clears, you get paid for your services."

"Just as Oscar pays me for cases I bring him," I said. I could have shut down the conversation but I was getting interested. It sounded simple. "Give me an example. How big of an income property? What kind of business?"

"We have very few investments in the United States and want to change that. Let's say you find a person like yourself who has...how many apartments do you have?"

"A little over a thousand units."

"A thousand units. We would buy that."

I shook my head. Not for sale.

She laughed. "Just saying you know what we want. We trust you to get the best price possible. You're smart. You know the market. You know people. Oscar told Pepe a long time ago of your drive, your hunger, how you work, not just reaching clients but also with lawyers in other countries. If the apartments you find have a mortgage or mortgages we can pay them off, and you try and get the seller to accept cash for the difference."

I'd never known that Oscar had talked me up that much. Maybe he'd had to go overboard to convince Pepe to find where I was being held in Venezuela. Maybe I would ask him about it when I got home. I was curious about what Oscar had said, but filed it away. Now I wanted details about this new deal I was being offered.

"Flattery is good, but tell me more."

Olga continued, "Let's say you get the seven hundred apartments for five million. If the seller will take all cash you get ten percent of the sales price. If the seller takes only part cash and the rest through a bank, you get ten percent of the cash amount."

Martin poured us both more wine. "Tell me more."

Olga talked for an hour, reciting the histories of properties Camacho owned, and the details of how they came to own them. The list of their enterprises was mind boggling. They had their fingers in everything from apartments to mining, and their interests were scattered all over the world.

"Camila does very well selling granite to building contractors in the United States like this project in Chicago. The stone is coming from Lima. She has a contact with an agent who sells granite and marble across the states. The stone company in Lima accepts cash. I don't know of anyone we've done business with in many countries that refused cash payment."

"Love it," I said.

"LAI wants businesses, income property. Amor, please you can do it. You can find clients for lawyers. You can find properties for LAI."

"I'm thinking."

"We know you don't need the money. Oscar doesn't talk about how much money you make, but we know you have an estate like one of Camacho's." She leaned over and kissed me. "I admire you. I heard how you got started, and how you're a master in karate and judo."

Olga had mentioned Oscar an awful lot in this conversation. Oscar had gotten Pepe to rescue me from the kidnappers. Oscar had introduced me. Oscar had recommended me highly to Pepe. I didn't need to be a genius to figure out that Oscar was behind my popularity. It began to fall in to place. I had met Pepe, then Camila. They sized me up. They liked me. They trusted my judgment.

"What is the downside?"

"I see no downside, Amor." She put on this big smile. "You'll get richer, Amor."

"I'm not rich."

"You are rich."

"Far from being rich. Just lucky."

"You're so humble, Amor."

I was still trying to get my head around the offer.

"Did Camila ask you to tell me this?"

"They both did. Pepe and Camila. They like you."

"So where does the money come from? No, don't tell me. I don't want to know."

"Amor, if this money was very dirty, do you think I'd be flying around the globe with it like I do?"

"I don't care if it's dirty, Baby. I'm sorry if I made you feel uncomfortable." I almost laughed at her denial that the money was very dirty. Slightly dirty, maybe, but not very dirty.

Olga kissed me, talked, and kept kissing. Every time I got a word out, she started another round of kissing and persuasion. I couldn't get an objection in edgewise, but I didn't stop trying.

"Think about it, Amor. No rush, no pressure. If you don't want to do it, no problem."

She let me up for a sip of wine. We clicked our glasses.

"And don't be mad at me for proposing this to you."

"Let me digest it. Why would I be mad?" She'd said this would be profitable. I wondered just exactly how profitable it would be. I needed to know that before I could make any decisions. "Assuming I get lucky, how much do you think I can make a year?"

"You can make millions, Amor."

I played it cool, but I won't deny that I found it damn enticing. "I'd love to make millions."

"Digest it, and then let me know."

"I'll do that. Sounds tempting."

"Good," she said, sitting up, then leaning forward, looking at me intently. She pulled a lightning switch of subject, or maybe she was just messing with my mind. "There are times when I see you look at me. I don't know what love looks like. Is there anything there?"

What was there was great sex. "Obviously this trip was for getting me to connect with you so you could make this proposal. Last year's trip with Camila in Rome was for bonding me with her. I got close to her afterwards, no question. But..."

"But what, Amor?"

"I feel closer to you."

"We have been close. Amor, there is no part of my body that you haven't visited in one way or another, and I've done the same."

I kissed her. "You're right. I love every inch of your body. I wish I wasn't headed home. I wish I could spend a lot more time with you." Or at least, I've certainly taken to her body, and she to mine.

"Amor, I feel the same way."

Her eyes had fallen to half-mast. She was staring at me like a cat stares at a bowl of cream. She wanted more. I was certainly willing to provide all the sex she could handle. There was no denying she was beautiful, but I wondered if she wanted some kind of declaration or commitment I couldn't make. I thought of my girls.

"Olga, I would be a lousy steady boyfriend or husband."

"I've been with a lot of women, but that's just ancient history. I've only been with three men in my life, and you are one of them."

I had no idea how many women I've been with. I took a wild guess. "Baby, I must have been with more than four or five hundred women. You would kill me if we ever got truly serious."

Her stare continued. "Tell me you love me, but only if you do."

"I love you," I said without hesitation. "I love a lot of women."

Our mouths met. When the kiss broke, she was the first to speak.

"I love you as well."

I had to find a way around what had become really serious talk.

"Should we do something really fucking crazy?"

"What, Amor?"

I turned her around on the sofa, face down. I pulled down her Camacho pajama bottoms to expose the fine ass I knew so well. I lay on her, my mouth against her ears, her hair. She turned her face and our lips met.

"Is this crazy?"

"It is if the attendants walk in on us."

She moaned, loud, for the attendants benefit, then yelled for all she was worth, "Fuck me, fuck me."

Of course, I complied.

"I love this kind of crazy," Olga said gasping.

I took a taxi from Van Nuys Airport. After refueling, Olga's plane would be taking off for Bogota. As the taxi took me home, I remembered my days and nights from the time I left Van Nuys to Rome to the moment I kissed her goodbye. There was no denying I was attracted. If she thought I was serious with Olga, what would Camila say? What would Pepe do or say? But that's not how I felt. I was not getting serious, and I was not getting exclusive. How could I be serious about people who had an agenda, and who manipulated me?

But I still owed Pepe my life. As for Olga and Camila, as long as I had my eyes open, and the sex was unbelievable, I was game, and going along for the ride.

When the taxi dropped me off, I lugged the suitcase from the gate and down the driveway, a long solitary walk that I took double-speed because it was so great to be home. The driveway lights were on, just enough to illuminate the pavement. Landscape lights were off. Porch lights were on. I didn't expect anyone to be awake. When I arrived, even though it was one in the morning, Letty was at the door to greet me, beaming and happy, and wrapped up like a Christmas present in a filmy nightie designed to send my temperature skyrocketing. The girls had gone home long ago to sleep in their own beds.

I shut the door fast because it was jacket weather outside, and admired Letty in her get-up.

"Boss, I fucking missed you!" She hugged me, her face pressing against my chest.

I kissed the top of her head. "I missed you, too."

"Are you hungry? I can cook you breakfast right now."

"I don't think so. I'll wait till breakfast."

I tossed off my jacket, trudged upstairs, showered and barely made it to bed. Before I closed my eyes, the phone rang. I got it before Letty did.

"Amor, I'm on the plane radio. Just taking off."

I was surprised how clear the connection was. The radio call meant our call was public.

"Safe travels, Baby."

"Amor, I wanted to tell you that this trip we just took together is something I will never forget. Thank you."

"Don't thank me. I thank you for inviting me. The trip was a treasure for me."

In our last encounter on the sofa, she'd been screaming and laughing. I had come close to telling her I was willing to try marriage if she was game.

"Amor, I want to see you more often."

"Me too, Olga."

There was a slight pause. The connection was degrading but still understandable. "I get goosebumps when you call me by name."

"I should be with you."

"I should have not let you get off the plane." Her voice wavered. I couldn't tell if it was the connection, or her reaction.

A few lines later, we said good bye. I closed my eyes, still holding the phone. Nodded off to sleep. I felt Letty take the phone out of my hand, and put it back on the cradle on the nightstand. Blearily, I dragged one eye open. My eyelid weighed a hundred pounds, at least, but I glimpsed her pretty face before she clicked off the lamp.

"I love you, Letty."

"I love you Boss."

It took forty-eight hours for me to get over overeating, overdrinking, getting to Rome, returning from Rome. I guess that's lumped in with jet lag. I was home for two days before I left a message at Melina's office that I was home. She visited me the next morning on her way to work, finding me in my breakfast nook in a sleeveless tee and shorts. I'd already taken a run around the neighborhood, worked out downstairs, and showered. My copy of the *LA Times* was dismembered across the table, and the classifieds were open in front of me. Next to my cup of coffee was a red pen I hadn't used on the paper yet. A second, untouched copy was already in my office on the conference table waiting for the girls to go through it.

Melina sat next to me, and pulled the front page toward herself, glancing at the headlines.

"Welcome back to the real world," she said.

Her welcome home kiss wasn't as passion-starved as it was after a month-long case-related trip, but fire burned under the surface, even if her mind was more on the day ahead than me. Her hands did linger on my biceps, and she mumbled something about wishing she'd gotten to bed early enough last night so we could have had a wrestling match this morning.

"I missed you." I raised my index finger to my lips, signaling her not to argue. "And don't say 'I didn't miss you.'"

"I missed you, too."

I took my pen, and drew a big circle around the headlines in front of her.

She grabbed my pen, looked over my classifieds and circled one.

"Mobile home teardown?" I quirked an eyebrow at her, and refilled her coffee. "Looks like you really need caffeine today." I laughed at the ad.

She emptied her cup and held it out for more.

"How was Rome?"

"A little cool, but nice."

"How was Easter Sunday mass?"

"The seats we had were to die for, first row, but we never made it to mass."

She was wearing a top hat and a scratchy green tweed dress with a nipped in waist. The green plaid with touches of red did wonders for her coloring. The hat reminded me of Sami. She'd had a riding hat, not the one with baseball brim, but the kind that looks like Lincoln's top hat. I pushed away the memory, and focused on the woman who was with me. With Melina, a hat usually meant some kind of meeting with someone outside of her company.

"You're all dressed up. You got something special going on?"

"I dress up every day. You just don't notice."

"You're always put together like a magazine cover, whether or not I say something about it. You don't come by every morning like you did back at the apartment." I reached over and tapped the brim, giving the hat a rakish angle. "The hat, Baby, you don't always wear a hat."

"You like it?"

She was sitting to my right. I leaned over and kissed her. "I like you.

And the hat."

She thumped my chest. "Why didn't you make it to mass? Too busy fucking her?"

"No, I think we were sleeping off the night before. I would hate to show up at mass at the Vatican drunk off my ass."

"Asshole."

"I'm just being honest, Cuz."

"If we were married, we wouldn't have that honesty between us."

"Are we cousins forever then?"

Melina laughed, a genuine laugh. "Kissing cousins. I can fuck a cousin. So yes. Cousins. Tight cousins. So tight that no one can break our bond."

It was written all over her face. "You mean that, huh?"

"Cuz, my being ten years your senior will always be in the way, no matter what."

"Is that all?"

"I don't want to get married, and you don't either." She got up and hugged me fiercely while I was still at the table. Almost pulled me off the chair.

"Check this out," I said. I had to clear the air. "Talking about truth. I came close to asking Olga to marry me. I have no fucking idea why. She didn't do anything to steer me in that direction, but I came close."

"Why?" Melina sat back down.

"I don't know. They are both different, and a fucking mystery attracts me like a magnet. But the days I spent with Olga were something else."

"Maybe she got a Bruja to put a spell on you?"

"No, she didn't get a Bruja to put a spell on me."

Melina did a fake grin. I could see she was putting on the cool, brave act and doing her best to be supportive, in spite of whatever she was feeling. That's what love was. No question. "Forget about the Bruja crack. Do you love her?"

"If I loved her, I would have asked her. I just love being with her, I love flying around in that big fucking airliner, and I dig the sex to no end. She probably would have told me to fuck off."

"Fuck, I'm not sure I like the truth," Melina said slowly, her voice so soft I could barely hear it. Her color was high but no ugly emotions leaked out.

"I'm sorry. I didn't have to bring this up. I think I needed to get it off my chest. Olga doesn't know what I was about to do."

"Strange things happen," Melina said. I could hear the honesty in her voice. I couldn't tell you what honesty sounds like, except that it sounded like Melina in that moment. "When I fuck someone else, afterwards, I wonder why I did it. It's a lot closer to regret than it is a proposal."

I swallowed. "Talking about truth. Damn." I pictured Melina bending over her desk and a faceless employee pounding her. I felt the green monster rise, and pushed him back where he had come from.

"Don't be a pussy. We both fuck around. You can be sure of one thing. I'm not asking any dope I fuck to marry me. If I ask any dope that question, it will be you. I gotta run." She was distant, her mind already at work. No more hugs.

"See you Sunday?"

"Of course, Sunday. We got a lot to chat about. Clear the air."

Then she was off.

On the third day after my return, I was three days into a tougher workout routine. Mostly, I ran. As much as I hate running, I'd forgotten how much I liked the course I set for myself, timing the run to coincide with the sunrise. Jogging has never been my thing at all. It was just an alternative till I was cleared for my usual workout. Jogging didn't quite mix with the karate and judo that Cosmo had inoculated me with. I followed up with a very light karate workout after with the girls. I wasn't wearing a helmet, and hadn't quite gotten a final carte blanche from the doctor. I cleaned up, and met Oscar for lunch at the restaurant on top of the Crocker Plaza. Just the two of us. He ordered a six-ounce strip steak with a loaded potato, and a Coke. I got a twelve-ounce sirloin, side salad with vinaigrette, and plain iced tea. We chatted about a few cases the girls were working on, and several that we signed before I left for Rome. Helicopter cases. One Cessna. A formally dressed waiter delivered our meat on a sizzling plates. It smelled almost but not quite as good as Miguel's. I started on my salad. Oscar went for the steak.

The ambiance of the restaurant was conducive to business. There were other businessmen around the room, quietly discussing whatever they were discussing. Brilliant white linens, spiffy waiters, a steady flow of early cocktails, lots of meat. Across the room, I saw an early bird couple looking over a dessert cart. My stomach growled loud enough for Oscar to hear, and he laughed aloud. I took a few quick bites of steak, and chased it with a whole glass of tea. The waiter showed up like magic to refill it.

"Oz, you probably know that I've been seeing Camila and Olga pretty regularly. Pepe not much, but the girls, yes."

"I didn't know," he said with a straight face. "What a lucky young man you are." He barked that laugh of his, and continued to carve his steak.

"Here's my problem, Oz. I have no one to talk to about this situation. I think we can talk. We are tight." Not as tight as I'd been with Harry, or Jake. Harry and Jake had never connected me with people like the Camachos. Oscar could have gotten Pepe to help with my rescue and not introduced me. But introduce me he did. Oscar was no dummy. Whatever consequences might arise with knowing the Camachos, he would understand all the possibilities, positive and negative, and he had still introduced me.

"Of course," he said, "What is it?"

"Pepe is or was your client. Camila and Olga both know you."

Oscar nodded in agreement and looked up from his plate to encourage me. "You can talk and eat, Mario. It's going to get cold."

Oscar had finished his steak, and started methodically on his baked potato. I had an instant of potato envy. I'd seen Cosmo for a few minutes on my first day home, and he'd growled and slapped me in the belly. No words from him, just the slap. No spare tire. Not even close. But I wouldn't want to lose the washboard I'd had for years. His actions decided for me that this would be a lean food week while ramping up the exercise again. I hadn't come here for the food, but I took a bite or two.

I could not tell Oscar that I was holding seven million dollars, but I wanted his input on the proposal to do acquisitions. Olga had not told me not to tell anyone, although she may have assumed I wouldn't. Fuck it. I told him their proposal, then worked on my steak as he formulated his response.

"It's a great opportunity for you as long as it doesn't get in the way of our business. I love the cases you bring me."

I nodded. "I have no plans of stopping aviation. We're kicking ass, and we're just getting rolling in aviation. But the nature of the business does leave me with a lot of time on my hands that I could spend earning more. I know what bothers me about it, and I know why I think it is a good idea, but why do you think it's a great opportunity?"

Oscar offered me a cigar.

I shook my head.

He stuffed the extra cigar back in his pocket, clipped one for himself, and went through the whole ritual of lighting it. He had cigar smoking down to an art form, so this preparation and lighting procedure took a few moments. I'd seen him at this before. It was a performance. He smiled at me, took a couple of puffs, sucking the flame inside the cigar just to get it going, then one real puff. He savored the flavor, than glanced back at me.

"Pepe's father left him a fortune. His father had a good business sense but nothing like his son. Pepe took over that fortune and continues to grow. I don't handle any of his business, but he's closed some staggering deals. I know that in Germany, he has a stadium that sits forty thousand people. He's all over the place."

"Are you saying I shouldn't worry where the money is coming from?"

"I'm not going to tell you that, but if it was me, I wouldn't worry about it."

I chuckled. "Oscar, no question. You're such a lawyer."

Oscar puffed away and laughed. "Indeed. If it was dangerous, I would tell you to play busy and pass. When you talk deals with sellers, keep in mind that many will believe cash is automatically dirty. Even if it's not. You're smart, if you encounter a stubborn person who talks the dirty money shit, walk. Just walk."

I was quiet as Oscar took a break from talking and puffed a little. Oscar loved his cigar.

"It's brilliant the way you work with the clients you bring me. As a people person, you should use your skills in negotiating deals for LAI. I've never checked, but I can almost guarantee that his companies are as clean as they can get." Oscar's lips moved on the cigar. "Don't forget we had his trial here in Los Angeles. The Feds thought they had him dead-bang, but I proved them wrong and a jury agreed and found him not guilty on all counts. In other words, the judge decided he was not the head of a cartel and there was no evidence he was importing drugs in to the United States, or conspiring to do so."

"Maybe the case was intended for the father but he was dead so they came after Pepe," I heard myself say.

"The Feds knew his father was dead. Took advantage of him during a trip he made to Los Angeles. Arrested him."

"I can understand why he doesn't want to come back."

"Because he's afraid they'd pull something like that again, he won't come back to the US. That hasn't stopped him from planting his company's assets in fertile US investments. Pepe will not jeopardize those assets."

"You'd think he would just stay away from the United States. The globe is big. Why mess with a country that has it out for him?"

"If he's so afraid the Feds would attach what he owns under the assumption that he is involved in racketeering and the assets have been purchased with dirty money, I don't know why he's expanding in the US. If I was advising him, I'd tell him the same thing you would. He can invest anywhere in the world." Puffs. "Wouldn't do any good. Pepe does what he wants. The man is as stubborn as he is brilliant. Don't let his appearance fool you."

"Appearance?"

"He doesn't run around in three-piece suits."

"No, he just runs around in great big airplanes."

"That's for sure. You look like you are tempted as all hell to test the waters of this proposition."

I took a long drink of tea, and covered the glass with my hand when the waiter magically appeared to refill it. "I am. I like the possibility of how much money I can make with him as his investment adviser." I set my glass down. "I'm sorry if my questions put you in a spot."

"You didn't put me in a spot. You wanted legal advice, not for information about my client or former client. Legal advice. That's my job. All is good."

"Thanks, Oz."

"No thanks needed. Remember." He pointed his cigar at me. "Do whatever you want but don't stop that case flow."

"I can't schedule crashes, or predict how many cases I'm going to get when they do crash, but I'll continue doing what works, no matter what else I'm doing."

"Mario, that spark you have, the people skills, that fiery ambition, it will take you as far as you can imagine."

"I can imagine a lot."

I raised my empty tea glass and clicked his glass of port.

The first time Oscar and I ever spoke was on the phone, after he'd asked Carson to get me on board with him. Oscar had offered me five thousand just to meet him for lunch. He wanted me to come on board that bad. I'd taken the meeting but not the money. The offer had certainly set that memory in concrete. It had taken Jake's untimely death to get me to work with Oscar. And now I could not imagine not working with him.

Chapter 6
May 1979
Rolling The Dice

Camila called from Bogota a few days after my meeting with Oscar and never mentioned the business proposal. Her call was followed closely by Olga's call, from another part of the world.

"Where are you?"

"I'm in Paris. Where is that bakery is that you told me about?"

"I forgot I told you about that. I'm still a partner. It's on the Champs-Élysées, a couple of blocks from–"

Olga's laugh interrupted me.

"Amor, I'm already at the airport, ready to board. I'll go with you one day when we come to Paris together."

"Okay. Where you headed?"

"I was thinking of stopping in Los Angeles on my way back home."

"I'm local, Baby. Do it."

"Flight plan is already in the works."

Camila must have told her I was home. "I look forward to seeing you."

"Me too."

A day later, I picked up the phone in my room.

"My pilots are off in a Burbank hotel taking a ten-hour nap. I'm totally naked and alone at the Van Nuys airport," Olga said. "Hurry."

In a minute, I was at the door with my keys in hand. The team was at the conference table looking through newspapers. I didn't look back.

Letty was coming out of the kitchen with a tray of snacks, and caught me at the door. She set the tray on the foyer's console table, and noticed the keys.

"I guess I'm not driving you," she said. "I bet that was Olga or Camila on the phone."

I nodded.

"I'll play dumb. Have fun."

"Baby, don't do that. Tell the girls I'm off for a few hours. The meeting with Olga is not a secret."

"Got it, Boss."

She picked up the tray and headed to the office. As I went out the door, I heard her say in a loud voice, "Who wants lemon ice box pie and lemonade?"

In private airports, I'd seen huge planes before, like an executive's 747. Olga's plane was bigger than most of the executive jets that used the airport, but not that big. Olga's plane was usually just off the tarmac a short distance away from the lobby of the airport operator. Today, I was taken by jeep about a mile from the lobby. The jeep's driver explained the plane's location, but I confess, I really wasn't listening. I just nodded my head.

I ran up the rolling stairs and embraced Olga. "Baby, so good to see you."

"Amor, please tell me you missed me like I missed you. Call me Olga, please."

I pulled back to see her face. "Olga, I missed you. I don't know what's come over me."

"Amor, me too."

No planes were around us. A taxiing plane at this airport would be lower to the ground than the aircraft we were in. Even if the shades on the windows had not been pulled down, I doubt that anyone would be able to see Olga prancing naked around the plane, or me when I joined her.

We played around in bed for about six hours. When we got up, I just put my boxers on. As much as I ached for a shower, water on board was limited. The plane had a shower, but I let Olga use it. I could shower at home.

No food had been brought on board yet, so we ate peanuts and packaged snacks we found in the galley. We found a couple of Cokes, too, which really hit the spot. We were relaxed in the sitting area. I was on the sofa, and Olga was stretched out across me in a pajama top. I laughed to see she was looking over the real estate classified ads from the newspaper she'd picked up in New York.

"What's so funny?"

"You're reading the classifieds." I laughed that she shared my pastime, but didn't explain. She rolled her eyes at me, and kept reading. "I want to be straight with you," I said.

"About what?"

"I didn't tell Oscar everything, but I mentioned the proposal to him."

Her smile told me it was okay.

"Did Oscar give you the legal advice you wanted?"

That just about confirmed that she had talked to Oscar.

"Not really."

"Does that mean you're interested, or not?"

"I want to roll the dice, and try this out."

She beamed. Her gleeful response felt spontaneous. If Oscar had talked to her, he hadn't given away my decision. Olga was jubilant. She tossed the newsprint aside. I got a big hug, a sitting hug, and a wet kiss.

"I'm so happy, Amor."

"So now what?"

She grabbed a wad of the newspaper she'd tossed aside, and shoved it in my arms.

"Here," she said, laughing. She was still draped over my lap. "Quick. Find something to buy."

I dropped the *New York Times* and held on to her instead.

"And when I find something, then what?"

"Find something. Then call me or Camila."

"Do I wait to get an okay from either of you?"

"No need. If you think it's a good deal, make it happen."

"What if the seller wants part of the money through escrow and not in cash?"

"No problem. I wire the money."

"The idea is to get seller to take as much cash as possible, right?"

"Right, Amor. That way, you make more. You get ten percent."

I really didn't even know how I'd start to work this out but trusted that I would find a way.

"Tell me more about what you want. Just apartments?"

"No, we are looking for any income producing property. Office buildings, anything you like. If you like it, we will like it."

"You are that sure?"

"Amor, you paid $1.1 million for your house. You put in a lot of money to make it gorgeous as it is. What is it worth right now in such a short time? Three million, maybe four? Down the road, worth much more. We're in it for the long-haul, not looking to buy and sell. We buy and lease out. Buy and manufacture."

"How did you know what I paid for the house?"

"I know, Amor." She kissed me. "I love you a little bit, yes?"

I returned her kiss and spoke into her mouth. "You just like the way I eat your pussy."

"Amor, *si, si.*" She sighed. "And you love what I do to you, *si?*"

"*Si* Baby."

She pulled my boxers off. We had a little over an hour left before the pilots would return, and made good use of the time.

Since I'd met him, Randy had gone from agent to broker. I trusted him because he's the one who taught me the ropes. I would not have as many apartments today if not for him. We didn't hang out together, or run in the same circles, but he was a friend. He was always hunting for apartment deals for me. What would I tell him now? That I wanted bigger deals for a foreign company I was doing some moonlighting for? I didn't call Randy right away. Instead I kicked around the best way to find deals.

I had always liked reading the classified ads and once in a while I did read about interesting items and property for sale.

I called Tricia in Las Vegas. After we talked through an x-rated conversation, I got down to business.

"If I want to find a list of properties in foreclosure, can you get them for me?"

"No problem. What you looking for?"

"I want to find apartment buildings and office buildings in my area. I'm looking for owners that are desperate."

"Boss, I can find foreclosures, but I won't know the owners are desperate."

"Wise-Ass," I threw back. "We can assume that the owners are desperate because they're in foreclosure."

"I have a fine ass. You keep telling me that."

"And I don't lie."

When she called me back the next day, I could tell she was at a public pay phone.

"Where are you calling from? It sounds like you're in a crowded bathtub."

She laughed. "I'm at a pay phone in the Los Angeles Hall of Records. This may take a while."

"Take your time. If you find something interesting, read everything about the property that might be there, and if necessary go by the property. Take pictures."

"Okay, Boss."

My team was sitting at the conference table. I hung up and saw them fixate on me with their 'what's up' look.

I got up from behind my desk and joined them. It took a long time to explain, largely because I was figuring it out while I talked.

"Is this fucking legal?" asked Pixie.

"Oscar didn't tell me it was illegal."

"Did he tell you it's legal?" asked Niley.

"I think I put him in a spot because he represents Pepe, or did," I said slowly, because I was remembering his very loop-holey sentence where he could almost guarantee Pepe's businesses were all entirely legal. "I believe that Oscar would have told me not to mess with it if he thought I would be vulnerable."

"I agree," Jo said. "It's not that I think that Oscar's an angel. But he sees Mario as a gravy train, and he wouldn't jeopardize that gravy train."

Niley looked a little shocked.

Jo patted her on the back. "I call it like I see it, babe."

"I think it's a great way to make extra money," Letty said.

Pixie giggled. "How the fuck would you know, bitch?"

"Call me a bitch again, and I'll kick your ass," Letty said. "I've been practicing that throw Cosmo was showing us last month, and I've got it down pat. I'm itching to try it out."

"Girls, don't mess with my brain right now. No distractions. I think I'm going to do some more investing."

"You're the Boss," Jo said, moving her arms like an orchestra conductor calling all the instruments to a halt.

"Right. You're driving the car. That's for sure. Always have," Niley said.

"Except for when Letty or me—" Pixie said, clapping her hand over her mouth when she got that Niley didn't mean it literally, and switching her sentence to "We'll help any way you want, Boss. Legal or not, who gives a fuck?"

The girls did a high five. Pixie, who was sitting next to Letty, put her arm around her and leaned in for a kiss that had no karate in it.

Tricia brought me a list of twenty-one properties in foreclosure, all in the final thirty days before the auction. She'd been working with the team as needed. She had begun calling me Boss, too.

"I went to see them all," she said. "And I have more foreclosure lists from a couple of banks, and an agent who handles FHA and VA repossessions."

"Good work. Bear in mind, I'm looking for apartment buildings and commercial buildings, not single-family houses."

I picked up the first file. Each file had one or more Polaroids of the property in question. She sat across from me, my desk between us. The team, in eavesdropping mode for sure, was sitting at the conference table looking ever slower through our endless supply of magazines and newspapers.

"Anything here that caught your attention?"

"Most of the properties are run down, but maybe that's because the owners figured they were going to lose out and gave up. I don't know. The one you are looking at is twenty units in Downey."

"It doesn't look too bad."

"Let me see," Pixie said, jumping out of her seat and running over to my desk.

"Hey, I want to see, too," Niley said.

"And what about me?" Jo ran over.

Letty stayed at the conference table. I waved her over. Then they all huddled around my side of the desk until I realized it wasn't going to work. We all moved to the conference table. I went through the pictures, then passed them around. They all studied the buildings intently and started pointing out the obvious merits and flaws of each one, and interrogated Tricia when they had questions. Letty wrote down the merits and flaws on a new sticky note pad product she had found at our local stationary store, and added her notes to the file.

I called the owner of one of the properties, and got his okay for me to come by on the next day.

"You do good work," Jo said to Tricia.

"Thanks."

At nine in the morning, I pulled in front of a home in Boyle Heights, my old neighborhood, except that the houses on Boyle were big nice houses, certainly a cut above the apartment I'd grown up in. This was the best street to live on in ELA, and this was where the owner of the twenty units in Downey lived. His house was not the best one on the street but the inside was okay. He'd introduced himself as Enrique Munoz. The house smelled like smoke and someone was cooking. He was friendly and talkative, and asked me to call him Ricky. The lines in his face were deeply grooved, and he looked a little like a pit bull, if a pit bull had a cleft chin, and graying black hair just around the edges of his mostly bald head.

"I've had a hundred calls," Ricky said, offering me a beer which I refused. "Everyone's offering me a thousand. One offered me five thousand to sign off. Is that what you have to offer?"

"I have no offer. If we make a deal, I promise to give you more than that nickel you got offered.

"I'd rather let it go than to sign off for anything less than $25,000.[12] There's a lot of equity there, but my credit is fucked, and I can't refinance." He led me to a couch in his den where the scent of smoke was very strong. "Sit down," he said. "That's a nice ride you got out there."

"Thanks. So are the payments." I always said this even though car was paid for.

Ricky laughed. "Yeah, I bet they are."

---

[12] $25,000.00 in 1979 had the same buying power as $89,155.10 in 2017

"I see three mortgages on the property, a first, second and a third."

"Right on. The first foreclosed. If the second and third don't step up and pay the first, they are out of luck."

The loans on the property totaled up as one hundred forty-five thousand. The rental income was $3,800 a month,[13] $45,600 a year.[14] The rule of thumb on rental property is that it was worth about eight to nine times the annual rental income. I wasn't that well acquainted with Downey, but I had been there many times when I was signing up regular car accidents. Tricia had said the area wasn't bad and the pictures showed an acceptable property.

"So how much you want, Ricky, to sign off, and I'll pay off the loans."

"I want forty thousand."

"I'll give you twenty."

"No way."

"You prefer losing the property? It goes for auction in eleven days."

"Fuck it. I have three other properties that are going too."

"Three other properties?"

"Yeah, three. I was flush once. I had apartments everywhere."

"What happened?"

"Wife split. Got a divorce. She took her half and left me to manage everything, and I ain't no manager."

"Fuck," I said with a gut full of empathy. I hoped this never would happen to me.

If I wasn't doing this for Camacho, I'd make this deal for myself. The property was a good buy. I had not seen it firsthand, but I would rely on Tricia's pictures. I returned four hours later with a grant deed and a quitclaim deed just in case. I also brought my broker and his notary public. I gave Ricky thirty thousand. [15] I knew I could have raped him by waiting longer, but I felt too bad for him. He hadn't had a break in a long time, I couldn't take advantage of

---

[13] $3,800.00 in 1979 had the same buying power as $13,551.57 in 2017

[14] $46,500.00 in 1979 had the same buying power as $165,828.48 in 2017

[15] $30,000.00 in 1979 had the same buying power as $106,986.12 in 2017

him too. When he heard I was going to pay him cash, he was thrilled.

"I owe the second and third to one dude," Ricky said. "I can call him. If you pay him cash like you did me, I think he'll give you a discount."

After I paid Ricky, I visited the property by myself. I brought the team the next day, before I paid off the second and third. I gave Miguel the go-ahead for a sudden celebratory dinner, and invited my broker and notary, my team plus Tricia. I breathed a sigh of relief when Melina couldn't make it, because I knew it would be impossible for her not to ferret out the details about cash involved. It was the first time I'd ever seen Randy tipsy, but even after four glasses of wine, he waxed on and on how I got a great deal. He asked no questions, and when I gave him a thousand dollars for handling the paperwork and filing, he left a happy man.

I paid Ricky's former friend $40,000 [16] for the first and second loans that totaled just under fifty thousand. He would have lost out anyway because he didn't have the money to pay off the first.

Randy and I walked in the lienholder's bank with a cashier's check from my bank and paid off the loan. I had the deed made out to Latin American Investments with a mailing address of a post office box in Florida that Olga had provided.

Olga and Camila both called to say the deal was fantastic. The cost of fuel for a couple of trips for Olga to travel would have covered the apartments in short order. Fantastic was a bit of a reach. It was a good deal, but at their level, I knew it was not fantastic.

"You are good negotiator," Camila said. "Oscar was right. But I knew it too."

"The truth is I almost hope you don't like it. If it's not to your liking, I'll buy it from you."

---

[16] $40,000.00 in 1979 had the same buying power as $142,648.15 in 2017

"Not for sale, Amor. *Gracias!*"

So, I figured I made twenty thousand for a few days work. I wasn't sure exactly how much, but I'd wait until I met up with Olga or Camila to figure it out.

I used their money from the safe to pay everyone, including getting the cashier's check. It was no big deal getting a cashier's check for almost a hundred thousand to pay off the first at my bank using cash. The girl didn't mind at all, although she charged me five dollars for the cashier's check. A bigger amount might present problems.

"Boss, you did it," Jo said, excited.

"Yeah. I don't know why I didn't look at foreclosures before this. Not sure why I thought of it and asked Tricia to get me the information. Maybe I just got lucky."

"This is a deal. For less than two hundred, you got twenty units," Niley said.

"I loved the deal. If I hadn't made the commitment to LAI, I would have bought them myself."

"Nah, Boss. Everything you own is around here. Why mess with Downey?" Jo asked.

The girls concurred.

"I would have given it to the management company just like I'll recommend to LAI to do."

"I agree with Jo, Boss. Buy stuff around here," Pixie said.

I followed through on that thought, and had Jo call our management company for a quote to handle the property. Two days later when they gave us a price, I called Camila.

"Amor, I should have told you. I retain a management company to handle anything you buy for us. May I give him your number? The name is Raul Gomez. A cousin from Bogota who works for Pepe"

I was surprised, but she'd never know it.

"By all means. Have Raul call me. I'll give him the information on the tenants, what they are paying, and anything else he needs."

"Oscar is right, you are one of a kind. I love you, Amor."

"I love you, too," I heard myself say, but I was starting to think Oscar talks too much.

I told Jo that they had someone to handle the management.

"All the better," Jo said.

"Why you say that?

"Buy. Close. Get paid. Done."

"Do you say that because you think the deal or deals are shaky?"

"Not for me to say, Boss."

I heard from Raul Gomez a day later. He had a young voice.

"Whatever you buy for LAI, instead of sending them to Miami, have the escrow company send me all the closing documents. I travel a lot, but I have a team here in Los Angeles who will handle anything you can throw at them for LAI."

I was impressed. "So if I buy a theatre?"

"No sweat. Buy it. My management team will take it from the moment you close the deal."

Raul was the next step. He was the person who would make whatever happen that needed to happen with the properties. They would be using the properties or businesses as fronts, pumping cash into banks. I did not need anyone to spell it out for me.

Across town from my old neighborhood was a large twenty-four hour bakery. Day or night, hungry people lined up to buy Mexican pastries. I heard that the owner Margarita Lopez was very sick and was thinking of selling the business. She employed a workforce of over a hundred, none of them family.

I visited Margarita in her gorgeous Montebello home. I was not surprised that she had money. I pulled up in her circular drive in a community built overlooking a golf course where each property was unique. A servant answered the door, and led me to her. I had my eyes open in the few rooms I walked through, and I was looking at a house anyone would be proud to live in. Marble foyer. Expensive antiques, lovingly curated. Plush carpeting. I'd had a devil of a time getting an appointment to see her at home, pulling out the stops, even using connections through my aunt's church, since it was through church gossip I'd heard she was sick. Before coming to see her, I had done my due diligence. I had Tricia canvas the bakery. For more than a week, she had taken pictures of the customer lines at all hours of the day and night. Twice she brought me samples of the pan dulce, delicious sweet bread, made in all shapes and sized to fit in your hand.

Although the property was across town from Boyle Heights where my aunt and I had lived, I'd heard of the bakery. My aunt had been a bookkeeper for a garment factory, but her sideline as a midwife took her all over town. She'd known of the bakery, and certainly she had shopped there when she'd been delivering a baby in the neighborhood. We weren't regulars by any means. ELA has a whole mess of bakeries that have pan dulce. Mexican markets like Melina's have a wide selection.

"Mrs. Lopez, I was told you are ill, but you look fabulous." She had to be over eighty, but still worked countless hours every week.

"*Nino grande*, you are so handsome, so tall. Please sit down. Have some coffee and pastries with me."

Margarita Lopez had chosen to meet with me in her living room. She was in a comfortable looking wing chair with a quilt draped over her lap. An elderly servant stood just behind and a little to one side of her chair waiting for her orders. He was as wizened as an old apricot, but spry, and quick to respond to his Boss's wishes. No sooner had the word pastries come from Mrs. Lopez's mouth than he rolled up a cart loaded up with goodies. It had been ready to go, and carried a steaming silver coffee service. I figured the baked goods, a selection of pan dulce and other pastries, came from her bakery. I could have cleared the tray by myself. There were no plates.

"Family style," she said, selecting a cookie for herself.

Mrs. Lopez accepted a scant cup of coffee her servant poured, took a second cookie from the tray, and dipped the cookie in her cup before she took a bite. I noticed a slight quiver in her grasp, and guessed that was why her cup was only half full.

I used a linen napkin to contain the crumbs.

"Excellent quality. From your bakery, of course."

"Of course."

She seemed pleased.

"Thank you, Mrs. Lopez for your hospitality. I've been a customer of your bakery since I was a kid. I was raised in ELA, not far from the bakery."

"I don't remember you, but I have thousands of customers. This business has been my life's work."

"You make the best bread in Los Angeles."

She flushed with pleasure, color rising in her face. Some people age and don't wrinkle. Not Mrs. Lopez. Her skin was like typing paper that was wadded into a tight ball and then flattened out, with a million tiny creases. It was easy to picture her slaving over a bakery oven. Her silver hair was cut short in a pixie-like cap. The room had spectacular windows, and was well lit. I could see light glinting in her hair as she turned to her servant. Margarita waved him away, and he tottered off, leaving the food behind.

"*Hijo, gracias.*"

"I heard you may want to sell the business?"

She frowned, reached for a tissue from the table next to her and blotted her eyes without removing her glasses.

"My two sons and three daughters have never wanted anything to do with the business. I have two managers that work two shifts, and I work a shift. My people know the business but they have no funds to buy me out."

"I have the money."

"You." She seemed surprised. She tilted her head and considered me, her gaze sharp behind those glasses.

"If I can have the managers to operate the business, I'm interested."

"You seem so young."

"I got an early start. Like you, God helped me succeed. I have almost a thousand apartments all nearby. I do very well."

I could tell she was impressed. I was impressed with her, too. I could see when her business gears clicked in. She might be a baker, but she also had chops as a businesswoman.

"I take in more than a hundred thousand a month. [17] I clear about thirty-nine percent after all expenses are paid."

I nodded.

She looked at me a little nervously. "Most people pay cash. I cannot produce books to show actual sales."

"I believe you," I said, looking right at her. She looked as relieved as I felt. I was glad to hear her cash problem meshed so well with Camila and Pepe's needs.

"The building is mine, free and clear. I haven't checked the value lately, but I believe its last appraisal was around eight hundred thousand. That's the building plus everything in it."

"How much are you thinking of asking, lock, stock, and barrel?"

"I think my bakery is worth two million dollars."

"What if I could pay you in cash?"

"I would like that." She thought for a moment and tested the water. "I would take 1.5 million in cash. Do you have that much?"

"If you let me speak with the two managers you have, and recommend them to handle the business, I can probably get the money."

"My managers are wonderful people. I trust them completely. One has been with me for fifteen years, the other over twenty. I would not feel right if I left them in a lurch. But I would love to give them the chance of secure em-

---

[17] $100,000.00 in 1979 had the same buying power as $356,620.38 in 2017.

ployment into the future, maybe even a possibility for advancement. Can you do this?"

"I think that would fit perfectly with our objectives."

I rolled the dice, and met with the managers Jaime Gomez and Arturo Cruz at my house over dinner. They arrived grim, somber, and in awe of my house. I fed them before we got down to the important talk.

"If the deal goes through and we buy the bakery, it is for a big investment company."

They looked worried. Both arrived in jeans and tees, both as husky as you might expect bakers to be. Miguel had heard he was cooking for bakers, and was excited to impress them. He'd outdone himself frying chicken, and fixing biscuits, cornbread, several vegetables, and a parfait-style dessert made of crushed pastries from their bakery, with whipped cream and berries. They ate with gusto, and bantered good-humoredly with each other about their respective shifts. They asked Miguel to come out, and complimented him, and said they were considering using his dessert recipe in the shop, which tickled Miguel to no end. Arturo was the day man, and Jaime, the night. I could see they were good friends, and that their mutual competition kept their work-lives interesting, but afterwards when we retired to my den, Jaime got to the point and spoke for both of them.

"Why are we here if you are going to put us out of a job? We are good at what we do. All we want to do is keep the routine that has kept us going for decades." He looked like he was in his late fifties, and though he wore his weight with a deceptive layer of softness, he was as fit as you would expect a man to be who regularly handled hundred pound bags of flour.

"The buyer is interested in long range plans, and the big picture, but not much in the day to day running of the business. They have a management company to handle their interests, but I could guarantee that you could remain in your positions. I can get you more money, and a possible bonus based on a percentage of annual sales."

"And we can stay in our kitchen, and not have to fool with office work?"

I assured them that would probably be the case. I knew the Camacho team would be handling numbers and paperwork for their own reasons.

"The two of you might put your head together and figure out who will be running the shift Mrs. Lopez usually manages."

"Chuy," they suggested, simultaneously. Chuy turned out to be Jesús, the swing shift's assistant manager. He was a youngster at thirty-eight, and had only been there for ten years, but knew the ropes.

When they left, they were optimistic, and chattering enthusiastically with each other.

I met with Mrs. Lopez a total of three times. In less than two weeks, we opened an escrow for the real estate, equipment and the business; escrow instructions stated for valuable consideration paid outside of escrow the sale was being made. I gave Camacho's management manager, Raul Gomez, an overview, including the promises to the two managers. The transaction details were not his business. His business was to sit in an office to supervise operations. I knew the bakers would be delighted over that.

"I know the bakery. My team can handle the office, and let the bakers do their jobs and have their space and their annual percentage. Have you talked to Pepe?"

"Actually, I haven't."

"Mario, thank you for giving me a heads up. Let me know if it happens."

I didn't tell anyone about my own conclusions. I figured that no matter what the bakery was making in a month, it would be Raul's job to feed substantially more cash into the bank accounts. I'm guessing Lopez had trouble producing records because she probably hoarded some of that cash income of hers, and only banked enough to handle the overhead. Raul would be doing the opposite, infusing as much cash as possible into the bank deposits and fiddling with the daily income receipts in creative math. LAI would pay taxes on the money, but once in the bank, the excess funds would be totally clean and available for anything LAI wanted to do with the money.

When LAI walked away with the title of the bakery a month later, I walked away with a cool $150,000 dollars[18]. Well, I actually got paid a couple of days later, but I earned it when the deal went through. That is a lot of money. That much profit for a quick transaction snagged my full attention. I'm not knocking my client development business. When Oscar paid me 1.1 million for a case, that's a lot of money too. I was on a winning streak.

After closing, we left the lawyer's office together. Margarita and I shook hands in the elevator on the ride down.

"What are you planning to do, now that you're a millionaire?" I asked, pushing the button for the lobby.

"Sleep late," she said, though I had a feeling she was kidding. "The money won't make a difference. I was a millionaire long before I became a widow, and I've been a widow for twenty years. We lived in a regular neighborhood close to the bakery up till my husband died. I moved up the hill for the view and built the house on the advice of friends. When Luis died, the house was a new beginning for me. I'm looking forward to the free time."

"You've earned it," I told her.

"So have you," she said. "Are you going to continue brokering deals for LAI?"

"Of course. They are always looking for investments."

"You're a good boy," she said in a grandmotherly way. "You remind me of my grandson. I think I have something you might be interested in." We walked out of the elevator into the lobby. She sat down on a bench, and dug around in her purse until she found a business card, which she handed to me.

---

[18] $150,000.00 in 1979 had the same buying power as $534,930.58 in 2017.

There was nothing on the card but the name Barriga and a phone number. The card reminded of the ones I used to carry when I was a kid working for Cosmo, the karate teacher, and then Harry, the lawyer.

"That's Pablo Barriga, the owner of a corn tortilla factory. He has thirty delivery trucks. Barriga Tortillas are in all the markets."

"Sure. I know the brand."

"You know I'm as old as dirt. Well, Pablo is five years older than I am. I did not tell him the details of our deal, but he's ready to sell too. Call him."

I kissed Margarita. "*Gracias, Amorcito.*"

When I visited her at Van Nuys Airport, I gave Camila an album filled with pictures of the bakery and a huge box of varieties of pan dulce. She whooped in hysterics over the samples she had not expected me to deliver.

"Just wait till you try it," I said. I thought she'd never quit laughing.

She had already heard from Raul.

"Amor, we love this. Pepe thought it was hilarious, but never questioned your decisions. After he talked to Raul about the place, he was ecstatic." Laughing, she thumbed through the pictures. "Wait till Olga and Pepe get a look at these!"

"Wait till they get a bite of these," I said, making her laugh again. "Are you really happy with the deal? I know it's not what you expected."

"Amor, I will never lie to you, ever. We love this deal."

"That means I can take my $150,000?"

"Absolutely. And I can think of a bonus I can give you right now."

"Bonus?" My ears perked up, along with other parts of me when I realized what she meant.

Camila got up from the sofa, took my hand. I followed her to the bedroom cabin aboard this aircraft, and we took care of business for hours.

For the amount of income this generated, this job was too easy. I loved this new line of work. I was happy. The Camachos were happy. Margarita was happy. I suppose Margarita's kids who hated the bakery business were happy that there was a bunch of cash now, and no more bakery headaches, whatever they might be. It was all good. I imagined that eventually the bakery would be a money moving machine for LAI in the hands of their management team headed by Raul Gomez.

Barriga Tortillas was located in ELA, a huge plant filled with gas operated machines that were cranking out corn tortillas and going through a process that ended with a familiar package of tortillas in one dozen, two dozen and five dozen bundles. Unlike Margarita, the owner, Pablo, had books and records, or at least he showed me a mountain of ledgers on his desk.

"Here are three years of our operation."

"Pablo, give me the bottom line. How much do you make a year?"

"After expenses, about two hundred thousand.[19] I pay for all my cars, a boat and many adult toys from the company account."

"Sounds like you don't need to sell?"

"I don't, but I want to."

"What is the building worth?"

He was evasive about an answer. The factory stood on 1.5 acres, with enough room to park another thirty trucks, and expand another ten thousand square feet to the plant.

"When the flour tortilla machine is out, we will add flour tortillas to our line. Soon."

"Interesting."

I agreed to return in two days to discuss a possible deal. I wasn't about to make a call and talk to a trio of Colombians who don't eat tortillas in their homeland about buying a tortilla factory, so I was on my own here. I had carte blanche, anyway. They'd already told me that if I like a deal, I should run with it. I was hooked on the value of the real estate alone. As land goes, the real es-

---

[19] $200,000.00 in 1979 had the same buying power as $713,240.77 in 2017.

tate was huge and on a great street, as great streets go in East Los Angeles. And I half believed what the seller told me the business was doing per year. Even if he exaggerated by fifty percent, it would still be a great deal but I didn't tell him that.

I consulted Melina.

"If you compare to the neighboring properties, the building alone has got to be worth a million," she said. "Get your real estate guy to check the square foot value of nearby commercial properties. The business is booming. My markets sell over a thousand dozen of Barriga's tortillas daily, and that's just me. It's a hot property and a thriving business."

Pablo agreed to sell for two million. It was three hundred thousand more than I wanted to pay but he'd managed to sell me on the imminent flour tortilla production line. Retailers from one end of LA to the other were already lining up to buy flour tortillas.

I gave Raul a courtesy call the day I opened escrow.

"Mario, what a great idea. You are a genius."

After that compliment, I figured we might become friends. I didn't know for certain, but anticipated that Raul would be the LAI team member I would be dealing with locally in Los Angeles, if he was the one who would be setting up and managing the various LAI offices here. We had never met. Beginning with Pepe, I called each of the Camachos about the pending purchase. I wasn't sure if they really liked what I had done, or were acting excited just to make me feel good. As an investment, I knew it was a good deal. The land would easily appreciate to what I had agreed to pay for the whole package. I shared that Melina's markets turned over twelve thousand Barriga Tortillas daily in her markets alone, and that the brand was everywhere. The deal taught me a lot about bulk sales.

It took thirty days to come out of escrow. Another fat paycheck lined up. $200,000. Boom. As before, I got paid in green.

Chapter 7
June 1979
Ugly Returns

Three months after paying off the bank, the development company offered Melina and me two million for the ugly building. All cash. Thirty days escrow.

"Let's take it. We double our money," Melina said.

"Now that we own the fucking place, let's just see how bad they want it."

"You're king of the negotiators," she said, laughing at me. "Go for it, tiger."

"You don't think I got all my apartments without a battle, do you?"

"Do you dicker like this for the Camachos?"

"I have to dicker to get good deals. I made $150,000 on the bakery, I loved that deal."

"Got to hand it to you on that one. I would have bought it."

"Barriga Tortillas was a prize, too," I reminded her. "That one made me a cool two hundred thousand." I was still jazzed over that deal. I guess I get high over successful deals the way some people get off on the lottery or Vegas.

"Proud of you, Cuz." Melina was beaming. She gets off on business, too, but she's a stickler. If she knew I was doing all this buying with cash, the proud attitude of hers might go south.

"You know what's crazy about this? I work on a commission. If I pay more for a property, I would make more. That means I should be okay with just giving what the seller wants. But I beat down the deals to what I would be willing to pay, if it was my money I was working with."

"That's why you get the big bucks." She laughed at her own joke that wasn't really a joke. It was true.

"Remember the Downey purchase. On that one, I made twenty thousand for a few days work. I hammered out a deal, saved a bundle by bypassing the auction."

"You don't know what it would have gone to auction. The bank holding the first was holding the cards. You could have walked, maybe, with whatever the bank was looking for without paying the owner and the second and third off."

She was right, but I didn't have to like it.

"Baby, don't ruin it for me."

She raised her eyebrows at me, and her lips quirked up on one side. "You're on a roll, and I love it."

I was glad to see the good mood. It was hard enough for her to accept that I was doing business with the Camachos at all. She only knew I negotiated their purchases. She was only happy because she was in the dark about these being cash purchases. At least with the ugly building, we were in complete accord. Two million was not as high as they would go. They had no choice. Melina had been right. We sat in the middle, and they owned the property on both sides.

We said our price was five million. In record time, we received their final counter of four million.[20] During the deal, she wore the austere, chilled features of a stranger, her eyes a chilled black, like an endless mirror. She looked bulletproof and untouchable, even intimidating me at a glance. I don't know how she did it, but it was a skill. We wore three-piece suits to the escrow closing. Mine was brown. Hers was red. She looked good in red, and knew it.

"Couldn't have done it without your inside info, Cuz."

---

[20] $4,000,000.00 in 1979 had the same buying power as $14,264,815.36 in 2017

She gave me a thumbs up, all warm and woman and accessible again. "Sorry it took so long, but our return on the investment is a home run. I made you a ton of money. You have to admit this is better than what you make for finding properties for them."

"Sure Baby, this is sweet, no question. I don't put up anything with Camacho. I put up half the money to make this deal. It's awesome. I made a ton of money. Thank you, Baby, for including me."

We walked down to the escrow company parking lot. Johnson was in her car waiting for her. Letty was in my car waiting for me. I gave Melina a big hug.

"Thank you, Baby. This was a fabulous investment. I love you."

"That's more like it." We kissed. I looked her over.

"I love you in red, but I love you naked, more," I whispered in her ear before I got in my car. Letty knew I didn't like her to open the door for me, so she waited in the driver's seat.

Johnson nodded at me, and held the door open for Melina.

She said, "I love you, Mario."

"Ditto."

She made a face, her tongue out. She hated me to ditto.

I laughed all the way to the bank with my two million dollars. I had put up five hundred thousand plus some interest we paid the bank until we paid off the note, but I was clearing a cool $1.5 million[21] minus a little bit for expenses. I was happy. I was over the moon.

Letty got the giggles when driving me.

"I know why I'm happy," I said. "What about you?"

She giggled again, and adjusted her chauffer's hat at a rakish angle.

"I love driving for you. It's like dress-up and playing hooky at the same time."

I grinned at her reflection in the mirror. She was cute in the chauffeur

---

[21] $1,500,000.00 in 1979 had the same buying power as $5,349,305.76 in 2017

get-up with her hair pinned up under her hat, and the little bow tie at her collar.

"Baby, you don't have to wear that uniform. It was your idea."

"I love the uniform Boss. I'm thinking I should wear it to bed one night. What do you think?"

I pictured her naked, with only the hat and the little bow tie around her neck.

"Try it and see. Surprise me."

Jo, Pixie, Niley and Letty had nothing to do with my ugly building deal, but I wrote four checks for five thousand dollars[22] and handed them the bonus during a dinner at the house. We ate by the pool. I was sitting on a padded bench, and except for Pixie, the girls were in various chairs, in their bathing suits. Miguel was such a great chef that we skipped the PDC ritual. We seldom did restaurant dinners like we used to except when we were out of town.

"I feel bad taking this," Letty said, after looking at the check. "What's it for?"

Pixie yelled from the shallow end, "Payment for all the pussy eating you've been doing." She was dripping wet, as usual, unable to resist the pool. I put the check in her wallet for her.

Jo said, "Shut up already." She looked at Letty. "Mario made a bunch of money on a deal and passed some of it on to us. You should know. You drove him to the escrow."

"Way too generous," Niley said.

"Yes, he's way too generous, but I love it," Pixie said happily. "And of course, I love you, Boss."

"I love you all. I want you to be happy. You can't be totally happy without money. Doesn't matter what many say about money. It's great to have it. And you earned it. I also feel terrible that working for me, you miss holidays

---

[22] $5,000.00 in 1979 had the same buying power as $17,831.02 in 2017

with your families sometimes, and—."

From the shallow end, Pixie interrupted.

"Boss, stop it. We had a blast in Portugal. Working jazzes us, and we had a nice little Christmas in the room. Lainey and Aunt Carmen did their thing on Christmas, anyway. And I love my rings from Brazil." She waved her hands, and I saw she was wearing some of the handcrafted Brazilian gold. "Our families are great. Our bank accounts are flush. Fuck, we rock."

The girls at the table did a high five.

"Go us!"

Pixie got out of the pool and made a run for me. Jo, Niley and Letty followed, wrapping themselves around me while I tried to finish dinner.

I thought about Margarita Lopez, ensconced in her great home where she no longer had to get up and run to work at the bakery. I was happy for her that the million plus she got for her business was just more of what she already had. Those managers of hers should have been bringing in enough that they would have been able to buy her out. She could have spread the wealth and still been rolling in her millions. Her way was not my way. My success wouldn't feel as good as it did if the people who made it happen didn't share my good fortune. It didn't matter that my team wasn't involved in this particular project. They were the cogs and wheels that made my life work, and without them, my life would have been very different.

Chapter 8
July 1979
Musical Houses

At six a.m. on July 4th, Tricia took off from the Ontario California Cessna case she was working, and took possession of a perfect spot on the sand next to the first lifeguard station and Santa Monica Pier where the fireworks would be exhibited that night. Letty and I led the way in the Rolls. Following were Jo and her kids, mom and nanny; Pixie, Lainey, and my Aunt Carmen; and Niley, her four kids and nanny. Melina couldn't get away from work.

Fire pits and cooking is not permitted at Santa Monica Beach, but Miguel was scheduled to arrive in my station wagon with ice chests and sustenance about two hours after our arrival on the sand. Tricia had arranged a parking spot a stone's throw from our umbrellas and chairs.

The beach, the sunbathers, and swimmers were beautiful. Even if the pier hadn't been there, I would have been able to guess our location by attire alone. Santa Monica Beach was nothing like Cannes or the nude beaches of Capri when I'd been buried naked. My team and Tricia looked gorgeous in knock-out bikinis. From under her own umbrella, my aunt watched all of us frolicking in the ocean, swimming and riding the waves. She even tested the water for herself for a bit.

A leggy woman running on the beach turned to look at me. Pixie noticed, and gave me the once over. I was in trunks that she'd picked out for me and attracting attention from women on the beach.

"Boss, you look so fucking hot in those short trunks," Pixie said, giggling. "I hope you get a hard-on."

I didn't get a hard-on, at least not right away. I had a beach towel over my shoulder, ready to wrap around myself, in case anything got prominent.

When Miguel arrived, he served us great submarines, and three different kinds of chips. We were parched, and chilled ourselves with icy sodas and cold water on tap. The cooler of beer Miguel brought sat untouched.

My team and I walked the pier, played games, got on the bumper cars. The girls had no worries, as the nannies—and the lifeguards—kept an eye on the kids while they played in the sand and rode the waves. I laughed until I was hoarse. We hiked away from the pier, following a boardwalk on the beach-side of homes fronted on Pacific Coast Highway.

The houses suffered a nightmare of traffic on Pacific Coast Highway, but I didn't care.

"I'd love to have one of these," I told anyone who would listen.

Jo looked at the traffic and made a face. "Boss, coming from Pasadena, you'd have to make a left to get into your garage."

"This is my first time in Santa Monica, and I can see that is dangerous shit," Letty said, frowning. "I'd hate to make that turn in the Rolls."

"I always admire these fucking houses when I drive by them," Pixie said wistfully.

"Me too," Jo said.

I kept looking as we walked. A ten-minute walk from where the umbrellas were set up, I stopped.

"Ready to head back?" Jo asked.

I pointed at a wooden FOR SALE sign and two OPEN HOUSE signs.

"I gotta see this," I said, walking between the house for sale and the one next door. I could see the traffic on PCH.

"Skinny houses," Letty pointed out.

The lots were about forty feet wide. This house was skinny but according to the flyer, it was three thousand square feet on three floors. Windows facing the ocean were floor to ceiling. Even the first-floor kitchen had a magnificent view.

"I dig the fuck out of this pad," Pixie said.

The whole team was buzzing over the house. I was getting excited. I focused my attention on the agent, a woman with helmet hair, and nice clothes. She was well padded, and sporting a shitload of costume jewelry that reminded me of my doctor. She gave me her card.

I asked the broker, "Why is it vacant?" I looked out of the third-floor window as a wave struck the beach, flattened into white foam and withdrew.

"The house was a foreclosure by the bank. It just went on the market last week. No problem with the house, just with the divorced couple who owned it."

The agent didn't care we were in skimpy bathing suits and covered in sand. She was treating me like I was in my best Italian suit.

"So the bank is the seller?" Niley asked.

"Bank of America."

"How much?" I asked.

"$250,000."[23]

"Lots of money for such a skinny thing," Niley said.

"It's three thousand square feet. Four bedrooms, three full baths and two half baths. And the land belongs to the house. And look at the location."

"Of course the land is included. When you buy a house, isn't the land included?" Niley asked.

The agent shook her head. "Along the highway, there are many homes where the land is leased for ninety-nine years. When you buy one of those, you only buy the structure. You pay a monthly rental for the land lease."

---

[23] $250,000.00 in 1979 had the same buying power as $891,550.96 in 2017

The team noticed that it was getting dark, and urged me to hurry up.

"I don't want to miss the start of the fireworks. Lainey will never forgive me," Pixie said. "Talk later. Walk now."

I promised to call the agent back.

The next day, I convinced Melina to see the house with me.

"I love it," she said with lots of enthusiasm. "But it comes with some negatives. PCH is a fucking bear. The noise, access in and out. If you are itching for a place here, why not look down the coast? A few miles away, you have Malibu."

"I like this house. I like being next to the pier. I like the boardwalk."

"Baby, you'll need a good burglar alarm system. You realize how vulnerable you are, sitting right on the sand under the nose of thousands of people every day?"

None of the drawbacks cooled my urge for the house. I made an offer of $200,000. The bank countered with $245,000, though I was told they were buried in the house and just wanted out.

"Write it up for $240,000. I'll agree to a two-week escrow, no financing necessary. I'll write a check. And by the way, I have my own broker, so you'll have to split your commission with him." That did not go over very well with the agent, but a sale is a sale. When the bank agreed to my offer, my broker took over, and made arrangements for insurance, setting up utilities, etc.

Melina was buried in her work, and Santa Monica was too far for her to come to mess with decorating. She hired a decorator, Carol Myers, who had ten years experience decorating beach houses.

The exterior of the house wasn't modern, but I told her I wanted it modern.

"It's going to take couple months. Maybe September."

I could look forward to September, still okay beach weather, though I didn't have to be in the water when I went out there. I wanted to walk the sand,

and the boardwalk. I wanted something different.

Back at home in the office, we had a meeting.

"Boss, are you going to invite us out to the beach?" asked Letty.

"Hell no. I will never invite you."

The girls all pouted simultaneously. I thought Letty and Niley were going to cry. Jo looked impervious, and Pixie looked like she was revving up to punch me in the jaw.

I held out my hand, dangling four little paper bags. They each got one.

"These are your keys to the beach house, and the combination to the alarm. No invitation needed."

The girls did their cheering and jumping routine. For an instant, I felt like cheering and jumping along with them, but I just watched. I could feel myself moving back into my shell. Whenever I faced the bright specter of happiness, I would feel the gray clouds looming. I might not be exactly haunted by the past, but I could not forget I lived in a world that had tried and failed to explode me out of it; and it had tried and succeeded in taking down Sami.

Melina had been concerned about the traffic around Santa Monica. I didn't know how dangerous crowds of beach walkers were, and I wasn't going to let street traffic determine whether or not I was interested in a property. The Bahamas didn't have the kind of crowds Santa Monica did, and that place had not been safe. At least it hadn't been safe for the two men shot at Pepe's house. I pushed that memory down, willing those secrets to disappear into the back of my mind. I wasn't going to let traffic patterns dictate where I was going to spend my time.

I went through every file that Tricia brought me this time around and found only one property that showed promise. I had Letty drive me to the fourteen-unit apartment building in El Monte. I walked around the exterior of the property, finding it clean and in good shape. I couldn't understand why the owner had let it go this far in the foreclosure process. It was up for auction in two days.

I asked my broker if I should I talk the owner into signing off, or show up and gamble on winning the auction on sheer luck. He thought anything I did to encourage things in my favor was good, as long as I didn't tip my hand that I was willing to pay more—not exactly news to me. The best bet was to get sellers to sign off, then do what I had done in Downey: pay off the loans and not take a chance of losing the property to a bidder. I didn't know what the rents were, but they had to be at least two hundred. The building looked good. I did the math. The minimum bid was $100,000.[24] The building was worth at least two hundred thousand, and even at that would be a steal.

On auction day, Letty drove me in the station wagon to El Monte City Hall. I didn't want to be seen in my Rolls at a foreclosure sale with a chauffeur, so I sat in the front seat, and she wore shorts.

I deposited a cashier's check for $25,000 with the clerk handling the sale, and I was handed a number so I could bid. Two others had badges like mine. I opened with the minimum bid plus one thousand. One of the other bidders bid a thousand more than my bid and the other bidder bid higher. As it started to get competitive, I covered up my increasing tension.

Paying cash to the bank was never going to work. If I took a chance and went in with a cashier's check as I'd done for the Downey property, I'd have to fill out an IRS form. This would be a good deal if I could buy it cheaply. I could just pay for it with my money.

The bid was up to $120,000. In my head, I drew the line. I'd go to $125,000 and stop. I needed to steal the building or nothing. I ended up buying the building for $124,000.[25] I was given twenty-four hours to come in with the balance of $99,000 or lose the twenty-five thousand deposit.

Letty and I were at the bank when it opened in the morning. She had

---

[24] $100,000.00 in 1979 had the same buying power as $356,620.38 in 2017
[25] $124,000.00 in 1979 had the same buying power as $442,209.28 in 2017

$49,000 and I had $50,000. I introduced myself to an officer at a desk, and told her I had two accounts there. She looked at a huge register on her desk, and then asked us to sit down. Between my two accounts, I had well over $400,000.

"I'm buying a building, and I need a cashier's check," I told her. "I prefer paying for it with cash, but I can write a check from my account if you prefer. Whatever is easier."

"Mr. Luna, whatever is best for you," she said.

I had planned for Letty to get a cashier's check with the cash I had given her, then I would get one with the fifty I had, but it was unnecessary. I paid a five-dollar fee, and thirty minutes later we were out of there with a cashier's check.

When I called Camila, I couldn't reach her, but got through to Olga right away. I updated her on the purchase.

I could hear her enthusiasm over the phone.

"I knew it, Amor. I'm so pleased."

"When am I going to see you?"

"Sooner than you think."

It was a damn good deal, another property that I would have bought for myself. I could buy them out if they balked, but they weren't going to balk.

My team knew what my deal was with Camacho, but Melina still did not know I was paying in cash. I felt guilty over keeping the secret. She'd be all over me if I told her. She also didn't know I was holding more of their money. I'd moved it to the bigger safe, the converted gun safe in order to squeeze in the additional three million I got from Olga when I returned from Rome.

I was sitting on so much money. At first, I didn't often think about how this came to be, but I now believed they had planned this. Oscar had introduced me; and they'd courted me, put the money in my custody, then slowly worked me, adding more money to the stash of theirs I was holding, and waited a year before Olga made me the offer of hunting for property in exchange for a fee. I'd preferred to keep thinking of Olga in bed rather than their methods of vetting people. I missed them, not just the sex I was addicted to. Sami was out of the picture but there were still three elusive women who consumed me: Melina, Camila, and Olga. And of course, my team.

Sunday, I was relieved when Melina showed up for brunch. I had not seen her all week.

"Baby, I fucking miss you." I gave her a bear hug, and she bear hugged back.

"I always miss you, Cuz." She boosted herself higher by stepping my shoes. We kissed.

"Are you hungry?"

"I'm starved. Let's eat. It smells great."

I felt good around Melina. She was like the queen. I messed around and she messed around, but on Sundays, we came together. Letty was all over us, hovering, working in the kitchen, taking care that we had plenty of everything though it was no longer her job. Maybe I was in love with Letty too, and didn't know.

"Anything new?"

"I bought a building in El Monte for them. Nice deal. I would have kept it for me."

"Cuz, don't spread out. Keep it close to home." She had the same opinion as my team.

"I wouldn't take a deal that was intended for them unless they were to reject it."

She kissed me. "You have lots of integrity, Cuz."

"It's good being with you," I said.

"Ditto," she said, laughing at her use of my word. "You still have that diamond ring?"

"I sure do. Why? Are you proposing to me?" I sat up, still laughing, and met her eyes.

"Cuz, I love our life the way it is. Even though I have to admit, I have my moments when I'm jealous."

"What?" I scooted closer. We were practically nose to nose.

"I get jealous of those two from Colombia because I know they are strong and I know you are attracted to them in a different way from other women. Probably the power of their wealth is a part of it. The whole mystique."

"Baby, you will always be the queen to me." I kissed her. I loved her body. I loved her breath. I loved her scent. I could not deny I wanted to own her, not as a possession but because she was like a part of me.

"Sometimes I wish we could be different people. I wish we could be like normal people."

"You don't mean that. It would be so boring not to be us. Wouldn't it?"

She sighed. "Maybe."

"I'm addicted to you," I admitted.

Melina smiled. "You are addicted to sex, Cuz."

"Oh, and what about you?"

"I plead guilty."

It was my turn to smile. "And what about us?"

"I don't believe in marriage." She pulled away from me just far enough that we could look each other in the eye. There was something compassionate in the angle of her brow, the corners of her eyes, the quirk of her lips that expressed tenderness I saw nowhere else. "But I do believe in love."

I felt a rush of warmth. "Maybe that's how I feel, too."

A hundred sayings crossed my mind, and none of them described my mindset. If it's meant to be, it will be. There is always tomorrow. When did I ever sit on my ass and let fate dictate my life? I agreed that I believe in love, but marriage would mean losing control of my life, especially considering the powerhouse kind of woman I was most attracted to.

Tricia walked into my office with a new stack of foreclosures and put them on my desk. She was always bringing me plenty of potential properties, but it was tough to find a match.

"You're here early," I said. I'd just finished what the girls called my daily triathlon: a run, karate, and swim, followed by spa and clean-up. I'd been pushing harder every day after the doc's go-ahead. Most days, whoever was there did one leg with me. Letty had taken up running since she was here in the morning. Someone always turned up for karate, the rotation so regular that I was thinking of asking Jo if she'd scheduled it. Pixie was always there for the pool, but usually in the way of conventional workouts unless sex counts.

"You're looking fit, Boss," she said.

"You too." She had a clean-scrubbed look today. No makeup, more college girl than military or Vegas. It suited her. A couple of the foreclosures looked really interesting at first glance.

"Thanks. Good job, by the way." I glanced at the clock. Not yet seven. I'd been up alone since five. Letty had gone back to sleep after her run.

"I finished up late last night, and went to bed at the hotel. Today, I was thinking of looking at some apartments."

"Apartments?" I held up the stack of foreclosures.

She shook her head. "Not those. I've decided to move to Los Angeles. I'm not doing anything in Vegas. LA traffic is a bitch but there's more business opportunity here for me. I feel it."

"Good idea. If you need a place to live, we can check with the management company that handles my apartments and check for vacancies."

"Boss, thank you. I've already started the process of getting licensed here and getting a gun permit like I have for Nevada. If you have anything delicate you want handled, you got me."

"Keep finding me good foreclosures. When you are local, I will find plenty for you to do."

"Thank you, Boss. I appreciate all you do for me."

She gave me a high five. I handed her a brochure the management company had made up that had all of my apartment complexes and their room plans.

"If you like any of these, let me know. I'll get you a discount. I know the owner."

Chapter 9
August 1979
A Winner

I found a fifteen-floor structure in Westwood, a very high-end area on Wilshire Boulevard. From that address, if you took Wilshire Boulevard west, you'd hit the Santa Monica Beach in twenty minutes depending on traffic. The steel structure was on a corner, unfinished. I don't know why I even went to the next step except that the address spoke to me. Tricia located the owner, Trent Joel, a contractor who'd run out of money. The construction loan he had was yanked because he drew more money against the loan than there was progress on the building. He wrote vouchers, but the total loan at any given time had to match up with the progress of the construction. I knew zero about progressive construction loans.

"Call me TJ," he said. "I have a million of my own money in land, construction plans and city permits. The bank won't budge. Bastards. No more time, they say. No one will come in with me on the project because they are afraid of foreclosure."

TJ's apartment was not far from the home I had just bought in Santa Monica. It wasn't anything special, but it was in a good neighborhood, close to everything, and cost effective. We got along pretty well. We had the same taste in neighborhoods.

"The old lady works close by," he said as we shook hands. He was in neat jeans and a button-down shirt. "She picked out the place." He was single but always had a broad living with him. His words, not mine. A woman clattering around the kitchen yelled, "The old lady has a name."

"If you bring out some fucking snacks, I'll fucking introduce you, old lady." He looked up at me, shaking his head. "Women."

I looked around. The furniture was neat, not outstanding. It was a respectable place. The most interesting thing was a twelve-foot photo of a surfer riding a wave. The picture was a gorgeous shot, and the surfer was a true athlete. "You have a nice place here."

"Thanks, but it's not mine. It's hers. I sank every penny I had into that money pit. If you think this place is nice..." He sighed heavily. "Man, if you check out the plans of my building, you'll see the plans of my flat at the top with a view of Santa Monica Beach." He sighed deeply. "I'm fifty-five, too fucking old to be left broke."

"You look younger," I said. He had a trim physique, and moved like he had an active lifestyle. "Was that your surfboard I passed coming in?" I'd seen one leaning against the wall.

"Yep." He pointed at the huge picture on the wall. "My glory days."

"Wow," I said. "Just...wow. That's you?"

He laughed. In the photo, his hair was flying behind him in long wild tangles as he balanced on water racing ahead of a curling wave, his body tanned and muscular. Now, not quite so tan, not quite so muscular. His hair was still jet black, now short, with a hairline that had receded about as far as one can go.

"So, you like London?"

"Favorite town in the word, after Santa Monica."

I laughed. "Me too, brother." Suddenly, I felt a deep compassion for the guy. Sinking everything into a project and having it go under. It could happen to anyone. I felt a cold chill. It could happen to me. It said something about him that he had been able to save up a million plus.

"The foreclosure is for 1.3 million.[26] Is that what it cost you to put up the steel we see there?"

"There's a lot more than steel already in. The floors are in. Conduit is run to most floors for electrical. There's a whole lot there you can't see. My whole life savings. When I think about it, it makes me feel physically sick."

The apartment was comfortable with air-conditioning full blast, but he was sweating.

His girlfriend came in with tall glasses of iced tea, one sandwich cut into four finger sandwiches, a cold hot dog sliced up and on toothpicks with mustard for dipping, a roll of crackers, and some kind of dip, all arranged on a tray. The girlfriend was about TJ's age, and introduced herself as JJ before going back to the kitchen. I heard water running, and the sound of someone doing dishes.

TJ ate a sandwich, and yelled into the kitchen, "Thanks doll."

"Don't mention it," JJ yelled back.

I dipped a hot dog into mustard, sipped iced tea, and had a sandwich about the size of a radish. It was a peanut butter finger sandwich, a contradiction in terms.

"Jif?" I asked.

"Is there any other?"

We laughed.

"So you like peanut butter," I said.

"Peanut butter and money."

TJ shoved the plate toward me to let me have the last sandwich, but I passed on it.

"How much will it take to finish the building. I mean turnkey?"

"About 3 million."[27]

"How much was the loan they yanked?"

---

[26] $1,300,000.00 in 1979 had the same buying power as $4,636,064.99 in 2017

[27] $3,000,000.00 in 1979 had the same buying power as $10,698,611.52 in 2017

"Four million."[28]

"Are you licensed?"

"Fuck yeah. I have an A & B License. I was doing the building."

"How much do you want to step aside?"

"I'd like to have what I have in it."

"In two weeks, you won't have anything." The auction was scheduled.

"What you got in mind with all these questions?"

"I may be interested, but if I step in, you have to finish the building or you don't get your money."

TJ lost interest in his snacks. His head jerked in my direction, and he swallowed his mouthful. "Tell me that again."

"Let me see the plans."

He unrolled the plans and lay them flat. I stared.

"What am I looking at, exactly?"

TJ was a good guy. He explained everything as we turned the pages. The elevator shafts, the elevators he had selected. Everything was planned. I figured it had to be for the bank to have given him the loan commitment. On the other hand, he fucked up drawing more than he knew he should draw. He was paying too much for something or stealing money for himself from his own loan.

I tried to put brakes on my thinking and even walk out and forget this big deal, but I couldn't. I was hooked. I spent three hours looking at page after page of plans that he spread out on his dining room table.

I went straight to Oscar, told what I was doing and who I was doing it for. Either he had to represent me with TJ or find me a real estate lawyer. Oscar turned me over to Charles Chase at his office. I'd never met him. Chase worked personal injury but not aviation, and had come from a firm that did real estate.

I spent two hours explaining to Chase what I had tentatively agreed to

---

[28] $4,000,000.00 in 1979 had the same buying power as $14,264,815.36 in 2017

do with TJ. I would give TJ $300,000[29] dollars upon signing over his entire interest in the property and commit to give him an additional one million dollars upon completion of the property within nine months. TJ had set the time table. I would pay him a weekly salary of $1500[30] as contractor to finish the building, cover the cost of all material and labor needed to complete the project in an amount not to exceed four million dollars, more than he said he needed. If he brought in the project for less than four million, I would split the difference with him, fifty fifty as a bonus. To get things rolling, I'd pay off the bank immediately to stop the foreclosure.

TJ joined us at Oscar's office, bringing with him all the paperwork on the building and meeting with Chase. I left them working together, heads bent over a desktop full of paperwork, and headed straight for my office to touch base with Pepe.

"This is bigger than I've been looking for, but the location is bitching. I wish you could see it. Anyway, the catch is this. I will need a wire to pay off the bank. I think I can swing the rest of the construction the way LAI prefers." I knew he would understand.

"Stop, don't tell me anymore. Do it." Pepe was instantly all aboard.

"I prefer telling you everything."

"Mario, do it. Never worry about a property being too big. Call Olga and give her the details for the wire to pay the bank."

"The contractor needs to sign the contract first. That may take two days. I want the wire ready to roll the minute I close with TJ. The auction date is too close for comfort."

"Okay, do it. You'll get paid for every day you oversee the construction. See to it."

"Do it?" I had it clear, but I couldn't resist teasing him. "Are you sure?"

"Do it."

---

[29] $300,000.00 in 1979 had the same buying power as $1,069,861.15 in 2017

[30] $1500.00 in 1979 had the same buying power as $5,349.31 in 2017

"Okay."

It took less than twenty-four hours for the contract to be approved and a done deal.

"Are you happy with this deal?"

TJ had the pen in his hand. "You saved my fucking life, man. And with this three hundred, I'm totally flush." I had already told him the money had to be in cash, and that most, if not all the labor and material would be paid for in cash.

"No one is going to bitch about that. Leave it to me."

"Okay, man."

"I need to hire an assistant and a paymaster," TJ said.

"Okay, do it." I laughed to myself at the 'do it.' Too bad Pepe wasn't around to hear.

When we were done with Chase, I met with TJ in an empty office to hand him a briefcase with $300,000 cash from my safe. Camacho money.

"Count it," I said.

He extended his hand to shake it. "No way, I trust you."

"I trust you, too," I told him. "I want you to finish that building. I threw in that extra million to make sure." Of course, he knew that.

Eight days after I paid off the bank, the building was back in construction. I took the team to check it out from every angle outside. We didn't go inside yet. Too easy to get hurt. Melina's visit was held off until one of our Sundays. She had peppered me with questions about the project.

"So, they wired the money to pay the bank?"

"Yep. The bank got $1.275 million of the four million original commitment." I didn't tell her about the $300,000 in cash I gave TJ or how I was funding the paymaster every couple days with green cash to pay bills.

I bought a big safe for the exterior construction office trailer where TJ could keep smaller denominations for exact amounts to the vendors and workers. I gave him $50,000 in twenties, tens, and fives, and $5,000 in singles.

Guards were at the property twenty-four hours a day to guard the office, the equipment. and building from theft and vandalism. Tricia had hired the guards and I agreed to pay her a percentage of what I paid them. I paid Tricia for hours she clocked monitoring the guards, and when she kept an eye on the security of the construction site.

The paymaster turned out to be a good bookkeeper. I wanted to send Jo over to check things out or even the girls to break the boredom of looking through newspapers, but I didn't want to involve them. Involve them? Involve them in what? Nothing I was doing felt illegal. It just felt like business. Is paying cash for services, fees and materials, illegal? I don't think so. The team tagged along with me daily when I went over to the building. We all wore hard hats. The whole thing reminded me of when Melina showed me around the first market she built.

I saw all sorts of tradesmen engaged in their professions: electricians, welders, carpenters, air-conditioning and heating, elevator techs, masons, granite and marble installers, glaziers, metal framers, plumbers, and a bunch more. Many of the men had worked with TJ before, especially his all-around personnel that could do plumbing and another trade. When the girls were with me, they got whistles and cat calls. Pixie responded to the attention, and gave as good as she got. Crews that worked regularly started to call me Boss, and some called me Cash. I didn't want to be known as Cash but there was nothing I could do about that. They were being paid in cash. When a cement truck poured their load, the driver went to the paymaster and was promptly paid. The cement pump person, the same. Full time workers got paid once a week. At one point, there were more than fifty workers scattered through the structure. I had nothing directly to do with them. All I had to do was keep money in the safe.

I hired a photographer to take pictures inside and out. He was to deliver me four sets of eight-by-tens once a month, visual records for Olga,

Camila, and Pepe. The first set of pictures were extensive, spectacular images, including views from different floors, some taken from scaffolding running outside the building, I think his best vantage point. He documented a complete panorama of the building outside and in. Some of the best shots were close-ups of the workers, TJ, and the paymaster showing his big crooked teeth.

Finally the building was enclosed. I donned a hard hat, and TJ gave me the grand tour, and updates on where everything was in terms of completion. I ran into Tricia when I went down to the ground floor, and walked through the building again with her.

"This job is great for me," Tricia said. "Thank you, Boss."

"You're family. No thanks needed."

She stopped, and so did I. We were somewhere between the sixth and seventh floor ascending the steel and concrete staircase. She had a mischievous look in her eye, and her hard hat was at a deliberately rakish angle. She hooked her hand in my belt and pulled me up short.

"I want to give you head right here, right now."

I kissed her. "The answer is yes, but not here and not now."

"Rain check then?"

"For sure, rain check."

We started up the stairs. Her offer had given me an instant hard-on. We hadn't had sex since Las Vegas, but Tricia is a hot chick. When she's around me, I can't help admiring her jeans-ass. That tough girl tomboy attitude she has is really sexy to me. It's like she has a chip on her shoulder, and she's daring me to knock it off, except it's not a chip. It's sex. Maybe the attitude was something she'd picked up during her military career. Where ever it came from, it sure as hell is a turn-on.

Melina finally went out to see the building with me on a Sunday morning. Only the guard was there while we poked around, both of us with hard hats.

"Fuck, Cuz, I could have built this," she joked.

She was kidding, but I remembered that she built her own markets. Of course she had her own TJ to act as the contractor but Melina was hands-on everything. It was just the way she was.

"How much is this going to cost?"

"If we're lucky, we'll be in it a little over five million."

"Those Camacho's should be pleased as all shit that you are doing this for them. That's a fucking deal. This is Westwood. Damn, what a deal."

"I'm sure they are pleased or will be pleased. Let me tell you something, I'm happy as hell. I'm making big dollars on this."

I smiled broadly, put my arm around her. "You like."

"I love it," she said. "Can we go to the top floor and fuck, or did you already do it up there with one of the girls or all of them?"

"Virgin building, Cuz," I said. "Let's break it in."

We walked to the fifteenth floor as the elevators had not been inspected yet. Everything was concrete, and no furniture in sight. There was no going horizontal, so we did it vertical fashion, though we might have bucked hips and rolled around on some carpenter's sawhorses that were conveniently close by. She leaned over against a bearing wall moaning and writhing, and I entered her from behind, our jeans around our ankles, our hard hats on our heads. It was hot as hell in Los Angeles.

Melina always worried about her age, ten years older than me. In this moment, way up on this building doing what we were doing, she looked to be in her early twenties. I couldn't say that, because if I mentioned it, she'd get started on the age thing and remind me that in the future she wouldn't age at my pace and would look older than me. Blah-blah. If she didn't have the age hang up, we'd probably be married now.

Johnson drove us to the beach house that the decorator was still working on.

"Looking good," she said as we walked through. The floors were stripped. The kitchen was an empty room. Another room had been demolished to make it larger.

"I hope she gets it done by next month as promised."

"What's the rush? Let her just do it. If you forget about PCH out there, the spot is gorgeous."

"The gorgeous part is the price, Baby. I got a deal on this place."

"You did," she admitted.

"I could pass it on to Camacho as a rental and make a commission on selling them my own place." I wasn't going to do that but I had thought about it.

"You wouldn't, but then it depends on how much you can sell it for."

"I feel the same way about all material things, even Casa Luna. If a person came in with a great offer, I would consider it."

To my surprise, Melina smiled. "I'm the same way. Even my pussy is ready for a fuck if the money's right."

"You are so dirty, Babies."

"I know."

I wondered if Melina would sell her markets.

I lifted her up, kissed her and said, "Let's fuck. We can face the beach."

"Deal." She giggled. Afterwards we went out to walk on the sand, and held hands like a couple of kids.

"Let's have some seating out back," I said, "so we can people watch. You pick it out."

"Sure thing. Won't take much. You only have that small space before you hit the boardwalk and sand," she said. It felt good to be here, not as a tourist, but as part of the landscape. The only conflicts we had in recent memory were about my Colombian friends. Today we were free of that, a couple of teenagers. No tensions, arguments or disagreements.

I looked around the empty kitchen. Knowing there was no refrigerator made my insides anxious.

"Hungry?"

"Starving."

We walked down the beach into the tourist area, and picked up street food from venders. Burgers and fries of course, but also Mexican corn, fruit on sticks, and funnel cakes, all of which we put in bags and carried home. We even got a cotton candy the size of my head which we were supposed to share. Melina dodged my hand when I reached for it, and devoured all but my first taste of it. I didn't miss it. I would have had to add a mile to tomorrow's jog. Her bright mood was worth it.

"I owe you." She laughed, waved around the empty paper stick the cotton candy had been wound on. There was nowhere to throw it on the open beach. She had no pockets, laughed some more, and shoved it into her bra.

"You're gonna pay," I growled, though I don't really have much of a sweet tooth if it's not ice cream. I hadn't seen Melina this playful in years. She never takes time off. She laughed and ran ahead.

"Now I gotta burn those calories off your ass!" I threatened.

She dodged me, and I pretended I couldn't catch her. Dusk was falling when we got back to the house. Night on the water can be pretty creepy, when the light disappears and you hear the water, but can't see where the sand ends and the water begins. It feels like you're on the brink of the world, about to fall off. I stood at the edge of the surf looking off into the darkest sky with no stars. No telling where the water ended and the sky began. I heard the door slam, or thought I did. I was out here alone with my pants rolled to my knees, my feet in the surf, my arms full of bags of food. I didn't want to drop anything and lose it in the rolling surf, so I turned back to the house, and made my way to the kitchen which had nothing to recommend it except walls, ceiling and a nice, new floor.

"Melina!" I yelled. "Where did you go?"

I walked through the house, scanning the rooms. She wasn't answering. Then on the second floor, there she was, standing in the door of a bedroom that had a brand new king sized bed in it, still wrapped in plastic.

Something was up. Melina was in the dark doorway of the dark hall, backlit by candlelight, wearing nothing but a camisole, which was showing off silhouette of her glorious body to great advantage.

I topped the steps, caught sight of her, and I admit, I stared.

"Hey Mister, I hear you're a man who likes to make deals." She strutted down the hall at me. If I'd been a dog, I'd have been drooling. She hooked her finger in my collar, pulled my face down and gave me a kiss that knocked my socks off, and me standing there with arms full of food bags. When she backed off, my mind was blown. I was standing, hard as the Rock of Gibraltar, without any sense of time or place.

"You need a little company tonight Mister? Let's negotiate."

I wasn't sure what I'd end up with for the Westwood building. Eventually it would be a nice payday, and the road to the finish felt like an adventure. It was going to be a profitable adventure. When Pepe had told me during one of his phone calls that I would get paid for every day I oversaw the construction, I'd shined it on, but I would definitely take him up on that. It was a long fucking drive from Pasadena to Westwood. The one good thing is that it was close to the Playboy Club in Century City where I often went with the team after checking on the building. We'd been dropping in briefly before coming home. I was surprised how often I saw Carson there. Every time I ran into him, we always ended up competing over a game of pool. I'd forgotten how much he hates to lose, and how much I enjoyed winning.

I didn't stop looking for foreclosure deals. By the end of September, I had bought two more apartment buildings for LAI, both at auction, short notice properties where there was no time to meet up with the owners to do it the other way. One of the buildings was in Monterey Park on my turf, thirty-five units. The other was twelve units in Eagle Rock, a stone's throw from Pasadena. I had to come up with three hundred sixty thousand in cashier's checks to pay the banks selling the property at the foreclosure sales.

Thanks to a heart to heart with June Lunati, the operations officer at the bank I have used for years, I was able to do this exchange of cash for cashier's checks. She had to approve deposits I deposited from Oscar if they were over a certain amount. Most were over twenty thousand.

I knew June. When I had to replace cash for my socks where I kept my business cash that I used for travel and other cash matters, it was June who approved the check I cashed against my own account. I kept it under ten thousand.

June worked behind the tellers, but had an office where the loan officers worked. That's where we met to discuss the problem.

"June, check my two accounts. I keep good balances. I'd have a lot more than I do if I didn't invest so much of my money in apartment buildings."

She smiled.

"You are a very good customer."

"I have been attending auctions for foreclosure properties. The auction houses require a deposit to get a chance to bid. If I get lucky and end up the high bidder, I need a cashier's check to pay off what I owe the next day."

She nodded. She got the picture.

"Is there any way I can bring in cash, and buy cashier's checks for this purpose so that I don't have to take it from my bank accounts?" It was a bold move, but I read June as a person who might find a way to help me.

"What amounts are you talking about?"

"Two or three hundred thousand at a time."

"That's lot of cash. We have a requirement to fill out an IRS form for anything over ten thousand cash per day."

"I know."

June studied me over her glasses. I studied her right back. She was probably in her forties, and had short dark blond hair, and eyes that were green, barely a shade darker than her hair. Square jaw and long face. I was aware of a clock ticking on the wall behind me, the noise of bankers and customers coming in through the open door, the empty coffee mug on her desk that had a spoon in it, the soft waft of a cool breeze as the air conditioning kicked into high gear. June held a pen in her right hand, and tapped it once on her desk before she put it in its holder beside a Zen desk garden with sand, a rock and a little rake. Someone had scribbled a dollar sign in the sand.

"What's in it for me?" she asked, without a hint of anxiety.

I smiled, the kind where my teeth showed. "Where've you been all these years I've been banking here?"

"I've been right here." She broke from my gaze to glance down at a mug on her desk.

"You got to tell me that doing this is not illegal, and we'll make a deal."

"I wouldn't do it if it was illegal, but it does violate bank rules. That could be construed to be a violation of something in the federal system. On the other hand, I don't remember the last time our branch filled one of those IRS forms. This branch moves a lot of cash."

"I love you, June."

She had a percolator on the console behind me. She walked over to it, filled two mugs, and with a casual kick of a doorstop, let the glass door to her office slowly sweep to a close. She put one coffee in front of me and drank from hers. On hers was written *I turn coffee into money*. On mine *Lawyer because badass motherfucker isn't a job description*. She had half of the coffee downed before she returned to her seat.

"Gevalia," she said. "I get it by mail."

I sipped the coffee. It was good and strong, but I don't have a real keen coffee palate. I noticed the writing on the mug. "I'm not a lawyer."

It was her turn to show me her teeth.

"But you are a badass, aren't you? Real estate agents and lawyers love that mug."

I laughed out loud.

June is older than I am but is a pretty woman I would fuck in a split second.

"Show me how much you love me. Tell me what's in it for me."

We agreed that if I came in to buy a cashier's check for $25,000 she got $100,[31] no matter what. If I came back to get another cashier's check because I bought the property, she got $500.[32]

"How will I know you bought the property. Do I need to trust you?"

"Of course. And you already trust me or we wouldn't be having this conversation."

"Okay, deal. Call me before you come in, and give me the amounts you need and who the cashier's check is payable to so it's ready."

"Deal," I said. I looked at her glass door, closed now, but I could see everything going on in the branch. Anyone could see in.

"Don't ever hand me anything," she spoke softly. "We'll figure it out how we do that. I can meet you for coffee somewhere or something. I'm not worried. I'll keep track of what I have coming."

I figured I may as well go for broke so I threw something else real quick. "June, you know I get some hefty checks from Oscar Cooke's firm, sometimes so big the teller has to get your approval before I deposit. It's never been a problem. Cooke's checks are drawn on this bank, if not this branch."

"You're a great customer."

"I said that because I may have another issue. Sometimes I get paid in cash and I may want to deposit the cash and the amounts will exceed ten thousand. Will you think how that can be handled when I need it?"

"Of course. We can figure something out."

"June, to be clear, Uncle Sam will get his taxes from—"

June interrupted me. "I don't need to know about your taxes. When you need to make a deposit like that we'll work it out." She smiled. "No prob-

---

[31] $100.00 in 1979 had the same buying power as $356.62 in 2017

[32] $500.00 in 1979 had the same buying power as $1,783.10 in 2017

lem."

I had just scored. My first thought was Olga. I bet she had friendly bankers like June across the globe. So if I was right, why did she bother to bring me into it? I would have to ask her or Camila. Or maybe not. Why did I care?

I finished the coffee June had given me, and got up. We shook hands. "June, I love you."

June smiled. "You told me that already."

Letty had waited in the car for me, under an awning close to the entrance. The windows were down. She didn't like to overheat the car keeping the air conditioning on while she was waiting, but revved it up as soon as I got in the back seat. I didn't say anything when I got in. I was thinking.

"Anything wrong, Boss?"

"No," I said. I had mixed feelings. Relieved that I'd solved that problem. Not so relieved that I had just crossed some line. I wasn't sure what the crime might be, but I think June had as much to lose as I did. Whatever cash I made from LAI would be reported on my taxes, and it wouldn't matter if the cash was sitting in my safe or I put it in the bank. I was ok with the tax part. There was more than enough to go around. Uncle Sam has to get his. And the State of California. Yes, gotta pay them too.

When I got home, the girls were still there. Letty joined us in my office.

"Sooner or later we're going to get a big crash again that takes us out of the country. I need to figure out how I'm going to fund the paymaster on the Westwood project. With all of us gone, I don't know how the fuck I can swing it."

I could confide in my team about this delicate matter, but I had to keep the cash aspect secret from Melina. I just knew that if Melina knew all the details about how cash was the currency financing the Westwood property and most of the purchases of real estate I had made for LAI, it would cause problems in our relationship. And fuck it. She didn't have to know.

"Simple shit, Boss. One of us has to stay back," Pixie said.

"You need all of us if the case is big," Niley said.

I used to work alone signing up case after case every day of the week. When Jo was first on board, she stayed in the office. I was handling car accidents and not aviation cases. Did I really need the entire team with me on a big case? As Pixie suggested, someone needed to stay behind. I didn't want to involve them in the Camacho deals, especially with the day to day. Damn. I had already involved June but I didn't know June outside the bank.

"Boss, penny for your thoughts?" Jo asked.

I came back and settled down next to her. "About this."

"We may not have another case for a long time," Letty said.

"Bitch, don't be casting your negativity," Pixie yelled.

"Fuck you, slut."

"I'm not in the mood," I said with finality.

Everyone shut up.

"I can do it," Jo said. "I'm the numbers person. You may need my expertise with the numbers if you are gone longer than usual."

I shook my head. "I'm not even sure this is all straight. I don't know where the money is coming from. I'd die if you got in trouble over something you were doing for me."

"Hey, Boss, I went to jail for soliciting at the hospital, remember?" Pixie said, taking a bow.

The girls laughed. She had gone to jail, but it had been over trumped up charges instigated by Carson to clear the field for whatever retainer he was chasing. Pixie's charges had been dropped.

"The money is coming from your safe," Jo said. "I'm not worried about it."

"Really?"

"Boss, after all these years, have you ever known me to say something I don't mean? Besides, I don't believe that the Camachos are mobsters. Mobsters don't fly around in huge jets and flaunt their money the way they do."

"I agree," Pixie said. "If they were crooks, they would be low key. You should see their mansion in Hawaii. Fuck."

I got up and went around the conference table. Jo was sitting across from me. I put my arms around her from behind and kissed the top of her head. She turned, still sitting, and faced me. I leaned toward her and we kissed.

"You are so hot, Baby."

"Boss, that line. It's so old already."

"So, I take it that Melina doesn't know you're paying in cash," Letty said.

"Hello?" Pixie squealed. "Where the fuck you been?"

"I been right here, and I'm going to kick your ass." Letty rolled up her sleeves, and got up from her chair.

"Stop it." I felt like a vice principal or a referee separating combatants. I knew they loved each other, but they went at each other like cats. So dramatic. I wondered if any of it was for real.

"You know what the problem is?" Jo said. "Boss, we don't fuck very much anymore."

I looked at her, then at the group. I stood up. "Are you kidding me?"

"Boss, when's the last time we fucked, all of us, together?" Niley asked. "Maybe she's right."

I tried to think of the last time. I think it had been on the last case, but I wasn't sure. Letty was a regular with me, and Melina was on Sunday. I assumed they were all free agents, getting laid on their own time, but as for us all together, Jo was right. We hadn't been together much.

"Change is in the wind," I said.

Pixie stuck her nose in the air, and sniffed.

"Change? I don't thank so. That's just yesterday's burritos." She made a little burp, and covered her mouth. "Definitely burritos."

"I'll be at Van Nuys Airport the day after tomorrow. Are you free?"

Olga's call had caught me walking out of the shower with nothing on but a damp towel. Letty was already asleep on her side of the bed and it was barely eight pm. The poor thing knocked out early ever since she'd been taking that five am run with me. I took the phone into the hall and shut the door to keep from waking her.

"I thought you'd want to see the properties," I said.

"Amor, wouldn't you prefer to spend the eight hours with me in bed or walking up and down stairs?"

Soon as I got off with Olga, I dialed Tricia, now residing in one of my Alhambra apartments.

"What's up?"

"Hope it's not too late."

"Barely eight," Tricia said. "I'll be up till midnight.'

"Get the photographer. I need eight by tens of Downey, El Monte, Monterey Park and Eagle Rock. In duplicate by eleven the day after tomorrow."

"I'll drive him around and make sure he handles it. Good thing he has his own darkroom. This gives us a whole day and a half. We'll get it done."

"Great, Tricia. Thanks."

Tricia had been thirty minutes late getting the pictures to me, met me at the door, jogged alongside, giving me the rundown of the shoot until I got to the car when she handed them over. I had her leave my copies on the desk in the office and waved goodbye from my car as she went inside the house. When I arrived at Van Nuys Airport, it was at the regular time. High noon. Los Angeles was blazing hot, so I'd dressed casually, in shorts, and sandals. I took a moment in the car to get the pictures in order. After I kissed Olga and manhandled her for a few minutes, I handed her four envelopes, one for each property Downey, El Monte, Monterey Park, and Eagle Rock, with the addresses underneath. I was keeping the Westwood envelope as a final surprise. I'd brought copies of the paperwork. The originals had been mailed to the LAI post office box in Florida. Just brought it to be prepared, in case there were questions. I hoped there were questions, because I was ready to wax on each one.

The fifteen-story high-rise in Westwood was taking shape, no longer just a steel structure. TJ was good at his job. He knew his stuff, and he had been teaching me, one reason I was so excited over Westwood. The photographer's images were brilliant and dramatic. I'd been very pleased with his monthly documentation of progress on Westwood. The new shots of the other properties were icing on the cake.

"Oh my," Olga said. Her jaw dropped. She beamed as she saw the first pictures of Westwood. I don't know why she was surprised. I'd been keeping all of them informed. I dropped copies of that project's paperwork on the table. I had a feeling she would want to have it side by side, and I was right.

"This is really something, Amor." She looked from the pictures to me, and back to the pictures. She sat down and spread the Westwood envelope contents out on the table in front of the sofa, and leaned over them, exclaiming over each picture. She looked at me again.

"We need more of these," she said, and then focused on the pictures again, as if she couldn't tear her eyes away. "Amor, find more big buildings. Look for seller who are foreign. It will be easier to dump cash. The majority of sellers will be local or within the states. Use your nose on those and maybe you'll get lucky. So far, you are doing great. The tortilla company, the bakery, all cash, very well done, mi Amor."

She caught me totally off guard about going for foreign sellers.

"Good idea," I said.

"The buildings don't have to be in foreclosure. I know you'll know what to do. Now, where were we?"

"Wait. One question."

"Ask me anything, Amor."

"Why am I doing this? Why not you, or Camila, or brokers you can hire to look for you? You told me of at least one friendly banker somewhere that you see often. I just made a contact at a bank. You have to have a bunch of these contacts."

"You're right, Amor. We need you."

"Camila does this in the world at large, not the US. My job is not to find property. I'm like you said, the banker who comes in, and lays out the cash."

"Got it."

"Is that all?"

I figured to ask now or never. "Did you plan this when you asked me to hold the cash for you?"

Her big smile never dimmed. "Amor, the original reason was to buy a house in Pasadena. We still want to do that. For now, use the money you have. There is plenty where that came from. If you see a house near you, let us know. We'll let you handle the purchase so you will make money on that too. Amor, be happy."

"I am happy."

"Amor, si."

"The paymaster at the construction site pays everything he can with cash, but once in a while a big delivery comes in from a big company and I will need to write them a check. I can give him some blank checks of mine to handle, then reimburse myself with cash. That means I have to deposit cash in my account." Now that I had June's cooperation at the bank, I could work that out. "Are you okay with that or do you want the paymaster to have checks that are drawn on LAI or another account you control?"

"I'll have Raul send you checks from an account he controls. That way you don't have to monkey around with using your own checks. It's a construction cost for us. Actually, a good idea to have some checks going into the project."

"Great. The paymaster will have an accounting so I don't charge the ten percent on expenses paid by check."

"Amor, stop it. Keep it simple. We're treating this deal as all cash. I will handle the check thing by tomorrow."

"You're dynamite, Baby." I felt better not having to use my checks then depositing cash to reimburse myself.

She smiled another smile, a carnal one, dripping with sex. Hooded eyes, pouty lips. Compelling stuff. Compelling enough that I didn't dig for the direct answer she had evaded. "Can we do it now? The clock is running."

I took her in my arms. "You may have trouble walking for a day or so."

"Amor, si. Yes please. I want you."

I decided to keep Tricia looking for foreclosures and recruited Randy.

"I'm no longer just interested in foreclosures and apartments. I want office buildings, too. Get on your multiple listings and find me a bunch I can review. Local. Commercial properties. The bigger the better."

"Right away." Randy beamed.

"Is there anything in the listing that states if seller is out of the country?"

He hesitated. I could see he was thinking it over. "Not that I've ever seen. Why?"

"Just a question. Priority to sellers who are foreign. If I find something I'm interested in, the deal is conditional upon me meeting with the seller, no matter where he or she happens to be, I will need to meet with him or her, personally."

"Okay." Randy agreed without another question.

Chapter 10
November 1979
Canary Islands

In November, two planes collided in the Canary Islands. More than five hundred people were aboard. No survivors. There was no way we were missing out on this case. We were prepared. We'd even prepped TJ about how we would handle it if I were pulled away on a plane crash. Jo would take my place here at home. Pixie took over Jo's slot for this crash while Jo and I went over what she would be doing with TJ and the Westwood project paymaster. Pixie worked with Tom Jones on the details needed to get retainers prepared. Tom always started with the same retainer, but revised it every time so the details fit the crash, location, date, time, the name of operator, etc. The brochure we used was already up-to-date, including the last crash we handled. This crash had so many decedents that we would have needed hundreds, and though we always took only a hundred or so brochures, we settled this time on taking a hundred and fifty. With added plane crashes and the quality of the heavy paper the printer used to make the brochure to look high-end, they were getting heavier. What didn't change was the cover with Oscar on it.

"Who will be running the project while you're gone?" Melina asked during our Sunday.

"Jo. I'll be calling in daily."

"You have a time zone problem, you know?"

"I know, but I can live with that. I have to do this crash. Besides, we've been planning how to handle this."

"You never mentioned it to me."

I kissed Melina. "It's not like we can really plan for a crash. Baby, when I say planning, I mean I brought up the possibility to the team some time back. Jo volunteered to stay behind."

"Good choice. I don't know what's involved, but if there are numbers involved, she's the greatest."

Melina did not dish out compliments about anyone. That was high praise for Jo.

"Cuz, I would have helped." She grinned at me. She might have taken it on if I'd asked her to, but she appreciated that I hadn't put her in that position. Then again, she didn't think much of my Colombian friends so maybe she wouldn't have stepped in.

"Babies, you got enough with your markets, but thanks for offering."

I didn't mention the upcoming Canary Islands trip to the Camachos. They might have offered a plane, and no way would I accept that. That would make me a real mooch. We could have taken Oscar's plane, but the fuel and rest stops were more than I wanted to mess with. Pixie had our travel agent book us with a stop in Washington DC. From Madrid, Spain, we secured a local airline to the Canary Islands. I've developed a taste for flying on private planes. These days, flying commercial airlines demonstrates to me why I've been getting spoiled on Camacho planes.

Letty's old staff quarters were available, but instead I had Tricia move into one of my guest rooms. I wanted her in the house. She picked a bedroom no one else had selected, Spartan compared to the others. The girls had all put in their own touches to their room, but Tricia's taste had been influenced by the military.

"That safe holds a lot of LAI cash for the Westwood project."

"Worry not, Boss. The premises will be secure. The burglar alarm will be armed, and I'm always armed."

"Boss, I can stay," Jo offered. "I'm always armed as well."

"Stay as long as you want, but I know you'll be taking time with your kids. Tricia has a gun and an assortment of shotguns and rifles."

"Hey, I bet I can kick the shit out of Tricia."

I didn't bring up Tricia's military experience, and her history of surviving actual hand-to-hand combat situations. Jo showed off some karate moves, and her impressive kick. Jo was trimmer and more fit than when she'd started off with me. No way would a stranger believe she, like Melina, was almost ten years older. Karate practice, and having a workout room and spa handy was having some side benefits. Then again, Jo is competitive as hell, and having Letty, Niley and Pixie around kept her on her toes. I complimented her on her style, but reminded her that karate only stops bullets on TV.

"Baby, here's the deal. Get here early every day. Stay as long as you want. If TJ needs money, you run it out there for the paymaster. I've hired Tricia as security full time until I get back."

"Got it, Boss. Any idea how long?"

"Baby, you know crashes as well as I do. We don't know that. Hopefully a month or less."

"That's nothing."

"Right."

"I'll stay in touch every day. If I don't catch up to you, you call me. Got it?"

"Got it."

"I'll be paying you whatever bonus I give the girls for this case, just as though you were with us."

"Boss, that's nice, but—"

"But, nothing. You're giving up your usual commission to take care of this other essential thing. So it's only fair. And I'm telling you now because I don't want any lip when the case is over. Got it?"

"Thanks, Boss."

Canary Islands turned us all into basket cases. It was draining to my team beyond anything we had been through. Or maybe we were really feeling the loss of Jo.

I talked to Jo every day. "Baby, you are lucky you sat this one out. It's a real bummer."

"What's different? Is it as bad as Amsterdam?"

"Nothing has been as bad as Amsterdam was." I took a breath. In Amsterdam, the local lawyers had brushed us off. No such lawyer problem in the Canary Islands. I already felt better. "For one thing, the Spanish families trust no one. What's different from Amsterdam is that once we walk away from the family, they come back looking for us, wanting to talk again."

"That's a good thing. I am sure you will find a way to make it work. Boss, I can tell your mind is not on that case a hundred percent. Stop worrying about this damn building. TJ is getting it done. It's going to be okay."

I was usually the one giving pep talks.

"Yes ma'am." As dreary and frustrated as I felt, the role switch made me laugh. Jo was right.

Two days after I arrived, I reached Pepe. I told him where I was, and that the building was under control.

"I'm not the least bit worried," he said, cutting me off before I could explain to my satisfaction.

Camila wasn't interested in anything about the building either. I don't know if that was a compliment to me or just an assumption of how she saw everything in the world always obeying her wishes. "I'm going to find you in Spain, Amor. Start sleeping with one eye open."

We laughed.

Apparently, I remained Amor to Olga, too.

"Amor, I'm going to fly there when you least expect it."

My priorities were shifting. Now that I was getting accustomed to finding foreclosures, I felt that being on this plane crash was costing me money. While I was here, I was missing out on foreclosure opportunities at home. At night when I was staring at the ceiling trying to find sleep, I would start on the math of how much I might make on this crash versus my take in buying buildings for LAI, but I'd fall asleep before I was done. When I was in school, math had been my enemy. It was a different story now. With all the cases I'd handled over the years, after talking settlements with clients and lawyers, numbers had become my friends.

After the helicopter case with the girls in Puerto Rico and the big case in Portugal, Letty was no longer a novice. When I wasn't right there to work with her, it was up to Niley and Pixie to bring her up to speed. Challenges are learning experiences, and these independent families were going to be good learning experiences. The families were from Spain, various points in Europe, and even some from the United States. None were easy, but there was no question that in spite of having the language in common, the Spanish families were the most challenging. I was still taking new approaches. The learning never stops.

I talked to Tricia and TJ regularly. In December, Tricia mentioned days when "…we spend a lot of time at the construction site. Gives me a chance to walk the floors and watch all the action by all those tradesmen."

This was news to me. I had been under the impression that they drove over only when necessary, and certainly had no idea they were walking the floors. "What do you mean by lots of time?" I was curious. I didn't picture Jo or Tricia as ever having the faintest interest in commercial construction. "When did you and Jo develop an interest in building?"

"It's not the building," she said, laughing. "It's the builder. I think TJ has a special liking for Jo."

"Really?" I was astonished. I don't know why I was surprised. Jo is a real beauty, and she always had a healthy interest in sex. She had not been interested in anyone since 'Nando. She'd never mentioned anyone being interested in her, but then maybe she wouldn't do that. Maybe she'd keep it to herself out of concern for my feelings. I don't know. TJ seemed a nice enough guy. I mean, I really liked him. But I didn't know if he was good enough for Jo. I didn't know how I felt about it. All this wasn't really what I was thinking in that instant. I was just feeling, I don't know, something that wasn't quite the big green monster.

"Jo dresses up to come out here like she's going to a fancy place to have lunch." Tricia paused. I pictured her counting on her fingers. "Actually, we've gone to lunch with TJ three times."

"Really?" I felt shockwaves in my guts.

Tricia said, "Don't say anything. Promise? I don't think it's a secret, but it is something Jo would want to tell you herself. It might not go any further than lunch out, anyway."

"Of course. I promise."

I hung up the phone, and looked up at Pixie, parked in my suite playing solitaire at the table where we ate. She looked up from her game, and looked down again as she turned over a card. "Tricia is a snitch."

"Oh, so you know." I looked her over.

"I know, and you don't." She put down the cards, and walked over toward me with a sashay in her step. She put one hand on her hip, and with the other, tapped me on the pectoral. "I know and you don't." One tap per word.

I made a grab for her and she stepped away.

"Unh, unh," she said. "I have bargaining power, now. I know, and you don't." Pixie played hard to get. She backed off again, and made it a little game. I tickled her. I lifted her up and swung her around in circles until she was too dizzy to stand by herself.

"Tell," I said.

She giggled, and looped her hands behind my neck for balance. "I'll tell you, but I need a one-hour fuck."

"Is that all?"

"Okay, two hours."

"Deal."

I would say Pixie got the better of me on that deal, except that the stakes paid off equally for both of us. Afterwards, when we were lying in nothing but sweaty sheets and a glow of contentment, Pixie told me all she knew. Which was that when she'd talked to Jo earlier that morning, Jo had mentioned eating lunch a couple of times with TJ and Tricia. Pixie's head for gossip made her nag Jo for more detail. Two of those times didn't count as significant in Pixie's opinion, because the lunch had been standing up at the truck that brought sandwiches around to construction sites. At least once had been in a sit-down restaurant.

We were gone for three months. December twenty-fifth approached. I told Letty, Pixie and Niley to go home for the holiday. We'd suffered no problems when Pixie and Niley had done that during the Puerto Rican hotel fire. They all refused. I took heat from my aunt, who said "No one should work on holy days."

Christmas day, I had feasts sent to our table, providing us a day of eating Spanish Christmas food. I'd gone to some local shops to pick out presents. I'd gotten each of my team her favorite perfume,

We retired to our individual rooms for a couple hours to make Christmas calls home.

I made the most difficult call first. Jason. He'd given me the running start on this case. We had talked often since I arrived, with no mention of Sami. Jason almost sounded normal to me. Even though it was Christmas, Jason talked business first. Now that it was Christmas, I was on shakier ground. I really didn't know how close he was to the holiday season. I took a deep breath, and jumped in.

"I miss her," I said. I didn't have to say her name. He knew.

"I miss her too. Not a day goes by when I don't think of her and wish we'd taken the leap and tied the knot."

"Hang in there, my friend."

"I am. Sami was a strong woman. She wouldn't want me feeling bad over her being gone. I remember her telling me she was not afraid to die, but she wasn't in any big hurry to be dumped in a furnace." Jason chuckled, but there were tears in his voice. "She could be funny."

"She was."

"Mario, my invitation is open whenever you wish. Call me the day before, and everything will be ready for you, and whomever you bring with you."

I was touched. I swallowed the emotion, so I could talk.

"Jason, soon as I settle down a bit, I'm taking you up on it."

"I'll hold you to that."

"Deal, my friend."

I called Carson to wish him a Merry Christmas, but maybe I shouldn't have called him.

"Ese, you could have taken me on this one. Oscar says you been there for months."

"Carson, ease up. You have a fabulous business going with all your contacts."

"Ese, I know, but the money, the big money is what you're doing. Let me in, Ese."

Maybe it was bad of me, but I was glad when he hung up.

I talked to my aunt for the second time this holiday week. Because I heard from Camila and Olga at least once a week and I also called them.

Camila, Olga and Pepe were together in Bogota. "You need to come visit. You've never seen our home, and our home is your home," said Pepe.

"Thank you, my friend."

I didn't mention the building and neither did they.

I talked to Melina on Christmas Eve for half of the night and on Christmas Day. Betty was at her house on Christmas day, and I talked to her too.

Then I called Jo.

"Merry Christmas, Boss!" she said. I heard Christmas music playing behind her, and lots of voices.

"Sounds like a party," I said. I heard lots of kids, but couldn't make out individuals.

"We're rotating," she said. "The kids are here now, and later will be at Aunt Carmen's, and on New Year's Eve, we're having a big sleepover here."

"Sounds fun," I said.

"I got your box of boxes," she said. "It got here yesterday, just in time. I made sure everybody got everything. Aunt Carmen loves the camelhair coat. Tricia says thanks, that the bathrobe is fabulous. She never wants to take it off. I want to thank you for the little black dress. I put it on and look just like Audrey Hepburn! And that check you sent Lainey, I put it right into her college fund. Johnson wants to know how you found a tux in his size. He looks spiffy. I can't speak for Melina though, because she refuses to open her present without you here. She's got something for you, too. Thank you so much Boss. Wish you were here."

"Me too."

"How much longer on the case?" she asked.

The music on Jo's end of the line stopped, and I heard a male voice.

"No telling how long. Who's that?"

She didn't answer, but gave the phone over.

"Hello Mario. What's up, dude? Merry Christmas. Loved the smoked turkey! Thanks man."

I recognized TJ's voice, though I'd never heard him sound so happy and cheerful before. Sure, it was Christmas, but I don't think it was the holiday that made him sound so upbeat. I wished everyone Merry Christmas, but I definitely had some petty vibes I wasn't sharing with anybody.

Niley, Pixie and Letty returned for our planned feast. I knew we'd all talked to Jo. Everyone was full of gossip from home, and I waited patiently for the topic of Jo to come up. It didn't take long.

"I think Jo has a boyfriend," Niley said.

"That's so fucking cool." Pixie high-fived with Letty, not letting on she already knew. I smiled, and kept quiet, squashing any jealousy I was feeling. Jo had a right to have joy and companionship in her life.

Neither Camila and Olga showed up in Spain, but I was fine with that. I got to enjoy Pixie, Niley and Letty more during our down times, though I had vivid pictures of Olga and Camila in my brain, in pictures that ran like a movie. My team was a turn-on, always were. My Colombian girlfriends were the extra spice.

We flew home on Oscar's plane. It was a pleasure not to have to make arrangements. Oscar's flight attendant Chastity coddled us all the way home. She knew the wines we drank and the goodies we liked to snack on, and stocked plenty of everything. If the pilots were allowed to fly longer hours, or if the plane didn't need to refuel as often as it did, it would have been great, but private planes just aren't designed that way. We appreciated not having to switch planes or deal with ticket counters.

Talking to families of victims is something you never get accustomed to. In our own lives, we are not so frequently touched by death; but when reaching out to families of victims, we end up looking death in the face, day after day. Not just death, either, but also grief, loss, pain. Deep emotion not only moves us, but also can make the family members crazy or agonizing to work with, and you can't help but empathize with their agony.

"We're solid, Boss," Pixie said.

The girls gave me a thumbs up. I thought they were all putting up false fronts.

"I don't believe you," I said, closing my eyes and almost immediately falling asleep, again. It wasn't all from work. The last night at the hotel, we had a major party. Pixie said it was making up for lost time. I planned to catch up on sleep on the plane.

As the trip had taken so long, we couldn't just hang on to the retainers. Doing so would delay the process, so during the Canary Islands accident, we sent the signed retainers weekly to Oscar and Tom by using a courier service that delivered to the airline cargo department. When the package arrived in Los Angeles, Tom Jones sent a messenger to LAX to pick it up. Mail was notoriously unreliable and would have taken as long as a month. Courier service only took a couple of days.

It was late. Letty and I walked in the house. Pixie and Niley got in their cars that had been parked on my property for three months, and drove home.

"Want me to stay?" Letty asked. "Or should I go to my apartment?"

"Stay Baby, but get some rest. Crash in your room where I can't bother you." She knew I meant the guest room that she used.

"You never bother me."

I hit the shower. When I came out, Melina was there in nothing but a towel.

"You look tired," she said.

"How did you know I was here?"

"I've got my ways," she said, mysteriously. "No problem. Do you want me to go?"

"No, I don't want you to go," I said. "So glad you're here." I pulled her close. I may have fallen asleep while I was standing there.

Melina nudged us toward the bed. I collapsed on it.

"I have an early morning," she said. "Let's hit the hay."

We spooned, and I had the best night's sleep, but I woke alone.

Jo was in the kitchen with Letty and Miguel when I breezed in for coffee.

"Boss, you should have called down and stayed in bed," Miguel said.

"Yeah, Boss," Letty agreed.

I ignored them and hugged Jo. "I missed you, Baby."

"I missed you, too, Boss."

Tricia joined us for breakfast. I had forgotten she was staying in a guest room to take care of the house and assist Jo with Westwood.

"The accounting of everything I paid out from cash is in the safe," Jo said.

"I'm sure," I said with a smile.

"Did you have fun?"

"I missed not being there, but this was cool. Tricia was great company."

Tricia said, "Other way around. Jo is great company."

When I had been home a week, I finally went to the office.

"You are marvelous," Oscar said.

"I don't work alone," I said. "My team is marvelous."

"They are, especially considering the competition you had on this one. Two hundred twenty retainers is amazing!" Oscar said.

"It started slow, but the end was worth it."

"We are grateful," Tom said.

I winked at them. I sat across from Oscar and Tom in the conference room.

"Let's see how grateful. How much, Oscar?"

"I'll give you the Learjet, plus five hundred thousand."

At first, I thought he was kidding about the plane.

"You love that plane," I said. "Why would you give up a plane you love so much?"

I almost fell for the idea of owning the plane. I loved flying. I loved not flying commercial. I figured Oscar paid a little over a million for the plane, so it was probably worth half of that by now.

Oscar shrugged. "I don't have the time to take it out. Mostly it sits in the hangar. Lately, you're the only one who uses it."

I wasn't convinced of Oscar's explanation, but I admit I was tempted. It took me two days to decide whether to accept Oscar's offer. I weighed it carefully. Maintenance, fuel, flight crew, airport fees, storage. My CPA assured me that I could write all of that off as business expense, but even if it was a good deal, it was still a steady draw of cash.

"You don't have to pay me all in one whack. How much will you give me if you keep the plane?"

Oscar wrote me a check for $1.1 million.[33]

"Kid, thanks for the offer of installments," he said, laughing. "I love you, Mario."

After a celebratory dinner at home, I gave the girls, including Jo, twenty thousand dollars each.[34] During the dinner, Tricia walked in in her slippers, wet hair, and the heavy winter bathrobe I'd given her for Christmas.

"I don't mean to bother you," she said. She was holding some papers about the investments that I'd asked her to check up on. Personally, I had a thousand and three apartments. If I behaved and didn't go crazy spending lots of money, I could easily retire, live in my big house, drive big cars, and have money left over just from my rental income. But of course, I was still hitting aviation hard, and barely scratching the surface of investing for LAI.

"Pull up a chair," I told Tricia.

Tricia said, "I'll put this paperwork on your desk."

"Do that," I said. "Then join us. Miguel has been cooking up a storm."

"Sure thing, Boss."

When she came back a few minutes later, the bathrobe was gone, and she was in long sleeved spandex, something she probably worked out in.

"Wrong outfit for one of Miguel's dinners," Pixie warned, patting her trim stomach that was hidden under a loose shirt.

---

[33] $1,100,000.00 in 1979 had the same buying power as $3,922,824.22 in 2017

[34] $20,000.00 in 1979 had the same buying power as $71,324.08 in 2017

It was Tricia's first time to be at one of these celebratory meals. She hadn't been expecting anything.

"Tricia, I told you to track all your hours."

"I did. Jo has me all paid up through last Friday. I'm cool."

I handed her a thousand in cash.[35]

"What's this for?" She looked down at the check and back up at me. Everybody was wearing a big smile.

"For being around."

She had to jump up from her chair and give me a big hug around the neck. Everybody laughed, and hugged, and eventually she made it back to her seat.

"It's going to be hard going back to my apartment after living like a princess here. Miguel has taken care of me. I eat like a horse, then I have to go work it out in the gym."

I smiled. "Welcome to the club."

"Speaking of clubs," Pixie said. "Hey, Tricia, are you into group sex?"

"I never tried it."

"You will dig it," Niley said.

"Hey, stop it," I said. "You are embarrassing Tricia."

"No way, embarrass. I don't know the meaning of that word."

"Do you eat pussy?" Pixie asked.

Tricia didn't say anything. In fact, she looked a little shocked.

"I do," Letty said, breaking the silence. "Do you?"

This time, Tricia blushed.

The next day, when the girls showed for work, the topic of money came up during breakfast.

"It's been a long time since you invested your money," I reminded them. "Letty, it's time you considered getting a small four-unit building or something

---

[35] $1,000.00 in 1979 had the same buying power as $3,566.20 in 2017

where you can live in one unit and rent the other three. Or even a duplex. I can't tell you how to spend your money, but Jo, Pixie and Niley can tell you that it feels good to own property."

"I can't fucking believe this check," Pixie said. "Boss, I am going to suck every inch of your body."

"I'm going first," Letty said. "I don't deserve twenty thousand dollars."

"You deserve it. All of you deserve it," I said. "You earned it."

Niley said, "Boss, when Letty finishes doing you, I will show you how thankful I am. That's more than six thousand a month, for three months straight. I can't get my head around it. I mean, that's in addition to our regular weekly pay."

Jo smiled without adding anything.

"Jo, you got something you want to tell us?"

Jo turned a little red, but she was a straight shooter. "I'm in love with TJ. He loves me and my kids, and they love him. He feels like family with us."

"Is it serious?" I asked.

The girls were silent, looking intently at Jo.

"We're getting married."

We all got quiet.

"Married?"

Jo nodded, she was beaming. "Mario, tell me it's okay with you. Tell me to do it, please. If you say no, I won't."

I won't lie. I felt a pang. A part of me was screaming *hell no.* "Of course, you do it, Baby. You gotta be happy." My throat filled up with some volatile roller coaster of emotion, and I could barely speak. I'd known this was coming, but not quite so soon. I'd thought maybe she'd ease into telling me she was dating. In three short months, things had moved farther along than any of us had guessed in Spain. The girls got up and clustered around her, hugging her, fierce in their congratulations and joy. There was a moment of seriousness, but then there was laughter, and jumping and squealing, and linking arm in arm the way they always have done. Then they parted, and Jo left them to come put her arms around me. I pushed my chair back, and gave her room to sit on my lap. She hugged me. I kissed her and rocked a little bit, though it wasn't a rocking chair.

"I hope you will give away the bride," she said softly.

"For sure I'll walk you down the aisle," I said, "but give you away? Never. You'll still be our Jo, no matter what. Now tell us, when is the big day?"

"Not too soon but soon. He wants to finish the building. He wants that bonus money you are going to give him."

"How's the job?"

"I have the current pictures."

She got up, and ran for her enormous purse. She pulled out a big envelope.

"Amazing. It's fabulous. Coming out even better than I'd hoped."

"TJ is such a character, and he's smart," Jo said with pride.

The lower floors had glass panes. Dark glass, sharp. Expensive looking. The parking garage beneath the building was still filled with equipment, but looked ready to be striped once they got everything out.

Miguel came out with dessert. We all sat in our own chairs again, though food had definitely taken a back seat.

"I guess we lost a bed partner," Pixie said, pretending to be sad. Maybe pretending, maybe not. She hams it up so much to entertain us, it is difficult to tell. She stirred her ice cream into mush. She might really be sad. It might mean real change was coming.

"TJ knows everything. He knows that even before 'Nando had his disability, I was no angel."

Pixie grew impatient. "Fuck, just answer the question. Did we lose a bed partner?"

"Let's play it by ear," Jo said. "I'm not expecting TJ to be an angel. He said he wasn't going to fuck around. If he doesn't fuck around, neither will I. Even if it's not easy. We don't have anything against open marriage, it's just that

I...we...are maybe more traditional than we realized."

"I hope he can keep up with your sex drive. You're one hot mama," Niley said.

Jo laughed. "Thanks, I think."

"So you really, really love him," Letty said.

"I really, really do." Jo smiled.

I saw the light of hope in her eyes. Jo was so willing to take the gamble on love that Melina and I had never dared. She'd been the best wife she could have been to 'Nando, and now she was getting another shot at happiness. In my heart of hearts, I hoped that TJ was the man for her.

"Are you going to keep working with us?"

"Of course, Boss. I want to remain independent. TJ's ex took him to the cleaners. I think he likes the idea of me having my financial independence. I told him about the trips we take, pointed out how long you were on this one. He's not crazy about being apart for that long, but he'll roll with the punches."

"If traveling messes with your marriage, no sweat. We'll find something else for you to do."

"I love you, Boss."

We all huddled and hugged.

I looked at my beautiful team, and once again, wondered what had I ever done to deserve them and this great life I was living. When I told them how fantastic their work on this case had been, I wasn't just saying it to make them feel good. I could never have brought home this many retainers on my own. Sure, I would have kicked ass and brought home a bunch, but not as many as we did together. My team worked every lead, spent hours with family members and were on point, start to finish. The twenty grand each I gave them was what they had earned. Even my newest on the team was kicking ass, especially after the first month. Letty was proving to be a die-hard competitor. She was the same about karate. Though her learning had started way after the others, and she was already trying moves Cosmo was just now teaching the others. I was proud of them all.

Chapter 11
January 1980
Compromises

Melina and I finally caught up with each other on our Sunday morning brunch at her house. The sideboard was full of breakfast meats. I scraped a film of butter across the hot surface of the Belgian waffle on my plate, and as it melted, I added a touch of pure maple syrup. Each bite was crisp and light and delicious.

"My compliments to the chef," I said.

Melina reached for the little glass bell that sat across from her. "Shall I call him in here?"

"Three's a crowd," I said.

"I'll let him know you liked the waffle."

"It's so fucking crazy," I said. "We live across the street and hardly see each other. We should have moved in together."

"You were three months gone. Canary Islands was a long time," she said.

"I missed you. That was a great welcome when I got home. I didn't wake up when you left, though. You're never there in the morning."

"In the morning, I'm off to work," she said. "Did you miss my pussy?"

"Not just your pussy. I missed you."

"Are you going to talk dirty to me like you do ... your Colombians?"

I heard the hesitation. Melina knew no one had ever asked me to talk dirty but Sami. I know she had almost said Sami, but had caught herself and switched it to Colombians to spare my feelings.

"If you want dirty talk," I said. "You know Sunday is always yours."

"I don't need dirty talk," she said. "All I need is you. And our Sundays."

I told her about the Learjet I had turned down as part of my payment.

"Smart move," she said. "A plane would have been a drain on your wallet. Cash is king, and you are making a lot of it. Raking it in with aviation on one hand, and..." She made a face. "...Colombians on the other."

"You must be making a bundle too," I said.

"Yes, I suppose so. I keep reinvesting in opening markets, so I don't have chunks of extra money floating around. But it is nickels and dimes. A stick of butter here. A pound of beef there. Food does not have a big mark-up, and once you subtract expenses, well, it is not a huge profit margin. You, on the other hand, work for three months, and get a check for $1.1 million. That's a whole lot of butter and beef. If that's not enough, you make a deal with two senior citizens, one to sell a bakery, the other to sell a tortilla factory, and you walk away with $250,000 dollars[36] in two months."

"Baby, that doesn't upset you, does it?"

Melina made a funny face. "Upset? You crazy or what? Sheer genius, that's what you are. I just hope you don't cross any lines with those people. Please don't."

"I won't cross any lines."

Her reply was a smile.

"Do you ever get lonely?" I asked. I'm healthy and in my prime, but wearing out four nubile women in their prime, I won't lie, I get tired. I want Melina, but when I am with Camila and Olga, I want them, too. Fuck.

"I don't have time to get lonely."

"You have to be kidding. You live in this big house with only the help,

---

[36] $250,000.00 in 1979 had the same buying power as $891,550.96 in 2017

and you don't get lonely?"

"Do you get lonely?" she asked.

"I do."

"But you don't get lonely when you're in Portugal, or Mexico, or some other far away land doing your work, right?"

"I don't have time to get lonely when I'm away. I work till I drop, get up, and work again."

"That's where I am. I'm so busy I don't have time to be lonely. I come home to sleep, but I love it here. It might be lonely, but having Betty available to come over on short notice helps me like you wouldn't believe. I never craved a massage before. She's no substitute for you, though."

"I'm glad you didn't leave me behind at the apartment."

We smiled at each other, and had a little moment of understanding. I think we were both happy to be in the here and now.

"Let's go do what we do best," she said, reaching for my hand, and getting up from the dining room table.

In her room, one of Melina's staff had left a bowl of cubed mangos and watermelon beside a couple of silver toothpicks and a shaker of chili powder. She gave the bowl a light dusting of chili, and carried it to the nightstand. I was already undressed and under the covers. She speared the fruit and offered it to me.

"You first," I said.

"Together."

She mounted me. We laced our elbows and fed each other. She teased me, and held it out of reach. A piece of mango fell on my abdomen.

"What a mess," I said, looking down. "It's cold."

"Oh no," she said, in mock concern. "What ever can we do about that? Shall we call Letty over from your house to clean it up?"

"I think we can manage one piece of rogue mango. Baby, don't be a wiseass about Letty. I'd be lost in that big house if she wasn't there."

"I'm sorry, I didn't mean anything by that. You should know I love her, too."

I smiled. "That makes me feel good that you love her, Babies."

Our eyes met. She leaned down, and lapped up the mango, not once losing eye contact. She sat up, and I saw a trace of chili on her cheek. I kissed it away.

"Spicy," I said.

"You missed my mouth."

I grinned. Picked up the bowl of fruit, and tipped half of it on to my torso.

"Oh no," she said, reaching for the pile of mango and watermelon sliding around on me. She grappled for control, but I seized her hands and held them over her head, flipping us over. I was in the dominant position, the fruit slipping and sliding between us.

We came out of the shower, and found Melina's staff had snuck in like ghosts. I never asked her about it, but I was sure that Melina must have a button to signal the help to head for the bedroom. The mango, watermelon and sticky sheets were gone. We faced each other, lying on our sides. She didn't have a mirror above the bed, but the position was good. It wasn't dark. The room was softly and romantically lit by the deep fireplace, flickering in red and yellow, and the lavender and peach of Melina's linens glowed soft and touchable. The moment felt new and at the same time, very familiar.

"You're beautiful."

"I'm getting older," she said, making a funny face.

"You look better than ever."

"Do you think we're going to ever do it?"

"What do you mean? Get married? Shack up?"

"Either."

"If we did, we'd fuck up what we have going for us."

"You really feel that way?"

"Only when you ask," she said. "The rest of the time, I am sure we will always be in sync."

She laughed and kissed me. Her hands were on my face.

"You know how I am. I run from the ones who want to control me. You do the same thing, running from commitment to one person."

"I don't want to control you." At least I didn't think so.

"You already have me. What would be different if we shacked up or got married? Are you thinking of children? I've already hit forty. Probably out to lunch in the children department."

"I don't think about that." I said it, though it wasn't totally true.

"You have Letty living with you. She's a perfect age. She can give you a kid for every bedroom you have."

"Baby, stop torturing yourself over your age."

"You eventually will marry someone. I fear that day because a wife would come between us."

"Mmm. Sounds sexy." I rolled my eyes.

She thumped me on the shoulder. "I'm not kidding. You have Camila and Olga. I forget their ages, but from my perspective, they are youngsters with the hots for you. I hope you don't marry either of them. Have you had another urge to ask Olga to marry you?"

I ignored her question. "Baby, I want it to be you." She didn't wear handfuls of jewelry like Olga and Camila. The 15-carat diamond ring in my safe—the one that Sami had given me—would go well on Melina's finger.

She gave me another kiss, more passionate. One thing led to another, until serious talk was the last thing on our minds.

I slept late. I went from Melina's to my Rolls. Without even going in my house, I drove to the Playboy Club, played pool with Carson and several bunnies, and nursed cokes. I ate a sandwich. I got home after two in the morning. The five o'clock inner alarm woke me, but I went back to sleep, until noon.

I broke with routine for the day. No workout. Not even a shower. I could do it later. I went in my office. Miguel prepared a late breakfast that I ate at my conference table, Letty next to me, refilling my tomato juice and keeping my coffee coming. No less than three cups. I looked at the lovely girl sitting next to me, and wondered why would I want to give up the freedom I adored by getting married. To get over being lonely? Nah. As long as Letty was there after hours, there were no lonely moments.

"Letty, I love you," I said.

I looked over foreclosure files and saw nothing interesting. I called Randy to let him know I was back in town, and that it was time to get the ball rolling again. By afternoon, his messenger delivered a box of brochures and handouts of commercial listings in Los Angeles and hot counties like Orange County that were having growth spurts.

I called Randy and told him I was going to look through the entire contents of the box he sent. "If I find something of interest, I still need access to the seller. You need to make that clear with the listing brokers. That's a must. I won't make an offer unless I talk to the seller." I'd have to feel them out for myself to see if they were open to cash deals.

"You told me that before. I got it, Mario."

The team, except for Letty who wouldn't listen, was at home, taking it easy as I had told them to, recovering from the long trip and catching up with quality time with their family. I was glad I wasn't paying to keep a plane sitting in an airline hangar. I wasn't glad that I had no building prospects. At four that afternoon, I met with Tricia in my office.

"Baby, find me something."

"You have sixteen new files there, Boss." She pointed to the stack on my desk. "There were a bunch that sold when you were gone. You were gone a long time."

"Turn your work clock on. Go find me something. I have Randy looking for commercial buildings."

"Good to know," she said.

I drove down PCH, stopped at a store and bought a bunch of bathing trunks and beach towels. I went a few more blocks down PCH, turned in the drive, and took a day at my beach house to see what the decorator had been up to. I lit a fire in the fireplace, put the trunks in my empty dresser, folded the beach towels convenient to the downstairs bathroom intended for beach guests, walked around naked to look at all the work the decorator had done, showered in all the bathrooms, watched television on the new modern couch. I found the couch's material was sticky next to my bare skin, but I guess fabric isn't practical on couches if people are going to be plopping down in wet, sandy bathing suits. I decided to ask Melina about it. Maybe I should have pressured her to do the decorating. I didn't feel like spending the night alone, so I let the fire go out, got back in the car, and headed home. At least when I left, the place felt like it was mine.

It wasn't Sunday, but a few mornings later, Melina showed up. She was in a robe, and so was I.

"I'm happy to see you. Taking the day off?" I asked.

She nodded. "Playing hooky." She looked over my shoulder as if she were checking the room for other people. "Any sleepovers?"

"Nope." Letty didn't count as a sleepover.

Miguel brought us coffee and Danish served on a silver tray I'd picked up at Harrods. We sat in the living room on one of the sofas she'd picked out. Hell, she'd picked it all out. It was all done by Melina. My house was Melina.

"Boss, let me know when you want breakfast."

I nodded, and Miguel left. Melina didn't say anything until we were alone.

"Do you love me?"

"I love you, yes."

"Is it love? Or is it like how you love everyone around you?"

"You are way more to me than anyone else," I said. As I said it, I realized that it was true.

"More than Jo, Pixie, Niley, Letty, and the Colombians?"

"Yes. My love for you is different."

"I love you that way, too." She put her arm around me. Her head rested against my chest. "Are you sure you really don't care that I'm a lot older than you?"

"Stop it already."

"Okay, I'll stop it."

"So now what?" I asked.

"Let's get married," she said.

"Just like that?"

"Just like that. If Jo can handle it, why can't we? If it doesn't work out, we can get divorced and go back to the now."

I waited for a sense of panic that didn't come.

"Why now?"

"I'm tired of waking up alone, too."

We were quiet as we kissed. For a moment, I was ready to take her right there on the sofa.

"I think I've always loved you," I said, thinking of when we'd met.

"I fell for you when you picked me out of that burning car," she said.

"It didn't catch fire till after you were out of—" I said. It was something I'd had to repeat a hundred times to reporters afterwards. She was laughing. She knew my buttons.

"I'm in," I said. "Let's get married." I pictured a frowning Camila and Olga, but I'll cross that bridge when I come to it.

Melina smiled. She did more than smile. She glowed. She looked happier than she had at the grand opening of the first market, back when we were partners.

"So should we have a huge wedding?"

"No," she said, "It's you and me. Fuck the big wedding. Let's go to Las Vegas."

"I'll call Oscar and borrow the plane."

"Let Johnson drive us. We can neck and let our fingers play."

"Are you sure? I mean, about driving?"

"Sure. It's four hours."

She made reservations at Caesar's Palace.

I called Jo. She had that gadget for conference calls. Within a few minutes, she got Pixie, Niley and Letty on the same line.

"I'm getting married," I said.

"What!" Pixie said.

"Melina?" Jo asked.

"Yeah."

"When?" Letty asked.

"Leaving in two hours for Las Vegas. Johnson will drive us."

"Why drive?" Niley asked.

"Melina wants us to go in her car." I didn't mention the sex.

I pictured my team as we continued to talk. They all sounded positive. But then again, what could they say? Maybe if they were alone with me, each one might say something different. Except for Pixie. Pixie always spoke her mind. If it was inside her head, it came out of her mouth.

"I knew you loved her, but I never thought for a moment you would get married," Niley said.

"If I could marry all of you, I would."

"You can marry all of us," Pixie giggled. "But I don't want to move to Utah."

"Are you going to invite us over right now to see both of you off?"

"I don't need to invite you. You should know that. You come over anytime."

I hung up the phone and paced the first floor of my house. Where would we live, here or there? There was so much to agree on. Fuck, it was Melina. So much to disagree on. I laughed, actually looking forward to it.

I thought about calling Pepe, Camila, and Olga but changed my mind. I could do that after.

There was no question whether or not I loved Melina. If jealousy was a measure, I was jealous of her in a way I was jealous of no other. I was jealous of her fucking others, about the times she'd been with Carson, maybe even the stories about her fucking the banker, and the butcher and anyone else she laid just to get off, so she could keep going without going crazy. I couldn't blame her for needing sex, just as I did.

Once I had thought I couldn't trust her because she was so secretive. It had preyed on me when she was fucking Carson to get Pélon to off that guy in prison. That hit never happened, though Pélon was still regularly fucking the guy up at every turn. That passed, and the reason that passed was because I love her. She needed nothing from me just as I needed nothing from her. But what we had, we wanted.

From the moment I pulled her from her wrecked car, she had been there for me.

I wondered if she'd expect me to be a loyal husband just as I expected her to be a loyal wife. She hadn't asked me to give up Camila and Olga, but I should make the offer. I just didn't want to say anything that would rock the boat. Jo was going to try and be straight as TJ had said he would do. Melina and I should probably at least try to do the same. But maybe not. Open marriages were a thing in California. We could be as open as we wanted, or not.

Two weddings coming up out of nowhere were a lot to digest.

Jo arrived first, and found me in the living room.

"I'm so happy for you. I assume you thought about this?" She was her usual mother-hen self, but gave me a very wet kiss.

"Actually, we did no thinking about it. It just came up. We both agreed. Just like that."

Jo smiled, her eyes a little watery, but she was totally composed. "That's kind of like TJ and me. We hadn't even been to bed yet."

I pictured TJ in bed with my girl Jo. I shook the thought and pictures away. She was not my girl. Not like that, anyway, any more.

Niley showed up, and ran into my arms.

"What a surprise! Congratulations, Mario," she sniffed, and her tears ran. "I want you to be happy." She looked at Jo. "Everybody's getting hitched."

I kissed the top of her head. Her hair always smelled so good.

We sat on the extra-long sofa. Miguel came in with white and red wine.

"Thank you," I said. "Please set the tray on the table. We'll wait for Pixie and Letty."

Miguel said that Pixie's car had already pulled up. Pixie flew in in double time, landed on her knees where I was sitting, pulled herself up and kissed me passionately.

"I want you to be happy my dear friend, my Boss, my lover, my love."

She started crying. I felt a rush of emotion.

Letty came in. She leaned over to me in my sitting position, and put both her arms around my neck. She pressed her lips against mine.

"Boss – Mario." She sniffed. "Congratulations. I will always be here for you, always at your beck and call."

They were all crying. I should have gotten a picture of them at that moment, with all the red noses, red-rimmed eyes, and hankies out. My team all around me, one on each side of me, two behind me. They looked more funeral than wedding.

"I love you," I said. "You are my family. Even with Melina in the picture, I promise she will smother you with love and respect as I do, and will."

Miguel passed Waterford crystal wine glasses around then held the white with his right hand and the red with his left, and poured in an amazing feat of dexterity. We stood up, held our glasses extended and clicked.

"To everlasting love and friendship," I said.

"To your happiness," Jo said.

"And to yours and TJ," I said. "Happiness for all of you. I love you more than you will ever know."

We sipped and sat back down.

Pixie asked, "Do you love her a whole lot? I heard what you just said."

"I do love her. Maybe it has always been Melina, but we are both so difficult and independent that I didn't think it was possible. We mess with each other's minds."

"You know, I thought you were falling for either Camila or Olga," Niley said.

Pictures flashed in my head of the Colombians. "It's hard for me to fall for anyone in particular. I'm attracted to Camila and Olga." I looked at Letty. "I'm attracted to Letty. She's here at night keeping me company. I'm attracted to Pixie whom I've known forever, and Niley, I've always been attracted to you, as I was attracted to your sister. And you, Jo, you know I've always had a special place in my heart for you." I wasn't trying to paint a maudlin scene, but I managed to get the girls' noses and eyes even redder, and the hankies all needed to be wrung out like sponges. My own eyes were moist. I sighed and stood. My team remained seated.

"Another toast," I said. The girls got to their feet. "To the future," I said. "May we always be together and always be family." We clicked glasses.

"Will it be an open marriage?" Letty asked. I saw her take a long sip of wine. "I'm sorry for asking that."

I laughed. "I don't have an answer to that, yet. I'm not discussing it with you until Melina and I talk about it."

"What's your vote?" asked Pixie.

"Pixie stop it," Jo said, probably sensitive to my tension because this was something she'd been working through with TJ. "They will figure it out, not us."

"We're friends. We're family. It's a fair question," Niley said.

"It's us. It's a fair question," I agreed.

Pixie had to be a wiseass. "Fuck, what's the difference? We hardly fuck anymore anyway."

"Hey, what about that non-stop two hours I gave you in Spain?"

Pixie brightened. "That was so fucking good. I could cum right now."

"You are so filthy," Letty said.

"Eat me, bitch."

Jo said, "Today is not the day, kiddos."

We drank a little more without a word.

"Did you call Auntie Carmen to tell her?" asked Pixie.

"I didn't, and won't tell her until it's a done deal."

"Is Melina coming over with Johnson and the car to get you?" Pixie asked.

"Don't know."

I looked at my watch. It had been almost three hours since Melina left. After the high of earlier, I was suddenly feeling very low. I had a bad feeling. She should have been back by now. I put down my wine, and without a word, and jogged to her house. Okay, I ran. I saw Johnson as I went inside. The Mercedes was ready to go by the front door.

"I been waiting for you guys to pick me up."

"Boss Man, she told me we were going to Vegas, then an hour ago she told me she would let me know when she was ready. I haven't seen her since."

"Where is she?"

"Her bedroom."

I went up the stairs.

"Come on in. Why do you knock?"

Melina was lying down, fully dressed in slacks and a blouse. She was on the bed facing me.

"Join me," she said.

She turned away from me, and wiped her face. I kicked my shoes off and lay beside her, spooning. I could feel her heart racing.

"Are you feeling sick?"

"No, but my head is all over the place."

I touched her head.

"Your head feels fine to me," I said. She wasn't in the mood for humor.

I kissed the back of her neck. My arms were around her. She took my hands. I felt the kisses on my fingers, my palms, my heart.

"I do love you, Mario. Very much."

My heart sank. I knew what was coming.

"But you got cold feet?" I said it with just a little of humor. I had my work cut out for me.

"Mario, I want to. The reality of the age difference drives me crazy. When you are forty, I'll be fifty. That's when it will start to sting you. When you're fifty, I'll be sixty." She started to cry. "Seriously, if you really want marriage, find someone your age or younger. I'll be there with you, no matter who you marry."

I couldn't believe what she said. "Baby, I don't care about age. Fuck age."

"It's everything. What if I can't ever give you a baby? I can't do it to you. Don't hate me. Please, let's spend time together like we do. You are my only family. I fuck around because I need to vent and you do it, too. You're the most important person in my life. Marriage as we know it will never work for us. Please don't be mad at me."

There was a long silence. I held her tightly.

"Baby, I'm not mad at you. I'll just have to put the fifteen carats back in the safe."

"I'm sorry. Eventually the years will get in way of happiness. I'm very sensitive about it."

I kissed the back of her neck again and again. "Don't be sorry."

She turned around to face me, our heads on pillows.

"Thank you."

"Silly girl, why you are thanking me?"

"For putting up with me." Sniff. "Besides, I have terrible fucking cramps."

"Aw, Baby, I'm sorry."

"When we got word about the terrorist bomb and that you were in the hospital, I totally lost it. I was beside myself on the plane. You were so far away. I took a sleeping pill that normally knocks me out in ten minutes, but it didn't work. I remember taking a second pill, and that didn't work either. My head was all over the place then, too. I thought about the times we talked about marriage, and how I fought off the idea. I hated myself, worried to death that if something happened to you, I would never know you as a husband."

"Baby, don't think about it."

"I have to think about it. I am fucking up again. We were both ready to take the leap, and here I am balking again. Hiding in bed, fucked up, fucking us up. If you get that feeling again about marrying Olga, don't let me stand in the way. Like I said, you and I, we're a thing. No one will ever pry us apart."

"Baby, stop. I'm part of that confusion. I'm as unsure as you are. I'm sorry for being the asshole that I am."

"Don't be sorry. We are who we are." She yawned, and buried her face against my chest. "Fucking sleeping pill."

"Pill?"

"Okay, pills." She yawned again.

"On a scale of one to ten, with ten meaning yes, if I was older or you were younger, would you marry me, today?"

"Marry you today, a five. Marry you in the very near future, eight."

"Baby, this is insane."

"Not insane."

She was fading. A few minutes later she was asleep. I leaned her away from me and tucked her in. I kissed her lips, then her forehead, and before I stood, I kissed each cheek. I am quite sure I heard her purr.

When I got back home, my team was where I left them.

Jo asked first. "Boss, what's up?"

I reached for the glass that Pixie poured me.

"Wedding is off."

"I'm sorry," Pixie said, moving closer. Niley leaned in.

"Our relationship is—"

"Fucked up?" That was, of course, Pixie.

"—complicated."

Letty said, "Boss, are you okay about it?"

"Anyone have a joint?" I looked at Jo. She shook her head.

Pixie said, "I got enough for three joints."

Letty, behind the sofa, moved close and hugged me. She kissed and nibbled my neck the way she liked me to do to her. "I'm here for you," she said.

"I'm fine," I said to all of them, though I wasn't fine. I was feeling shell-shocked. I was hoping for another mood change from Melina when the sleeping pill was out of her system.

"Let's move downstairs."

We converged in the wine room. Pixie took nickels from the jar on the bar and fed the jukebox. Neil Diamond came on. We sat around my favorite table in the deep seats. Pixie lit the first joint and passed it to me. "Maybe one day I'll know good from bad stuff," I said taking a deep drag, holding it in my lungs.

"Boss, I only get the best. Dude knows I ain't going for fried ice cream."

"Okay," I said, "Not that I know what that's supposed to mean. It just makes me want fried ice cream."

I put my hand on her thigh. She moved my hand up.

Miguel closed the shutters, lowered the disco ball and dimmed the lights so that the room looked as intended, like a disco. We got up from the table and started dancing. Or maybe we were practicing karate. It was hard to tell. We were all wasted. I guess this was my version of two sleeping pills failing to put my mind at ease. Melina and I are so much alike. I felt a strong urge to go tell her, but she was asleep, and it would more words than I had command of to explain.

The phone rang. Pixie got it on the second ring.

Pixie yelled over the music. "It's someone named Brenda."

"Get a number. Tell her I'll call her back. I'm in a meeting."

I could hear Pixie. She was as nice as could be. I saw her write down the information.

"Who is Brenda?" Pixie asked, handing me the paper she had written on. I tossed it in the trash and sipped my great red.

"A Playboy Bunny."

I tried to picture her but couldn't recall her face. I remembered only that she was hot, but if we passed on the street, I wouldn't know her.

The girls and I drank a lot. We continued dancing and working out. The drunker we got, the more the lines blurred between kata and rumba. Letty yawned, and I sent her off to sleep. Didn't tell her where. I didn't want the others to drive, so they each headed off to their rooms, leaving me alone with my thoughts.

I went to bed alone, got up at five from a bed that was rocking like a boat. When I went through my routine, I excreted sweat that smelled like wine. I showered like a zombie. By the time I sat down for breakfast, Letty was pouring me coffee.

"You're up early, Baby."

"I wanted to pour your first cup and butter your toast." She was behind me and kissed the back of my neck. "You okay?"

I still felt the urge to go next door and tell Melina how alike we are. I shrugged. "Join me. Are the others sleeping?"

"I haven't seen them."

By the end of my coffee, the missing trio walked in wet from their showers. Their faces were flushed and they were moving like they'd had a good workout.

"Good morning, Babies. You look wonderful." They looked better than I felt. In spite of the workout, shower and coffee, I was still lit from last night.

I got a kiss from each. They took their seats. Miguel came in with their favorites. For Niley, fava beans and scrambled eggs with cilantro, an Egyptian dish Miguel had dug up from somewhere. Pixie had a quarter of a Belgium waffle covered heavily with sugared strawberries and two inches deep in whipped cream. Jo had a bowl of cereal, and black coffee, though she did pilfer some of Pixie's strawberries for her cereal.

"Boss, are you good?" asked Jo. I guess she had noticed I wasn't really eating.

"The question is are you good? Have you talked to TJ?"

"He's cool."

Pixie said. "Tell him we behaved last night. No sex."

"Already told him," Jo said with a laugh.

No news yet from Randy on buildings that were good deals. No news yet from Tricia about more foreclosures. No calls from Jason. The down time was like waiting for the next crash.

The cases would happen when they happened. We needed a break from the stress. Correction. I needed a break from the stress.

"I have an idea," I said. "I'll borrow the Lear. What do you say we head out to New York for a couple of days of R and R?"

I got one *grito* and three high-fives. The girls stopped eating.

"Jo, I don't want to put you in a spot with TJ."

"That sounds like you don't want me to go, Boss." She made a sad face.

"I want all of us to go."

"Then count me in."

"Maybe you should call him and make sure," I wasn't really pushing, but.

"Boss, a trip to New York is nothing."

"Are you going to participate in bed?" Pixie's voice, a little daring.

"Fucking-A."

"Okay, enough. You know how cold it is here right now, so figure NY is real cold. Pack light, I'll buy you clothes there."

"Fuck, I'm coming," Pixie squealed. "I can't stop. I'm sorry. Oh, I'm soaked."

"You slut," Letty said. "Why you gotta announce it like that?"

"Eat me," Pixie fired back.

"Spread 'em and I will."

I stuck my fingers in my mouth and gave an ear-splitting two-finger whistle to break it up.

"Girls, let's make arrangements. Get packed but keep it light."

The girls disappeared down the hall, but I could hear their excited chatter.

My call caught Melina at the Montebello market.

"You ok? We—" she said.

I interrupted her. "I feel lousy and fucked up. I'm sorry about yesterday."

"I feel lousy and fucked up, too," she said. "And I'm sorry too."

"I got wasted last night, and all I could think about was how alike we are. Not that you were in the hospital or anything, but you took sleeping pills, and I got wiped out, and all because of the same thing. I'm not explaining it very well but it made sense at the time. And we both want to get married and don't want to, at the same time."

She hesitated, and said, "I'm okay if you're ok." She didn't sound like she understood about how alike we were, but that was okay. I wasn't too sure I understood either.

"Were you really ready to do it?"

I thought for half a second. "I took the 15 carats out of the safe."

Melina laughed. I pictured her standing in the middle of her office, perfect hair, perfect makeup, perfect dress, that grin on her face, and the cheeky dimple that ruined the perfection and made her so irresistible.

"Just give me the fucking ring already. Why does there have to be a catch?"

"Baby, there doesn't have to be a catch. I'll give it to you in a second if you want it."

"I'm kidding, Cuz. Someday, you will need it for the lucky girl."

"Baby, don't close the door. Leave me some hope."

"Asshole, don't throw it all on me."

"Hey, yesterday it was all you and the age thing."

Pause. "I know. The age thing is not going away."

"Love you," I said.

"I love you, too."

"I'm heading for New York on a pleasure trip. Wanna come?"

"Love to," Melina said. "Don't think I can get away. See you when you get back. Kiss the Statue of Liberty for me. And have a blast." I don't think she was referring to the statue in the harbor, either. "Tell those horny bitches of yours to leave some for me."

After we hung up, it occurred to me that if I had gotten married yesterday, there would not be a trip with my team to New York today. Or—I had the crazy thought—maybe the team would have come on a New York honeymoon with us. I doubted Melina would have liked the fantasies that popped into my head. Melina was no angel and all of us had been in bed together, but if Melina and I were married, who knows what she would expect. With this age thing, I don't think it will ever happen.

By four, I'd parked my Rolls at Van Nuys airport. Tricia was on patrol at the house, watching everything. Although I didn't think she knew about all the cash I had, I knew if she was there, the money would be safe. An hour later, we were cruising at thirty-five thousand feet. Jo had reserved a suite for us at

The Plaza Hotel. It was renowned for being lavish and extravagant, but when we walked in, I found it nice but not the most gorgeous suite I'd ever seen. It had two bedrooms, three full bathrooms and one-half bathroom.

"Boss, this is one bedroom too many. Don't order any connecting rooms," Letty said, awed by the space.

"It's perfect," I said. "But not enough bathrooms." I don't like sharing my bathroom.

"Three bathrooms is plenty, Boss," Pixie said. "You pick the one you want, just for you. We'll share the other two. The half bath will be here for convenience."

"Deal."

I had been right about the weather in New York. The suite was perfect, but the ride from the airport in the limousine was cold even with the heater on full blast. We got in late but had room service bring us a feast of a little of this and that. We had three bottles of 1970 Chateau Mouton.

"This is bitching," Niley said. "A slumber party in New York City."

"Dig it. Tomorrow we can buggy ride across street in Central Park!" Jo said.

We slept in the master bedroom, and though it was huge, it was not as big as mine at home. As bare as when we were born, we cuddled under the covers of the king size bed. It was dark. No candles. The hotel had really mastered black-out drapery. There was plenty of light outside since New York never slept, but none of it made it inside. It was different from back at home, but had its own charm. There was a lot of touching but no sex. It was hours until there was silence and everyone was asleep. It was still fun.

We didn't have a case. We were free. We were on vacation. I didn't think about foreclosures or buying buildings, or Camacho money, or Melina getting cold feet on me one day ago.

After showers, we went to a restaurant on the lobby level and had a huge breakfast that wasn't half as good as Miguel's. Ours was the noisiest table in the packed establishment. We didn't care. We were from California, land of the loud.

When we came out of the restaurant, we came upon the fur shop in the lobby of the hotel. The girls wanted to try on full length furs, and spent an hour driving Mindy, the shop girl, crazy. They thought they were just window-shopping. I pulled out my Carte Blanche Credit Card.

Mindy fell all over herself to make the sale.

"Do you want to have them wrapped and sent to your room?"

"No, but send up garment bags, and put those on my tab." I said.

They kept thanking me, but I told them, "You've earned it. And you look fucking hot."

We decided to cross the street to the park where horse-drawn carriages were lined up. We all squeezed into one buggy. By the time we made a circuit, I was done. It was a big mistake. I was squashed, and my ears were frozen solid. I realized that the girls' ears must be cold too.

"Let's go back to the shop," I said, when we got out of the carriage. I led the way. The girls were confused.

Pixie clutched her lapels. "Boss, I don't want to give it up," she wailed. "It's mink!"

"Is something wrong?" Mindy asked when we walked though the door. I am sure at that instant, she was seeing her bonus fly out the window.

"Smile when you see me," I told Mindy. "The girls need hats to match the coats."

It took a second for what I said to register, then she smiled till her face was all teeth. "Yes sir!"

Only Jo protested. "Boss, you already spent too much on us."

I paid cash for the hats.

Half an hour later, my team was happily ensconced in a large carriage, and I was in the smaller buggy ahead of them. There was too much of me to fit on a four-person bench with four girls in big coats. Besides, Central Park is a haven for girl watchers. The best thing for me was how the girls were having a blast. If it is true that laughter is healthy, the girls would be living to be a hundred and ten.

The carriage ride was just the beginning. We got into the serious tourist business. We visited the Statue of Liberty, took the Staten Island Ferry, went to the top of the Empire State Building, walked New York Botanical Garden in snow, spent an hour each at the Metropolitan museum and the Museum of Modern art, and then Madame Tussauds. Pixie had us all in stitches, mimicking all of the wax figures. We stopped off at Saks Fifth Avenue and I got the girls a dozen pairs of boots to ship home, and finished off with a night of clubbing. The next day we took a helicopter tour of the city, and an open-air bus tour, before we ended up back at Saks, where the girls shopped their hearts out. It reminded me just a little of Harrods in London. The big difference was that I wasn't worried about anyone blowing up the store.

Years ago, Jake had given me a Rolex which I always wore, but the snap on my band was not shutting right. We were walking along Fifth Avenue, and I saw the Rolex store. I had to stop in. While the watch man checked my watch, the girls and I looked around. I bought Rolex Gold oyster watches for the girls, each one sized and adjusted on the spot. I kept the extra links of gold.

"In case you guys gain weight and need to make the bands bigger, I'll keep the links in my safe." I laughed.

Pixie punched my stomach. "I love you, Boss. I'm never going to get fat."

"I'd love you fat. I'll love all of you no matter what."

The storeowner was so happy that he didn't charge me for the watch band repair.

On the fourth day, I called Oscar, and asked him for a ride home.

"I'll cover the cost," I said.

"I'll send the plane right away. Stop the nonsense about paying me." Oscar laughed.

We had so many purchases, some of them were buckled in with us in the cabin. There was no more room in the baggage hold of the Lear. Pixie said that if we hadn't shipped the boots, one of the pilots would have had to walk back to Los Angeles.

Chastity was a good sport, and offered the buckled-in packages their choice of food and drink. The girls made up names for our merchandise passengers. "Mister Badass Belt Buckle." "Miss Fine-Ass Spandex, Won't Betty Be Green with Envy." We laughed over it all the way home. I hadn't noticed that Betty wore that much spandex.

"Does everyone realize we only had sex once in all these days?" Niley said.

"Fuck, we had a blast," Pixie said. "I didn't even miss sex."

An hour or so after we arrived in Pasadena, Jo, Pixie and Niley drove themselves home with all the booty from New York shopping spree including their minks and Rolex watches—minus the boots which had been shipped. Letty stayed with me.

When I came out of the shower, Letty had the fireplace burning, candles lit, wine open, and she was wearing the mink coat with a big smile. I walked in front of her. She looked up at me and the coat came off. She was naked, except for the Rolex and Sax boots.

"Groovy," I said. "You're so hot."

"Groovy?" Letty laughed at me. "Boss, you are so Sixties sometimes."

"Far out," I said. "You bet your sweet bippy. How does that grab you?"

"Put groovy, far out, and the bippy back in mothballs, Boss, and get with the Eighties."

"You're still a hot chick."

"I'll let you slide on that one."

"Sliding is good," I said. "Let's do that."

We spread the coat on top of my bed so that the mink was up. I picked her up, placed her fine naked ass on the fur and we practiced a little sliding, and it was very good. I also did to her what she had done to me so many times. I kissed and loved every inch of her body.

We should have gotten back from New York all rested and raring to go, but when the girls showed up the next day, everyone was off tempo.

"I feel jet-lagged," Jo said.

"Sex-starved," Pixie said.

"Can we call Betty to come over to give us a massage?" asked Niley.

"Good idea."

Niley didn't start dialing fast enough to suit Pixie and Letty, who started pecking at each other.

"Don't be such a spaz, Niley. Boss said yes. Do it."

"Spaz, my white ass."

"Your ass is not white. It's brown."

"Enough already," I said, putting a stop to it before they got rolling. They could go on and on like that. Fortunately, Betty arrived. She clocked a whole mess of hours, and beat us all into shape, until New York was but a memory, and the vacation was over.

Randy found a property with twenty storefronts with parking, three hundred feet facing Valley Boulevard in Alhambra, a stone's throw from my house. For the past two years, the occupancy factor had been less than twenty percent. The biggest store, Javier's, sold liquor and food, employed a dozen people each shift, and was open 24/7. The owner, Javier Barcelona was originally from Durango, Mexico, and he also had several meat markets. Javier sold Mexican food products on a small scale compared to Melina, but he had done well. He wanted to move back to Durango, and when I sprang the possibility of paying him in cash, he didn't even try to hide his enthusiasm. For the Alhambra stores that he owned free and clear, I gave him 1.2 million [37]in cash.

---

[37] $1,200,000.00 in 1980 had the same buying power as $3,777,293.35

Randy and the listing broker were paid by Javier. The escrow closed in less than a week, the time it took to get a title policy. The only money that went through escrow were broker fees, cost of escrow and title.

I purchased his other two centers, one in Montebello and one in MacArthur Park, in record time. Montebello had ten storefronts and MacArthur Park eleven. I paid him one million for both properties. Javier figured a way on his end to pay off the mortgages without me having to buy cashier's checks. There were no brokers involved.

Randy dropped by my office, as I was sending Tricia and the photographer out to get pictures of the properties for the Camachos' packet. I gave Randy five thousand dollars[38] for taking care of my interest in the short escrow.

"How are you paying Javier Barcelona?" Randy asked.

"He signed off on the property, right?"

"Yes, of course."

"Then don't worry about it, Randy."

"Yes Boss."

---

[38] $5,000.00 in 1980 had the same buying power as $15,738.72 in 2017

Chapter 12
End of February 1980
Payoff

I met Pepe and Camila in Tijuana aboard his DC9, the same plane I had first flown in when he invited me to Rome. I handed them the pictures of the three centers, nothing like the Westwood property as far as curb appeal, but the deal was great.

"I like the way you operate, Amigo."

"Thanks," I said, "It's not hard when you have the money."

"That's not always true," Camila said. "Most don't want cash."

Pepe agreed. "Okay, let's do a fast accounting."

I handed Pepe a listing of each property, the cost and exactly how much I had taken from my safe where I started with seven million. There was Downey, twenty units; El Monte fourteen units; Eagle Rock twelve units; Monterey Park thirty-five units; the three centers in Alhambra, Montebello and MacArthur Park that together had forty-five storefronts. Westwood was unfinished.

"I'm holding one million for the Westwood contractor that is part of the 1.3 million I agreed to pay him for signing off. He gets it when the job is finished. I am working with a four million cap that should finish the project. If he finishes for less than four million, he gets half the savings. If everything comes in as planned, you will have a fifteen-story high-rise in Westwood for

$6,575,000[39]."

I was proud, smiling so big it almost hurt my face.

Camila and Pepe were thrilled.

"I love you, Amigo."

"Ditto," I said.

Pepe looked at Camila. She explained. "That means he loves you, too."

"I only wish I could see it for myself. I have many buildings, bigger, but this one has a story that makes it mine. This building was abandoned, construction stopped. I like that we are completing it. It feels more ours." He changed the subject. "Olga made some deal about five percent if you don't pay cash. Too complicated. Can you live with a flat ten percent of the selling price?"

"Of course. Are you sure? The other option is a better deal for you."

"He's sure," Camila said. She was thumbing through the new properties' paperwork, her long red nails bright and sleek against the photographs. A heavy gold chain around her wrist clinked softly with her every move.

"Do you want me to pay you for Westwood now?" Pepe asked.

"Not till it's finished."

Pepe showed Camila the paper I had given him. The total was two million eight hundred fifty-six thousand.

Pepe said, "We owe you $285,600. Let's round it up to three hundred thousand. I like round numbers."

"Very generous, but I owe you so much."

"Three hundred thousand," Pepe said with finality. "Do you prefer to take it from the money you are holding, or do you want to take it with you now?"

I laughed a little. "I'll take it from my safe, and show it on my accounting."

"I think you will run short," Camila said. "We don't want that. You

---

[39] $6,575,000.00 in 1980 had the same buying power as $20,696,419.82 in 2017

need more money to finish Westwood. Right now, you are short $1,156,000 [40]or thereabouts."

"Wow, you did that in your head." That sounded stupid coming out. I wished I could take it back.

Camila looked at Pepe. "Olga and I told him to take a hundred thousand for holding the money for me."

Pepe shrugged. "Take the hundred."

"No way," I said. "I owe you my life. Thank you but no."

Pepe studied me. "You have integrity," he said.

"A hundred thousand is nothing compared to what you have done for me."

"You will make more money with us than you can ever imagine," Camila said.

I wasn't sure about that. I can imagine a whole lot. But I said, "I'm game."

I wanted to fuck Camila. I could tell she was feeling it, too. I could feel the vibes. We were like a couple of magnets, attracting each other, but Pepe was obstructing us, like a big wad of insulation, interrupting our current.

---

[40] $1,156,000.00 in 1980 had the same buying power as $3,638,792.59 in 2017

Chapter 13
March 1980
Carwash King

No big airliners crashed anywhere. The girls came over daily, worked out with me, worked the newspapers and made phone calls. Pixie and Jo went to Phoenix, Arizona on a helicopter crash with fatalities. It was a long shot, but not all cases are dead on.

I would have been bored with all the waiting, except that Tricia came over every day with new prospects. She'd honed her skills. She'd gotten herself a network of agents who let her know when they had something huge or interesting. She was bringing me bigger properties, not just foreclosures. Sometimes I'd snag Jo with her brain for numbers, and we'd talk about a building that interested me, in terms of these huge investments for Camacho. Randy didn't know about the Camachos, didn't have to know. He knew LAI, but that was a company, nothing more, a name that appeared on grant deeds and title policies.

It was dark when Olga called to say that she had just landed in Ontario. She only had a few hours. "I'll be right over," she said.

The girls were long gone. It was almost nine that night when I opened the gates for Olga's limo. The bright headlights blinded me as the driver pulled up. Letty had already voluntarily disappeared upstairs. I waited for Olga at my front door.

She walked in carrying a suitcase. When I closed the door, she dropped the suitcase in the foyer, and flung her arms around my neck. We did the hug that we hadn't done at the door.

"You smell so good." I said, "Want a drink or something?"

"No, Amor, I have to get right back. I wanted to deliver this to you instead of you bringing it from the airport."

"How much?"

"Five million."

"Can I keep the suitcase?"

She laughed.

"I'm headed to Nassau. Need to be there early in the morning."

"I got to see you more often, Baby."

"I promise," she said. "I feel like you have a spell on me."

I kissed her all the way to the waiting car.

I buzzed Letty on the intercom to meet me in my office. I was in the safe room when she walked in.

She stopped in the door. I had the suitcase open, and was opening the safe.

I heard her say "Oh my God," under her breath, but after that, she did a pretty good imitation of being unrattled.

"What?"

"Nothing," she said.

"Come help me put it away," I said, swinging the safe open, and pointing her to a shelf that needed filling.

I did not count the cash, but added five million to the account balance.

My three hundred thousand—a lot of green for me—was already in my small safe. I figured that if I paid taxes on the cash, it would be perfectly legal for me to accept it as a finder's fee. I hadn't yet figured out how to tell my CPA about it.

I drove to Westwood every weekday, even if the paymaster was good on cash. This part of Wilshire Boulevard was starting to look spectacular. The building was gorgeous from across the street. I would look at it just as I did when I bought a new apartment building. All the buildings going up around us were upscale high rises, most taller than fifteen stories.

Sometimes I was at the job site for a little while, and sometimes for hours. I really got into learning about the trades involved in construction, and paid attention to details, like how the drywall people hung drywall on metal studs instead of nailing it on lumber. The new codes required fire sprinklers. Each floor had two, three-bedroom apartments, three two-bedrooms, and one one-bedroom. The plan was to offer one and two-year leases. The management company I used for my apartments gave me a bid to handle the building and recommended an unusually high amount for the rent. The going rate for a two-bedroom apartment in the area was less than three hundred dollars; a new fifteen story high rise with amenities could command higher rent. The management company was talking about three times more.

I was worried about the budget, and kept calling TJ on his work.

"I don't see why we need separate meters for everything. It's extra expense.'

"Trust me, Boss. Condo conversions are coming," TJ insisted. "When they became legal, everything will be in place. Now is not the time to cut corners."

"Dude. You don't have a crystal ball," I said. I didn't see condos in the future. I only saw that each unit did not need a separate electric meter, natural gas meter, hot water heater and air-conditioning/heating unit. All that metering hardware and installation was driving up costs. I understood how common areas such as exterior, hallways, and the pool on the roof had their own meters so management could keep a handle on expenses. The only thing not metered separately was water.

Jo sided with him. I threw my hands up.

"Do you really think you're going to finish this by May?" I asked TJ.

"Fuck yes, Boss. I'm already working a couple crews 24/7."

"I don't want you going over budget."

"No worries, Boss. I got it."

"That little thing?" Melina squinted at the *LA Times* classified ad I had circled and shoved in front of her. "I don't see the appeal, but I can see you're excited over this. I trust your instinct." She sipped the black coffee she'd brought over in a thermos, some dark roast that I felt had been roasted about an hour too long. It tasted like someone had put a cigarette out in the cup, but it was a new line her market was offering and I didn't want to hurt her feelings. After one taste, I topped my cup with whole milk. Not subtle of me, I know. It was almost palatable with the addition of the milk and the freshly toasted LAI brand pan dulce accompanying it.

I knew why the ad had caught my eye—a long ago fling with a cashier at the car wash in Monterey Park where I used to wash my car. But that wasn't what got me excited. I felt a thrill of recognition when I saw it, not for nostalgia's sake, but for the possibilities for Pepe. He could wash a lot more than cars at a car wash.

"I never saw you as a car wash magnate," she said, her eyes on the ad. She looked up at my face. "No, you don't like the day to day running of a business. This is an LAI deal." She grinned sympathetically like the business predator she was, and chugged the last of her coffee. Her mug went on the table, as she pushed off of the bench. "Go for it, tiger. Have fun making your next million off of this one."

"Not that much," I speculated as I walked her out the front door where we lingered on the landing above my front steps. "Maybe a hundred thousand."

She made a noise that sounded like she was turned on. We exchanged a pan dulce-burned coffee kiss that was also flavored with citric shampoo and the essence of something fruity and delicious that was just her. I growled, my best tiger imitation, and almost managed to make her stay, except that Johnson found that exact moment to pull up, get out, and open the door.

As I walked back through the house, I saw Miguel had the coffee thermos open and was sniffing it, a perplexed look on his face.

"You can toss that out," I said, grabbing the classifieds, "and bring some regular coffee to the office in one hour."

I was impatient, and had to wait a few hours to make the call, long enough for the March sun to wake up Los Angeles. I'm glad I had the time for my workout to burn off the sound of my eagerness. I didn't want my determination to win this deal to make the seller confident enough to play hard to get.

"I'm calling about the car wash you have for sale."

"Who are you?"

"My name is Mario Luna. Who are you?"

"Joe Cooper."

"Your ad is so small I'm surprised I caught it."

"Did you call to criticize my ad?"

I nearly hung up, but I'd caught the scent of that deal, and I wanted it. After ten minutes of pulling hair, I got the address, and arranged the visit with Cooper at the property on Ventura Boulevard. It was car wash weather, but when I pulled up, I saw few customers and no line. It was a partial automatic and manual wash, in so-so shape. The condition hardly mattered. It was what it was. I handed over my keys for a manual wash, and told them not to scratch the Rolls, and showed them the twenty dollar bill that would be their tip for a perfect job. Johnson would have flipped at using a commercial wash, but then, Johnson didn't chauffeur for me. He babied Melina's cars like they were made of fine porcelain and eggshells. Through the glass window displaying the manual car wash line, I watched the crew converge on my Rolls while I talked to Cooper about the property.

"So how much you want?"

"Hundred thousand."

"Does that include the land?"

"Luna, you funny. Fucking land is worth five times that." He pointed to the street as if I didn't know where we were. "Ventura Boulevard."

I made a face. "Selling the building, keeping the land. You want rent."

"Join the club."

"How many cars do you wash a month?"

"Depends on the month."

"Show me the books."

He snorted. "My managers manage. They don't bookkeep. My books are lousy."

Cooper was at least twice my age, sucking on an unlit cigar, and wearing a red sport shirt that smelled faintly of sweat and soap. He spoke in short sentences, and something about him irritated me. I reminded myself that I had driven all the way from Pasadena because LAI could do wonders with a car wash pumping cash into the banking system. I had already decided this was a done deal but Cooper didn't know it yet. Bad books was a good sign for me. He would be amenable to cash. I could sense it.

"Tell me what you want," I said. "Your sweetheart deal."

"I'll take a hundred thousand, and rent at four thousand a month."

"Is this your only car wash?"

He shook his head. "Five more just like it. All in twenty-five square miles."

"Sit down, Joe. May I call you Joe?" I stepped forward, and shook his hand, maneuvering him into a chair. "I'm not here to rent. I'm here to buy."

I didn't trust Cooper. It had taken all my patience to get the hook set in his mouth. There came a point when I all but refused the deal. I called my office. Letty picked up, mystified.

"Looks like we'll go with the other deal," I said on the phone. Cooper was behind me, but I could feel him listening. He shut the door to make the room quieter, but he stayed inside the office with me.

"Cash," I said on the phone, "we'll have to go with the other deal, the one with cold hard cash."

"Have you been drinking?" Letty asked in my ear. "What the hell are you talking about?"

I could feel electricity in the room the instant I mentioned cash. Cooper could hardly wait for me to hang up. I thanked him for the use of the phone. Turned to go. Had my hand on the door knob when he stopped me, physically put his hand on the door as I was opening it, and he snapped it shut.

"What's this about cash?"

As soon as he said that, I knew he was mine. All that was left was to reel him in.

It didn't happen in one day or a week, but I bought the Sherman Oaks car wash and the property it was built on. I also bought the other five car washes, three with the real property and two that were on leased property. I gave Cooper one million dollars. I paid off the mortgages on the four properties where he owed on the land. The leases LAI signed with the owners of the other two car washes included an option to buy the real property at fair market value within five years.

I hated the drive to the San Fernando Valley. When I closed the deal, I was happy there would be no reason to return. Raul Gomez, Pepe's management company was happy with the prospect of LAI car washes washing a whole bunch of money into LAI bank accounts. The management company had it under control the day escrow closed.

Chapter 14
March 1980
San Diego

A plane crashed in San Diego in our own back yard. It might have been the first big one ever that the girls and I heard about before Jason called me.

Before long, Jason did call with priceless info.

"There are victims on the ground. I have some contact information."

We'd never had anything this big this close to home. Within twenty-four hours, I had Juan flying in from Puerto Rico to San Diego.

"Valita learning English pretty good but she help with Spanish speaking families. Should I bring?"

"Don't need to ask," I replied. I agreed that her English was improving. I already knew because she and I regularly talked on the phone.

I called Melina to let her know I was leaving.

"I'm here for you," she said. "But you have four hot little bitches to keep you company."

"Three. I'm leaving Jo behind to handle Westwood, and Tricia will be staying at my house for security."

"Is TJ going to bring it in on time?"

"He says May."

"Good deal. That project is a big mother."

"It's beautiful. We have to go out and let you take a look again."

"When you get back."

"For sure. Besides, I'm only two hours and change away. I almost feel like driving it every day."

"Silly man. Put the driving hours in the case, and get in and out."

I said, "Love you, Melina. You're my queen bee."

"Love back," she said. "Try not to wear your eraser down to the nub. Call me every day, asshole." With that, I knew she was back to her usual self.

"If I only knew the market where you would be, I'd call you all the time. It's just San Diego, not behind the iron curtain."

"You can find me. Good thing I have Betty and her massages."

"Betty is addicting, I love her, too."

"Not sure how we managed without her before she surfaced."

By air courier, Jason sent me a manifest listing all the decedents and contact information.

In San Diego, the best hotels were filled. The airline operators got the families of victims into two hotels side by side. It was convenient to be here in the US in so many ways, except that our directions in this case were different. I lectured the girls.

"Tom Jones reminded me to be very careful approaching any family."

"We handled it in New York," Pixie said. "We all know, Boss. Big plane is no different from the helicopter and small plane crashes we handle here."

"This is bigger," Niley said, stating the obvious.

When I couldn't find a hotel I liked, I looked at what else was available. I rented a beach house. March in California is not exactly beach weather, but we weren't there on vacation. This place was more than three times the size of my vacation house in Santa Monica, and only fifteen minutes from the hotels where the families were. We planned to have our meetings at another hotel near the families, but we would be staying in nine thousand square feet. It was ten thousand[41] a month, fully furnished. It wasn't plush, but it was roomy. Inside, except for the fantastic ocean view, it reminded me of a lodge, with lots of unpainted real wood paneling. A moose was hanging over the fireplace, but Pixie took him down, apologized to him, and put him in the closet. Lots of wooden furniture, unpainted wooden walls, wooden ceiling beams, and more room than furnishings. The bedrooms weren't fancy. Just beds and nightstands that looked like they might have come from a thrift store. On the plus side, all the bedrooms had balconies. Lots of bedrooms, more than we needed, in fact. We only used the ones that faced the beach, and it was right on the water. It was the first time we stayed in a house during a case. It took days to get situated and into a routine that worked. I took the girls on a quick guided tour. I took the master bedroom, which had a regular king-sized bed, was downstairs, and had a bathroom suite, and a patio instead of a balcony. They picked their rooms, like I said, all facing the ocean, and told me about how they took Valita to the salon at her hotel.

"First time in her life she had her hair styled."

"She didn't need it styled," I said. She had a style of her own. I liked that thick, long, rope braid of her dark hair, and how it curled softly when she let it down.

"And the manicure. And the pedicure. She didn't want to get it done, but she loved it, afterward."

"She wouldn't let us color her hair," Pixie said. "It would have been so cool."

"It's too bad we're here on such a sad mission," I said.

"Look at it on the positive side. When we get back here every night, we'll enjoy the fuck out of this."

"Pixie, you're right," Letty agreed. "We should have brought our minks."

"Fuck, for sure," Niley agreed, "We were dummies not to bring them.

---

[41] $10,000.00 in 1980 had the same buying power as $31,477.44 in 2017

I'll drive back in a couple days and pick them up."

They all high fived that.

"Mink in San Diego on the beach?" I asked.

"Boss, chill. We can use them when we're out," Letty said.

"You aren't wearing them to the hotel or with the families. Enough about the coats."

"Of course not," Pixie said, shooting a look at me like I was a dummy to think that. Letty slapped her head in understanding.

"We all brought our watches," Letty said, holding up her hand. "I hope that's ok."

"Watches are okay," I agreed. "If you get a compliment, say it's a knock-off."

This was our first crash where planes had collided airborne. The Portugal collision had involved two planes on the ground.

In that first week, I got back from meetings and gave Melina a call.

"This place is much bigger than my beach place, but it's decorated in early attic. There's not a fiber of carpet in the whole place. The girls take turns sweeping the sand out."

"Get doormats for the sand, and take your shoes off at the door. I seriously doubt you can get a house that big right on Santa Monica Beach," Melina said. "Be grateful with what you have. Your beach house is gorgeous."

"I'm grateful, and you're right. My house is gorgeous. By comparison, this place is pretty bare."

"You hardly use your beach house."

"The girls go out there on weekends whenever they have a chance. Oscar says that owning a second house is like owning a yacht. You never really get a chance to use it much. Maybe when spring hits, we can spend some weekends there."

"Sounds like a plan."

Every meeting I had with families consumed me. All the meetings were individual; we didn't do any group meetings. We even held off on individual meetings until after the local funerals. Many bodies left with families to other parts of the country, Baja California, or Mexico.

Our first retainer was signed three weeks after the tragedy. One Tijuana family brought us eight other families that they hardly knew, but who lived in Baja. It wasn't Juan's style to stick around during meetings, but Valita did. She fit in with the girls like they'd been carved to fit in the same puzzle.

I listened to her after she got a little coaching from Niley.

"Only way to get even is to take everyone responsible to court where a judge can throw the book at them. If they get hit hard enough, it may prevent another tragedy. Your loved ones would want this, I'm sure."

With just a little practice, Valita was primed to fall right into the business. Her charm was very persuasive with those who spoke her first language. As I watched her now as a polished young lady, I could also envision her back at the plantation, unpolished, rustic, and lustful. Pixie had shopped with her, and the new outfits delivered the look of a young assistant advocating for fair compensation of families of victims. The girls had taken her under their wing. As for me, I missed the old Valita.

We made it a point to have dinner at the beach house, even if it got late. The girls worked out whether we were having it delivered, or if one of them was picking it up. No matter what was ordered, it was a feast. I stocked up on wine. Letty had the kitchen stocked with plenty of peanut butter, beverages, chips, nuts, cheeses, dry fruits, and all sorts of snacks.

"Okay, I need to say this," Pixie said, lifting her glass and looking at the rest of us around the table to do the same. We raised our glasses. "I want to offer a toast to Letty. In the short time she has been in the field, she has learned to be fucking terrific. She signed a case today that I had figured would never sign. Salud!"

We drank.

"Hear, hear," I said. "Coming from Pixie, that's a real compliment."

Letty blushed, looked at Pixie and said, "I'm going to give you the fucking best head ever."

"Aww," Pixie squealed. "I just came."

Pepe never called much, but Camila and Olga were regulars.

"Amor, wish I was there with you," Olga said.

"Where are you?"

"I'm in London."

I could not separate Sami from London, so instantly, pictures of Sami filled my brain. The sharp flash of grief knocked me off my feet for an instant. Then I heard the voice on the phone again.

"Are you there?"

"Sure," I said, speaking into the silence. "I love London."

"Even after that horrible accident, you still love it?"

"I do love it. It wasn't London that set off that bomb. It was the IRA."

"Amor, I'm sorry to bring that up."

"Please don't apologize."

"*Te amo, Amor.*"

"I love you, too," I replied. I wondered what business she had going in London, but I wasn't going to ask a question like that on the phone.

Camila called. "*Amor, te estrano, muchisimo.*"

"Me too, Baby. I miss you a lot and love you."

"You tell that to everyone."

"But I never lie," I said. "I do miss you, and I do love you."

"Amor, you're so sweet. I wish I was there with you."

"Where are you?"

"I'm in New York, headed to Marseilles."

"Nice," I said.

"Quick trip, wish you were joining me."

"Ditto, Baby."

Lately, the flirtation among my team didn't go anywhere, but we talked a good game. X-rated conversations and hot talk, but no action. My team and I were hard at work, so we got home exhausted, people-watched the beach if it was still daylight, watched television together, had dinner, drank wine and crashed, not necessarily in that order. With all the glass and no carpets, the beach house was cold, even with the central heat on, except for when we had a good fire going. Once we were home, the girls stripped off their work clothes, and put on flannel underwear, socks, and slippers, like we were a bunch of polar bears in Alaska. The clothes lasted only until I got a good fire going, then the flannel came off. Most nights, we were mostly naked in front of the fireplace, watching TV, wrapped in blankets, and drinking wine.

I got up early, and by the time the sun came up, I'd jogged a couple of miles on the beach. In spite of the cold, it was a killer run. There's something about the waves, the sand and dawn over the water. Every other day, the girls joined me on the sand for karate moves. They'd start out in bathing suits and goosebumps, complaining about the cold, and end up dripping sweat. They were getting good. Each had her own style. Pixie danced around like the sand was on fire. Niley dodged like a boneless otter. Letty was a novice, but she was scrappy, an aggressive fighter with a boxer punch. She'd gotten very close with Tricia. Since they started working out together, Letty had picked up some vicious military defense moves.

Twice weekly, Jo drove down to visit, bringing Tricia's foreclosures and Randy's properties. She stayed over, then left early in the morning with whatever retainers we signed, and delivered them to Tom Jones. Pixie drove home with Niley about once a week to see their kids. At least we were close to home. I stuck around and looked over foreclosures. It was difficult to work with an owner of a property on the phone, but I made the effort. Randy stayed in touch, but I didn't like any of the office buildings he presented. His listings had pictures and detailed information about the property, but none of them struck me as a particular deal.

Before dinner, the girls would bundle up and sit on the wicker furniture behind the house, watching people on the beach. Not many people, too cold. The girls had different names for the different body types, thanks to Pixie, who had names for all of them. A Bro, for example, had burly muscled arms, and chicken legs. A Marilyn was a sexy blonde, male or female, underdressed for the weather. After a good dose of beach walker watching, we sat down to dinner at the round table. Usually the talk was of cases or problems.

Even though there is good Mexican fast food on every corner of San Diego, one night early on, Pixie had cooked some ground beef and provided a spread of self-serve tacos on the table. She said it was because she had driven by a truck selling produce, and the tomatoes and lettuce started calling her by name.

Everyone sat around the table, and started making their own tacos.

"I don't know what to do, Boss," Letty said, with a mouthful of avocado. "This family I was working is telling me they have lawyers who are offering their services for twenty percent. Can we match that?"

"We can't charge one client a fee that is less than someone we already signed."

"So, what do we do?" Letty asked, chasing the avocado with iced tea.

"I've been running into that too," Pixie concurred. She'd packed her taco with peppers and was downing her second glass of water.

"You let the family know that this firm does not negotiate attorney fees, but we can promise that our attorneys shoot for maximum compensation. Show them the cases we are handling and have handled in the past. Use the book."

"That's all?" asked Niley.

"That's enough. Believe me, I know."

"Okay, Boss. Got it," Pixie said. "I'm going to start being more generous with the firm's book of cases but we may need Jo to bring more."

Randy called.

"What a surprise."

"Mario, I think I have a good one there in San Diego. One hundred twenty units. I had never seen it or I would have sent it to you. It's been on the market four months."

I was excited but my voice was not. "How much?"

"Listing price, eight thousand per unit. Vacancy factor 30 percent. It still pencils out."

I took the address, and at noon the next day while the girls met with family members of victims, I found the address in the Thomas Guide and headed over. I knew nothing about neighborhoods in San Diego but the location looked as good as Monterey Park where I had a lot of apartments. I walked the property. Three swimming pools. A playground area with swings looked like a park. Lots of kids playing and moms looking over them.

I walked up to a mom who was sitting on a bench watch her two kids on the swings. I handed her a card. "I'm sorry to bother you. My name is Mario. I hear this property is for sale and I came over to take a look." She looked at my card.

"I didn't know it was for sale."

"I assume you live here and I was looking for an opinion about living here, the neighbors."

Her name was Connie. She was twenty-eight. Connie was cute, but what girl isn't cute? I love them all. About twenty minutes after we met, she showed me her apartment, a three bedroom on the first level. She paid $200 a month rent and had no lease. Her husband was at work.

"If I bought this place, what would you ask me to do to your unit so that you'd be happy?"

"That's easy, Mario." She smiled. "Don't raise the rent. We love it here.

We've been here three years. It's quiet, lots of kids, proximity to good schools, and that playground is just as nice as any park around here."

Buying apartments and talking to families of victims doesn't mix well. My team took care of business. They were good, but sometimes I wondered if they could handle a big crash like this without me. I was there, but my head was on the apartment purchase. A hundred and twenty apartments would be a goodie for LAI and for me. I had Randy working up an offer.

"Be sure the listing broker knows you can't submit the offer until I talk to the seller."

"Already told him. He's on board."

It took more than a week for that meeting to take place in the lobby of the San Diego Hilton Hotel where Miguel Angel Cardenas, a resident of Mexico City, was staying. Randy and the listing broker arranged for me to speak with Miguel by telephone. It took ten minutes to let him know I was a serious buyer who needed to see him in person. He agreed to the meeting.

At the hotel, we had a friendly chat. Then we got to business.

"Mario, if you brought me over to negotiate the price, you are wasting your time. My broker knows the price is firm. It is a steal for an investor."

I was good humored when I said, "If it's a steal why has it been on the market for four months?"

He shrugged. "The price is firm, Mario."

Cardenas was over sixty-five and not hurting for money. I felt like we'd known each other much longer than thirty minutes. The price seemed right, the comps Randy had shown me were few but they were for more money per foot than the asking price. These old guys had seen prices change drastically in their lifetime, and often they undervalued their properties. I figured the apartments needed work but at eight thousand a unit, there was room to put money in to the building and raise the rents accordingly.

"I'll give you $900,000 cash."

"Of course, it will be cash, you put a down payment and the bank puts up the difference. A loan on that property should be easy."

I smiled and showed him my teeth. "I mean green cash."

Miguel was holding his glass with Chivas on the rocks. He didn't have much left but he drained it in one gulp and was cool as could be. "If it's green, I need a million dollars."[42]

I laughed. "Miguel, your asking price makes comes to $960,000."

"I know but if I accept cash it has to be a million. The difference of forty thousand dollars is nothing if you have this much money. I have to get very creative to accept the cash and pay off what I owe on the property. And getting that creative is going to cost me. A million and you got a deal."

"I'll think about it."

"I'm going back in the morning at eleven."

I remained silent and so did he, but not for long. "Let's order another drink," I suggested.

"Excellent idea."

"Your English is perfect Miguel."

"I lived here all my life until two years ago." I didn't ask why he moved and didn't ask why he wanted to sell, but that last drink made him eloquent. He admitted he'd had a long-term girlfriend in Mexico who died a couple of years ago, leaving him with a family he hadn't known about. He had mixed feelings about the girl he'd considered there just for good times who had never told him about his three sons. He probably would have insisted on and paid for abortions, but even though he'd met the boys as angry teenagers, he was crazy about them, and with being a father. He got drunk and sentimental, drinking to their mother's eyes, which apparently were light brown with gold specks. He was so wiped, I had to walk him up to his hotel room, but by then, he was crying on my shoulder, and we were best buds.

Miguel did not leave the next morning. I took another day off from the crash case my team and I were working and met Miguel at an escrow com-

---

[42] $1,000,000.00 in 1980 had the same buying power as $3,147,744.46 in 2017

pany where they knew him. Miguel worked it so escrow would have enough to pay off the mortgage, costs, including broker commission. We agreed that when escrow closed I would hand him 1 million dollars in cash outside of escrow at the Hilton. I wrote a check from my personal account to open escrow in the amount of $25,000. The escrow officer wrote in the LAI details as buyer.

Eighteen days later Jo brought me a million dollars from my safe and the next morning I met Miguel at the hotel and gave him the money. He gave me back $25,000 to reimburse me for the check I had written. Our meeting was short but extremely friendly. We hugged tightly and said goodbye.

In the lobby of my hotel I met up with Raul Gomez, head of LAI's property management division, who had spoken with me on the phone but this was our first face to face meeting. I handed him a package of closing documents with details of tenants and everything he needed to take over the property over.

"I hope I didn't mess you up buying this out here in San Diego." I knew he was in Los Angeles but didn't know for sure. I know he had an office there.

"Not at all. I drove by and looked at the property on my way over there. Damn good, Mario. Pepe is right. You're a star."

Well, I'll be darned. I'm a star. I believe that was twice he had complimented me. "You are too kind," I said.

We signed fifty-two families of decedents. We also signed eleven injured who were not on the plane, and two decedents who were in their homes when the planes rained debris on their properties. After forty-five days, the families left the hotels. The families we had met but had not signed gave me contact information. I also had the contact information of families we hadn't met who had not signed with a lawyer. We'd be in touch later when the time was right.

"If we don't sign another case, I'm still jazzed. Your work has been righteous," I told my team. Juan and Valita turned down my offer of the beach house and elected to go home. I told them to say hello to Lobo for me. They made their goodbyes and headed back to Puerto Rico, leaving me with unfinished feelings because Valita had been here in reach for over a month and I'd never made a move. I knew I was being an asshole, but I was still a slave to my urges. I was compelled to make love to her again, even if it meant I would have to bide my time.

Niley and Pixie were pooped out and didn't argue when I told them to split for home and their families. I was only halfway through the ninety-day lease on the beach house. "I'm going to stay a few days," I announced.

Pixie's last word to Letty was "Hussy, don't get too comfy with the Boss. I'll be right back."

"Yeah, me too," Niley promised. "And don't you go falling for any Bros or Marilyns."

"I'm going to spoil the Boss like no one has ever spoiled him," Letty said, giving them the finger.

"Bitch," Pixie said, and got in the car.

"Takes one to know one."

"I'm going to kick your ass when I get back," Niley promised. She kicked the air over her head.

"Show off, bitch," Letty yelled out, smiling. "That's not karate. That's ballet."

We'd bundled up and spent an hour sitting on the sand while Letty described the difference between a 'bro' and an 'Arnold.' I believe that the bros were the ones with chicken legs. The whole body-type naming thing had been a Pixie invention. I found it very entertaining, but didn't have the body types down. We went inside when Letty got cold. She fixed some hot tea, and talked about plans for dinner, settling for steaks on the grill.

"Growing up, used to be having a steak was a big deal, maybe once a year, until Miguel got a job in a kitchen and started bringing home leftovers. Now we have steak whenever we want. How does it feel to have enough money to do anything you want?" Letty asked.

"I wouldn't go that far. I can think of things I can't afford." Like Pepe's lifestyle, for example. I couldn't afford that, as much as I would like to.

She laughed at my answer, and shook her head in disagreement.

"You're rich, Boss."

I disagreed. I considered myself solvent, but not rich. But I said, "I have enough going on for me." That didn't mean I was content. I was still on track to make much more. There was no such thing as being too rich.

The next best thing to sitting on the sand was the fireplace in the living room. The big appeal of this living room was the floor-to-ceiling glass that over-looked the sandy beach and the waves. The furniture was rustic, and on the verge of uncomfortable. Wood framed couches and vinyl leather-look cushions that fit the lodge-style decor, and not much else. There was barely enough seating when everyone was here, but Pixie often curled up on a blanket on the floor to watch TV. With just Letty and me, there was plenty of seating, but we usually ended up in the same couch or chair.

"You showed us that check from Oscar for over a million dollars. You cannot tell me you're not rich. And now you are making all that cash with the Camacho."

"It's sweet, no question," I said. "But between taxes and overhead, a chunk will disappear before it gets to my wallet. It doesn't all stick."

"When you say that, I feel guilty for being part of the overhead."

"You're not overhead, Letty. You're part of the engine. Don't feel bad. Melina calls it incentive. My CPA calls it something else."

"Mario, thank you for sharing like you do. I feel like a queen, especially when I'm alone with you like this."

I kissed the top of her head.

"How do you feel when all of you are together?"

"Like everybody's handmaiden, because they have seniority, and the girls keep me so busy." She suppressed a giggle.

"Letty, I need to ask you something, but don't get pissed."

"I can't imagine getting pissed at you."

"Well, Jo, Pixie and Niley get pissed every time I bring this up. You know how pretty you are. Why don't you have a boyfriend?"

"That's what I'm supposed to get pissed about?" she giggled. "I'm happy doing what I'm doing. I have a nice apartment I can go to, and you share that beautiful mansion and the girls with me. I travel everywhere we go on a case. I have money in the bank like I never imagined. I'm not interested in finding a relationship right now. Maybe there's someone out there for me, and maybe I will find her, but I'm having too much fun. Why you ask?"

"Keeping me company is not in your job description."

"It's a perk."

"I'm serious. Pixie, Jo and Niley had all had relationships that ended badly. You haven't. I don't want to take advantage of your situation."

She rolled her eyes, and looked around the room we were in. "I like my situation. How else do you suppose I could be staying in a place like this with my very good, very hot friend and Boss? Mario, I'm happy. I enjoy the girls, and you too. Don't ruin it for me." She gave me a punch on the shoulder, luckily not one of her boxer punches, then jumped up and ran into the kitchen.

The tall stack of pillows and small fake fur rugs had been Pixie's doing, because of the lack of furniture. They were normally beside the fireplace, but tonight had been scattered on the floor so we could lounge around the hearth. I felt the loss of Letty's warmth as soon as she moved. I took the moment to poke the fire, and managed to get it burning hotter. I looked toward the umbrella stand Niley had moved by the fireplace where we kept our marshmallow roasters, a bunch of metal hangers that had been straightened. We had started off with just one, but each time we got around to making s'mores, one of us had straightened another hanger until there were enough to go around. Letty came back with graham crackers, chocolate bars, and marshmallows. The big treat for me was that she came back wearing only her panties.

"I know what you're doing. Distracting me with chocolate. It's not going to work," I said, grabbing one of the metal hangers.

"Chocolate always works. It's the universal language."

"Chocolate," I said, admiring her nakedness. "Right."

We toasted a couple of marshmallows, and got messy with s'mores. Letty was the type who always got too close and burned hers, but she was always happy with the result. She sighed and fell back. Against the nubbed weave of the pillow, her skin was silk.

"Fuck me, Mario. Right here. Right now."

I tugged off her panties, lifted her ass onto a cushion, and moved inside her. I heard her whispering.

"I dig this so fucking much." Her words were just loud enough.

The words lost their coherence, and turned to moans that reminded me of Valita. I worked wildly till we were both spent. Pictures of Olga and Camila flashed through my head. The three of us in bed, in Paris.

Letty went into the kitchen and returned with a damp, warm kitchen towel. We made a game of sharing it to clear off the marshmallow stickiness. I headed for the bathroom, and when I came back, she said, "The cushion under me. It was so intense." She closed her eyes and appeared to clench.

"Are you okay?"

Letty started laughing. "I just came again thinking about it."

"You've been spending too much time with Pixie."

On Saturday, Melina called to get the address of the beach house.

"I heard the girls came home and you stayed. I need to see what's keeping you."

"What a great surprise. Is Johnson driving you?"

"Fuck no, I'm driving. I got a new Jag."

"What about the Mercedes Limo?"

"What about it? It's in the garage. I heard Letty is with you."

"She is."

"How cozy."

"Come over Babies and be cozy with us. I can send Letty home."

"No, let her stay. Letty doesn't bother me. Been ages since she went down on me."

"Baby, you have such a dirty mouth."

"I do, and you love it," she said with a laugh. "I'm just horny. I heard you closed the deal on the apartments."

"I did and we did great on the case."

"Cuz, you are the best, no question."

The next week with Melina and Letty was any man's fantasy, except for the running. The girls thought I was crazy, but I still did my runs in the morning in frigid weather. I also did my sit-ups and pushups, sets of three hundred. Cosmo would never let me live it down if he ever found out I was doing them inside on the pillows by the fireplace.

When Melina and I were alone, I said, "I can't recall a time you were gone from the markets this long except when you were in London, caring for me while I was in a coma."

"Oh, don't remind me of that, Cuz."

"Okay, forget London. I can't remember you spending as many nights with me, period."

"We had a week together last year, I think." She mused. "Maybe the year before. I don't remember exactly. I love being with you, Cuz." She nibbled my ear. We were watching television, sitting on a sheet-draped sofa in the family room.

"Letty has grown up so much since I first met her when she was with Miguel looking for a job."

"Is that good?"

"Fuckin-A – and she eats pussy better than before."

"You are such a slut."

"I know." She bit my earlobe. "And I know you like the images that puts in your head."

"Ouch."

Daily, Jo connected us via her conference call gadget.

"I picture it exactly. You got a threesome going. Gotta be good if Melina is not going to the markets," Pixie said. I didn't deny it, but I didn't admit it either.

"Melina hasn't even *mentioned* the markets."

"I wish I could be there at least to watch," Niley said. "Letty is so lucky."

"Why don't we come visit you?" Pixie asked.

"We're going home any day," I said.

"Not fair, Boss," Pixie complained.

We sat in front of the fireplace that night after sharing a bottle of wine.

"You know what? My life is like a beer commercial," Letty said, striking a beer commercial girl pose. It was quite a feat, considering her head was resting on Melina's stomach, and Melina's head was resting on my stomach. We were all lying down. "Who are you?" Letty asked.

Melina was quiet for a minute, but I could tell the wheels were turning. "I am woman, hear me roar," she broke out into the Helen Reddy song, so loud that Letty and I both jumped, and made Melina break down laughing.

"What about you Mario? Who are you?" Melina asked. Both of my girls rolled to face me.

I had never thought about it. I'm just me. I couldn't think of anyone offhand who was like me.

"Hugh Hefner," I guessed.

"No way," Letty said. "All he does is sit on his ass."

"He's no you. Try again," Melina said.

"James Bond."

"Too British," Melina said. "Mario, you don't have a stick up your ass."

"You tell me."

"Okay," Melina said. "You're like a guy in a book I haven't read yet. Each tragedy you work is a chapter, and each of the victims are like those red shirt crew guys on Star Trek who get killed when they go to the planet."

"William Shatner?"

"Too short," Letty said.

Melina cleared her throat. "At the end of each chapter, the field work wraps up, and you and your team all go home to hang with me. And wait for the next tragedy."

"Oh, oh, oh!" Letty sat up. "Oscar is Mrs. Moneypenny. She never leaves the office and she always tells her Boss where to go next."

"Not quite," I said. I pictured Oscar in the role of Moneypenny and chuckled. It was pretty close. Like Moneypenny, Oscar was always there. I tried to picture Oscar in a dress, wearing red lipstick. Cigar. Not a good image.

"Too much 'theory of Mario' for me," Melina said. "My brain is dry. This calls for more wine."

Letty hopped up and ran for the bottle she'd left in the refrigerator, because she liked it very cold. While she was in there, the phone rang. We all got still, facing the answering machine, like it was the last monster at the end of the fairy tale.

"Turn it off," I said.

Melina and I just lay there, frozen. The caller turned out to be one of Melina's managers, rattling off a list of problems. I looked down at Melina's face. She was still using my abdomen as a pillow. I felt the tension rise in her. She rolled face down and covered her ears with her folded arms. I felt more than heard a muffled "Nononono" moaned against my stomach.

The next day, Melina and I put Pixie's floor pillows in the trunk, and set off for home in Melina's new car. Letty packed what was left in the house and drove it back in my Rolls. When I was driving off, I saw a huge mass of seagulls descend to the beach, chowing down on our leftovers, which Letty had tossed out on the sand.

Chapter 15
April 25, 1980
All Good

The day after I got home, I gave Jo a week off and drove to Westwood. In the money log, she had tracked every dollar she gave the paymaster, and verified every receipt.

The views from Westwood were fantastic, each floor better than the one below. The marble and tile flooring was complete. Reception was in the building lobby. Management would post a rental agent to handle applicants. Till the building was at capacity, three agents would be showing the apartments to prospects.

TJ was showing me around. They had done a lot of finish work already.

"Not bad," I said, looking at the lobby desk.

"Raul Gomez came by. Gomez is the Colombian who runs the management company chosen by LAI," TJ told me. "He had idea about how he wanted the cabinets arranged." He laughed good naturedly.

I'd known Raul was heading to check out his new offices, but not about TJ being directed where to put furniture. I nodded to TJ like he was telling me something new. TJ would have no way of knowing the management company was in the Camacho family.

TJ talked a little about Gomez's people, his team who would handle the task of renting and managing the building. He showed me a walk-in safe hidden in what would be the management office, then led me up the stairs, floor by floor, though two of the four elevators were fully operational. The elevator installation foreman said they had another ten days to call for an inspection, at which point the elevators would be declared finished. In addition to the management office, the first floor had retail space. Apartments began on the second level. We found painters there and on the next four levels. The apartments were shells, but the apartments at Bunker Towers where I had once lived had once been shells. I pictured what these would look like complete. They were going to be spectacular. On each floor, I felt a rush of pride. It was cold outside for April, and on the rooftop, it was windy. The pool was being plastered.

"Looks like you are going to make it. TJ, you the man. No question about that."

TJ beamed.

TJ had estimated three million to finish. I allowed him four million, but four was not going to cut it. Turn key was going to be about five hundred thousand over what I had planned. The extras were easy to see. Predicting cost was a science. In some cases, prices dropped, but usually they rose. Sometimes the cost of fixtures went down, and doors went up. I trusted TJ more now than ever, and Jo had a lot to do with that trust. I didn't plan on disturbing the bonus promised to TJ.

They say a watched pot never boils, and I had been watching closely these last excruciating weeks. By May 15, 1980, the cleanup crews had finished detailing the entire building. The office trailers were off the property, the three levels of parking under the building were cleaned and striped, and the security gates were in and working. Landscaping had been finished a week before. The city had issued a certificate of occupancy. TJ's obligation was fulfilled, though we went over budget by six hundred sixteen thousand.

I had a little dinner at home. It was Pixie's idea, a surprise for Jo, though it's no picnic to keep a secret from her. Melina's store made up a huge gift basket for TJ, and more baskets for his top staff, paymaster, head electrician and the like. It was all set up as a roast of Jo and TJ, the theme being mostly that Jo was going to be marrying TJ and Westwood, and now they were finally divorcing Westwood so she would have TJ for herself. They even had a surprise for me. The photographer presented me with a poster size photograph of the building, framed beautifully. At the end, Niley faked that there was a crash coming in, that turned out to be a stripping fireman; and now TJ was going to have to share Jo with her work too. Melina was not there, but her staff brought me TJ's basket to present to him, and the other baskets for him to present to his staff. Everyone had a blast. Melina had sent a photographer to capture everything so she could see it later.

When everyone had cleared out but Jo, TJ and the team, I gave TJ a million dollars he had not been expecting as he'd gone over budget. Pixie brought an aluminum briefcase made by Zero. The hundred-dollar bills fit inside perfectly.

"We have to do this again," I told TJ.

"I'm already looking, Boss. Stay tuned."

The team left after midnight, and Letty crashed in the guest room she used when not in my bed. I took a good thirty minutes to hang the photograph of the building in my home office assisted by Yolo, trying every wall. I thought of passing it on to Pepe but I knew it wouldn't mean as much to him as it did to me.

I wasn't awake when I got the early morning call, but the ring woke me.

"Hey Amor. Sorry we missed the wrap party. We had business in New York, but we're here now," Camila said.

"I missed you," I said. "It was a nice party."

"We're here in Van Nuys. What are you going to do about it?" Olga yelled in the background.

"Tell her I'm on the way as soon as I grab a shower," I said, getting to my feet. "I can't wait to show you the building."

"Take your time," Camila said. "We're going check in at the Beverly Hills Hotel. Let's meet you at the building at ten."

Here I was escorting two beautiful LAI women to their LAI building that I knew they already approved of, but I was as anxious as a teenager. We passed two red on white FOR LEASE signs posted next to the front entrance, and six people, probably prospects, talking to the management personnel on duty. I waved at the house manager that Raul Gomez hired, who greeted me crisply and professionally, and handed me a couple of VIP badges. I introduced Camila and Olga as two of the building owners.

"Do you want keys?" I asked. The manager was beside himself trying to impress them.

"No need," Olga grinned and winked at him. He staggered like he'd been hit with a twenty-year supply of pin ups. Camila and Olga shook his hand, and thanked him for his service, leaving him in emotional shambles.

"Let's walk up," Camila insisted. "I've heard so much about it from you. Now I want to see for myself."

We made our way up, randomly stopping and looking around the floors. There were so many managers on hand that keys were unnecessary. We compared the three-bedroom apartments with the smaller ones.

Looking at their high heeled boots, I kept saying, "Are you sure you want to walk?"

"Amor, we're fine, I promise," Camila said. She was on my right, Olga on my left. Walk we did, all the way to the roof where we emerged to a spectacular view that hit me like a fist between the eyes. I'd seen the pool area already, but it was as impressive now as when I'd first seen it finished. They loved the pool, cabana, and outdoor lounging furniture. Abundant Ficus trees placed with other potted greenery made the bare concrete feel fresh and tropical; a couple of arched walls provided both a view of Los Angeles and protection from the sun at strategic times of day.

"It was either a pool or a helipad," I said. "I don't think renters who will live here will have a helicopter."

"I'm so proud of you," Olga said. "I saw the pictures every month. The transformation is lovely but the pictures hardly do justice to the real thing."

"Pepe and I, too," Camila said. "Can we do this again, maybe bigger?"

"Sure. We have the contractor, TJ. He's going to be family soon. He's marrying Jo."

"You mentioned this before," Olga said. "Will Jo continue to work with you?"

"I think so. She doesn't plan on traveling. She covered for me here when I was in Portugal and San Diego. She's a smart cookie. And she's a human calculator."

"From what I've seen, she's brilliant," Camila said. "And you trust her. That's so important."

"That's key," Olga said. "Trust."

I knew what they meant.

Letty was at the house. I had driven myself. Camila dismissed the hotel car and they rode with me for the first time in the Rolls.

"I like your taste," Camila said, though she was looking me over more than the car. She was on my right, and Olga, sprawled with her legs wide-spread, was in the back. She was posing for the rear view mirror.

"I bet you have it because you fit better in this car than a little sports car," Olga speculated.

"You hit it."

"Amor, you are so big," Camila said.

"All of him is big," Olga added. Camila reached over and put her hand on my crotch.

"*Amor, eres un gigante,*"[43] Camila laughed, "I hope you don't have plans this afternoon."

At the Beverly Hills Hotel, they had a two-bedroom bungalow, a beauty. I had never been in the bungalows here. We sat in the living room and had a glass of wine.

"First, I want to tell you that Pepe sent you this for the Westwood property."

Olga handed me a suitcase.

"Do you have these Louis Vuitton suitcases made for you?" I asked.

"No, but we should," Camila said.

"There's a million there," Olga said.

"You don't owe me a million."

"Pepe said you would say that," Camila smiled. "It's close, Amor. We are very happy. No telling how many hours you spent going back and forth to the building. That counts, too."

I had been geared all along to charge Pepe for the time going back and forth. He'd said from the start of the project I would be paid for that time, but a million dollars was considerably more than I had coming under the ten percent agreement.

Olga left the wall she was leaning against, and she sat on my lap. She put her arms around me and kissed me. "Take the fucking money. It's yours. You earned it."

Camila looked on with a big smile.

"Let me get some of him, too," she said, heading in my direction. "Got enough for us both?"

"We will wear him out," Olga said, laughing, over my head.

"You shouldn't challenge me like that," I said.

I don't know if my excitement was from Camila and Olga being determined to both seduce me, or if it was the million dollars I had just been paid.

---

43 Love, you are a giant

I did know my dick was so hard that I had trouble squeezing out my jeans. I fucked my two Colombians like there was no tomorrow. It was much later when Camila breathlessly called for a break.

"If you don't take a break, I'm going to pass out."

Olga wasn't out of breath, but agreed. "A break is in order, Amor. I won't be able to walk for a week."

I sat up on the bed and kissed Camila then Olga.

"Bellas, you are so delicious."

"I'm Bella," Camila said, still out breath. "Find something else to call Olga."

"Pay no attention, Amor. Call me Bella, too. I quiver all over when you do."

Olga rose to a sitting position on the bed and kissed Camila like her life depended on it. It was a little bit of a shock to me, even though I knew they really aren't sisters. Sisters don't kiss each other like that. There was more going on there than society would approve of. Then again, none of the Camachos gave a flying fuck about the dictates of law or society.

When I had come out of the coma, I had been weak. One of my fears had been that my dick would stop working, or that I'd lose the staying power I always had. At least now I knew that my fears had been groundless.

Chapter 16
June 1980
Mexico City Medical Plane Crash

I sent Juan to Mexico City. A medical plane from Texas picked up a wealthy patient in Monterey, Mexico, for transport to Dallas, Texas for a heart transplant. The plane crashed right after take-off killing two paramedics, two pilots, and the patient. Once Juan told me the funeral had taken place, I flew to Monterey, Mexico with Pixie and met up with Juan. It took two days to get the family of the patient to come around and sign. I made a deal with the family lawyer in Mexico who recommended the family hire the American firm.

Juan was staying on the lower floor of my hotel. Valita had stayed in Puerto Rico, much to my regret; but Pixie and I had been having breakfast with Juan in my suite, and using the time to discuss the case.

Pixie pushed back from the table and chugged the last of her coffee with a smacking noise.

"Ah. Backwash," she said. "Dibs on that tortilla if neither of you eat it before I get back."

"Don't forget your..."

She hit the door at a run, and it slammed behind her.

"...key," I said, holding up her key.

"She's in a rush," Juan said.

"She promised to get presents and forgot to go shopping for them. So she's checking the gift shop for something that says Mexico and not tourist," I said.

"I'm glad she step out," Juan said. "I want to talk man to man."

His concerns had nothing to do with the case.

"You know Valita real good, right?"

I nodded. "Pretty well. I guess so."

Juan said, "We live like a married couple. I ask her to marry. Valita refuses. I don't understand."

I nodded. "Back in Caracas, she told me her people pick a mate but they don't go in for monogamy."

"She tells me the same, over and over. I ask her again and again." He was laughing, not like it was funny. It was a laugh just this side of despair.

"She loves you," I assured him. "I talk to her on the phone. She tells me that all the time."

"I believe she love me. She not marry me."

"Give it time."

"Boss, I have no choice." He sighed.

I patted him on the back.

Juan brightened and stood.

"Maybe I ask Pixie to find gift for Valita, says Mate and not Tourist."

"Good idea," I said, though I thought what he needed wouldn't be in the hotel gift shop. I had mixed feelings.

Juan flew back to Puerto Rico.

Pixie and I flew back in Oscar's Lear. It is great to fly in a private plane. Using the Lear was becoming routine on short jaunts to Mexico or within the United States.

Pixie sat across from me, a window to her right and one to my left. When we reclined, the seats did not touch, but I could put my feet up to rest on her lap or on each side of her. I saw her in subdued light, the shades drawn on all the windows.

"Boss, I've really enjoyed this trip. Just you and me."

"We did good," I said.

Pixie positioned my stockinged foot between her legs, her closed eyes and changing expression a reflection of her arousal. I watched her face in the cabin's changing neon night lights. This week her Farrah hair was blonde, but now it reflected the colors shining on her.

After a while, she opened her eyes as if she felt me watching her.

"I love you, Boss."

"I love you, too."

"I know you love me. We've been together so very long. You're like the brother I never had."

"If I was your brother, you couldn't deep throat me, and we couldn't fuck, and my foot wouldn't be so hot right now it might as well be on fire."

"Is that a suggestion bro?"

Pixie licked her lips. Her latest look emphasized her beautiful features, her slim form. "I'm going to give you head," she said in a low voice I barely heard over the roar of the engines. She put her hands on my ankles, slid them up to my knees, and slipped between them. On her knees, she looked up at me. The hunger on her face made me hard as a rock.

Chapter 17
June 1980
London

Jason called me, not about a crash, just to talk. I couldn't remember the last time he called just to chat. I could tell he was feeling pretty good. It seemed like he was in good spirits. It had been a year and a half since Sami passed away, not that that was enough time for him to get over her loss. I doubted if he would ever fully recover. I wasn't over her, and I'd only known her a tiny fraction the time he'd known her. He asked me what was going on.

"I'm in between," I said. "Just tied up a medical evacuation in Mexico. Haven't found a big investment to jump into."

"It's the right time to come to London then, for a visit. I suppose you don't have to stay at the penthouse, but it's just sitting there. Bring your lovely team. I met them at the hospital. Come on. Get on a plane."

"Sami used to say that to me all the time, a little less politely," I said with a little humor.

"No doubt she said to get on a fucking plane and get your ass over here."

"Right on. Exactly."

It wasn't that I had a change of heart, or anything. I didn't have any rea-son *not* to take advantage of this down time.

"When can I come?"

"When do you want to?"

The girls were excited at the prospect of going to London on a real vacation and not on a plane crash. "If we have half the fun we had in New York, fuck, let's bolt!" Pixie declared. "Boss, can I take a shot at Jason? His accent is the best, ever."

"Whatever you want," I told Pixie, laughing at her enthusiasm.

"Should we take our minks?" asked Jo.

"Mink in June?" I laughed. "It's warm, but what the hell. Bring the mink if you want."

"Boss, are you sure you aren't going to freak out going back to her house?" Niley asked.

I had no idea. "I won't know unless I try."

"Jason says it's been mostly redecorated."

I tried picturing a laughing Sami. A wild Sami. A loving Sami. I didn't want to picture Sami sick, or dead. Those were the images that haunted me.

Oscar pushed me to take the Lear at his expense. He was delighted with the new business, and knew Jason was part of it. It was largely thanks to Jason that Oscar's aviation case load was worth tens of millions of dollars. The problem was that the Lear had limited space for luggage. As we gathered at my house to plan the trip, the Lear had become a bone of contention.

"Fuck it. Let's go commercial. Pixie, get us seats."

"Boss, are you sure? Oscar already agreed to let us have the plane."

"On the Lear, you have to travel light. Pretend we're on a case. That light."

"No sweat," Niley said. "I prefer the Lear. Boss, you always exaggerate about how light we have to travel."

"I like the Lear better too," Letty agreed.

Jo called to back out. TJ's family was in town, and she couldn't get away. "Boss, I love you for asking me, but I need to take a rain check."

I would miss her presence. "You can bring TJ," I offered.

"And his mother?" She laughed. "Love you for asking. Are you going to be okay staying at her house?"

"I'll be fine. I hope she's a ghost, so I can see her again."

"Boss, don't say that," Letty shrieked.

"Pussy," Pixie said, giggling. "I hope her spirit comes in when we're sleeping."

"You freak."

"I'm okay with ghosts," Niley said. "I still see Tanis."

That caught my attention. Niley's big sister Tanis had been an ER nurse, one of my case sources. She and I had been lovers before I'd ever met Niley. I missed her, but she didn't haunt me any longer. "Really?"

"I do, Boss."

"Can we stop talking about ghosts?" Letty asked, shivering.

We landed in London at a private airport, dealt with customs, and entered the arrival area. Sami had never met me here, but I could not help remembering when Sami would run up to meet me at Heathrow. I'd pick her up, our lips locked, her legs wrapped around my waist. We never cared about the circus we were putting on. I saw a familiar figure, and blinked twice before I recognized Ginger waiting for us. Her red hair was hanging loose and frizzy, and I hardly recognized her, except that it was her. I hugged her without a word. I held her tight for much too long. My eyes watered. It was almost like holding Sami, by surrogate. I heard Pixie clear her voice impatiently, and finally introduced her to Pixie, Niley and Letty.

"I parked right in front," Ginger said, trying to help us with our suitcases, but we didn't let her get any. The Rolls limousine was just as I remembered. Unlike my Rolls, Sami's limo was massive and stretched, with jump seats and lots of room in the trunk, and of course, the steering wheel was on the right. I tried to recall if we were in this car when Ginger took us to the pub where the explosion had changed our lives. I really couldn't remember. I willed myself to stop thinking of Sami, a stupid thing to do just before going to stay in her residence. I could feel her spirit everywhere and growing stronger as we neared her place.

The girls loved the penthouse, the view, the grandeur, everything. I felt good about their reaction, or maybe it was because I felt her spirit all around me.

"Reminds me of Melina's house," Letty said. "In a way."

"Sami was a lot like Melina."

I saw the changes in décor, but most of the art and ornate items remained, just in different places. Same artwork, statues, metalwork, porcelain pieces here and there. Fabrics, wall colors, arrangement, and some big pieces of furniture were different. It still had Sami's stamp, and I was glad of it.

Ginger introduced Chef Crispin to the girls. I gave my friend a hug.

"Welcome, Mr. Mario. So good to see you."

A few minutes later I was telling Jason we'd arrived.

"I want to see you," I said.

"Get settled down. Don't try to pay for anything. The pantries are filled with enough food for months, and I had Ginger visit the greengrocers."

"Jason, you are embarrassing me."

"Sami would want you to make yourself at home."

"I will call you in couple days, and we'll set a date for dinner. In the meantime, Ginger and Crispin will take good care of you. Enjoy London."

I stayed in the master bedroom where everything had been changed, including the bed and massive tufted headboard. The master bedroom's furniture was now all white antiques, the fabric what Pixie called French toile, though I told her that to me the fabric looked like the Delft pottery I'd seen in Amsterdam. The wing chair beside the bed was lower and wider than the one Jason had sat in when he watched Sami and me making love. I wasn't sure how to feel about that, but I crashed without taking my clothes off.

The first night, Sami visited me. I woke in my bedroom, a huge yule log afire in the fireplace, casting warm light on everything. My dresser set gleamed with red lights. We were on my bedroom floor on Sami's mink blanket, inches from the fireplace. I smelled everything, her fragrance, those cinnamon biscuits she favored, wood smoke. A crackling chunk of wood jettisoned on to the mink we were on. I grabbed it painlessly and tossed it back into the hearth.

"How do you like my place?" I asked her. I'd never managed to get her to visit me, but now that she was here, I was proud. I was full of emotion that she had come to visit.

"How's my boy?" Sami asked.

"Where have you been?" I asked her, forgetting that she'd been dead, marveling at her healthy color. Her breathing was back to normal. Her doctors must have been magicians. "I have missed you more than you can imagine."

"You can't see me, but I'm watching." A worried look crossed her perfect face. She looked over my shoulder at the bed where my team was sleeping, and she grabbed my face with urgency, holding hard with both her hands. "Take care of your team, my boy. You're on a roller coaster."

I did not understand the roller coaster reference.

"What do you mean?"

I sat up. Alone.

Alone. Fully dressed. Alone on Sami's bed in Sami's redecorated room in London. Sami had never set foot in my house. I could still feel her hands on my face.

I checked the black-out curtains, to find it was still night, pulled off my clothes and got back in bed. No cinnamon. No smoke. No Sami. But it was a long time before sleep found me.

I stopped feeling like a leech after twenty-four hours. The girls had their own rooms, and circulated as if they'd lived there forever. Ginger and Crispin were beyond hospitable. Crispin practically lived in the kitchen preparing one thing or another for all of us to eat. We were short on clothes, but Letty packed peanut butter jars for a month. It wasn't unusual to find me walking around with a jar and a spoon.

For the first three days, we never left the penthouse. At night, Sami slipped in and out of my dreams, like some composite of a wraith and a pure goddess of sex. I dreamed of the girls, and Sami was with us, weaved into the action like the sheets we were sleeping on.

In the day, Ginger had four masseuses come to the penthouse. Two males and two females, who came in every day to pamper the girls, and of course, me. The spa was in constant use; Ginger brought in a young pair of dancers to give dancing lessons. The girls spent hours dancing with each other and the dance teachers. It went over so well that on the second day, a second couple came in.

"This is bitching," Letty said. "I always wanted to learn how to do something besides rock and roll."

Pixie was in her element as she danced around with one of the guys, and then switched to one of the girls. Letty too.

"Ginger this is so great. I need to pay for all this."

"Sorry, Mr. Mario. You need to take that up with Mr. Jason."

"Baby, I feel like a mooch."

Ginger laughed that statement away. "Mr. Mario, that's funny. You're not a mooch." I thought of the massages I'd gotten from Ginger and how I made sure she was content when she was done with me. "Tell me, Ginger, does it bother you that I have my team with me, sleeping with me? Do you think it's disrespectful to Sami, or you and Crispin? Or even Jason?"

Ginger took my hand and placed it on her lips, and gently kissed.

"It is not disrespectful. Sami wouldn't mind. You know how she was. She'd go in the bedroom and spend the night with Mr. Jason, and make sure you had me as a substitute. She cared so much about you. She would not want you to be without gratification."

"I love her, even now."

"We all do," Ginger said with authority. "She knows."

"I feel her presence here," I told her. I'd not mentioned it to anyone else.

"Me too," she said softly. "She's very much alive here. Sometimes when no one else is here, I talk to her."

We had a little moment of connection over Sami.

I told Ginger, "The girls are my family. You've made them feel at home. I don't want to do anything that makes you uncomfortable."

"Enjoy your stay. This is your home away from home, Mr. Mario."

"Okay, but stop with the Mister. And thank you."

"You can thank Mister Jason. As for Crispin and me, we are grateful you're here. This place needs the life you bring. You are the first visitors since the funeral. I doubt Mr. Jason will invite anyone but you, Mr. Mario."

"Stop with this Mister shit, Ginger. We know each other better than that."

"Yes, Mr. Mario." She dimpled up at me, and slipped away before I could say more.

The night Jason came over, dinner was a feast. Right from the beginning, my team flirted with him and took over his attention. The girls knew Jason from his many phone calls and had met him at the hospital when he had come visit me during the coma and after. They must have felt he needed some payback. He and Jo had hit it off on the phone, but she wasn't here.

"Finally I have a face to tie to that sexy accent," Pixie said, as soon as they were face to face.

Jason took to Pixie fast. Niley and Letty flirted with him too, and made a big thing over his accent. Maybe I should have felt jealous, but I was happy to see the girls so playful. I could see the eighteen months or so since the bombing had been hard on Jason, but once the girls got going, he looked almost carefree.

One chair was empty. Sami's place at the head of the table. Her place was set, and a bottle of Cristal sat waiting as if she was going to arrive any second. Her glass of Cristal was poured and waiting.

About an hour after dinner, around the time when Sami and Jason would disappear for the entire evening to the master bedroom, Jason and Pixie disappeared to sit on the balcony where I had spent hours with Sami. The evening was beautiful.

Niley, Letty and I didn't join them. We went to different balcony facing another angle of Hyde Park. Ginger and Crispin made sure we had plenty of Cristal to keep us feeling good.

"I love London," Niley said. The night was balmy and beautiful. One of those famous London fogs was rising from the street, giving a lovely, mystical ambiance to the spring night. Not that I was paying much attention to the night. I was eaten up with curiosity about Jason and Pixie.

"I was surprised to see Jason looks so much like you. What do you think they are doing?" Letty asked. "I'm dying to know. Shhh, and let me see if I can hear them."

There wasn't any sound from the balcony that made it over London's night sounds. Distant traffic hummed and beeped, though everything seemed muted by the fog.

"I don't know any more than you do but I'm just as curious," I said. "After dinner, Sami and I would sit on the balcony just like this, except for the nights when Jason came over."

"What happened then?"

"I'd go to the spa, mostly."

Niley and Letty glanced at each other, but didn't pry. We kept whispering in the night, mostly about Pixie and Jason, but also about plans of what we might do as tourists in London. Ginger returned to see if we needed anything, and brought a message.

"Mr. Jason didn't want to interrupt you. He said he will send Miss Pixie back in a little while. Miss Pixie was interested in seeing his house, so that's where they've gone."

"Ginger, thank you," I said, smiling at her.

"Can I get you dessert now?"

"I'm stuffed, but I'll take a little of everything."

"I'll eat from his plate," Letty said.

"Me, too, Ginger. Thank you," Niley said.

Ginger pushed out a cart with many different dishes, tiny portions but three of each. A spoon here, a spoon there. Crispin had outdone himself, so it didn't take any convincing for us to taste everything. I don't know what any of it was, but it was all delicious.

When we finally retired to the master bedroom, it had been two hours since Ginger had announced that Pixie and Jason had gone. Candles were lit throughout the bedroom, making it look like a completely different place. Letty was on my right, and Niley on my left, engulfing me in their light fragrance. They were both wearing lavender, I think.

Letty said, "They're not back yet."

"Jason is a good-looking guy," Letty said. "I hope Pixie has a blast with him. How old is he?"

"I have no clue. He never said, and I never asked." I figured he was ten years older than me, just about Sami's age.

I pictured my Pixie on top of him, fucking him. I wasn't sure how I felt about it. Not good. I wasn't jealous the way I'd be if it was Melina.

"Are we going to talk about them, or are we going to do our own thing?" I said.

It turned out that we were going to do our own thing. But not for long. We got interrupted with a knock on the door. I got up, naked, and opened the door.

Ginger was unfazed at my nakedness. "You have a long-distance call from Madrid."

"Thanks, Ginger. I'll take it in here."

I heard Olga's voice.

"Hey, Baby. If you're in Madrid, you are close," I said.

"I know. Just a jump and I could be in London. Are you game?"

"Fucking-A. I'm in bed with Letty and Niley, and we have plenty of room. Pixie is out on a date."

"Really? Good for Pixie."

"Are you coming over?"

"Maybe," she said.

"Come to the penthouse. I want to show you this place. I keep hoping that Sami will appear. She loved to get it on with others."

"I hope you're okay there."

"If I had any hesitation at all, we'd be at the Mandarin."

Fifteen minutes later, Camila called. "Olga is going to see you tomorrow. *Me da gusto que vaya Olga. Yo estoy en Bogota. Y estoy muy ocupada si no, allí me tuvieras contigo.*"[44]

Pixie never came home that night. A car dropped her off in the early afternoon on the next day. We passed on the sidewalk. She was coming in as I was on the way to the airport. She told me in passing about Jason's estate, a one-hour drive outside of London. I didn't have time to find out more because Olga was waiting.

"I never imagined he was so loaded. I figured he was a lawyer representing insurance companies but how much can a lawyer like that make? You would not believe his house!"

I tried to leave, but Pixie was hanging on for dear life. I stopped and faced her.

"I've never been to his house but I knew he, like Sami, came from money. You'll have to tell me all you did when I get back."

"Where you going?"

"Meeting up with Olga."

"That bitch follows you everywhere."

---

[44] I'm happy that Olga is going there. I'm in Bogota. I'm very busy, if not I would be there with you.

"Easy, Babies."

"Sorry, Boss." I could tell by her grin she was the farthest thing from sorry.

I kissed the top of her head, and we parted company.

As in the states, my Olga time was spent on the plane in the airport as she was between locations. Then I was back with the girls playing tourist during the day and romping nights at the penthouse under the benevolent eye of Sami's spirit.

It was dark and silent, but something had jolted me awake. I waited a breath, and there it was. A shrill, strange ring cut through the night. Phone. A different ring from my phones at home. That's what grabbed my attention. I reached blindly and clicked on the bedside lamp, revealing the redecorated guest room in Sami's London flat. Midnight phone calls are never good. They are always news you don't want to hear. Death is only a phone call away. It took a moment to orient my head.

Pixie sat up in bed holding her clenched hand over her mouth as I answered.

"Mario Luna speaking."

"Thank God I got you, Mario. I'm at the end of my rope. I tried your other numbers but they go to—"

"What's up, Tom?"

Tom was breathless as if he'd been running, and his voice was ragged.

"Two masked men got to him when he was on the way to his car. His man got two shots out, killed both motherfuckers. One shot each right in the face, right through their fucking masks."

"Who is he, Tom? Who got shot?"

I couldn't make sense of what he was saying.

"It's Oscar. He's hanging on, but he's not conscious."

My heart stopped for a second, a painful jolt. I looked toward Pixie.

Her face had gone white. She mouthed the word, 'who?'

I told Tom, "We'll get the first flight home."

I hung up and looked over at Pixie.

"Oscar's been shot."

I said the words, but the reality hadn't really hit me yet. So much has happened since Sami died, and now this. Sometimes I wonder just how I got here, but without a crystal ball to see the future in, what could I have done to make things different? All I could do now is hope and pray for Oscar to pull through.

Pixie got out of bed and pulled our suitcases out of the closet. She opened them both and started packing. I heard dresser drawers slamming behind me, as I ran to Niley's room and opened the door. Niley sat up. I could see her in the dark.

"Oscar's been shot." I heard her gasp of shock. "He may not make it. No time for the Lear to come back. Book us the first flight out. If no room in first class, book us economy."

I opened the door to the guest room next to Niley and woke Letty.

I called Camila. The assistant who answered cross-connected us.

"I tried reaching Pepe. I left a message for him. Oscar was shot a few hours ago. I'm told he may not make it."

"*Amor, lo siento muchisimo.*[45] Pepe will be shocked by this news. He always held him in such high esteem, not just because he was a good lawyer. I will reach him. Give me a number where he can call you."

"Where are you?" I asked.

"I'm in Guatemala City, and Olga is in Bogota. Amor, please try and be calm. I will reach Pepe and have him call you at the penthouse."

Before Pepe, Olga called. Camila had reached her. "I can fly out of here and postpone my errands and take you to Los Angeles."

---

[45] Love, I am very sorry

"No way, Olga, please."

"Amor, talk to Pepe. He should be calling you in a few minutes, then I will call you back."

Pepe was in Caracas. The connection was miserable. He had to call me back twice to get a line good enough to talk.

"I am so sorry," said Pepe. "I love that man."

"I love him, too."

"Damn, I can't take a chance and travel to the United States."

"Pepe, I just wanted to give you the news. Oscar wouldn't want you to travel there."

"I have nothing against me there, but I hate the agency that arrested and prosecuted me, knowing they didn't have a case. I can't give them another chance at me."

"Pepe, I understand."

"I will send a plane for you. It will be in London at noon tomorrow, ready to depart for Los Angeles."

"Pepe, I can't—"

He interrupted me.

"No arguments, Mario. Because I cannot do anything else for Oscar, I must do this for you." His voice was firm.

"Pepe, thank you." It was all I could say.

"Stop with the thank you. I will have Olga give you the details later on. I will call you. It is too difficult to get through to me in this stupid city."

"Pepe, who do you think did this? It was a deliberate attack."

"Oscar is a criminal lawyer. He has many enemies."

"What about those asshole lawyers who kidnapped me? They and their henchmen have been in prison almost five years. The day I got Valita out of prison, I saw them locked up in a cell, awaiting transfer. They hated me and hated Oscar. Maybe they are behind this."

"Why would they wait till now? They could have ordered a kill from prison."

"I don't know. Can you check if they are out of prison?"

"I will check on them, and I let you know next time we talk."

"Gracias."

The next day at noon we boarded a Camacho airliner, a Boeing 720 with two private cabins, one much bigger than the other. The smaller was for the crew to sleep. There were four pilots. One of the two captains greeted us at the door. Camila and Olga would not be aboard.

"I have to figure how to pay Pepe back for all this attention," I told the girls as we sat on the sofas and buckled up. Two minutes after we asked for cokes, the refreshments were in our hands. There were two stewardesses.

"Camacho's are loaded, Boss. You're helping them get richer with the property you buy for them. Take what they give you." Pixie said.

"Do you think Jason has more money than Camacho?" Letty asked.

"Good question," Pixie replied. "I gathered that he has lots of property, but I don't think Jason has planes like this." She waved her hands around indicating the big plane. "Imagine owning just one of these. Pepe owns a whole fleet from what the stewardesses said."

"He does," I confirmed. "I seriously doubt anyone has more money that Pepe."

"Fuck," remarked Pixie. "How did we manage to get around all these big shots?"

"I keep asking myself the same thing," I said.

"Our fuel stop and customs will be Washington, DC," announced a male voice from the cockpit.

When I talked to Tom before leaving the house, he'd indicated Oscar was in critical condition in intensive care. Oscar's wife and Tom had been at the hospital continuously since he'd been taken there. Oscar was unconscious but not in a coma. I could hardly wait to get to Los Angeles to see him.

When I called from Washington DC, I learned there had been no change in Oscar's condition. He was still unconscious. It was a grim flight, none of us talking much. We tried sleeping, but we were all restless, and in a dark gloom. The girls were somber-faced and unsmiling. The atmosphere was bleak. It felt like we were just getting rolling with Oscar's firm. I did not want to think beyond that. Oscar must survive this. He was a tough and vivacious man. I could not picture him downed, even by a bullet.

Melina's Mercedes picked us up at the airport. We were close to Pasadena. Pixie, Letty and Niley picked up my car from Van Nuys Airport and drove it to Casa Luna where Pixie and Niley got their cars. Johnson took me directly to Cedars Sinai Hospital. When he pulled up, Melina's Jag was parked in the red in front of us. We found her in the lobby with Tom Jones.

"Only two of you can go in at a time," the nurse said.

Melina waited outside the room. Tom and I walked in.

Oscar had tubes all over him. His eyes were closed. His face was not clean-shaven like I was used to seeing it, but had several days' growth of beard. I took one of his hands. He was warm. I took that as a good sign.

"Oscar, I'm so fucking sorry this happened to you."

I felt Tom's hand patting my back as I leaned over my friend. I kissed his forehead.

Outside the room, Tom talked to Melina and me about the latest prognosis from his doctors.

"He has a fifty-fifty chance of pulling through. That's day and night from what I was told when they brought him less than an hour after the shooting."

"Let's pray that he makes it," Melina said.

"Yes."

We were in a small waiting room outside intensive care. Oscar's floor. It had been busy earlier, but now it was empty. The small gray room was furnished in cold metal furniture with thin gray cushions. Hard couches and too short chairs. I could not help wishing it decorated in a happier color. Gray was not a color to induce hope. I stared at the carpet. A thread by the door had come up, and the whole edge was unraveling. That was not far from how I felt. Melina went to the cafeteria to get us coffee.

Tom's face was haggard, as if he'd aged ten years overnight. I doubt he'd slept since the shooting. Then again, I seriously doubted that I had more than three hours sleep in the last twenty-four hours. I had never noticed the creases in his face, or so much gray in his hair, but he could not have changed so much so fast. He'd been at Oscar's side, or in the waiting room ever since Oscar had been shot. Oscar's wife had been by his side, sleeping in the room, and the doctor had strict limits on who could come in to see him, and when.

I saw Oscar's wife in passing. Tom introduced us. We shook hands, and she joined him in his room. It happened so quickly, she barely registered in my brain. I don't recall what she looked like. Frankly, I'd been busy worrying about Gustavo Martino and Lario Flores.

I told Tom, "I asked Pepe to find out if the lawyers are in or out of prison. I have a sick feeling they are behind this."

"I don't think they will ever get out of prison," Tom replied. "If they are as powerful as we're told, what happened to Oscar could have been ordered at any time, in or out of prison."

"Pepe said the same thing. I will try to reach him when I get home and find out if they got out."

"They're in Venezuela, and we're here, I just don't think they are behind this," Tom said. "It's all speculation at this point."

"You're right."

My words agreed, but only because Tom looked like he was already carrying the weight of the whole California Bar on his shoulders. I did not agree. I could still picture the rabid vindictiveness of the lawyers behind bars, their yells echoing in their rude prison. I thought that while they were behind bars, their goal would be getting out. They would be saving their revenge for later.

I didn't see Oscar again before Melina and I left. We said our goodbyes to Tom. On our way out of the hospital, we went in the chapel. In my head, I had a little talk with God about revenge. Somebody needed to find justice for Oscar.

Melina took me home in her Jag. She declined wine, and went straight to bed. My bed. She was still awake when I left a message for Pepe. He returned the call in minute. In a low voice, I gave him an update of Oscar's condition.

"I am very sorry to hear he is so badly injured."

"They aren't letting many people in to see him," I said.

There was a silence on the phone. I didn't have to ask.

"The lawyers were released a month ago."

I felt a quick flush of rage as I leaped to the conclusion of the lawyers' guilt. I tried to focus on Pepe, who was still talking.

"I am looking into the matter, and will keep you informed."

"It hasn't even been five years," I said. I tried it keep it down in case Melina was listening. I could hear the fury in my own voice.

"Their release is no surprise. The family has money. The wives have money. Time goes by fast, in a few months it will be five years. I'm surprised they didn't get out before this."

"What can I do?"

"Nothing, *amigo*. Just be a little careful. If there is a hit out for—"

I interrupted him. "I will be cautious, my friend. If I see it coming, they don't stand a chance."

I heard a soft laugh, and an apology in his voice. "Forgive me. My friend may be dying. I know this is no time to laugh. Just...Oscar told me how you handle your enemies. Stay positive."

-

I slipped under the covers. Melina reached for me, but didn't talk. We clung together like two children tumbling in a riptide.

"Thank you for always being here for me."

"Nothing is more important than being here for you," she said.

It seemed to me that night that I could feel the love in her, like a tangible thing, warm and kind, surrounding us. I don't know if it was heartbreaking or healing. Probably a little of both. She woke me before she left. I don't know if it was intentional. It was early, nearly five when I am primed to wake up.

"Do you need me to stay? I will stay if you want."

I could not see her face in the dark.

"I know you have work. You go. If I'm too wiped, I'll have Letty drive me to the hospital. I will check with Tom before I go."

She kissed me on the forehead and left.

I skipped breakfast. I called Jo to let her know what was going on, but she told me not to worry about her. She'd been in touch with Pixie already. Then Letty drove me to the hospital.

I tried making calls with the stupid car phone, but only managed to snag the mobile operator's attention once. I used that one connection to call Jo back, and let her know they should all stay home until I asked them to come in. I told her to have them ready for a conference call once I got to the hospital. So I called her again from a pay phone near the waiting room, and we had a brief group call.

"Please stay in touch, Boss. We love Oscar, too," Pixie said.

"We should be there," Niley insisted.

"Rest up. I'll call you." I cut it short with my stubborn team, knowing they wouldn't give up. "The intensive care unit waiting room is way too small and we'll just be taking up room that others can use. Besides, they will not let all of us in to see him. I only saw him for a few minutes yesterday then they wouldn't let me in a second time."

I went to Oscar's room. The nurse leaving the room said his wife had gone home to change clothes, but she would be coming back soon. Oscar was still unconscious, pale and grizzled against the sheets. I talked to him anyway, over the rattle and thump of the machine that was breathing for him. One of the bullets had pierced a lung. He needed surgery, but his doctors did not believe he was stable enough yet to undergo it.

I didn't stay long. The waiting area was small, and the chairs were few. The room filled with people. I gave up my seat. At least I'd gotten a chance to see him and talk to him, though the conversation had been one way.

On the way home to Pasadena, I dreamed I was in a courtroom. God was the judge, and I was Oscar's lawyer, pleading for God to let Oscar get strong enough to survive surgery. God wanted to know what I was doing acting as Oscar's lawyer when I was totally unqualified. A long string of character witnesses testified on his behalf, former clients of every stripe, many of them very shady characters, plus some of our worthy aviation clients and their decedent relatives. Just when I felt we had turned the tide in our favor, Pepe burst into the courtroom pursued by a bunch of Federal agents, and rushed up to me with a case of cash to give the judge, who was God. God was not happy to be offered a bribe. Hellfire started to rain down on Pepe and me. I was screaming that it wasn't Oscar's fault. That's when Letty woke me up.

"Sorry for this terrible time you are having, Boss."

Letty was dry-eyed and focused on the road ahead.

"Letty, thanks. I know you must be jet-lagged as all hell."

"I'm fine. I want to be with you."

I closed my eyes, this time falling into a dreamless sleep, and didn't wake up until we were in front of my house. I got out and stared up at the gray sky. It was chilly for June in Pasadena. Caro opened the door for me. I nodded a hello, and went to my office to return a beep from a number I did not recognize.

It was Carson, more upset than I'd ever heard him.

"Is he going to make it?"

I tried to calm him down but don't know if I had any success. Carson's call pushed me toward unwanted thoughts. It was the first time in ages that I spoke to him without his bringing up that I should bring him into aviation with me. I suppose he saw the good life he was leading in jeopardy. He had vehicular cases coming in. I had aviation cases coming in. Not every lawyer is good with what we do. He and I need a lawyer that has the money to take the cases and pay right away. Without Oscar, I'm not saying I'd be on a breadline, but I'd be back out there looking for another lawyer. If it came down to it, it would be my fourth lawyer association. Harry had taught me the ropes and been my mentor; Jake had swiped me from Harry, and brought me to the big leagues. Oscar had just fallen into my lap, like a cosmic gift from the universe. But without Oscar, I had no idea who would be next. I didn't think Oscar' firm could handle Carson and me, not without Oscar himself at the helm.

Oscar was the man for Carson and the man for me. We were both in trouble.

Chapter 18
Still June 1980
Bad News

Pepe had said to stay positive. I tried it. I told myself and others who asked that Oscar would pull through. Oscar was my friend. Deep into my bones, I wanted Oscar to recover to live another hundred years. When Jake had died, I had bonuses coming for many high dollar cases. I lost that money, not because Jake was not solvent—he wasn't, a secret he had kept well hidden—but because the lawyers who took over Jake's firm were not obligated to pay me anything Jake promised. I learned my lesson. With Oscar, the arrangement was cash and carry. Oscar owed me zero dollars. But I owed Oscar my loyalty.

Tom Jones kept in touch with the detective on Oscar's case, and told me that the two hit men were presumed to be illegals. There was no identification on them. Their fingerprints weren't on record. They looked Hispanic.

"Let me see the pictures," I urged. "I know what those fools look like." It was too much for me to expect Gustavo and Lario who'd been shot. I knew they were lawyers, not hitmen, but maybe they'd sent their hired goons I knew only too well.

I was upset when I talked to Pepe. All I could think of was my certainty that Lario and Gustavo were behind Oscar's shooting. They had threatened him when they were behind bars, and now, just when they were released, he ended up shot? It was too much of a coincidence, and I told Pepe so. I was talking like a thoughtless hothead, but at least I didn't mention them by name.

His response, or at least the lack of specific names, made me realize he was being careful what he said on the phone. We were speaking in Spanish, which Pepe often did. His English wasn't bad, but his Spanish was better.

"They are at their farm. I understand both families are there."

I figured the farm had to be the coffee plantation.

"I assume your source is reliable that they are there?"

"Count on it."

"I thought the government confiscated the planta—the farm when they got arrested."

Pepe coughed, maybe to muffle a laugh. "No matter. They had the money to buy or bribe it back. And don't forget how isolated it is there. Communication is terrible. They don't have the infrastructure to just order the Oscar situation."

That made me pause. Pepe would know exactly what kind of framework would be needed. His business was massive.

He laughed. "They just got out of prison. They're probably making up for lost time in the sack."

"Pepe, thank you for calling to let me know."

Silence on his end of the line. "You don't sound convinced."

"I believe anything you tell me. It's not you I mistrust. I just remember how worked up they were the last time I saw them. Get Valita's account, or the subordinate to your friend the general. He heard them going off like bottle rockets."

"Someone will go see them. I'll get back to you."

"I'll make it up to you," I said. "If they did this, I'll personally take them out. I've already sent three souls to the cemetery. What's another four?" Nobody with half a brain trusted phones, not since Watergate.[46] I guess I had half a brain in that moment. Or was just so pissed off, I didn't give a shit.

---

[46] Watergate was a political scandal in the early 1970s when the government administration performed clandestine and often illegal activities such as tapping phones.

"Mario, calm down."

I took deep slow breaths. "I shouldn't joke around like that, eh?" I managed a laugh that sounded lame even to my ears.

He switched to English. "Go find some more buildings for LAI. The San Diego property is a real prize. Thank you."

"I'm on it," I promised. As I hung up, I doubted that Pepe had a clue how serious I was about taking these assholes out. If I allowed myself to think of the kidnapping, all I could feel was how much misery I owed them. The only kidnapping and intimidation would be by me and not to me. Oscar's shooting was related. I was certain. Then again, maybe Pepe had a clue. He must have alerted his whole family because I was about to get an earful from the whole crew. Camila called me immediately.

"Amor, are you okay? My brother says you were really mad when he talked to you."

"I'm not mad at Pepe. I hope he doesn't think I am?"

"No, he knows. Let him handle the matter. Promise me, Amor."

 "I promise, Bella."

"*Besitos, Amor.*"

"Kisses back," I said.

Then Olga called. Ten minutes more, but all the same content, rerun. There was no question that the Camachos were in touch with each other.

Once I got them off the phone, I reached out to Randy and Tricia, nagging them to find me more properties. I wanted them to find me something out there, a project big enough to take my mind off of my inability to do anything to help Oscar. My temper was a big dog on a short leash. I was taking my stress out on everyone, not that I meant to.

Melina didn't come over every day, but we talked on the phone many times during the day and at least once a night. I brought her up to date with what Pepe said. I even told her how stupid I was to be on the phone and said what I said about taking the bastards out.

"I wouldn't worry about it. A best friend may be dying. You can vent. You're allowed."

"Remember *The Godfather* when they brought in mattresses so the guards could sleep in the house to protect the family?" Melina asked.

I laughed. "I remember. I loved that movie."

"Get some men parked over there."

"Baby, I don't need guards. Please stop worrying."

"Then promise me you will start using the alarm system."

"I promise." I meant it too, at least while we were talking. I followed Melina's philosophy. I could handle anything if I saw it coming. I believed the alarm was all the warning I would need.

That night, Letty parked her .357 Magnum Revolver in a bedside table drawer that she left open. "I talked to Melina. I'm sleeping all night with you from now on." Her look was too serious for me to argue or laugh. She had become a sharp shooter and favored this huge gun.

"Just don't shoot me when I'm coming out of the john at two in the morning."

"Deal, Boss."

Valita called with the same caution as Melina.

"Mario, please don't take this lightly. Be careful."

"I promise I am not taking this lightly."

I nagged Tom until he got pictures of the shooters from the detective in charge, and came over with them.

I was full of certainty until he put them on the conference table in front of me.

"It's not them," I said, disappointed. How stupid of me to hope it would be the lawyers in person, or even the goons who had been imprisoned with them. Of course, they must have hired guns. Tom already knew it wasn't them. He'd seen the four lying on the warehouse floor where I had put them. Almost five years since the rescue from my kidnappers, but I could picture that day perfectly.

"It wasn't easy getting the pictures but I wanted you to see for yourself."

Valita was not surprised when I told her about the pictures. She'd thought all along they would hire some professional hit man, and not Toothless and company. It seemed too simple a solution. She wanted to know if I had seen Juan around, if maybe he'd come to Los Angeles.

I told her no. I asked the girls if they'd asked Juan to do some research or a job, but no one had.

"Mister, you tell me if you hear from Juan, okay? After he hear about Oscar, he disappear."

I made it to the hospital every day. Sometimes I met up with his wife or bought her the swill that passed for coffee in the hospital cafeteria. Our chats were brief but extremely friendly. She was a pretty woman, younger than Oscar. She had probably been a trophy wife, but she was a good wife, as far as I could tell. It seemed that she loved Oscar deeply.

Oscar was not conscious, but his color looked better from day to day. The odor of sickness and disinfectant, and the tick and rattle of the machines drove me up the wall, so I didn't stay long. In the hallway at the hospital, I cornered Oscar's surgeon, who confirmed that Oscar was getting stronger. He was confident he would make it through the surgery. We were all beginning to feel a little more optimistic. I went home secure in the knowledge that he would be getting out of surgery early in the morning. But then I got the call. During surgery, Oscar died.

I felt grief, and rage, and everything I had tamped down after Sami's death. I felt a tangle of emotion I could not separate into all the threads. It was not the time for me to think of finances but I suppose I'm human so that's where my brain went. I had depended greatly on Oscar, but still, I was set. Even if I never got another case, I could easily live on the rental income from my apartments. I had money in the bank. I had a million plus in green cash that I had recently made with Camacho. I planned to keep buying assets for them so for as long as they wanted me to buy for them I would be making money on that. Big money.

But I wasn't giving up aviation. I would miss the action. I would miss the money. Still, with aviation, I had a bigger problem.

Without Oscar, where would my future aviation cases go? Where would Carson take the cases he was still getting from my old sources? Would Tom Jones have the capital to handle the cases? If he didn't, then I had to worry about the people I'd signed. I didn't even know who was designated to take over upon his death, or became too ill to work. It wouldn't be Tom in charge, but one of several attorneys who had been with Oscar a lot longer than Tom Jones. Suddenly, I felt like a heel, thinking about business with Oscar not even cold in his grave.

Working out helped my brain. I'd finished my late workout, and was nursing a glass of wine at the conference table in my office when Jo called. At least Jo was sitting pretty. TJ had moved from his ex-girlfriend's Santa Monica apartment by the beach to Jo's very nice house that had been paid off when her husband died. She had income from apartments she had purchased. She had money in the bank from her work with me, 'Nando's life insurance policies, and now she had TJ. TJ had the million bucks I'd just paid him, and, if he was smart, he still had some of that three hundred thousand I'd given him when we made the deal.

"Boss, should I be worried about you?" Jo asked.

"Why would you ask that?"

"We talk," Jo said. "I mean Pixie and Niley and Letty and me. This thing with Oscar has us worried."

"No need," I said.

"We're still concerned. If we weren't concerned, we would have quit karate a long time ago. We wouldn't be going to Melina's practice range every Wednesday night. We wouldn't be headed over there now, to camp out, and guard you."

"Hold on. What? What was that? Who's coming to guard me?" I stood up, knocking over the chair I'd been sitting in. I righted it, and sat down again, elbows on the table.

"Everybody."

"Everybody who?"

"Niley and Pixie. Me too. We're putting the kids to bed, then we're all coming over, armed for bear."

"You stay where you are," I said. "You got your mom, your live-in, your kids, and now TJ to worry over. I'll be fine."

"But Boss, somebody's got to be there to cover your back. And who better than us? We don't want you to have to be alone. Someone was gunning for Oscar, and now he's gone. What if someone is gunning for you?"

"Letty is sleeping with her huge gun at bedside and then there is me with twenty years of karate and judo. It's covered, Baby, really."

There was a long pause. I could hear the gears in Jo's brain.

I convinced her to stay home, and thanked her for giving me a heads up regarding Pixie and Niley. I almost regretted convincing her. Jo is the best buffer when Pixie and Letty get started on each other. I felt like calling her back and having her here too, but I'd made a resolution to at least try to step back now that TJ was in the picture. I had the feeling when I hung up that she was hoping I'd convince her to come too. She is accustomed to running the team, and I am accustomed to letting her do so. She's a good conductor.

The girls arrived all in a bunch, their belongings with them, packed like they were going on a trip, but they were in jeans and t shirts. They converged in my office.

"Boss, we decided. We're here to stay."

"Where is Jo?" Pixie asked. "She's supposed to be here."

"She warned me you guys were on the way over. I told her to stay put. I'm touched that you care enough to move in to watch over me. But what about your kids?"

"My kiddo is thirteen going on twenty-two," Pixie said. "And the only one she listens to is Aunt Carmen, so that's where she is."

"Mine are know-it-alls. They like the nanny more than they like me," Niley said.

"I'm so happy you will be here for a while. It will be fun!" Letty was all smiles.

"Bitch, you're just saying that. I know you want the Boss for yourself, going on forever already," Pixie said.

I wouldn't mind having them around, but I couldn't think of them as 'protection.' No need to tell them that, though. Arguments, competition, and hurt feelings would ensue. I felt the urge to protect them twice as much as they wanted to protect me. It was a sad state of affairs.

"Go get settled, and we'll eat up a storm for lunch."

I saw the identical green camouflage duffle bags that Niley and Pixie had. I saw the matching gun bags that Caro carried for them to their rooms. It looked like they'd gone shopping at the Army Surplus store. Tricia had been having an effect on them.

"Remember, those guns are not supposed to be around where I have access." I didn't mention Letty's gun, and no doubt they already knew Letty was sleeping with it nearby.

"Got it, Boss. We know," Pixie said, without looking back.

"No worries, Boss. You won't even know the guns are here, except for Wednesday nights when we take them over to Melina's for target shooting."

Jo, Pixie and Niley had licenses to carry a concealed weapon and Melina was working on getting Letty her license. I'm not much on guns, with good reason. If I wasn't an ex-con, I'd have a huge collection and I would know how to use them, but the government has laws about that.

After they scattered to their rooms to settle in, I went in my bedroom and shut the door. I got through to Pepe to give him the bad news. "I really thought he was going to make it," I said. "I talked to the doctor yesterday and saw Oscar for a little bit. He was looking better."

"I will miss him," Pepe said.

I talked over the huge lump in my throat. "Me too."

"He was a good friend. Forgive me that I cannot attend the funeral."

"He would be the first to tell you not to come. I just wish he could rest in peace. The coroner still has his body on ice. Makes me sick."

"You want peace for Oscar," Pepe said, with a strange note of emotion in his voice. "Or maybe revenge. Remember what I said the last time we talked. What if I told you I sent a helicopter with ten of my best men to the plantation?"

"Are you saying you did that?" I asked, untwisting the long phone cord before I sat down on the bed. All the phones had two twenty-foot coiled cords (one from the phone to the wall, one from the phone to the receiver) but they tend to wad up.

I parked my ass on the bed. "What did they find?"

He didn't answer right away. He took so long I stood up and walked around my bed, turned and walked back. I remained silent and began to think we got disconnected. The silence grew on Pepe's side of the line. I waited. As secretive as he was about his actions, Pepe was usually an excitable, passionate kind of guy, his feelings right out there in the open. Well, as open as he could be, on the phone. He finally continued. When he did, his voice was cold, unemotional.

"I waited for my men to check in. Thirty minutes. An hour. A day. No hails from them, and no answer on their end."

Hails referred to the cockpit radio communications. I knew his pilots always kept in constant communication with Pepe's base of operations. His pilots had shown me how it worked. This had to be very bad.

"These aren't guys who fuck up. These are soldiers who get the job done, soldiers I trust with my life. They didn't return within the time frame. They didn't respond to hails. They didn't call. I waited until I couldn't wait any longer, then gathered up some of my second string of soldiers in Caracas. Not that they are any less trustworthy, but they are younger, less seasoned. I sent them on a flyover in broad daylight. My soldiers had both doors to the chopper open, at ready to shoot below as we hovered low over the plantation. Over the landing field."

I was so excited I had to sit down, knees week, hand shaking. I knew something big was coming. I asked, "What did you find?"

"The burned carcass of my helicopter on the helipad. A debris field. Nine bodies. Not burned, still clothed. Arranged in a straight row, like they'd been placed there, like they probably were. Nine corpses in a straight row. Are you seeing it? As they hovered, one of my men, the tenth man they let live for some reason, named Julio was waving at my pilots. My pilots feared a trap but they took it down. Eight soldiers aboard were armed and ready. Just as Julio boarded, I heard the shots." He cleared his throat. "I heard the shots through the radio. I was listening. Remotely."

"I see," I said. I realized with another jolt that Pepe had been there in person. He was lying. He was still talking, and I tried to focus on his words.

"Julio was hit. My soldiers shot randomly, but there were no visible targets. They pulled up and took off. My men lay Julio down on the floor of the chopper. He was barely alive."

"Did he make it?"

"No, he did not. But he breathed long enough to give me a message from Lario."

My heart was racing. I could feel the adrenaline spilling into my veins.

"That Gustavo, Lario and Lario's brother knew I worked with the General to plant drugs at his plantation. The General's days were numbered and so were mine. My soldiers asked Julio if Lario mentioned anybody else. Julio said no."

"Pepe, I'm sorry you got involved in this all to get me freed."

"Mario, stop. No one forced me to do anything. Oscar asked for a favor and anything that happened after was on me and so it is today. You think this was the first time I had dealings with this family on my turf? No, it is not. They are bad people."

I remained silent. My mind raced. Five years ago I had asked Oscar if Pepe had planted the drugs and Oscar brushed the question off. We never talked about it again. Valita had been Lario's maid, and she'd told me more than once that there was never any drugs at the plantation. It wasn't like they were innocent. The lawyers regularly kidnapped people for ransom. But drugs were not their crime of choice. Valita had said all along that the soldiers who raided the plantation had planted the cocaine and heroin.

"I'm going in," I said, standing up, already looking toward the closet where my suitcases waited. "I have to face those bastards."

I tucked the phone between my ear and shoulder, walked over to my closet and jerked down a suitcase, the phone cord trailing after me as I tossed it on my bed. I jerked open my dresser drawer, but his next words froze me in place.

"Amigo, it's too late. I got it from a good source that sometime after the flyover, bombs and grenades were dropped from choppers. The entire plantation is a ruin. The jungle surrounding the property has been burning for days."

I knew Pepe always kept layers and layers of hierarchy between himself and anything that had the appearance of crime, but going on something in his delivery told me this one had been personal. I'd bet that Pepe had personally dropped the bombs or had been an eye witness, but I wouldn't know the truth until I asked him in person. He would never say so on the phone.

I remembered my prison, the warehouse, the shower, the impenetrable jungle. I pictured it, and the fire burned in my head, an inferno. The jungle, ashes. The plantation house, ashes. The trees and fields, burned blackened shadows, ghosts of what I remembered, all ghosts, including Gustavo and Lario. I know what too late meant. Too late meant that the lawyers were dead. Pepe had killed everyone who could tell me the truth.

I would never know for sure if these bastards had ordered the hit on Oscar.

I was so pissed off, I nailed the grip with a roundhouse kick. It sailed harmlessly across the room and smacked against the wall. I was shaking with anger, focused on my breathing to get ahead of it. I heard a patter of feet come up the steps, and Caro peeked in my open door.

"Everything okay, Boss?" Caro asked, her voice timid.

I covered the mouthpiece of the phone, and snapped, "I'm fine. Go."

"Did I lose you?" asked Pepe.

I waited till my help went back downstairs. I waited till I had control of myself before responding.

"I'm here. Sorry."

Pepe laughed, a harsh, hard crack with no humor in it. I heard a dark mixture of spite, revenge, cruelty, and malice. I would not want to be Pepe's enemy and the target of that ruthlessness.

"They deserved what they got. My men were killed in cold blood. An eye for an eye, my friend."

"How do you know they were there when the cavalry dropped the bombs?"

"Amigo, they were there." He didn't have to say the words that he'd been there, but the answer was in his voice.

"But we don't know for sure." I felt a cold rage in my gut. If they were dead, I had no way to hear their confession that they'd had a hand in shooting Oscar. If they survived and were hungry to get me killed, I was going to be right there in their face for them to take their best shot. Pepe took the words right out of my mouth.

"Amigo, tell you what. Get on a plane. Come to Caracas. When the fire is under control enough to land choppers, the Federales will be going in there to make a report. I see no reason why you can't ride along with the General's men. I feel certain he will have no objection."

"Deal," I said.

I had no idea what I would find, but I needed to be there. I needed to see for myself. With any luck, they had been clever enough to stay alive, and for me to find.

"I'll meet you in Caracas," he said, and hung up.

I walked over to the bag and picked it up. I started packing. I didn't ask Pepe about Julio, did he make it? I thought about Pepe and the General also being targets based on the message delivered by Julio. If the lawyers were really dead, did the risk die with them? Was Oscar's death going to turn out like Jake's death, unsolved? That would be a fucking tragedy. First to lose him and second to never know why he was killed and if it was a hit.

The phone rang. It had been about fifteen minutes since I'd talked to Pepe, and I thought it was him calling back. I was wrong. It was Olga, doing Pepe's bidding.

"Amor, Pepe wants me to pick you up. I'm headed home anyway, and it will be great to see you."

I didn't even put up the fight I normally do. "Is Pepe pissed that I'm pushing this?"

"He's pissed all right, but not at you. He doesn't like to get his hands dirty. All he said about you is that you are a stubborn *cabron,* stubborn enough to be a Camacho."

Of course, Camila called as soon as I hung up with Olga. The three of them seemed to be joined at the hip.

"Take care of yourself, Amor."

"I'm not Superman, but I do okay. Besides, Pepe said I'll be going in with the soldiers."

"There will be plenty of them, though I don't think there is anyone left at the plantation after the fire."

In the morning, I told my team and Melina that I was going to Caracas, and I was going alone. I warned them in advance that I wanted no lip. I expected them to give me a bad time, and they lived up to my expectations. That's what happens when the people you work with are family. They forgot that I do what the fuck I want. Melina and I had a fast fight on the phone. She hung up on me. I was in the office, and the girls had been listening to my side of the conversation. Not even pretending not to.

I faced opposition from them all, even Letty.

"Right after my rescue I returned to Caracas to get Valita," I reminded them. "I can handle Caracas."

"Yeah, but then, the motherfuckers were in prison already," Pixie said.

"This is better than that. The motherfuckers are dead. I just want to see for myself."

I put my head down on the table. I was feeling exhausted from the arguments, and sad, and missing Oscar. Someone put a hand on my shoulder, and I looked up.

"Boss, all that is left of those bastards are their ashes, I feel it."

Pixie seldom looked this serious.

Melina called as if the hang up had never happened.

"Let me send some security guards to keep an eye on the girls while you're gone. I know they go home at night but just in case."

"No guards."

"You are a stubborn asshole."

"I am. I'm in a hurry, talk later. If you send guards I will throw them off the property."

"I'm not going to send guards if you don't want them. Fuck you, asshole."

"Okay. I'll take you up on that when I return."

I had Tricia move in for additional security, and told her to call Melina after I left to let her know she was there.

"If Pepe killed those motherfuckers, good," Niley said. "And if he didn't, if they come here, we'll kill them, I promise."

"Easy, Niley, we know nothing yet. Not for sure."

"It was them," Pixie said. "I have a feeling."

We landed in Caracas at Maiquetía, which is what everyone in Venezuela calls Simón Bolívar International Airport. Olga came down the stairs behind me in white Greek lace-up sandals and a sleeveless white dress with huge bright splashy flowers placed asymmetrically at a diagonal across the skirt, and looking gorgeous as always, though she'd cut her hair short. She was carrying a suitcase. Salvatore was waiting for us. He'd put on some muscle since I'd last seen him, and had lost the boyish look.

"Mr. Luna. Miss Camacho," he said, and shook my hand, then Olga's.

I'd been ready to introduce them, but I guess I shouldn't have been surprised that they were already acquainted. The general was a friend of Pepe's. Neither Pepe nor General Maldonado did things directly. They were both busy men who always sent substitutes. Maybe Lieutenant Salvatore was the General's Olga.

"Your helicopter is waiting. I could have driven us to the military base to join with rest of the fleet on this mission, but this seemed more efficient."

"Thanks Lieutenant Salvatore," I said. "I appreciate being included."

"Miss Camacho, will you be joining us?"

"I'm sorry Lieutenant, but I have a meeting..." She looked at her watch. "...in an hour, and then I am going home. I do believe Pepe will be meeting Mario at La Estancia at seven this evening."

Olga went her way, and I went mine, which was behind the Lieutenant to the military chopper. I've done enough MEDEVAC rescue crashes that getting aboard one of these things always makes me a little apprehensive. I guess I was more tired than I thought, because once I was strapped in and the loud blades had sucked us up into the sky, I fell asleep. I can't blame it on jet lag though. It was all Olga, who had been on a mission to purge my grief in a hundred variations of the mile-high club. I do remember the Lieutenant telling me something about the helicopter we were in, and the next he was shaking me awake.

"Look out the window sir. We are here at the plantation."

"Enough of this 'sir' business. Call me Mario," I said. I was groggy, and felt half deaf from the roar of the helicopter. Silently, I looked out at the blackened skeleton of jungle beneath us as we circled. One of the soldiers aboard was taking pictures of the carnage. I recognized nothing except the pavement of the runway as it rose to greet us. Nothing was left except the pavement, and even that was burned. The walls of the cinderblock warehouse where I had been held captive were intact but charred. The burned husk of what had been the roof had collapsed into the building's center, which was still smoking. It smelled sickeningly like French roast coffee, which I will never be able to drink again.

"Mr. Mario," Salvatore said, "My men will walk around the compound for an hour or so. I doubt it will take us longer than that to assess what is left. We are just the first team. A second squad with a coroner is on the way to collect remains from the ruins."

Our flyover had revealed total destruction. My walk-thru confirmed it. I saw up close the iron gate through which Valita and Raton passed my rations of food and water. I had a memory flash of Valita and me engaged through the iron bars. Nothing remained of the compound except five or six adobe cinder block constructions, including the warehouse, all coated in inches-thick soot. Everything that could have burned, did. The manor houses were gone. I found what was left of Pepe's chopper, but the remains of his men were not where he'd said. His second string must have recovered them. Up to the minute that we got in the helicopter to leave, I'd been expecting Pepe to show up; but I guess our meeting would be at the restaurant. We took off a short time later, and did another flyover of the entire compound, impossible to distinguish from the surrounding jungle, which was also burned. No villages were nearby. I wasn't surprised about that. Ratón had told me the natives were nomadic, and followed where ever work could be found, building their homes of local indigenous materials. I could only hope there had been no migrant crew living on the compound when the fires began. A narrow unpaved mud path snaked through the burnt landscape, all that remained of the route trucks had traveled to haul coffee to Caracas. Valita had said that most of the cargo was taken by plane. I could see why. From the helicopter's perspective, all that remained of the plantation was a black, skeletal oasis, barely a drop in the vast tropical rainforest that looked like it went on forever. At least as we were flying over in a chopper.

The helicopter landed at my regular hotel. I'd made no reservations, but they were thrilled to see me, and treated me like visiting royalty, though I only expected to be there overnight. I showered, dressed, and met Pepe at seven at the restaurant as planned.

I had not been to La Estanza before, but I'd heard of it, a local place with a reputation of being one of the top steakhouses in Caracas. It perfumed the neighborhood. As I approached, the smells were delicious, though the smoky odor reminded me unpleasantly of the essence of smoldering timberland I'd just washed off my skin. I always find it difficult to get the stink of a fire out of my head. A waiter led me through a happy, hungry crowd of eaters. Savory dishes, steaks, shish kabobs, all being happily devoured. Pictures of famous guests on the walls. Tables with pink linen with white linen over that. Pepe's table was in a corner at the junction of a wall and a window, something I'm sure he requested. It was a large table, but that was not unexpected. Everything Pepe did was big.

As I approached, he got up from his table. We hugged.

"Pepe, it is good to see you again, my friend. Today has been most illuminating."

"No thanks needed, Amigo. Now you have seen for yourself."

We sat down.

"I hope you do not object, but I have already ordered for us. Several dishes. Steaks for us both, and paella, which is not excellent, but which is very good; and brisket, which is better than good. A couple of lobsters to start. There is a sommelier but I have gotten us a pitcher of sangria. I hope your palate is not insulted, but I find their sangria refreshing."

I sipped the sangria. As he had said, it was refreshing. "Very nice."

A waiter arrived with an armful of plates, and arranged them in front of us. Nothing could be more different, ambiance-wise, from PDC, but still, it reminded me of when I ordered feasts at PDC for the girls on our big paydays. We started on the food.

"Try the lobster," Pepe said.

"It is excellent. I came here in such a rush, and didn't realize how hungry I am." I chased the lobster with a small strip steak, and a taste of brisket. I hadn't realized I'd been so hungry. I had walked through piles of ash and bones that were no doubt the remains of humans. It was disgraceful that I had an appetite at all. I poured more Sangria for Pepe and myself.

"They are dead. Believe me," Pepe said. Pepe's eyes were sincere. "There were two main houses on the plantation where the two lawyers lived. Both houses were destroyed with R79 grenade launchers. No one could have escaped that." I knew he was convinced that they were dead.

"How about your man, Julio?"

"He died minutes after giving me the message."

"You were on the helicopter, weren't you?"

"I didn't want to say so on the phone."

"I'm sorry." I nodded.

"I am sorry as well."

"Do you think they ordered the kill on Oscar?"

"My information is that they went straight from prison to the plantation where communication is impossible other than radio. I don't know if they had Oscar hit. I told you what Julio said, what they planned to do with me and the general. Julio said they mentioned no one else."

"I'm sorry," I repeated and wished I hadn't.

"Stop it, Mario."

I changed the subject. "I've seen some small properties that are of interest, but still looking for the next big deal. My agent has made overtures to banks with foreign investors. He is…" I switched to English. "…keeping his ear to the ground."

He laughed at the English idiom, and cut a piece of brisket with the side of his spoon. "This is so good. I hired away one of their chefs to work in one of my homes. He's a wonder with meat." He savored the bite, then put down the spoon. He pulled over the paella, and picked out some bits of seafood from it, ignoring the rice. "Mario, put your heart into finding these investments. You will make a lot of money with me." Then he noticed I had stopped eating. "What's wrong. You don't like the food?"

"It's great, but I walked that plantation for over an hour. I haven't gotten over it, yet."

"I understand."

I looked at him, still eating. I could not do justice to the paella and did not even try.

"I do plan to put my energy into looking for investments. I have two reliable associates on the search for motivated sellers, one of them full time."

"When are you headed back?"

"Tomorrow. I'm going to check on flights."

Pepe took a big swallow of sangria. "It is good you don't stuff yourself," he whispered like it was a secret. "I have a dessert sampling coming."

Dessert I could handle, especially if it didn't have coffee in it. The smell of the burned coffee warehouse was still in my head. Pepe signaled the waiter who quickly cleared the table, freshened the linen, and deposited duplicates of the entire desert menu.

I groaned loud enough for him to hear. He laughed at me, and used his fork to sample everything, settling on some fruit concoction. "Friend, do not worry. My driver is taking the leftovers to a small orphanage." He sighed deeply, and I sensed in him a change of mood.

I wondered if he was thinking of his dead soldiers. I wondered if he had made provisions for their families. I asked him.

"I was just thinking of that because of the orphanage. My soldiers had families. Their children are fatherless," Pepe said, his expression grim. "I make provision for the widows."

I pictured Olga knocking on some widow's door, and rejected it. Oscar considered Olga a sister. He would never have her doing something that could be construed illegal, though I doubt charity to widows and orphans is illegal. It might not be illegal but it could be a way to track events back to Pepe. But who knew? They dealt in cash, which was hard to track. So, maybe she did bring them money. I might ask her next time I saw her, if the question was still on my mind. A guy in Pepe's racket must have lost hundreds of employees. What racket it was, though, I don't know and don't want to. I know zero about his actual business other than investments.

"Camila is in Europe, so her Learjet is available. Forget about checking on flights. I'll have a plane take you home."

"How am I going to ever repay you for all this?"

"We are friends." He reached across the table and patted the top of my right hand.

"Thank you, Pepe."

If Pepe was right and these assholes didn't kill Oscar, who did?

I was back to square one.

The Learjet made a fuel stop in Miami where I cleared customs. From there, I slept all the way to Van Nuys Airport. To my surprise, Letty was waiting for me.

"How did you know?"

"Olga called the house and told me."

I sat in the passenger seat, then hugged and kissed her. "You always smell so good."

"Boss, I missed you."

"I was gone fewer than three days."

"I know."

By ten that night, I was at home in bed, but before that I spent a very long time in the wet steam. I wanted my pores totally cleansed from the plantation. I would never admit it to anyone, but I was sorry I went there. I accomplished nothing. I did get a chance to speak with Pepe in person and learn that the two houses had been bombed with grenades. He didn't tell me that on the phone. Pepe would have made sure they were dead because his life had been threatened.

I felt like I was letting Oscar down by not promptly solving the mystery of who killed him. I had failed to nail it in Venezuela and hoped the cops were having more success. Oscar had come into my life unexpectedly, and he had been too good to be true. Now that I was back, and the reality of losing him was setting in, I had to mourn. I paid a visit to church, and lit candles over Oscar, and prayed for God to give me vengeance, first hand.

I could never forget how Oscar left his safe, luxurious LA home to brave the wilds of Venezuela to rescue me. The flight over that immense jungle impressed on me just how impossible it would have been for me to find my way back to Caracas from the plantation in the middle of nowhere. Fuck. What would have happened if the rescue had not happened? I'd overpowered my kidnappers. Maybe I would have gotten through the jungle, but I'll never know.

I credit my survival to Oscar. It was Oscar who enlisted Pepe's assistance. Without either of them, I would not be here.

I had trouble staying asleep since Oscar died, though I slept better on the plane than in my big bed. Melina had brought over sleeping pills that she used. I'd had enough when I was in the hospital in London and the two times I got shot in Los Angeles. I didn't believe in them, but I found myself taking a sleeping pill here and there. I tried to keep a lid on it, though. I knew too many people who relied on pills to put them to sleep at night and get them up in the morning.

The funeral date had been delayed till the coroner released the body to the family. I'm not one to brood, but I spent hours brooding. Wondering what I could have done differently. I had moments of being pissed that Pepe had closed the door for me being able to question the lawyers. I didn't want to think of how many innocents may have been killed when those bombs were dropped on the plantation.

I wondered if I'd done something that had led to Oscar's shooting. Oscar's death wasn't the only loss on my mind. I thought about Jake; the man who had shot me at the motel; the intruder I'd tossed out of my high-rise; and Hugo, who shot me before I threw him too, out my high-rise apartment window. I needed to bury Oscar. I needed to know he was out of that freezer and resting in peace. His death was an airless barrier between me and the rest of my life.

No airliners crashed. The girls were reading newspapers in search of small aircraft crashes. I kept myself busy with the mounting pile foreclosure files that I had nagged Tricia to find for me, and which she delivered for me to review. I was depressed, but my best outlet was always work, and I dived into it, with what little energy I had. The last thing I felt like doing was talking to an owner of a property that he or she was about to lose, but I would cross that bridge when I came to it. I was glad that Pepe, Camila, and Olga did not bug me about my hunt for buildings. I did have TJ looking for a business property that we could remodel or build from scratch.

Daily, my team reminded me how happy they were that my trip to Venezuela was short and uneventful. Uneventful like I had not been kidnapped, shot or killed. I spared them details about the killing field, knowing I would not be able to hold back my emotions.

I'd started chatting with Janice Cooke to see how she was doing. Every day, we made small talk, usually in the morning. On the days I did not call her, she called me. Betty, who was massaging Oscar's widow three times a week, came over to give us our much-needed massages, and told me that Mrs. Cooke appreciated my checking in with her.

"I don't remember ever talking to her when Oscar was alive," I told Betty. "But, I did talk to her at the hospital when we were there at the same time. I think she was sleeping there, I never asked."

"She says you are very nice. Oscar was very proud of you. He bragged to her about you all the time."

"I'll never tell her I went to Venezuela in search of the suspects."

"I can dig that," Betty agreed. "She's an empty-nester now that her step-kids are grown. She lives alone with a couple who does the housework and land-scaping."

"We must be wearing you out with coming over every day, seeing Melina every night, plus whatever clients are pulling at you."

She swatted my bare ass. "Boss, I love it. I'll tell you when I'm worn out. And I'm not there yet."

"You just love the money," I said.

"Boss, thank you. The money is good. It makes a lot of things possible for me, like eating."

Pixie, Niley, Letty and I drank more than usual, and smoked pot almost every night. No one had to drive home. Night would find us sitting at my favorite table as a joint made the rounds. I'd always avoided smoking pot and drinking wine to shelter me from a life event—except for when those thugs were shot in the Camacho villa in the Bahamas. I was not sure where the girls got their supply and had no reason to ask. It's not even like the hits from the joint were even fun. Pot just dumped a load of confusion on top of the misery I was already feeling. Pot is not a usual thing for me, but I didn't refuse. It was just too much trouble.

Every morning, Melina came over early. If I wasn't working out, we'd have coffee together like we did back in the apartment days. If I was working out, her arrival was a good reason to quit, and go upstairs for breakfast and Melina.

"Are you sure I can't send some security guards?" she asked me, every morning. That woman is nothing if not persistent. She reminds me of me.

"No," I said, every morning. "Cream and sugar?"

"Stubborn asshole," she said, holding out her cup. "No sugar. Diet today."

Melina kissed me and waved a goodbye kiss to the girls seated at my conference table across from my desk. I dragged myself downstairs to work out for an hour, but it was the sauna and steam that made me feel better. I could smell the alcohol coming off of me. After a shower, I rejoined the girls in the office. The days felt long, and the girls, including Letty, broke up their hours with an afternoon workout on their own. Betty was a lifesaver for us, especially now, while the girls were camping out here. She was another way to break the day into stages. I was feeling better, physically, but a shower didn't bring Oscar back to life.

I called Tom hoping to find out when we could lay Oscar to rest, but he said that the coroner would not commit to a date. Along with everyone else, I was left hanging, wondering how much longer it would take before his body was released.

So this was how we were these days, in the home office: Pixie was hooked over a chair, her back against one armrest, feet over the other. A stack of magazines was on one end table beside her, and a magazine in her lap along with a pencil and some scissors. She was looking out the window. Her bright hair was the only color in the room, but even it seemed washed out today. Niley was in another chair. Letty was flitting around running point between Miguel and the office, even though we had a perfectly good intercom. When Jo called, I kept telling her we were dying of boredom, though it was really sadness.

I promised myself I would look at foreclosure files, and I did but my heart was elsewhere.

"Are you sure you want me to keep bringing you these every day?" Tricia asked.

"If you want your twenty-five an hour, you better." I didn't mean it to sound like it did. "I'm sorry, Tricia. I'm all fucked up."

"It's okay, Boss, I understand. By the way, I've been billing you fifteen an hour for a while now, not the twenty-five anymore. I haven't been doing much."

Pixie laughed. "If Jo was here, she would have been on that like stink on shit. She's the number cruncher."

It was true, but I ignored Pixie. "Thanks, Baby, but bill me regular, don't worry about it."

"Don't worry. My price goes up when you put me to work again. Besides, I owe you, big time."

"After the funeral, consider coming over to join us in bed," Pixie said.

"Pixie, that's not funny," Niley said.

"I know it's not funny."

I didn't even get involved in that one, and neither did Tricia.

"Sure," Tricia said with a dose of Jo's sarcasm, after the girls stopped snapping at each other. "I'll make sure to bring my happy suitcase filled with adult toys."

"Oh, you're one of those," Pixie said. "Bring them over. Fun!"

Tricia gave me one of those looks like she wondered who the hell 'one of those' was, and no way did she have a happy suitcase, and Pixie had jumped on a joke that had fallen flat.

Tricia walked over and put a hand on Pixie's shoulder. "Pixie, I don't have a happy suitcase," Tricia said.

Niley laughed. "Guess we have to get you one."

Tricia shook her head. "You guys. I kind of prefer the real thing."

Letty had newspapers spread on the floor. She had a finger on the newsprint, and was dragging it across the page. She didn't read as fast as the others. She folded up the paper, and went down the hall.

I heard a knock. I didn't bother getting up. I wasn't expecting anyone. I heard Caro answer the door, and then Jo walked in.

We had a big moment of excitement that lasted about fifty-five seconds.

"Well, you are a productive bunch," she said, sarcastically. "I'm just here till dark."

Once everybody was settled down, they were back to staring into space. Jo parked herself at the conference table to go though the most recent stack of publications. She didn't use a finger; she put a piece of paper down on the page, and slid it down the newsprint. She said it made her read faster, but after a while, the cloud of doom fell over her too, and she kept stopping and moving the page to the top of the same article.

Letty brought in coffee and slices of coffee cake, and hung around watching us eat and drink, then took the dishes to the kitchen. She returned with lemonade. I put my glass on a coaster, and told her to sit down. She made a face at me, but returned to her copy of today's LA Times.

"Check the want ads for commercial properties and foreclosures," I reminded them.

"Right, Boss. Yes, Boss. Sure thing." They chimed together.

When the phone rang, shrill and abrupt, we all jumped.

Pixie answered.

"Casa Luna. Pixie speaking." Then she screamed and jumped up. The pile of junk on her lap went flying.

"It's Juan!" she squealed, and shoved the phone at me. Pixie dropped the extension into the speaker phone holder, and said, "Juan, we can all hear you."

The girls all chimed in. "Hi!"

"Where are you?"

"Home, Boss. Sorry I worry you. I was so sorry about Mr. Oscar's death that I got on a plane and went to Caracas. I was drinking. I went to see the vet who took care of Lobo, and I stay with her."

"You had Valita and us worried to death. And why would you go to Caracas?"

"I think with drunk head. I think I would run into the lawyers, and I figure a way to kill them."

"Don't do that again," Pixie yelled.

"I'm surprised you would worry us all like that" Niley said.

"Valita told me that a Bruja she went to told her she saw you dead, lying in an alley," Pixie said.

"Valita, she is going to Bruja to get money back," Juan said, "I tell her to leave it. We no want curses."

I broke in to the conversation. "Juan, a lot has happened. I just got back from Caracas. I saw with my own eyes that the plantation has been burnt to a crisp. All reports say that the lawyers are dead."

Juan swore on his end.

A week later there was still no funeral date. I was back to work, going out every day to look at properties. I had some small foreclosures in the works, and a shopping center that Randy had found.

"Babies," I said, focusing on Pixie, and Niley. "I love you being here, but you need to go home at night."

"I'm moving in permanent," Pixie said.

"I, too," Niley said.

Letty remained quiet. She was already as close as could be to being a permanent resident. She was never at her apartment, a ten-minute drive. I had less guilt with her around. She had no kids at home.

I was never much good at keeping track of birthdays and ages of anyone, not even my aunt. I knew Lainey was around twelve now. Jo's kids were older, certainly, than ten. By the time I was ten, I was out hustling business for Cosmo, home alone with a television or at Pélon's house where his mother was supposed to be looking out for me until my aunt came from work. Pixie and Niley had trustworthy live-ins who had proved their value over the years, and the kids loved their nannies. What I'm getting at is that I felt guilty about having their moms away from them, but not as much as I told everyone.

"I found a bodyguard to drive you around," Melina said.

Melina wasn't done with trying to protect me. I frowned at her. "You plan on hiring a driver for me that I haven't even met?"

"Yep. He's fifteen years older than you are. He's burly, licensed to carry a weapon, and he can watch your back."

"No."

Melina looked at me with impatience. "What about Tricia? Last Wednesday, she came over with the girls on their weekly shoot, and Buck was impressed. He said she's a marksman from the get-go."

"Buck, the retired cop who is coaching them?"

"He says Letty still needs some coaching but she's a fast learner. Anyway, Buck says that Tricia is a natural."

"It's the military in her," I said.

"Probably. So what do you think?"

"Sound like you are lobbying Tricia, and not the other guy you first came in talking about."

"It's your choice." I was going to kid Melina by thanking her for letting me choose but I let it go.

I thought of having Tricia driving me around. I also thought of just having her. We had fucked in Vegas like mad, and only done it twice since she moved to Los Angeles. That had been so quick we could have passed for bunnies.

"I'll ask Tricia," I said.

"I already did. I didn't promise she had the job, but she had no objection to being on your regular payroll."

"Baby, you are way too much. How do you find time to do this for me and take care of your hundreds of employees and markets?"

"I work my ass off. That's how."

Tricia was all for it. She agreed to continue working property searches and anything else I needed in the private investigator department.

"Do you have a problem if Tricia takes over the driving?" I asked Letty

"You the Boss. I'm good. If you're happy, I'm happy."

The last time Tom Jones had been to my house, one of the girls had given him the ten-cent tour. This time, Caro led him to my office, and we sat at the conference table.

"I asked the girls to be here," I said. "I have no secrets."

"Of course," Tom said.

The girls joined us, greeted him with a kiss, then took their seats, Tom at the head of the table, me at the foot. To my right was a vacant chair for Melina.

When Miguel came in to offer refreshments, Melina walked in behind him.

"I'm sorry for being late. Traffic is bad."

Melina shook hands with Tom, then leaned over and gave him a kiss.

"My condolences," she said.

No one wanted any drinks. I rarely drank around Tom. I knew he was a former alcoholic. It looked like the girls were following my lead.

"I'm way past temptation," Tom said. "Please feel free."

"Thank you," Melina said. "I can use a drink of something."

Miguel brought a bottle of sparkling water, ice and lime for Tom, and bottles of red and white for the table.

By habit, I drank the sparkling water. I saw no reason to start drinking around Tom now.

"What happens next?" I asked Tom. "Are you taking over? What's the arrangement?"

Tom coughed. "Bill will be in charge of the criminal department much like he's been doing. It will get extinguished when the pending cases are closed. Oscar has two bigger cases that he was personally handling. Those need to be dealt with. I will control the personal injury cases and aviation. The idea is to keep the ship tight as possible. I don't plan to hire new lawyers or more personnel. When the criminal department becomes history, I will negotiate to return to one floor of office space. That will cut the overhead substantially."

I took a drink and asked, "What is the financial situation? You have Carson bringing in a ton of soft-tissue cases. We have aviation that comes and goes, but until the cases conclude, they consume a whole bunch of money."

Melina asked, "I assume you have met with the principals, and you have written instructions from Oscar?"

"We do have written instructions. Oscar's personal attorney will be working us in the transition. For now, it's business as usual. There are a lot of complicated financing arrangements with banks that need to be handled. Our aviation caseload is fantastic. The run of the mill personal injury cases are bread and butter for the cash flow. We have a ton of cases."

"What will you do for capital? What are you doing right now to make payroll and cover expenses?" I asked.

"The accountant says there are issues but we can make it for a while."

"That doesn't sound very encouraging," Melina said.

"Not too long ago, I walked out of Oscar's office with a check for $1.1 million. Before the next big one, I need to know if it's business as usual or what."

"Mario, I know exactly how much you get paid, but it's too soon for me to have a feel of the finances."

"Of course," Melina said to the ceiling. "We're just tossing it around right now. Oscar forgive us for all this back and forth. We haven't even buried you yet."

I smiled at Melina. A real smile. "Thanks, Baby. I should be ashamed of myself." I looked at Tom. "I trust you my friend. All I ask is that you level with me. Get situated. I'm there for you. I want to know you are there for me."

"Don't worry about transparency," Tom said, getting up.

He shook hands all around, and I walked him to the door.

"I'm not worried. I said I trust you, and I mean it. Come over for lunch when you're in the neighborhood. You should see what Miguel can do with food."

"I will do that," Tom said.

"You are always welcome, my friend." We hugged, and I closed the door behind him.

I walked back to my office where I left Melina and the girls.

"He's a good guy," Melina said.

"I know," I said. "He's been great to work with. He's taught all of us so much about aviation. I can actually talk it now."

"Me too," Niley said.

"Waiting for the coroner to release the body is driving me batty," Jo said.

"It was the same with Jake," Pixie reminded us.

"It's a homicide," Melina said as she got up. "Lots of red tape."

"Horrible," Letty said.

I pictured Oscar smoking his cigar, filling the room with a cloud of smoke.

"Who killed you, Oscar?" I asked aloud.

No one answered. It was like the girls were expecting Oscar to say something. I toyed with the firm's aviation book, one with his picture on the cover. It was such a good picture. I half expected him to talk. It was exactly how he looked with his cigar.

The phone rang. We all jumped. I guess I wasn't the only one who felt like it had been Oscar making a call from the great beyond. The call was from somewhere a whole lot closer. Carson, wanting to come over. He must have called from close by, because minutes later, he landed in my home office. Miguel gave him a beer. I had a bottle of wine open I was thinking about drinking, but it was unpoured.

"What are you doing with cases?" I asked him. I could see how torn up he was over Oscar's death. He had deep shadows under his eyes, and looked like he hadn't slept in a month. His clothes were a mess. I'd never really seen Carson disheveled. He's been meticulous about his clothing from an early age.

"I turn them in every day."

"Are you getting paid?"

"Yes, I'm getting paid. What I'm worried about is that without Oscar, what's going to happen? I'm dealing with the head of PI, but he's nothing, and he knows nothing. I give him the cases, and he gets me a check. You must have a better idea of what's coming."

"I know nothing more than you do. Tom Jones is as high as you can get, and he doesn't know how things are going to work. Let's bury Oscar first. Then we'll dig deep."

"I'm making more money than ever before, but none of it sticks. We spend it all. I have so much going out to the contacts that send me cases. I don't know how you did it and lived the way you did."

"Hey, I did what you are doing. I lived where you live now. What are you talking about?" I suspected Carson had a hole in his pocket. And by that, I mean some habit other than clients that sucked money out of him, like gambling, booze, or girls, possibly all three. I didn't think it was drugs.

Carson sighed and took a deep drag from his beer. "I worry about tomorrow's cases."

"If Tom can't take my aviation cases, I'm out to lunch, too. Your cases are different. They turn faster than aviation. Bread and butter for the firm. Hang in there. You're getting paid. Stop fucking eating yourself alive over something that hasn't happened yet."

I got up and shook his hand. I buzzed Miguel to come up with a bottle of wine, corked, the same that I had breathing on my desk.

Carson was really stressed. "I got car payments, big rent, the wife. Sure, I'm getting paid now, but what if it stops? I can't go long without an income. I'm not living from paycheck to paycheck, but I don't have much in the bank to keep me going if the gravy train goes off the track. And you know how much goes to keep the sources happy. Ese, if you had let me in aviation, my bank account would have a whole lot more than it has now."

I nodded. He'd always overspent on knockoffs he couldn't afford, but usually they hadn't been top of the line. I noticed he was in upscale clothes that matched the upscale firm. Though I felt bad for the frame of mind of my friend of so many years, I didn't believe Tom would stop taking his cases. I believed they will soon be encouraging Carson to get more. Those small cases of his can turn over quickly, and provide essential income. My cases were expensive. My head would be first on the chopping block.

"Carson, you have a gold mine. Don't forget it. Those cases of yours can easily go somewhere else. You don't ever have to be broke again. As long as you keep signing cases, it's money in your pocket. Finding a home for your cases if Tom won't take them won't be like finding a home for my aviation cases. You should be happy that I didn't let you in the aviation. You still have the gold mine I turned over to you. They're going to have to cut me loose. Me, they can't afford."

"Ese, you were always the brains."

"Right, and don't you forget it," I said with a laugh, patting his back. "Want another beer?"

He didn't try to stare me down, but we locked eyes for a few seconds too long. I looked deep, and in him saw the shadow of so many Carsons. The four year old who had been my best friend, the seven year old neither of Señor Chapo's dogs had trusted, the ten year old who had been a sneak, the sixteen year old whose hunger and competitive nature had driven him to fake the kind of cases I'd worked so hard to find, the young adult whose desperate behavior led me to suspect he'd been up to more evil than he had been.

"I'll have another beer, thanks."

I poured myself a glass of wine and drank with him. We reminisced for a while about the bad old days growing up across the street from Hollenbeck Park in East Los Angeles. I saw unfallen tears reflecting in Carson's eyes, and reached for the unopened bottle.

"Your wife has champagne taste, right? Bring this home to her." I looked around my office, and found one of the small bouquets of lavender that Melina had delivered regularly to my office because I like the scent. I handed it over to him. "This too. You'll have a good night, and feel better about things tomorrow."

He swiped at his eyes with the sleeve of his impeccable jacket.

"Thanks *ese*."

Every day was another day of unrest for me, but after Carson left, the feeling stuck with me that maybe I'd done some good.

Pixie hung up the phone. "I phoned in a classified, Boss. 'Wanted to buy, commercial property. Don't let them foreclose on you. Any condition. Quick turn over. Send pictures to agent. Ask for Randy.' It's all in Spanish and I coordinated it with Rosy, the Cuban receptionist in Randy's office."

"Good," I said. I was glad to see new approaches in action.

"Stupid question. What if we get a big case before the funeral?" Pixie asked, folding the real estate classified section she'd been studying. It was a free local paper in Spanish that I thought might have some possibilities, but it turned out not to have a section for commercial property. It was what had given me the idea for the ad.

"I'd pass."

"Gotcha, Boss."

"I may need to find another law firm."

"It will come together," Jo said, looking at her watch. "Betty should be here within the hour."

"Cool." I stood up at my desk. "Tell her I'll be in the spa."

I went downstairs, did some stretches, and hit the steam and sauna.

I asked Betty how Oscar's wife was doing. I hadn't called her in a couple days, and I had no calls from her.

"She's going to be better after they bury him," Betty said.

"That goes for all of us," I agreed. "It's good for her that she's still your client."

"I've been over there every other day. Poor thing is so stressed. She's beautiful. A classy lady. Very much like Melina."

I turned on my back. I had not asked Betty to match my nakedness lately. I was still moved by her gorgeous legs and body, but my dick didn't have a whole lot to celebrate.

"I hired Tricia full time as my driver at large. Melina and I should just hire you for us," I told Betty. My voice came out vibrating with Betty's rhythmic thumping.

"Just say the word, Boss."

"You'd give up your clients and come to us?"

"Nothing is forever. Clients come and go. But I have to keep doing Oscar's wife."

Nothing is forever? Hadn't it been Harry way back who told me that?

"I don't want to get ahead of myself, but I'm just spoiled and love to have you around. Melina is the same. We've never discussed it. I just threw it at you. I know our hours would drive you nuts."

"If you want it to happen, we'll make a deal."

I laughed. "You sound like we would need to negotiate."

Betty slapped one side of my ass, and then the other. "Yes, we'd have to negotiate, but I'm easy."

The massage was great, but I still felt the weight of the world. Oscar's death was a downer that I just couldn't jump free of. It wasn't just losing him. Not knowing who was responsible weighed me down.

It was early on a Monday. It had been a strange morning. Melina had called and told Caro to give me a message: Navy Blue. I hadn't been able to reach her anywhere, and the question of what she meant had been bugging me all morning, and making it impossible to concentrate. If it had been Pixie's message, I'd have been worried that something was going to get painted that I didn't want painted, but with Melina, I just flat-out had no clue what she was talking about.

We were all in the home office. Pixie, Niley and Letty were working on some kind of information scrapbook about different planes. Everyone was still wearing black or a black ribbon. Jo was dealing with numbers, as she usually did, but she shoved her ledger aside and stood up.

"I've got something to say. Is everyone free for lunch?"

"It's early for lunch," Letty said. "I'll tell Miguel to—."

"No," Jo interrupted gently. "Please sit down. I have to apologize, because I've been keeping a secret."

Letty complied. We all dropped what we were doing and faced her. I felt some dread.

"If everyone is free for lunch, then maybe you can drive me to city hall.

With Oscar's passing, it just didn't seem right to have a big ceremony. We're holding off on the honeymoon till we feel like the time is right. But this is all planned. TJ and I are tying the knot today. You don't have to come, but I'd like to have you there as witnesses. You don't have to call Melina. She's meeting us there." Jo smiled at me, cautiously. "I expect she's wearing navy blue, and wants you to match."

I responded with a bunch of mixed feelings, but at least the blue question was answered.

"Today?" Pixie squealed. "Fucking A. Wild horses couldn't keep me away."

The air of misery in the office suddenly lifted. Jo was suddenly in the middle of a cheerleading section, with Pixie, Niley and Letty jumping and squealing like mad.

"I have a dress for you! It's perfect!" Pixie ran up the stairs, followed by Niley who was going to do a search for old, new, borrowed and blue. Letty headed to the kitchens, no doubt to order a feast for our return from the office of the Justice of the Peace. I was left alone with Jo.

"Well, you're finally doing it," I said.

"I hope you will give me away, even if it is just in a judge's office."

"Whatever makes you happy sweetheart," I said.

The JP's office was roomy enough for all of us, though Jo and I went outside so I could take her arm and lead her to where the judge and TJ were waiting, and Melina and the girls were lined up. I put my elbow out, and she walked in on my arm to a wedding march playing on the judge's eight track. He'd done this before.

The girls had taken this opportunity to wear what my aunt would have called their Sunday best. Their mourning clothes were scattered around my house, and they'd chosen a batch of pastel cocktail dresses. TJ was looking very fit and very tanned in white tails. Dressed in Pixie's white mini covered in sequins, Letty's stiletto sandals, Niley's blue Lapis choker and garters, and an old wedding ring that had been in TJ's family for generations, Jo became Mrs. Trent Joel at eleven in the morning, with the rest of the team, her kids and Melina (in navy blue) watching on. I can't lie. I cried like a baby. Even if I was happy for Jo, the heartache of losing her hit me at once. I knew she wasn't really going to be lost, but it was still an emotional upheaval. The judge's secretary got weepy, and took lots of wedding pictures. No charge.

TJ joined us back at the house for the feast of lobsters and wedding cake Miguel had drummed up, but before we ate, he grabbed me in the foyer with a fierce hug. He whispered in my ear, "Don't worry Boss. You're not losing Jo. You're gaining a fucking brother-in-law."

Chapter 19
July 1980
Last Rites and Unfinished Business

The funeral, when it finally happened, was three days after the coroner released Oscar's body. The widow had had far too much time to plan everything. After the long wait, the sudden funeral announcement was almost a shock. He was to be buried at Forest Lawn Cemetery. The formalities progressed quickly. Camila was in Turkey, and Olga in Buenos Aires, too far away to reach Los Angeles in time.

Olga called from Buenos Aires to apologize. "Amor, Camila and I planned on attending the funeral but this is too quick for us to make it. I am so very sorry."

"I understand and I will let everyone know. Did you ever meet his wife?"

"No, never. Pepe wanted us to attend. He was very fond of Oscar."

"I know he was. It will be okay."

Tricia drove the girls in my car, including Jo accompanied by TJ. Johnson drove Melina and me in her car with the divider closed. Melina and I sat in the privacy of the back seat. It was good to have her there. We held hands like a couple of kids going steady, but it was more than that. Whatever our relationship was, it consoled us both. We were definitely a couple, but just didn't know, a couple of what?

"The coroner held on to Oscar much longer than Jake."

"I'll be glad to know that Oscar will be resting in peace instead of in a refrigerator at the morgue."

Melina squeezed my hand. Her head rested against my left arm.

Jake's funeral had been one for the record book, but Oscar's was extraordinary. The girls gawked at the flowers. Melina knew them all. There were white lilies, gladioli, carnations, chrysanthemums, roses, orchids, daffodils, hydrangea and tulips, in baskets and bouquets, and massive arrangements, all in various shades of white. The only time I've ever seen more flowers gathered in one place was once at a tulip market in Amsterdam. It was a gray day, and the flowers were the only brightness in it. The grass was dull and grim looking as if even the lawn were in mourning. The funeral drew a huge crowd. Oscar's office staff alone numbered more than a hundred, and they were all there. When Janice Cooke and I talked on the phone, she always talked about Oz, never herself. All that I knew (from Betty) about her was that she was step-mother to three grown children from Oscar's earlier marriage. They had families of their own, and his ex had not attended. I saw Carson in the crowd, making his way through Oscar's family, and working in my direction.

"I met her at the hospital. Since then, we talk on the phone sometimes," I told Melina. "She's so young. Much younger than Oscar." Her makeup and the way she did her hair was more rigid than the girls, but I found her to be beautiful. She looked good in black. Not much could be seen of her hair now, though, since she had on some kind of widow's cap with a black lace netting over her face. The net was decorative, and didn't hide her features.

"I'd say she's five years older than me," Melina whispered some time later. "If I'm right, she's fifteen years older than you." She had stored up a lot of whispers, because I'm too tall for her to reach my ear until we were sitting down.

"Always worried about those years," I whispered back.

"Cuz, I know you. Maybe you have a thing for older women."

Oscar was turning out to be a secretive piece of work. I just hadn't expected him to have a trophy wife. Yes, she looked sad and a little drawn, but radiant compared to our first meeting during Oscar's hospital stay when I returned from London.

"His wife is a knockout," Carson said. "She's a babe." He had made his way to our group around the gravesite.

"Your wife will hear you," I whispered, sending a wink at his wife who stood next to him. She winked back. Carson still looked stressed, but the two of them seemed as wrapped up in each other as the newlyweds they were. I was happy for Carson. I had days when I really got pissed at myself for having hated him so much and blaming him for everything that went wrong, including Tanis' killing and my getting shot. Melina told me I should forgive myself. Someone had been trying to kill me at the time.

The casket was closed, given the length of time that had passed and the autopsy. I weathered the funeral service pretty well, but when I placed my flower on Oscar's casket, I was overcome. I couldn't bear the feeling of him so close, so still, so unreachable. When we finally had the opportunity to pay respects to his widow and his older children, I had trouble holding back the tears. Oscar had been more than a business associate. He'd been a mentor. He'd been a friend.

"He really loved you, Mario. He talked about you all the time." I kissed her right cheek then her left.

"I loved him, too, Mrs. Cooke," I said.

"You must call me Janice, as you do on the phone," she said, again, stepping close for a hug. "Tom has a big job ahead of him. Please help him out."

I wasn't sure what I could do for Tom, but that didn't seem to be something I could say to the widow. I replied, "Count on it, Mrs. Cooke."

"Janice," she corrected me again. "I'm the same Janice as on the phone," she said, patting my hand.

"I will do everything in my power, Janice."

"The flowers are incredible," Melina said.

"Aren't they? They were a complete surprise. Most of them were from a couple of Oscar's clients. Pepe and Camila Camacho," Janice said. "The rest of what they sent are at the house."

Melina and I exchanged a look. They hadn't been able to come, but Camila must have denuded a dozen florist shops getting this many flowers in their stead.

I had driven by Oscar's house, and the holiday parties he'd invited me to always conflicted with either my own event, or my aunt's, or I'd been out of the country. I hated that I had never seen Oscar in his own place. The house was a different architectural style from Melina's and mine, and looked to me more like a vintage public library than a house, with a grand entry, big columns in front and no Mediterranean influence. There were so many flowers here too that I wondered if the Camachos had cleaned out all the florists in Los Angeles county. The after celebration of Oscar's life was here instead of at a church or public venue. I stopped gawking, and paid attention to the objective of the gathering, did the room with Melina and the girls. I knew most of Oscar's staff, not well, but by sight. There were many hugs, many people flowing through the foyer, den, living room, parlor and out into the back-garden patio. Betty was one of the guests.

"Look how Betty sticks with Oscar's wife," I said to Niley.

"Mrs. Cooke needs someone to lean on right now."

"For sure. The ever-so-fucking-long wait for the coroner drove all of us nutty. Imagine what it did to her," Pixie said.

"I see no family around Mrs. Cooke," Letty said. "Oscar's older kids were around her at the cemetery, but I don't see them hovering here."

Melina announced in a whisper to our group that the wine was fabulous.

"Trust Oscar to have the best in his cellars," I said.

"Remember we went to La Fonda after Jake's funeral and got wiped?" Pixie said.

"I can remember the hangover," Jo said.

"Ditto," I said with pretended anguish.

"I missed that one," Letty said.

"La Fonda is great," Niley said. "When we get back to normal, we should go back."

"Normal. What is normal anymore?" I asked. We did not go to La Fonda.

Chapter 20
After the Funeral
July 1980

Our next meeting with Tom Jones was at the office in one of the larger conference rooms, an opulent space filled gleaming mahogany, wall-to-wall shelves filled with huge, serious leather-bound law books, and a conference table with twenty-four plush chairs. The massive window provided a breathtaking view of Los Angeles, or at least it would have been if it hadn't been the grayest of days. I had never been in this room before. I wonder what else might be on this floor that I hadn't seen. Two whole floors in that building is a lot of office acreage for one firm.

Tom was at the head of the table. Melina was at my side.

"All of you are like a family, so I'm not going to hold back," Tom said.

"Tom, we are not like a family," I said. "We are family."

Tom's great smile was not up to his usual shine. He seemed troubled.

"Before I begin, I want to call Denise in here. Mario, you recall Denise, our in-house accountant."

"Of course I know Denise." I wondered what this was about.

"Denise handles the money. We need her here," Tom said.

"Go for it," Melina said, looking for a sign from me of an objection. She had slipped into lawyer mode.

Denise was a small woman, all glasses, business, and prim aspect. She took twenty minutes to explain that the firm was deep in debt. Oscar's lines of credit at Crocker Bank and Security Pacific Bank amounted to $4 million, and those lines were maxed out.

"A five-million-dollar line of credit with a private attorney lending firm in Florida is also maxed out. The monthly interest alone is fifty thousand dollars.[47] That credit line will be paid off by a life insurance policy that Oscar took out for purposes of paying off whatever amount was due the credit line up to his limit of five million."[48]

Melina interrupted. "Are you saying that the lender required a life insurance policy just in case Oscar died?"

Denise said, "Correct. Crocker Bank also has a policy, but that insurance policy is only a million. Not enough to cover what is owed the bank but it will help."

"The five million credit line, is it current or delinquent?" I asked.

"The monthly interest payment was delinquent, three months."

"So, now, the insurance will pay five million?"

"Yes. Depending on when they pay, I figure it will just be enough to pay the balance of principal and interest."

Trust the lenders to cover their asses first.

Jo, Pixie, Niley, and Letty were silent. Melina was beginning the pen tap that indicated she was thinking. She had a grim expression on her face. That life insurance policy sounded almost like a bounty to me. Our eyes met. She nodded her head at me. I wondered if she had the same thought, and made a mental note to ask her later.

"What about assets?" I asked. "Is there collateral on the lines of credit that can be liquidated?"

"There is, but we're talking about a blanket chattel mortgage on office equipment and furniture. Unless we liquidate, that doesn't even count. Oscar's

---

[47] $50,000.00 in 1980 had the same buying power as $157,387.22 in 2017
[48] $1,000,000.00 in 1980 had the same buying power as $3,147,744.46 in 2017

house and his other real estate is all mortgaged to the max. The plane is included in the blanket chattel mortgage that Crocker Bank used to secure their credit line.

"If you feel uncomfortable talking about Oscar's personal accounts, we don't need to hear it, right Mario?"

"Right," I said. "Denise, what is the bottom line?"

"Before I get to the bottom line, Tom has advised me to tell you everything."

"There's more?" I said. I had a sick feeling in my gut. Based on Denise's presentation, and Tom's expression, it couldn't be good.

"It's about the client trust account."

I actually saw Melina's face change color. Her tapping stopped. I knew that a client trust account existed, but not really what it was, other than that it was a checking account that pays clients and doctors. I never got paid from that account. I always got paid with a check from the general account.

"Is the trust account upside down?" Melina asked, leaning forward, with the same horror on her face as when we'd watched Juan's uncut recordings of the Palomar Hotel fire, with burning people leaping from their hotel balconies trying and failing to land in the pool.

Denise continued speaking as if tears were not running down her face.

"It is. Mr. Cooke used the trust account to fund the general account when we needed operating capital. With credit lines maxed out and new cases continuing to come in, the money had to come from somewhere."

"Denise, wait. You have a ton of cases. Cases settling all the time. What about that money?"

"We have a great deal of money coming in every day from cases that are being settled, yes, but the overhead and expense are greater than the cash flow." She flushed, and said in an embarrassed voice, "We've done this before and managed to get it paid back. We have upside periods when we have replaced funds that belong to the trust, but now, the trust is in bad shape."

"How bad? Exact numbers please?" Tom asked. I could tell by his face that he already knew the answer.

"If we were to pay everything that hasn't been paid from trust, we would be short 4.2 million dollars."[49]

I had more Camacho cash than that in my safe.

Melina stood up. She looked at Tom. "Did you know about this?"

"Of course not. Denise will tell you I don't have a damn thing to do with the money. Denise only does what she is told. Oscar was not a person you say no to."

His choice of words made me look at him twice. Carson had said something similar in the beginning when he'd suggested my first meeting with Oscar.

Thank God I was not owed any money. I knew Carson had said he was bringing in cases and had been paid since Oscar passed away, but the financial burden of his cases to the firm was significantly smaller than aviation would be.

"I get the picture," I said. "The firm can't afford any more new business from me. My worry is the cases you have here that we brought in. What will happen to the clients you currently represent?"

"I'll find a way to work them to the end," Tom said. "Personally, I don't have the kind of money to finance the operation, but there is money out there. I wanted you to hear this from Denise directly so you'd understand why I can't possibly take another case and pay for it up front. There is no money, and I'm certainly not going to continue robbing the trust account. I'm just hoping there will be enough from cases as we settle that we can replace what's been taken fast enough to prevent problems."

Problems could be bad. I would have to ask what kind of discipline the bar offered for breach of fiduciary duties, and whose living shoulders that discipline could fall on.

Denise leaned against the wall as if she would fall without its support.

---

[49] $4,200,000.00 in 1980 had the same buying power as $13,220,526.73 in 2017

I felt bad for her. I felt bad for all of us.

The last time I lost my lawyer, I sold my contacts to Oscar, took off for Europe, and the girls took over the management of my apartments. I was hoping I would not have to change course again. That probably wouldn't be necessary thanks to the new business with Camacho. As long as they kept wanting to buy, I could probably make some serious money. I would still have to find myself a new lawyer to work with. I sure as hell wasn't giving up aviation.

"I don't know how I can help, but I'm your friend, Tom."

I got up, and gave him a big hug.

"I need to get home and digest this."

I walked over to Denise and tried to comfort her. I put my arm around her, leaned over and whispered in her ear. "You did nothing wrong, Denise. Remember that."

She nodded in agreement, wiping away tears.

Melina had gotten a call from a manager and left for one of her markets, but promised to check back later. In the elevator, the girls and I were speechless. We crossed the parking lot, and rode in the Rolls with Tricia at the wheel. In the continued silence, I pictured Oscar, reflected on how he boasted of his successes, but never complained of the cost. Now I see the Learjet in an entirely different light. He'd probably purchased the plane for cash using his credit line with Crocker Bank. When he sent me out on that plane, he'd always insisted that I not worry about the expense, but of course, I always worried. He might have breathed a little easier if I'd accepted the plane as payment when he'd offered it, getting those expenses off his back. Although the firm owed far more than what he paid me, I felt personally responsible for the disaster that Oscar had left behind. I thought about my recent checks, especially that one check alone for 1.1 million dollars. Oscar may have had his eyes on the prize, the long-term goal when those cases settled, but he should have just told me no more cases.

The girls and I entered my house and went straight to the wine cellar.

Miguel and Pixie lit candles. We all said yes to wine. Miguel poured, then left us alone.

"Are we fired?" Letty asked, looking in Jo's direction.

Jo glanced at me. I shook my head the tiniest bit.

"Of course not," she said, reading me like a book, or coming to her own parallel conclusion. "I have a feeling we're going into real estate again, until Mario finds a new aviation lawyer."

Jo had hit the nail on the head.

"Right," I said. "Rest easy. Tomorrow, you're on investment watch, just like Tricia and Randy."

"I've never been so flush," Niley said, sitting next to Pixie. "I'm just worried where your head is at, Boss."

"We all have property now, and we have money," Pixie said, patting the wallet in her pocket.

"I don't have property, but I'm not hurting. I'm better off now than I've ever been," Letty said.

"Tomorrow, we start planning your investments too, Letty," I said.

"Thanks, Boss, but I'm happier with cash in the bank than being a land-lady."

"Bitch, you'd make more in the appreciation of the property than what the bank is paying interest."

"Cunt, don't bitch me."

"Behave," Jo said calmly, standing up. "Don't stress out the Boss. I'm going home." She made a round of the room and kissed us all. "Going home to my hubby and kiddos unless you need me to stay."

"See you tomorrow," I said.

The girls were so quiet that I heard the front door close. I looked at the set of their worried faces, and felt the need to make them understand that their well-being was not threatened.

"If you are tired of working, I don't blame you, and won't be pissed if you decide to quit, but you should know that the last thing on my mind is to let you go. I have assets. I have great cash flow from my apartments, and I'm working this new business with Camacho that has proven to be very profitable. The only thing I owe on the apartments are a few mortgages. More than half are paid off. Even my house is paid off." It felt good to say this aloud. I'd dropped a couple of those hefty paychecks on to the mortgage and saved hundreds of thousands in interest, and a decade of debt. "As long as we have cases, we are never going to know bad times. If cases slow down, I've got the bucks to keep us floating for a very long time. The investment hunt for the Camachos is an extra failsafe to keep us sitting pretty. I love all of you. As long as I'm in the black, you will be too. I wouldn't have what I have without you."

"Not true," Niley said. "You made the money. You're the dealmaker. You always have been."

"I remember when you were making deals at ten," Pixie said.

Letty changed the subject. "I wonder if Mrs. Cooke knew what financial shape her husband's firm was in, or if Oscar kept her in the dark."

"No way to know, and we're not going to ask," I said. "Hopefully he played it smart and kept a nest egg for her that only she knows about, and the creditors can't get." I thought of Pepe's friendship with Oscar. If Pepe paid Oscar in cash, she might be sitting on her own safe full of cash.

"Here's my take on this fucking mess," Pixie said. "I think Tom will make millions off your cases and pay everyone off, and Mrs. Cooke and the law firm will live happily ever after."

I said, "My aunt would be saying 'From your lips to God's ears.' Let's toast to Tom's success." We clicked glasses.

"Here's what I know," Niley said. "I haven't been laid in more than a month. Crisis or no crisis, I think we should get back in the groove."

"I remember when you were so quiet," I said.

"Boss, let's take the wine to the master, and do a number on each other," Letty said.

"I'm so fuckin' horny too. Horny is how I cope," Pixie said, heaving a huge sigh. "I'm like you that way, Boss. I've been such a freaking basket case, so the vibrator doesn't work for me."

Letty said, "I've been here, and Mr. Happy hasn't shown his hard head. But I admit we haven't put much effort into it. Didn't seem respectful, under the circumstances."

I'd put no effort into it, although Sundays with Melina had not stopped. Once we'd even gone to the beach house and fucked on the living room carpet next to a sliding door fifteen feet from the boardwalk and sand.

"You're a fucking exhibitionist," I'd told Melina at the time.

"Not particularly," she said. "Didn't you like it?"

Sex with the girls was at zero lately, and I had been okay with it. They were in the mood to correct all that. Pixie and Niley got on either side and hauled until I was on my feet. Letty got behind me and pushed. They maneuvered me to the stairs.

"I promise an erection in sixty seconds," Pixie said, "I know your buttons better than anyone."

Letty was not to be outdone. Once we were in the bedroom, she dived at Niley, planting her head between her thighs. In an instant, both of them were moaning, and rolling around on the bed in a sudden fit of sixty-nine. I had what felt like a California redwood in my pants.

Pixie looked from Letty and Niley to me, and gave me a little sideways grin that was more sad than happy. I know that girl pretty well. She was still thinking of Oscar. "Girl on girl. I knew that button," she said.

I made it through the night. Oscar was buried. His law firm seemed to be fucked. I found myself thanking God for allowing me to escape death three times, and for giving me all I've got, and granting me so much success. Not only the material things, but also my family, my skills, and the understanding that I needed to look past Oscar and move on. When the time came, I would find a lawyer who wants what I've got, on my terms. In the meantime, I was going to put my heart in buying up buildings that were good deals for LAI. Time to put away the credit cards and use cash like Camila and Olga did.

Chapter 21
Late July 1980
King of the Hill

I was in the office, sprawled out with my feet on the desk in exactly the way that—when I was a kid—would have driven my aunt to whack me on the back of the head with a rolled up newspaper. She might still do it, but she wasn't here. I was scrutinizing a list of lackluster properties, and none of the addresses inspired me. These were Tricia's finds, but I was expecting a call from Randy. When the phone rang, I reached for it without excitement.

"Hey stranger," Camila said. "I've been here for two days."

My pulse snapped to attention. Excitement factor on the rise. I swung my feet off the desk and planted them on the floor. Letty looked up from the classifieds, a question in her eyes.

"Great to hear from you. Where is here?"

"My hotel in Beverly Hills. I had meetings since I arrived. I almost called at least twenty times."

"Cool. So when do I see you?" My mind was already sending me a snapshot of traffic from here to the Beverly Hills Hotel at this time of day.

"I'm done with business now."

"How long can we play for?"

"For as long as you want me."

I knew damn well she didn't mean that. What she meant was as long as it was convenient for her, but let it pass because it was convenient for me, too. "Are you coming over?" I was already excited.

"Can I bring Olga? She can hang out with your team. Are they there?"

"They are here. Of course you can bring Olga. Tell me what you'd like for dinner."

"Everything. Anything as long as you're on the menu. We will be there no later than six."

When I hung up the phone, Letty already had a notepad in her hand.

"What are we having for dinner?" Her pen was posed above the pad. "How many for dinner?"

"Letty, no need for notes. Get Miguel to drum up a little of everything. Get Caro to set the table with three extra places. Olga's coming, too. Find where Melina is and get her on the phone for me."

She dropped the pad and started dialing. "You got it, Boss."

A few minutes later, I was telling Melina, "Camila and Olga are in town. Going to be here at six for dinner. Be great if you can make it."

"Papi, that's six hours too early for me today. I'm so sorry."

My breath caught for a minute. Tanis used to call me Papi Grande.

"I like Papi, Baby. Is that my new handle?"

She laughed warmly. "Maybe, just between us, eh?"

I let the girls know Melina would not be attending and the three extra place settings went down to two.

When Camila and Olga arrived in the hotel limo, the girls and I were outside to greet them. Olga carried one of her LV suitcases. After a round of hugs, kisses and condolences, we went inside.

"Three million," she whispered in my ear.

In the foyer, I took the suitcase from Olga and handed it over to Pixie. I'd gotten over my reluctance over these cash-filled suitcases. I guess you can get used to anything. They say necessity is the mother of invention, but maybe it is also the big motivator of acceptance. If a deal came up for LAI, I needed to have the cash ready.

"Pixie, put this on my desk, please."

We moved down to my wine room for a while, and tested Tricia's bartending skills. She mixed Margaritas for Camila and Olga. In the kitchen, Miguel had Chete, Caro, Memo, and Yoli hopping. Two more for dinner was a very small party. Maybe it felt like a big event because it was in the dining room. We usually eat in the office, breakfast room, wine room, den, or by the pool—everywhere *but* the dining room. Our little group stayed in a cluster at one end of the ridiculously huge table, still huge without all of the extensions. The last time I'd eaten at this table, Melina and I had sat down at opposite ends for a Sunday breakfast, yelling our conversation like there was a small country between us. It had been for fun, and funny, but we decided not to repeat it unless we got some old cans and string, and made a 'phone' to test out.

I sat Camila at the head of the table. I was to her right. Olga was on my other side, and the girls were facing us.

"How was the funeral?" Camila asked.

"I am so terribly sorry we couldn't make it," Olga said.

"My apologies to all of you," Camila said.

The girls launched into a description of the flowers, the crowds at the cemetery and Oscar's big house.

"Janice mentioned you got flowers," I said. "Flowers, flowers, and more flowers. I think you got every bouquet in Los Angeles. Flowers at the service, at the cemetery, at Oscar's house, even at the office. Oscar's home looked like it had been strafed by a WWII bomber filled with lilies, carnations, roses, orchids and tulips."

"It was the least we could do. I'm sure we weren't the only ones," Camila said. "Especially with being unable to be there in person. At least with the flowers, we felt like we were making an appearance in spirit."

"Janice is so young and beautiful," Pixie said. "So much younger than Oscar."

"Not as young as she looks, but she was once the trophy bride. I feel bad for her," Olga said. "Oscar was a good friend. He stayed with us a few times after he handled Oscar's case."

Caro and Yoli served and removed a salad course, and filled the center of the table with an array of vegetables and breads. Miguel used the buffet as a carving station, and sliced a standing rib roast into thick slabs and paper-thin slices. Caro brought the meat around on a tray, and then placed the tray on the table with us, repeating the process with a ham, and a smoked turkey. A dozen crystal jars of various sauces made the rounds. My favorite was an avocado aioli. I was heavily into protein lately, but I saw everyone was enjoying the breads. Pixie frowned when she didn't see tortillas, but she went into the kitchen, and came out with bowls of chopped cilantro, salsa, crumbled Cotija, and a plate covered with a red clay cloche.

"Dibs on the tortillas," she said. She put the bowls on the table, in easy reach.

"Where will your cases end up now?" Camila asked, lifting the red lid and grabbing a tortilla. She dabbed it with salsa, cheese and cilantro, rolled her turkey in it, and chomped down. "You must have a lot of hungry lawyers dying to get cases like you guys bring in."

I'd never seen Camila eating anything so pedestrian as tortillas, but she was next to Pixie and had the first one downed before Pixie had managed to get back in the chair. She was keeping up with Pixie who was munching through the stack of tortillas as if they were in an eating competition.

Olga was a slow eater or maybe it just seemed that way by comparison.

"Not sure," I said. "It will give me more time to work on building acquisitions for LAI, providing that you still want to buy more."

Camila had a mouthful, and swallowed before responding. "Of course, we want to buy," she said.

"What gave you the impression we don't want more property?" Olga asked.

"I was just confirming."

"Go for it," Camila said.

"Unless I give the girls time off for good behavior. Maybe they'd like a vacation."

"No way," Pixie said, looking up from her plate. "I can't go without working. I'd start doing shit out of boredom, and get into trouble."

"Everyone needs a break some time," Camila said. "Maybe you should take a vacation. Tell yourself you are on a case."

Jo smiled. "That's a nice thought, but we're pretty amped up about finding your next big deal."

"We were once gone three months," Niley told Camila. "Nanny Delores said they were a terror when I was gone, but the kids were fine when I got home. They were angels for weeks." She laughed.

"If you need anything, you can count on me," Camila said. She rolled another tortilla full, this time experimenting with finely sliced beef.

The meat trays were emptied and replaced and emptied again. Caro and Yoli cleared the plates, serving dishes and silverware, and brought carajillos as after dinner drinks all around.

"Are you still doing karate?" Camila asked.

Pixie giggled. "Can you tell by how much food we put away? The best thing about exercising so hard is that we get to eat like sailors getting home after being stranded for a week on a deserted island."

"I didn't do so badly myself," Camila said.

Niley said, "We work out here or at the karate studio near home every day, unless we're on a case. We take classes too, from different places, just to switch it all up. On a case, it's pot luck. We do what we do with whatever is handy."

"And then, there's the coach," Pixie said.

"Who's the coach?" Olga asked. "A karate teacher? A…" It took a few moments for her to come up with the word. "Sensei?"

"He's a sharpshooter. Name's Buck. We've been practicing for years with him. Tricia's started practicing with us too, but she was a marksman before Mario hired her."

"Tricia?"

"She's our man of all work," Pixie said, "Except she's not a man. She's a private eye, does title research, chauffeurs, and hangs out as a guard. She fixed your before-dinner Margarita. Probably does other stuff too."

"Yeah, because of coach, we trained and have permits to carry a concealed weapon," Niley added.

"I don't have a permit to carry," Letty said. "Yet."

"You have more body guards than Pepe," Olga said, laughing.

"I doubt it," Pixie said. "How many does he have?"

"Pix, don't be so nosey," I said.

"Sorry."

Camila said, "He has a lot of protection. In Colombia, they like kidnapping people who live in big houses and drive expensive cars. So we take measures against it."

I remembered that Julio's last words had been to deliver the lawyer's threat to Pepe and the General.

"They like to do that in Venezuela." I nodded. Precautions were in order.

Pixie put her hand up to her ear, as if she was straining to hear. She looked expectantly toward the kitchen, smiling broadly. A moment later, Memo rounded the corner pushing a full dessert cart.

Jo said, "I'm on my second wind, but I'll be leaving soon. I hate to eat and run, but TJ's waiting."

Jo still did her work, but she'd quit hanging around after hours. I just wanted her to be happy. I'd have to kick TJ's ass if he ever did anything to hurt her.

Niley took a slice of sponge cake, and covered it with strawberries and a little of her cocktail. Camila and Olga took pieces of cheesecake. Jo and Pixie had flan. I passed on all of it, but sent Memo back to get me a cold scoop of Miguel's homemade peanut butter ice cream with candied pistachio nuts on top.

I looked at Camila. She had polished off two pieces of cheesecake. I don't know where she put it, but it sure didn't show up on her ass. She lit up a joint. She pushed the dessert plate to the side.

"What kind of trouble should we get into tonight?" she asked the girls, and passed the joint around. We did some experimenting, all of us, but Camila and Olga flew out that night.

Later that week, I was in my office studying Tricia's latest foreclosures. Everything was small potatoes. I put a couple of choices aside as possibilities for Letty. Caro turned on the intercom, and I heard her let in two sheriff homicide detectives. They stood near the front door while she came to me for directions. I had her to escort them to me, and was behind my desk when they walked in. I got up, and shook their hands, and offered them something to eat or drink. They declined, but if I know Miguel, some kind of drink and snack would be arriving on a tray within minutes.

I had never seen these two detectives before. I would put them both in their mid-forties, with the clean-shaven look typical of their profession. One of them wore thick black glasses, had a hawkish nose, and the physique of a body builder. He took the lead in the questioning. His name was Solé. The second detective, Ramos, had a pug nose, and a lantern jaw. I didn't catch their first names, but they weren't here for friendly chit chat. Ramos focused on his clipboard, and never met my eyes. He was busy writing down every word out of my mouth. I believed them when they told me it was a routine interview. I knew the routine. They were interviewing everyone connected to Oscar Cooke. Ramos pulled a chair from the conference table.

"Mind if I sit down?"

"Please do."

Ramos sat in the chair and continued writing.

Solé was still on his feet. He made no move to sit. In fact, he walked to the office door, and without leaving the room, looked in the direction of the front door down the path the housekeeper had led him. It's not a convoluted route, but it did give a general sense of the size of this level of my house. It's not a cracker box.

"Did you work for him?" Solé asked.

"I wasn't an employee. I did consulting work for him, and he paid me for my services."

"Services?"

"I was an advisor handling foreign aviation cases, and maintaining the foreign caseload from here."

Solé glanced down the hall again, and walked back in my direction. I noticed how he ran his fingers along the surface of the pieces of furniture as he passed, as if gauging their quality.

"You must be very good."

I heard admiration in his tone.

"If you are curious, it's all on my tax returns." I smiled, not a wise-ass smile, a genuine smile.

I told them I knew nothing, but that I was interested in learning more since Oscar had been my friend.

Miguel arrived as I anticipated. He had coffee for me, and for the officers, glasses of ice, canned soft drinks, and a small tray of pigs in blankets with a side dish of yellow mustard. By his choice of hors d'oeuvres, I could tell he was being a smartass. I didn't say anything to him, and both officers accepted their drinks gracefully, and polished off the hotdogs.

"If I can do something to help the investigation, let me know." I handed each detective my personal card with my exchange number and home number. In the thirty minutes they were here, they never mentioned Jake or Tanis's death, my shooting and my killing the shooter, or anything about the two intruders whom I had thrown out of a high-rise. That told me they had not checked on me, yet. I was certain they would be back as soon as they checked on my history. I thought about being proactive and calling Mike Sanchez, the detective that had worked on my case when Hugo had been gunning for me. After my aunt delivered his first kid, we'd actually turned into good friends and hung out sometimes. Today, though, that might be pushing my luck.

Melina came over and stayed the night. I'm pretty sure she dragged me up from the wine room and put me to bed. I remember waking in the night some time and crying in her arms.

I came out of my morning shower, naked.

Melina sipped from her chai and gave me a hungry look over the mug's rim.

"Nice suit," she said. "Who's your tailor?"

Since I was still naked, I took that as a compliment. I took the cup out of her hand and dragged Melina out of bed.

"Missed you," I said, pushing her up against the wall. Her kiss tasted of mint toothpaste and chai.

"I can always tell when you're lying out of your ass," she said.

Midnight sex is secret buried treasure. Morning sex is urgent and quick, pressed for time because someone's on a clock.

"Now I've got you pinned against the wall, what am I going to do with you?"

"Pin me like you mean it, Papi. Lay one on me," Melina said, challenging me with slanted, hooded eyes.

I did my best. It wasn't a marathon. It was more of a sprint, but we were both panting and covered in sweat when we were done, and had to follow up with a mutual shower. I toweled her off, and sat down for her to return the favor. She worked the towel, and everything would have been fine, but she had to work her mouth, too.

"You have to stay alert, Mario. You can't be drunk like you were last night and expect to be able to protect yourself and the girls when they are here. If you can't stay sober, I'm going to send guards."

"If you hire guards, I'll throw them right out. I'm working like a crazy guy during the day trying to locate hot properties with potential. I'm not sitting around drinking and getting high like before we buried Oscar."

"Baby, you were shitfaced last night. I peeled you off that table and dragged you upstairs. You can't let your guard down like that. Do you really feel you are out of danger now?"

I grabbed the towel she was holding, looped it around her, and used it to pull her into my lap. "I believe that they died in the fire. Besides Pepe doesn't think they had anything to do with Oscar."

"So we are back to square one on whoever ordered the hit on Oscar."

"Wrong. I'm back to square one," I said. "You're back to your markets."

"Your business is my business, Cuz. I'm not going to stand here doing nothing like a Hollywood bimbo letting the hero take all the heat. *We* don't know who killed Oscar, and don't know if they're going after you. I'm not going to let some shithead shoot you and break my heart. I have to do something." She looked at me earnestly.

"Look, the lawyers are in all likelihood dead, burned up crispy critters on their plantation. Why would Oscar's shooter be after me? I had no connections with Oscar but the aviation. It's his criminal clients who are next in line as suspects."

I knew having the girls as bodyguards was not a solution. Maybe I was a little pissed off because she was a little bit right, and she was pissed off because I wouldn't acknowledge she was a little bit right.

"All this trouble is because of those Colombians."

"Nothing is their fault. And they have names."

I was getting irritated. We didn't argue it out. We dressed silently. She left without another word.

I steamed out the liquor. The more I thought about it, the more I realized that Melina was right. Hers was the same advice Cosmo always urged on me. Be alert at all times to see it coming, whatever "it" might be. I wasn't going to give up drinking, but I resolved not to get drunk again until I knew who'd gone after Oscar, and they were safely behind bars or six feet under.

Tom Jones and I stayed in touch. Though their visit had been a week before, at our standing lunch date at PDC, I told him about the detectives,

"They've been here too. They are interviewing every employee, even the ones that are no longer here. I hope they find who did this."

We were not at the usual big table the girls and I shared for our occasional PDC feasts. We were at Tom's favorite table for two, with a surface barely big enough to accommodate our iced tea and strip steak plates.

"Speaking of overactive imaginations," Tom said. "Jack Fino's group got paid off by Oscar's life insurance."

"Jack Fino?"

"You know him?"

"I know *a* Jack Fino. Criminal attorney that represented Pixie on a bullshit charge."

"Bullshit charge?"

"Back when Carson was an independent and our competition, he and Pixie were working the same hospital. Might have been a bus crash or highway pile-up. He told a hospital security guard that Pixie was a hooker and they hauled her to jail. They dropped the charges, of course, but it was Fino who represented her." I grinned. I could laugh about it now, but at the time, I had been sure Carson had been up to much worse than that. I had beaten him down a couple of times, and had never really figured out if I'd been right or wrong in doing it. "I don't think that Jack Fino has five million to loan out."

"That's probably him," Tom said, swallowing a grin. "I can picture Carson doing that. He can be kind of sly and cutthroat, while charming your ass off. I'm glad he's not a lawyer."

"Carson was like that when he was in diapers. Hasn't changed a bit." I took a sip of water, and stared at the twist of lemon floating in the glass. "Jack never struck me as particularly wealthy."

"Jack is a criminal lawyer. He has investors, and makes loans to attorneys. The interest rates are high, but no bank will make loans for the amounts Fino makes. Oscar had a five million dollar loan[50] with him."

I remember Denise telling us about a credit line that would be paid off by a life insurance policy.

"Paranoid? Oscar had life insurance to cover the loan. If Oscar didn't live long enough to pay off the loan, he gets offed and Fino gets paid." I started laughing at my own logic and the absurdity of it, and saw Tom wasn't laughing. He had seriously considered it as a possibility.

"Fino is good people. He's not a killer," Tom said. "Matter of fact, he called and offered to give me two million to help the cash flow."

I stopped laughing. "If you take it, will you need life insurance?"

"I will. I don't have to wait though. He's going to advance the money next week but I need two of the old timers to sign for the firm along with me."

I thought about giving him a million cash for him to pay me back when one of the plane cases cleared. "Don't die, Tom. I've lost too many friends. Oscar was Italian. Fino is Italian."

"I'm not Italian, and I have no intention of dying," he assured me. "We're both just being paranoid. We're not living in a Godfather movie."

I couldn't picture Jack Fino. I had only met him that one time when Pixie, Jo and I went to see him about handling Pixie's case. His office was nothing like Oscar's classy high rise. It was just a small office. I also remember a message he left on my answering machine after I had thrown one of those fuckers

---

[50] $5,000,000.00 in 1980 had the same buying power as $15,738,722.29 in 2017

out the window. He said he was just calling to make sure I was okay. I don't think I called him back.

"Unless things have changed a lot since the last time we talked, two million won't cover what you are short in the trust account."

"I told Fino about the trust account shortage. He wants the two million to finance the caseload. As cash comes in on settlements, we can start paying people who are due money from the client trust account. Hopefully we can buy time, maybe even keep ahead until we are solvent, or anyone starts complaining to the state bar."

"As long as the clients get what they got coming from the settlements, I am happy."

"That's the plan. Two million will get us through. I am cutting personnel by half, and getting out of the lease for one of the floors. That cuts the shit out of the rent."

"Sounds good, my friend. It's going to help that you won't be paying me for new business."

"I'd take your new business in a split second, but I can't pay up front. Have you signed anything lately?"

"Nope, haven't signed a thing. I haven't been looking. What about Carson? I haven't heard from him."

"He's bringing in small stuff. We have a deal that the case has to be checked out before he gets paid. Can't afford to take risky cases right now. But he brings in a steady stream of cases that turn over fast."

"Is he okay with that?"

"That's the best I can do."

"If he hated the deal, I would have heard from him," I said. "At least you didn't cut him totally off."

"His cases are small, but they are bread and butter, you know that. They settle and keep us going. The big cases take time."

After my conversation with Tom, he went back to the office. I sat there nursing a glass of wine. Tom and I had made a joke of it, but I kept thinking back to Fino's group, the five million loan, and the five million dollar life insurance policy that was more like a threat than collateral.

I thought of the men who died after Pepe ordered them on a mission to the plantation. That they were killed did not prove those motherfuckers were responsible for Oscar's death too. They were in a whole other country. The problem was that when I thought about the lawyers, I knew they were responsible. But when I thought about that loan paid off by life insurance, I was sure it was Fino.

On the drive home, I realized how paranoid it was to blame Fino. Demanding insurance to protect assets was nothing new. I shouldn't be making up conspiracy theories out of my imagination. If Tom had taken his own suspicions seriously, he wouldn't be getting a loan. I should respect the man who had gotten Pixie's case dismissed without her even making a court appearance. On the other hand, her case had been no big deal, a tiny misdemeanor. The two thousand I paid was overkill, but at the time, I'd been worried. After all it was Pixie, and she had a real history of hooking, even if it was supposed to be in sealed juvenile records. Carson had no business ratting her out to the guard at the hospital.

Back in my office, I managed to reach Pepe for the first time in a while. Because it was on my mind, I told him about the five million credit line getting paid off by an insurance policy that was required in order to get a loan from this attorney who made loans to attorneys in need.

"There's another suspect," he said.

"He was a friend of Oscar's. Criminal lawyers, both of them."

Pepe came up with the name on his own. "You're talking about that Italian. Fino?"

"You know him?"

"I know everybody. When Oscar was representing me, I met Fino. Good guy."

"You don't think he's a suspect?"

Pepe laughed. "I don't think Fino is a good suspect, no. Talk to Olga and Camila."

When I was working locally signing auto accident cases, I was so busy, there was no rest. Work continued day and night, 24/7, and I loved it. I worked my ass off, but I loved what I was doing. I sold that source list to Oscar, and that became the business that Carson took over. In aviation, an existing client doesn't call me to refer a case unless it is another family of a victim in an ongoing case. When there wasn't a big airliner crash, we kept busy looking and sometimes getting lucky signing small aircraft crashes. Our hunt for small crashes was not productive, currently, but we weren't really looking. There was no point when we didn't have a lawyer lined up to work our cases. It was a good thing I had an income stream from Camacho if and when I closed a deal to add a property to their LAI corporation.

"Business is fucked," Pixie said. "Can't remember it being this slow."

"If you mean aviation, we don't have a lawyer to send the cases to."

"You could get one," Letty said.

"I could, and I will. We're not done with that business."

We were in the sunroom, a glass room that overlooked the sloping yard and pool area. Melina had noticed that if a room didn't have somewhere I could work in it that I neglected it. She bought the sunroom a new beachy table that fit against one windowed corner, with solid high-backed benches on three sides, and four chairs for the odd side, like a restaurant booth, but painted with a thin coat of distressed white. It was the dead of summer, and the sunroom was heavily air-conditioned, chilling us after a sunning-swimming break. From my vantage point, I could see Chete vacuuming the pool. Memo was tending some of the tropical plants behind the lounges.

Jo asked, "What if you let me take over the management of your apartments for a fraction of what you are paying your current management company?'

I spilled my coffee. "What?" I sopped up the mess with a handful of tissue, and punched the intercom for Miguel. "You just got married, and you want to get into a business that will consume more of your time than this does?"

"I can have an office close to home. TJ can help me with all the trades he arranges to service the apartments. Plumbers. Handymen. Cleanup crews."

Miguel saw at a glance what had happened, and came back with a fresh cup, and towel to clean up the mess. The cup was unnecessary, because there was nothing wrong with the other one. A full carafe of coffee sat in the middle of the table beside a pitcher of sweet tea. He checked the levels of the drinks, and was in and out like a ghost. A tray of brown bread sandwiches was partially depleted, the basket of fruit next to it mostly untouched. Jo had started peeling an orange, but now it sat forgotten on her plate. She sat at my right shoulder by Niley with their backs to one window. Letty was on my right, sharing my bench. Pixie was across from me on the third bench. Tricia had been sitting at one of the chairs, but she left to take the car to get it washed.

"I get the picture," I interrupted her. "I have over a thousand apartments now. Tenants will drive you crazy. You'll work harder and longer hours than you do now."

"It's okay. Sooner or later, TJ will start some big job and be working long hours. I saw on Westwood that he is not an eight to five person."

"Billing, banking, notices to tenants to pay rent or get out, evictions. More things than I know. Are you going to be doing this by yourself?"

"We did it before when you took off for Europe," Niley said. "You didn't have as many apartments, but we had a taste of management."

"You did very well,"

"I was on that management team," Pixie reminded us.

"You were," I said. "I remember how you handled collections." Everyone laughed except Letty who didn't know how Pixie had picked up a homey at Hollenbeck Park to muscle a delinquent tenant.

"What does TJ say about this?"

"I haven't told him. It's not up to him. He and I have a deal. We work, and we do the best we can with our jobs to spend as much time together as we can."

I thought a moment. "If I could make a deal with Melina like that, we'd probably be married."

"Making the deal is easy, Living up to it is a different story, " Jo said. "I don't mean that as a criticism of you, Boss. I'm saying it's going to take effort from TJ and me. And he's like you, with projects and down time. No one could handle Melina's job running all those markets of hers."

Pixie frowned, but didn't say anything.

"Boss, are you here?" Jo asked, and laughed. The other girls laughed.

"I was spaced out for a second. Wondering if I could manage the marriage thing. Melina and I are both such workaholics." I looked across the table at Jo. "You ask me for this. There is no way I can say no."

"No pressure, Boss."

"If this is what you want, show me the plan. If it will help you, I'll do it."

"It will help us both."

"If you approve, I am part of the plan," Niley said. She reached for another sandwich half, and a couple of ripe cherries.

I wished I had a mirror to check the look on my face. I was trying to be cool about it, but I had alarm bells going off in my head. "Anyone else?"

"Not me, Boss, I'm here to stay." Pixie said. She patted me on the hand, and grabbed the last chicken salad sandwich half, and a handful of green grapes.

"I'm with you, too." Letty wrapped her arm around mine and leaned against me. She'd polished off a cold meatloaf sandwich with a layer of ketchup on it. She smelled like ketchup, and oranges and chlorine with a hint of shampoo. Niley smelled like nothing at all. Jo smelled like the orange she'd been peeling, but she'd showered off the chlorine. Pixie still had the pool on her, and Coppertone sun lotion. She smelled like summer.

Jo said, "I will form a management company with Niley as my partner. We will hire the services we need to get things done. We've done this before, only now I have TJ to help me get every tradesman I need, when I need it."

"We invited Pixie, but she wants no part of it. She says we are abandoning you. Called us rats," Niley said.

"I guess this makes me the sinking ship." I looked up for their response, but they weren't laughing. "If we do this, there is no coming back when I need you on a case," I said, thinking to talk them out of it. Of course, if I found a lawyer and went back into aviation, and they wanted to come back, how could I turn them away? I wanted them back already, and they hadn't even left yet. "My apartments are a big deal to manage. You already know this."

"Mario, we are not abandoning you," Jo said. "Your ship is not sinking."

"How much will I save by using your company?"

The smiles on their faces were a sight.

"We figure if you pay us half of what you pay the management company, even after expenses, it will be a ton of money for us to split. Your savings by having us manage is probably enough to cover the house expense here, the beach house, and Pixie and Letty, Tricia, and the household help." Jo pulled out a folded batch of papers from her huge purse. "Do you feel up to checking this out right now?"

I wasn't, but I'd be a fool not to want to pay half of what I was paying for management. I knew Jo and Niley would be assets.

"Sure. Let me see," I said.

For two hours, I grilled them. Jo was as well-prepared as always.

"You're going to give up traveling on cases and probably give up a whole lot of your time with your kids, and TJ. A thousand families calling you every time they see a bug, have a leaky sink, low water pressure, noisy neighbors, have a parking dispute, or need to move in or out. The pressure will be greater than any pressure you have experienced running with me on cases."

"It's a challenge. We want to do it. We plan to hire people just like the management company does now. You don't think that two people manage all of your apartments?"

"Go for it," I said. "If it doesn't work out, forget what I said. You can always come back."

They attacked me right where I sat.

"Thank you!" Jo said.

"We won't let you down," Niley promised.

"TPI will have twins when they know they are losing your business," Letty said.

"They're giant. They won't miss my thousand units."

"Yeah, they will," Pixie said with a giggle.

Jo and Niley incorporated in July. Jo-Ni Management immediately consumed them. The first month's report since their takeover made me very proud. They had already begun a policy of refurbishing the vacated units that needed work, and filling spruced-up units with solid tenants with deeper pockets. TJ had a crew getting familiar with maintenance. They had taken out some cheap radio ads that had new tenants beating the doors to move in. Good for me. They were making more money in management than I had been paying them even with the bonuses they received after a big case. Good for them. Not using the old management company, TP1, was a win for me.

I hadn't yet looked for another lawyer to handle our future aviation cases. I don't know why I kept putting it off, but I was busy looking for buildings for LAI. Pixie got there early in the morning. Letty lived with me, no strings attached, her apartment empty most of the time. We sat in the office and looked for properties. Tricia and Randy searched for properties, too, Tricia from public records and Randy from property listings. When we found something promising, we'd check it out early, come back and cool off in the pool, and finish off with more searches, or handle paperwork.

I purchased a twelve-story office building in Hollywood for one million dollars.[51] The Hollywood Boulevard address was irresistible. Vacancies were at eighty percent of the building. I sent TJ in to clean up each floor, install new drop-ceilings and lighting, and anything else needed to make the building suitable for professional tenants. The building's exterior looked like travertine. TJ had two crews hanging from the roof washing crud off to reveal the building's beauty.

I met Olga briefly at the airport, exchanging money and paperwork for the building. Olga was happy with the initial eighty percent occupancy, but I assured her that the figure would go up under proper management.

"Of course, we want as much of the building as possible to be occupied, Amor," she said, but what caught my ear most was Olga mentioning using the building to channel money into the bank.

I realized that LAI buildings received rental income. Deposits could be made to the LAI account as though they were rental income. I pictured an assembly line of suitcases filled with cash rolling in to their bank accounts. I couldn't understand how they could deposit green cash all the time and call it rental income. Not all tenants would pay in cash. Their management company guru would have his hands full.

"How did you manage to get the seller to accept cash?" Olga asked.

I told her about the seller.

"All I did is wait a couple of days. The seller was an elderly lady, about seventy. She owned the building outright. No broker. All she had were three signs on the ground floor, For Sale by Owner."

"So you saw the sign and approached her."

"Nope, Tricia told me about the sign and gave me the number. When I called the owner, she wanted two million, but when I went to visit her a few

---

[51] $1,000,000.00 in 1980 had the same buying power as $3,147,744.46 in 2017

days later, she accepted a million in cash. On the spot."

"Just like that?" Olga said.

"Just like that."

"Very nice," Olga kissed me. I followed her into the cabin. In two hours, the crew would return to fly her away.

"Pepe mentioned Jack Fino. You know him, right?"

"I do," Olga said. She turned away from me so I could unzip the back of her dress, an orange sleeveless linen that emphasized her tan. She shucked it off. The cabin was cool, but she did not reach for the black pajamas.

"I told Pepe I suspected Fino of having Oscar killed. You know that Fino makes his borrowers get life insurance policies to cover their loans? He made Oscar get a five-million-dollar life insurance policy, and Fino's company is the beneficiary of—"

Before I even got the whole thing out of my mouth, Olga was laughing. I tossed my clothes over a chair, and got into bed beside her. New sheets. Cotton, I think. I liked them better than the silk ones because the silk kept sliding off the bed, plus they got hot and sticky when we were hot and sticky. Cotton seemed to, I don't know, I guess you'd say it breathes.

"Amor, you watch too much TV and it makes you paranoid, yes? We do a lot of business with Jack. He's a fine person. Yes, if you don't pay, he goes after you—"

"Aha!" I interrupted.

"Not with a bullet, silly man. He draws a lawyer faster than John Wayne can pull a rifle. I don't think he kills the borrowers in order to collect life insurance."

I caught the 'she doesn't think' part. To me, that was practically confirmation. I'm so used to lawyers and what they call plausible deniability.

"Business. What kind of business?"

She reached for my hard-on. "Amor, get your big verga in here and stop talking business."

She slid on top of me, and we commenced a whole other kind of transaction.

I cleared a neat ninety-one thousand, cash, on the LAI deal, gave Tricia a five thousand bonus, and Pixie and Letty two thousand each. The seller didn't realize that I'd been willing to give her the entire two million she was asking. She accepted the million offer and made it clear she was doing it because it was conditional on it being green cash, accepting the building as is, where is, with no contingencies other than clear title. At two million, I could have made a bigger commission but I was going to get Camacho the best deals I could. I knew there would be deals that were harder to land out there.

Chapter 22
August 1980
Holding Pattern

An airliner crashed, killing nine and injuring over ninety passengers, some of them very seriously. He knew I didn't have a lawyer to work with, but Jason called to tell me about it. I loved the South of France, and was sorely tempted to take the case, but I passed on it. What was the point with no lawyer to take the case to. Besides, I was busy with Camacho business. This was the first time that I had turned down a big aviation case.

"I don't blame you," Jason said. "Take it slow. Come live in London for a while."

I hung up the phone. Pixie, who was at the conference table behind a stack of real estate flyers, crossed her arms and pouted at me.

"I take it we're out of the crash business," she said. "I think—"

I never got to hear what Pixie thought because Letty interrupted.

"No, we're not." Letty replied for me. "We need a lawyer."

"Bitch, I know that."

"Hey, don't bitch me, bitch."

I ignored them as their argument escalated to the physical. It wasn't unusual. They had gotten good at martial arts floor work. I knew they were just having fun, but sometimes the action looked serious. Pixie was several years ahead and while she could jump like a pro, Letty was getting there. They took off down the hall. Something crashed. Caro shrieked, then scolded them in rapid Spanish. In a dustpan, Caro brought the three pieces of a Moroccan vase Pepe had sent me. I called Memo to put it back together. He was good at that kind of thing.

It was not unusual for Pixie to spend the night with Letty and me. We went out together to clubs in Hollywood and we'd do the Playboy Club at least two, sometimes three times a week. Tricia drove us so there was no chance of driving under the influence. Wednesday nights were reserved for Buck at Melina's shooting gallery.

In the morning in my breakfast nook, the girls were showering when Melina said, "You're a happy bachelor sleeping with two pussies."

"Baby, when you come over, I'm all yours, you know that."

"Asshole."

On Sundays, Melina and I had this conversation:

"We getting married this weekend?"

"I love you," Melina said. "You got me. Why do you need a ring?"

"So, not this weekend."

She patted my hand. "Maybe next weekend, we hit the honeymoon chapel in Vegas. Eh?"

Melina opened another market in late August.

I stopped buying apartment buildings for myself. Most of my mortgages were paid off, but I told myself it would stretch me too thin to keep getting more. Jo and Niley had their hands full with the units I already owned. Why should I buy something that I'd have to maintain for years before a profit appeared, when I could make something off of an LAI deal and not have to maintain anything? I owned enough. I concentrated on building the property portfolio of LAI.

Pixie spent some time redecorating her own investment property when someone moved out. She ripped out cheap paneling. Painted. Shined up the hardwood floor. Got new kitchen appliances. When she was done, she realized she liked that property better than her unit, so she moved her family next door, and started redoing her old apartment. She got the place rented for more money.

Jo called to let me know Jo-Nil Enterprises had a full staff of nine, one of whom was a former football player with a bit of brain damage. He did the heavy lifting, and sometimes the collections. The four person clean up crew that had been hand-picked by TJ for multiple expertise, which included a master plumber, journeyman electrician, bricklayer, roofer, painter, welder, and landscaper. The other two employees stayed in the office.

"We're training our crew," she said. "Niley and I have this real estate management thing covered. We're set up now that when you go back to aviation, we're available."

"Good to know." I was glad to hear it.

Tricia and Randy were bringing over mountains of paperwork causing a problem was the office. For Letty and Pixie, looking through piles of papers for properties was torture and they let me know it at every opportunity. They weren't academic and they sure as hell weren't into analysis or math. They just couldn't get into looking for property. They did it, but they moaned and groaned and belly-ached over every boring word they had to read.

"We need a case, Boss."

I opened my eyes. Both Letty and Pixie were staring at me. I had my feet up and my left hand was just resting on the neck of a full wine glass. It was after work hours. The girls had waited to corral me when I was in my favorite place to relax, in those deep chairs. Music on, disco ball off. We all had wine glasses, and Miguel had brought down a cheese plate for us. A couple bowls of different cubes of cheese, toothpicks, and various herb mixtures to dip them in.

I stabbed a piece of cheese with a trident-shaped toothpick and dunked it in the pepper bowl. Jalapeño and pepper jack were not a match with wine, but I liked it anyway. The cheese melted to cream on my tongue, and the jalapeño burned with its peppery kick. I chased it with a sip of wine, and put down the glass.

"We need a lawyer with lots of money," I said. My mouth was still burning, but my tongue was craving more heat, not unlike my feelings for all my girls. I used the same pick and readied another piece of cheese.

"Let's find one," Letty said.

"Of course." I wasn't sure I meant it. I was doing okay with this line of work. Finding the properties wasn't fun, but I was the one who made the connection with the seller, and got them to accept cash. That's where I could shine. It was just enough of a challenge and had plenty of reward.

"You miss Jo and Niley?"

I nodded, sipped my wine. The jalapeño kicked the wine's ass. It would probably go better with cold beer, but my tongue was okay with the combo.

"I miss them as much as you do. Jo got in touch with me. She and Niley are set up to go with us if we have a plane crash."

"A case? Please? Find a lawyer, Boss," Pixie said. "We can't turn another case away like you did Cannes."

I looked at my sad sack team, and agreed.

Pixie let out a whoop, and jumped up and down. She leaned over and grabbed me by the lapels to give me a deep kiss. She froze, looked at me with horror, and chugged her glass of wine.

"Your mouth is on fire," she panted, staring at the dish of jalapeños.

I laughed, and prepped another piece of cheese.

Chapter 23
September 1980
Aftermath

When Tom Jones called, I was having a late breakfast. Nothing much, just black coffee, scrambled eggs, and a side of classified ads. Caro answered the house phone and handed it to me while I was in my breakfast nook.

"Jack Fino wants to meet with you."

"Why?"

"He knows you're the source of our aviation cases. I think he's impressed. He remembers that matter he handled for Pixie."

"You don't think this dude offed Oscar to get his five million back from the insurance?"

"I still don't think he had anything to do with it. If I'd thought so, I'd never have taken up his offer."

"Did your insurance name him as your beneficiary?"

"Yes, I got the insurance. Yes, if something happens to me, two million gets paid to his company."

"I'll meet him. Give him my home number, on one condition."

"Which is?"

"Do not get me insurance."

Tom laughed.

"Are you sure you don't want to call him?"

"Fuck no. If he wants to see me, have him call."

"I'll give him your number."

Fino called immediately. He sounded very friendly. At the sound of his voice on the line, I remembered he'd left me a message asking if I was okay way back when I had a shooter break in my apartment.

I agreed to meet him for lunch at the Pacific Dining Car.

Jack Fino didn't look like Jake, but he dressed like him. We both arrived at the PDC in three-piece suits. I don't know where Jack's tailors were. His clothes looked ok.

We shook hands in the foyer. Jack had a firm handshake, but not too firm. He was at least two decades older than me, trim with salt and pepper hair. When we were shown to a table, I took the seat across from him. Neither of us faced the door, which was to my left, and his right. The waiters greeted me with nods and pats on my shoulder. My old friend Ramon was our waiter.

"Welcome back, Mr. Mario."

I ordered sparkling water. Jack ordered the same.

"So, you are the miracle man with new cases?"

I nodded. "You're the miracle man that lends lawyers what the banks won't give them."

"Not always," Jack said. "I have a group of associates who feel as I do, that a lawyer is a good investment. Loan him what he needs to keep his cases moving. I fund sixty percent of the loans from my money reserves. My associates come up with the forty percent."

"Pixie told me to be sure and tell you hello for her."

"You must give her my best. She is a cutie."

"She is, and she knows it," I said with a grin. "Any particular reason you wanted to meet?"

"From what I've learned, you have got to be the most savvy and successful person in your line of work. I'm a lawyer, and you're a good man for a lawyer to know."

"Thanks," I said. "I'm between lawyers right now."

"I am aware of that," he said. "Pepe Camacho told me you are doing some consulting work for him. He speaks very highly of you." I didn't show my surprise at his mentioning Pepe, but at least their business connection was out in the open. Olga had confirmed they did business with Fino. Now that Fino was telling me about talking to Pepe, I felt that he was too weaved into this group to be a suspect.

"That's very nice of Pepe."

"His sisters are knockouts. I hear you are good friends."

That was an understatement, but it sounded like he knew how close we all were. I chuckled. "I am a lucky man."

"Tom says you live in Pasadena. So do I. Been there all my life."

"Good to know."

I lifted my sparkling water as he did. We clicked glasses.

In the next fifteen minutes, Jack told me about how he started out much like me, having worked from early childhood. He lived on Linda Vista. I'd driven down the beautiful tree-lined street where there were small houses butting up to mansions sitting far back from the street.

"You must come over one day," Jack said.

"Love to. You must come over as well. I have a dynamite chef who will cook us up a storm."

Jack was easy to talk to. I sympathized with his story of growing up in Pasadena. His mom worked as a nanny and housekeeper after his dad died in a explosion at his work, and she'd managed to keep the house by taking on boarders. As an adult, he'd bought surrounding properties.

I cut into my steak with gusto.

"What are you doing with your new cases? I'm just curious," he said. "Tom mentioned he's not taking new aviation cases, not until their books are straight. That could take years."

Of course, he would be privy to the details of Tom's finances. He would know that Tom couldn't afford to pay me. I focused on my steak for a few moments.

"I haven't signed a single case since Oscar died."

"That has to be hurting you."

"Not at all. There's only been one airline crash abroad that I would have gone over for. I haven't lined up a lawyer that can handle my volume when we get busy. I need a lawyer who can afford me. I haven't been watching the skies the way I usually do. I'm pretty busy with Pepe's acquisitions."

"I don't want to intrude, and I don't know if you even want to go back to aviation. Are you still interested in client development?"

I put down my fork and knife and looked at him. He met my eyes directly.

"Client development is my bread and butter," I said. "Always has been. I have promised my team that I am one lawyer away from our next case. If I had the right lawyer..." I let the words hang in the air.

"I may be able to help," he said.

"Shoot," I said, hitting the baked potato. Fino's plate was already empty. He ate fast.

"Lawyers across the country borrow from my group. I'm thinking of a firm in Chicago. Their volume of aviation is a kernel of what Tom Jones has from you."

Was I ready to go back to work? If we got a case, I could have the whole team together.

"Sure," I said.

"Sounds good," I said. "We never know when the next crash will occur. It would be good to have a lawyer already lined up. I hadn't thought of looking outside of California, but why not? I could have gotten by going to Oscars a dozen times a year. I don't need to live in a lawyer's pocket to work with him."

We exchanged cards, and walked to the parking lot together. His driver waited for him in his car just as Tricia waited in mine. She looked the part in a chauffeur's hat with her sharp straight blonde pageboy underneath. It was cut to the length of her chin, and shorter in back.

He wrote his phone number and home address on the back of his card and I did the same.

"I hope your lunch was successful, Boss," Tricia said, her voice gruff.

"Successful and filling," I told her. "I need to burn off some potato and cheesecake. If you are up to sparring with me in the gym for an hour, I'd consider it a good deed."

"I don't pull my punches like your girls do, Boss. The only sparring I can do with you is in bed."

"Hey, it's been a long time for us," I said. "I'm up with that. But first, drive past this address."

I flashed Tricia the card, and she headed for Jack's house. I looked out the window, and watched the neighborhoods in Pasadena go by.

I felt silly snooping like this, but I wouldn't have been surprised to find he was doing the same. She pointed it out, and circled the block a couple of times. Like on my lot, you couldn't see the house from the street. A big double-sided iron gate with Ficus trees trimmed the height of the gate made up the front of a very wide property. The neighborhood was a mix of old, remodeled, and new residences. A neighborhood heavily in demand. I couldn't see the house, but what I could see of the grounds, it was huge like mine, maybe bigger. Tricia headed home, about a ten-minute drive. Fino had a mansion, no question. A banker, a lawyer of many years. It's expected he'd have a large residence. What was my excuse? I had a house to die for and I was no lawyer or banker. With a smile, I closed my eyes during the short drive.

The more I thought about it, the more a part of me was jumping up and down at the prospect of securing a lawyer, and getting into the thrill of the chase. My girls were anxious but I didn't need them to help me with the LAI acquisitions. I had Tricia and Randy. If nothing came out of it, I was out nothing; and I had just made friends with a heavy-duty attorney loaded with money.

Oscar had owed him five million dollars, and now Tom owed him two million. Even if it wasn't all his money, it was impressive that he had that kind of pull. He certainly wasn't a pauper. I was surrounded by wealth. No one had as much cash as Pepe though. He was in a class by himself.

Pixie and Letty were in the media room watching television on my projection TV at the house waiting for me to return, but I buzzed past them. Tricia followed me to the spa.

We didn't even bother to dry off, I reclined on one of the spa beds. and Tricia got on me. She was buff. Her breasts were firmer than I remembered, her waist tiny. We were sweating like pigs when we were done. I felt better than I had in weeks. Aviation was bringing me back to life again; and I had definitely left that potato and cheesecake in the spa.

"Hey Babies," I said, walking into my media room, where the girls were watching. "Enjoy the vacation while it lasts. We might be going back to work before you know it."

"We've been working," Pixie protested half-heartedly.

"Yes, Babies. I'm talking about aviation."

Letty brightened. "I can dig that, Boss, tell us. What's up?"

Jack Fino called a week later.

"Let's meet for dinner," he said. "I think I have something interesting for you."

"Let's have dinner here," I invited him.

"Love to."

"Tell me when," I said.

"You're hosting. You tell me."

"Tomorrow at seven?"

"I'll be there."

"Are you coming alone or with the Mrs.?"

"I'm not married. I'll be alone."

"Jack, I have a team that works with me. They're family. I have no se-crets from them. Are you okay if they dine with us?'

"Most certainly."

When I hung up, I called Jo. She put me on the speaker so Niley could hear.

"I'm having a dinner with a lawyer tomorrow here at the house. I'd like to have you here. If you're busy, no pressure."

"Boss, how the fuck you figure we're too busy? We're never too busy for you," Niley said.

I swear I could hear Jo nodding her head. "Of course, we'll be there."

"Can we fuck after the lawyer leaves?" I heard Niley yelling out.

"Jo has a lock on her pussy," I joked. "But as far as I know, you don't."

"Hey Boss, I don't have a lock," Jo said.

"I was kidding."

"No you weren't. Do you miss fucking me?"

"Yes," I admitted. "Are you thinking of cheating?"

"Not yet," Jo laughed. "But it's cleared with my hubby. Sex with you is not considered cheating."

"I just got hard," I told my absentee friends. "You're on."

The team and I had a glass of wine before Jack Fino arrived. I an-nounced that Jack might be providing us our missing lawyer connection. "I don't want you to think I'm pressuring you. I want him to meet all of you. Be-sides, you're familiar with my theories on meeting dynamics. With you here, it's five against one."

"Mario knows this," Jo said to Pixie and Letty. "We have a staff of nine. We're not working alone. We already planned to come back whenever we're needed. We hired Angie as our assistant manager, as a back-up to take our place if we need to be out. She's good and she's hungry and..." she looked both ways and put her finger in front of her mouth, and her voice dropped to a stage whisper. "...we poached her from TPI."

"She's experienced, she's quick to pick up our style, and she's almost as bossy as Jo is. We never really left," Niley said. "We'd still be coming here every day for karate if someone wasn't so paranoid about it."

Someone my ass. She was staring straight at me.

"So what? I worry. Don't forget Oscar was shot and the crime has not been solved. I don't want you hurt."

"Mario makes me call when I get home, like I'm his teenaged daughter. He doesn't care that I'm carrying a .45 in my purse to defend myself." Pixie laughed. "What I really want to do is forget the drive home and do everybody tonight."

Jo and Niley gave each other a high five.

"Boss said we'd have a fucking good time after the lawyer left," Niley put one arm over Jo's shoulder, and the other over Pixie's. She was beaming.

"Cool," Pixie said. "I have the hots for you, Niley. I missed you."

"You have the hots for everybody, Pix," Niley said, affectionately.

"So I do."

Letty walked in with a couple of bottles of wine she'd fetched from the cellar, and caught sight of the girls on the couch.

"What did I miss?"

"Party planning," Jo said, patting the cushion beside her.

Letty squealed, and they made room for her.

Seeing them like this gave me a testosterone jolt, in spite of the dark cloud hanging over me. Maybe it was time for me to start believing that no one was after me and my loved ones. Maybe it was time to accept that Oscar's killing had absolutely nothing to do with me. I was jazzed. Looking forward to the evening, I sat quietly and watched the girls and their planning. There's no fucking end to how they move me. All that was missing was Melina, but she hadn't confirmed she was going to be here.

Caro showed Jack Fino to the living room where we were seated.

Miguel had come out in his full chef regalia to serve the wine that Letty put on the sideboard. Jack accepted a glass of red from Miguel. Tricia walked in behind him.

"Join us, Tricia," I said.

Jo patted the seat next to her, and Tricia sat down.

I introduced the team.

"Do you all live here?"

"I wish," I said. "Jo and Niley are part of my team. Now they have a management company and handle my apartment rentals. They figured I had retired, and left me for more money." I chuckled.

"We've never really left," Jo said. "That's not even funny."

"We just wanted to be busy," Niley said.

"How many units do you have Mario?" asked Fino.

"Just over a thousand." I kept my facial expression neutral. I didn't want to sound like I was boasting. "I have buildings in South Pasadena, Monterey Park, Alhambra, and Montebello."

"Impressive," Fino said, taking a sip of wine. He was seated where I had been earlier, on a long suede tufted sofa, a twin of where we were all sitting, facing him. Between us was a huge glass top coffee table.

"Pixie and Letty are full-time, but if the case is big enough, Jo and Niley are available. Tricia here is a private investigator and my driver. In Puerto Rico, I have another private investigator and his wife who assist on most cases abroad."

"And some cases here," Jo said.

"Quite a team you have, Mario."

I heard a ring at the door, and Caro's footsteps to answer it. Melina stepped in carrying a dish she handed to Miguel as she walked in the room.

"I'm so glad you made it," I said, standing up and looking her over. She was wearing some kind of fitted suit, all in a fine suede that hugged every inch of her delicious self.

"I'm Melina," she said.

"Part of the team?" Jack asked.

"Well..." Melina said, slowly, drawing it out.

I stepped around the coffee table to get next to Melina, and hugged her to my side.

The girls chimed in before Melina got to whatever words she was going to say.

"She's his sweetheart," Pixie said.

"And his lawyer," Jo added.

"And she's got that ginormous place across the street," Letty said. "But it's not like she's a neighbor. They moved out here together, and got places across the street from each other."

Everyone looked at Niley, who looked like she was aggravated that she hadn't come up with something else about Melina, but then she said, "And you know Marron's markets? They're her."

Jack laughed, and bowed over her hand. "Pleased to meet you, Miss Marron. You are quite the loveliest market I've ever seen."

"It is good to meet you too. I just was passing through, but wanted to look you over, Mr. Fino. Make sure you do right by our Mario." She sounded so serious that I couldn't tell if she was kidding or not.

She turned to me. "Of course, I really do have to run. But Soledad made some peanut-butter and honey ice cream for you, and I wanted to bring it over. There are also some peanut butter cookies to crumble over the top of it."

"I am looking forward to it. Maybe I'll skip dinner and have it instead."

I excused myself and walked her to the car where Johnson was waiting outside. I gestured for him not to get out, and put my hand on the passenger door.

"I was planning to stay," she said, "Honest. But one of my managers had a heart attack on the job. I have to make a showing at the hospital, get to the store, tie up loose ends and re-order the ranks. Everyone goes up a rank, starting with assistant manager. Temporarily I think." She gazed off into mid-distance and tapped her chin, thinking. It took a second or two for her to realize she was still here, but as soon as she did, she stepped in my arms and she gave me a kiss that would keep me hard through dinner. I almost forgot where we were. When she ended the kiss, I turned to open the door, and she swatted my ass.

"Have fun tonight. I hear you've got a hell of a night coming."

"You're invited," I said hopefully.

"They'd never forgive me," she shook her head sadly, then laughed at herself. Then she was gone.

When I went back inside, Miguel announced that dinner was ready. We walked to the dining room.

"You have a beautiful home, Mario. Great taste."

"That's Melina's doing," I said. "She decorated."

I wasn't counting, but Jack Fino had four glasses of wine and a little port after dinner. He drank like a connoisseur. He was neither rushed nor a talker, though he seemed interested in everything we talked about. He laughed hard at some of Pixie's spontaneous jokes. We were all at ease. He'd been personable and likeable on our first meeting. On the basis of our two social meetings, I liked the man.

The conversation turned to the firm in Chicago that wanted to talk business with me. Fino assured me they could afford me. If it got too expensive for them, Fino's group would help them finance the new business.

"They are solid," Fino said. "They don't owe me any money, but I wish they did. That's your job." He laughed, but he wasn't really kidding.

Before Jack left, he invited all of us to dine at his home, soon.

We all walked him to his car. His driver jumped out of the car to open the door. A moment later we waved goodbye.

His driver pulled the car out, and the gate closed.

I looked at the girls, and they looked at me.

"That went well, don't you think?" I asked. "I think he provides us with a viable alternative for a lawyer. What do you think?"

No one answered. I looked from one set of sparkling eyes to the next.

"I thought he'd never leave," Pixie said.

They all had mischievous grins and impish expressions. I turned and started moving, but got tackled before I even made it to the house.

Chapter 24
Early October 1980
Leslie Gonor

Les Gonor was the senior partner of the Chicago law firm. He called me, and I agreed to meet with him. Five days later, early in October, Pixie and Letty traveled with me to Chicago, though they did not attend the meeting with Gonor. This was their first trip to Chicago, and they wanted to see the sights around our downtown hotel. I gave them spending money to go out and get jackets as their California systems weren't prepared for Chicago in September. They could have brought their minks, but it had been so nice back home that no one checked the weather.

It was not a huge firm, but they had aviation experience. The office was on a grand scale, but not as magnificent as Oscar's had been. Les Gonor was no wet-behind-the-ears kid. He had been practicing law for twenty-two years.

Closeted in a meeting room with Gonor and two partners, I sat facing big windows that overlooked the gray-skyed concrete forest that was Chicago. Gonor and his two partners were across the table from me, their backs to the view.

"Fino said we can trust you completely," Gonor said. He had to be in his fifties at least, but the thick black glasses he wore reminded me of Buddy Holly.

"Fino said the same about you."

"We need to know in advance how much we're going to pay per fatality that results from a plane crash. Fino has made it clear that you don't want anything on the backend. That's perfect for us."

It was a dicey question, but I didn't break a sweat. I'd been selling since I was ten years old.

"A fifty-year-old physician who dies will yield more compensation for the family than a fifty-year-old car salesman. That makes it difficult to pin a fixed amount on all decedents. You also have the situation of minors. The parent or parents will be paid very little for that kind of loss unless it's a single child. You have to figure that every soul sitting in a seat will not bring equal compensation of the person sitting beside him or her." I talked around the issue without ever saying flat out that it was all about income.

They would know this, but it was important that they know I know it too.

He wanted a flat formula. I gave them a different rule than what I'd used with Oscar. Instead of evaluating each case, I would get ten thousand[52] for each adult who died and five thousand[53] for a minor. If I had to associate a local lawyer where the crash occurred, the firm had to pay any upfront fees, and if we had a local attorney, he would get twenty or twenty-five percent of the attorney fees. I might have to negotiate a fee in order to get a local attorney to cooperate. European clients hiring my US attorney always felt better knowing there was a local attorney looking out for their interest.

I didn't close the deal during that first visit. We had a second meeting. At the third meeting, I reminded them about my expectations that their law firm would hire personnel to speak the language of the client. Client maintenance was important, especially with foreign clients.

"I know you didn't rise to the level of the success that I see without

---

[52] $10,000.00 in 1980 had the same buying power as $31,477.44 in 2017
[53] $5,000.00 in 1980 had the same buying power as $15,738.72 in 2017

properly taking care of business. It's easy to lose a case over bad communication. Whatever the cost is of having a translator always available to handle a phone call, it is worth the cost. There might be expenses or seed money, but we can discuss that if it comes up."

"All good points, Mario."

"There is no rush to make a decision. At the moment, I don't have a case to run to. Take your time. We don't have to cut a deal faster than you're comfortable with."

Gonor looked at his two partners who nodded at him. I'm used to reading the temperature of a room. It was obvious to me that they'd already decided this. "No reason to delay. We're in."

I shook hands all of them.

"That's our contract," I said. "You're friends with Jack Fino. This is what we need. A handshake."

"It's a pleasure," Gonor said. "We are going to do big things together."

"I'm sure. When we get back home, I will have one of my assistants, Pixie, call you. Please put her in touch with the person who will prepare retainers for us to take on a case. She will send you an example of what we've been using. You can decide the look and contents. Personalize it to your firm however you choose. The retainer should be both in English and the client's language. The retainers we have were prepared by Tom Jones. Fino told me you know him."

"We don't know him personally, but we know his reputation. The man is a real aviation wizard."

"He is," I agreed.

"I'll expect Pixie's call," said Gonor. "Whatever you need, you got. Let me know if you need funds up front against payment of what we will owe you."

"I've got it covered. All I want is the agreed amount when the case comes to you. I handle the rest unless it's a prepayment for a local lawyer. If something special comes up like a memorial, a special meeting, transportation to the site of the crash if we can't get the airline to cover it, I will let you know ahead of time."

We shook hands. We were all somber faced, but I could tell inside we were grinning fools, having secured points we all wanted with very little negotiation.

I took off on the four-block walk to my hotel and we left that night for Los Angeles.

In a taxi headed to the airport, Pixie complained, "We didn't even fuck."

I saw the taxi driver's eyes in the mirror. They got really big. There was no question but that the driver heard her.

"He's tired of us," Letty said.

"I love you both," I said. "I'm not tired of you."

I put my arms around them both. I turned left to Pixie first and kissed her deeply, then to my right and kissed Letty.

I felt hands grab me, but I wasn't about to let their mischief loose. It was night outside, and pretty dark in the back seat, but it's never that dark. The driver was watching us more than the road, reminding me a whole lot of Pixie at the wheel.

Pixie went home as soon as we got to LA. Letty was like a wife. She went to the guest room she used as hers, showered, and came out looking like we had not just returned from a long trip.

I called Jo and Niley to let them know I had a lawyer. I thanked them again for the great job they were doing with my apartments.

"If you need us, we're there. We have it covered here," Jo said.

"It's a good idea for you to have an Angie or more than one Angie to cover for you so you can have a life. But don't do it just because I'm going to yank you back here to go out on a case with me."

"I miss you, Boss," Jo said. "When can we roll around in bed again?"

"I'm recording this and plan to let TJ listen."

"Go for it," Jo said. "He'll want to come over too."

"I miss you," Niley said. "I love doing what I'm doing, but I miss you. And I'm still dazzled by that night after Fino left."

"You guys don't need an invite. Come over anytime. I didn't take away your keys. Love you, Niley, Jo."

I checked my watch, and headed up to my bedroom. From bed, I called Jason in London and gave him the Chicago firm's name.

"I don't know them, so they must not do too much aviation. It's not brain surgery unless they have to try the case."

"A friend recommended them. Told me they are solid."

"Now that you're looking for cases again, I'm here for you, Mario. I'll be in touch the minute I hear something."

"You're the man, my friend."

"Ditto," he said.

"That's my line."

I hung up, switched on the television, and Letty padded in, naked except for her giant rabbit paw slippers. She was an animal lover, so they were made of fake fur, but they looked real, if rabbits were five-foot seven and a hundred and ten pounds.

"Where am I sleeping?"

"Where else? Get your pretty ass over here."

She parked her rabbits at the door. I held up the comforter up, and in a split second she slipped in.

"You smell so good," I said, hugging her.

Pixie and Letty got back into the swing of searching newspapers for small aircraft crashes. The conference table in my home office was still perfect for the girls to spread out their newspapers. Gonor wasn't limiting us to airline crashes, so they were searching for broader possibilities. I covered the bases from New York, Miami, Houston, San Francisco, Los Angeles and Chicago, but I admit I got distracted because I still enjoyed the miscellaneous sale items, and I had a tremendous appetite for finding properties that fit what LAI was looking for.

Finding a property was not the hard part. Finding a seller that would accept cash or most of the sale price in cash – that was the hard part. I'd been finding small apartment complexes, but I was still on the lookout for one bigger than the high rise in Westwood.

"I got a helicopter in Frisco," Pixie said.

"Didn't you get one before up there?" I asked.

"That was a crop duster. Niley and I went up to sign a crop duster, but it wasn't in Frisco."

"Pixie, you're so smart," Letty said sarcastically.

"Bitch," Pixie struck back.

"Girls behave. Work the helicopter case, Pixie. It's good practice. Check with the coroner's office."

"I know, Boss, I know, already."

Within a week, Pixie and Letty signed two widows who had lost their husbands in a chopper that had lost power and dropped out of the sky. It had been a charter flight taking them to the airport.

"I don't know how you got it so fast," I told Pixie. "It's best not to talk to families that fast. Best let them bury their loved ones first."

I had said this before; they both knew this, but I repeated it anyway.

"We didn't solicit them at all. We attended a vigil, got to know the wives, and then you know the rest. They liked us."

"And they needed money," Letty said. "We gave them five hundred each to help them out, and bought their coffee at the pancake house."

"In that case, perfect."

"Gonor took care of their end. They sent us the retainer overnight by American Airlines cargo courier. He also sent some blanks, you know, like we used to do the PI cases, where we can fill in the information about the crash. He said it doesn't have to be typed out."

I watched Pixie, feeling proud. She'd come a long way from the pregnant illiterate teenager I'd brought home to my aunt. I could tell Letty looked up to her. Pixie loved being top dog, and sometimes I could see her pretending to be Jo. She and Letty argued a lot, but it was mostly banter. It was their thing. Because Pixie had been trying to beat Jo's tight budgeting, they had stayed in a cheap hotel, and they'd eaten fast food without passing the expense on to me. I only knew about the costs because while they were bickering, Letty called Pixie a tightwad. There was practically no overhead on this one, especially compared to those fancy European hotel bills.

"So, are you going to fuck us as a reward or what?" Letty asked.

They both started making sexy faces at me—or maybe it was just faces they thought were sexy, shoving each other out of the way.

"You nervy bitch. You got him every night."

"I'm going to do more than fuck you," I said.

I ran to the bedroom and they ran behind me.

The next day, I told Gonor, "I have no clue yet what caused this crash. Not sure if I should charge you as much as an airline death. With an airline, we know you're going to collect no matter whose fault it is."

Gonor laughed.

"This is the same. These two men chartered the helicopter to take them to the airport. They have insurance to cover the cost. Whatever you do, don't sign the pilot's family. It could be a conflict."

"I wasn't thinking," I said with some embarrassment. "Of course we have a good case no matter what. No worries about the pilots."

"Good boy," Gonor said, "Courier the retainers. I'll send you a check for twenty grand."[54]

---

[54] $20,000.00 in 1980 had the same buying power as $62,954.89 in 2017

I couldn't remember anyone calling me 'boy' before. Kid, but not boy. It made me feel like a golden retriever, but he could call me anything he wanted, especially when he was sending a check for twenty grand.

"Sure," I said, "I'm not worried about the money. I appreciate it."

"I'm the grateful one," said Gonor. "Stay in touch."

Pixie put together the paperwork and took it to air cargo at LAX the next day. The package had pictures of the widows and their families, birth certificates, marriage certificates, birth certificates of three children for one decedent and two children for the other. Normally, families didn't have this documentation readily available, but I figured that Pixie had something to do with prying this out of them. She'd saved the lawyers some legwork. Upon receipt, Gonor would be in touch with the two families, assign the case to an attorney, and the case would be off and running. I had to give Pixie props for getting the paperwork early. I gave the girls a well-deserved bonus of one thousand[55] each. I didn't wait until the check arrived, but just gave them the cash, which I rarely do. At the moment, I had a whole bunch of cash in my safe. I don't mean the Camacho cash either.

"I love working for you, Boss, and I love when you pay me in green," Pixie said.

"Remind you of when you were a corner girl?" Letty asked.

"You bitch!"

I punched the intercom and got the kitchen involved. Two cups of herbal tea, and one tray of Miguel's goodies had them purring like kittens, then they settled down, and got back to work. The crumbs were cleared when I was at the conference table checking foreclosures, and saw Letty on the phone talking to someone.

"Family?"

"One of the widows," she whispered with her hand over the phone. When she hung up, she called the other widow.

---

[55] $1,000.00 in 1980 had the same buying power as $3,147.74 in 2017

"Nice of you to stay in touch," I said after she hung up. "But it's not always possible."

"I know, Boss, but these women are right here in California. Pixie and I got close to them."

I kissed the top of her head.

"I saw you do this all the time when we had forty new cases a week. Where've you been, Boss?"

She was right.

"Proud of you, kiddo," I told her.

Jack Fino invited us to his home for a late lunch that Saturday. Melina couldn't come with us. I know Saturday is a busy day for her, but wondered if it was like when she declined when Camila was around. At least she'd met Fino. Anyway, Jo, Niley, Pixie and Letty were with me in my Rolls with Tricia behind the wheel.

Fino's house sat way back from the street so you couldn't see it. I didn't tell the girls that Tricia had driven me by here the day I met him for lunch. His place, like mine, had a long driveway. It was a Mediterranean villa, beautiful but the exterior walls needed some love. Or maybe it was supposed to look distressed. If Melina had come with us, she'd have known. I didn't know where the old house ended and the remodel began. A housekeeper let us in. We followed her through a huge entry with ceilings taller than mine, took a three-minute walk through a living room, and game room, passing a kitchen somewhere on the right side. We passed through a tall glass door that led outdoors. One center of attraction was a huge pool, nestled amongst tall oak trees, but I was more impressed with the big gazebo built of pink stone and stucco. The eight supports of the gazebo were not entirely surrounded by open walls. Two of them at opposite ends were solid stucco, with portions painted Mediterranean gold, and others left as bare weathered wood. The slick red tiled roof was gorgeous against the sandy texture and color variations of the pink stone.

The corners were massive stacked rectangles of sandstone or granite. As we walked into the friendly shade under the roof, I felt the breeze from a ceiling fan that turned in a leisurely fashion. I could hear and smell meat sizzling on the grill and see sweating wine bottles chilling in silver ice buckets on a built-in counter. A woman in a chef's coat was moving down the row of wine bottles, one by one, spinning them in the ice buckets. The aroma caught my attention too. Succulent.

Jack was standing at a grill built into one long wall. The opposite wall housed a fireplace, and in between was a long table, at least twenty feet long. It appeared to be made of a single piece of gray and white marble polished like glass and set atop a stuccoed base. I wondered how anyone could transport a piece of marble of that size, and thought of Camila's stone import business. There were just enough wrought iron chairs for us to use. The extras—there had to be more for a table so big—had been whisked away somewhere unseen. The result felt surprisingly cozy and welcoming.

Jack said, "Make yourself at home. I'll be right with you. Park yourselves around that table."

"This place is spectacular," I said. "I'd swear we're in old Italy."

Jack smiled. I could see how much he loved this place.

"You been to Italy?"

"I sure have," I replied. "I loved it." I felt a pang, remembering Venice and Fae. I could never think of Venice where I had found her, nor of Rome where I'd lost her.

He wore a white apron, and pointed out the table with a pair of chef's tongs. He was cooking.

"Can we help?"

"I got it." The female cook who'd turned the champagne took over. She put her hand out.

Jack relinquished his tongs and walked over to us.

"We have steaks on one grill. Fish and chicken on the other two."

I could see the sections he was referring to, though it was really one huge grill nearly as long as the table.

"I wasn't sure what your pleasure might be. If any of you are vegetarian, we'll have to work it out." He hugged the girls as though he'd known them for a long time, and he shook my hand.

"Beautiful place, Jack,"

"You're the one with the beautiful place," he said. "I haven't done much here in years."

"Big house," Niley said, looking over to the main building.

"I think it's about the size of Mario's, but not as beautiful."

"You're too modest," I said.

"Somewhere in all that rock is the house my parents owned," he said.

Within twenty minutes of our arrival, we were drinking and eating. Jack had taken off his apron.

"Who lives here with you?" I asked.

"Four macaws, two cats and two dogs."

He cut into his ribeye. Like mine, the inside of his slice was perfectly rare.

Pixie liked hers as well. I was afraid at any minute she'd scream that she was coming. Not that she's actually orgasmed from food before, but with Pixie, you never can tell. Letty's eyes had practically rolled back in her head.

"I think the girls like the steak," I said. "No vegetarians in the bunch."

I recalled he'd already told me there was no wife. Apparently, Pixie didn't. Or maybe she was making conversation.

"No Mrs. Fino?" Pixie asked.

"None," he said. "I do have three housekeepers, a cook and a driver. They live back there." He jerked his head in the direction opposite the street, but I saw nothing. "I won't deny I thought about marrying my cook. But she doesn't get along with the birds."

It was impossible to tell if he was kidding.

He pointed past a football field of grass where there were taller oak trees. "Behind the trees there are quarters where they live."

His setup was like mine. You couldn't see the building where the help lived. Like Melina, he was alone, but then, I have my team. I wondered who he had. Maybe the cook he'd mentioned. I was kicking myself for not paying attention to her when she'd been by the grill tending the meat.

We didn't talk very much business while eating, but afterward, Fino and I took a short walk around the grounds.

"I'm a good criminal lawyer," Fino said, "but Oscar was king. He had the ability to sway a jury over his way. I've seen hard-nosed judges take his side on cases that were totally questionable. When I started loaning money out to lawyers and put the group together, Oscar was an investor. He raked in big bucks from heavy criminals who hired him or in some cases hired me. Many times when I couldn't cut a deal with the prosecutor, I'd give the case to Oscar to try the case. He was a lovely friend. I will miss him."

He sounded so sincere that my theory that Fino had offed Oscar to get his five million decayed even more.

"Jack, so how did Oscar go from being an investor to a borrower?"

"He slacked off on his criminal practice, spent a fortune in rent to be in that showy office building and he got into personal injury. PI is a path to destruction. Branching into aviation cost him a fortune. Not just to pay you. His overhead got immense in a short time. You know those cases take forever to settle."

"I feel partially responsible. He paid me a lot of money."

"Tom has millions and millions of dollars worth of cases that you brought them. If he can weather the storm, the firm will have deeper pockets than you can imagine. It may take a few years, but I have high hopes. Tom Jones is one smart cookie."

"Oscar was also smart."

"Oscar stopped being smart when he switched his practice after all those years of doing criminal work and taking on PI. Every lawyer that owes me money is a PI lawyer."

We stopped walking for a few minutes and sat on a bench along the path.

"Jack, you sound like you hate PI. And that's what I do."

"I love PI, because lawyers are pushed to borrow from me. They max out at the bank and I'm the last resort. Let me tell you something. Most of the borrowers see it through. They pay me off and tell me to fuck off because my interest rates are too fucking high. I wanted Oscar to be one of these lawyers, but someone took him out before he could turn around."

I didn't say anything for at least a minute, and neither did Fino.

"Damn. Sometimes I feel like I helped him go down."

I thought how Oscar had chased me to send him business. "You know before we ever met in person, he offered me five thousand dollars just to meet with him. I did meet him, but I didn't take his money. I didn't know if it meant I was going to owe him something."

"Nonsense, Mario. You had nothing to do with it. He was doing PI before you two cut a deal. I know."

"An old friend of mine, Carson was sending him business before I came along but I don't think it was very much business."

I took a deep breath and asked what I had to ask. "I heard you got the money he owed you through a life insurance policy."

"Yes, five million. I didn't kill him, Mario."

He said it casually, as if it was a question he'd heard before.

"Of course not," I said. We continued to walk the grounds.

"Am I overstepping to ask what your business is with Pepe?"

"Not at all. I met Pepe when he was in trouble and Oscar was representing him. Oscar got him off. You probably know this?"

"I do."

"He went back to Colombia. And he hasn't been back since. He thinks they might arrest him again."

"Would they?"

"I can't imagine why, but it was a bad time for him. I understand his caution. Anyway, I told you that when I make a loan part of the money is mine and forty percent or so comes from a pool of money put in there by investors like Pepe. I have an aunt in Mexico who is also an investor. Not really an aunt, just a close friend of the family, used to work for a banker here in California."

"I see."

"And by the way, you can tell Pepe I told you this. It's not a secret."

"Jack, I had no right dropping that question on you. Sorry."

"Ask me anything. If I can't answer the question, I'll tell you so."

"Got it."

I realized this must be another way for Pepe to dump cash then get paid by check. I didn't know how it worked, but knowing what I knew of Pepe's business affairs, I was probably right.

Chapter 25
October 1980
Chicago Crash

As soon as I picked up the phone, Jo started in. I could tell by the lack of a hello and the excited timbre of her voice that this was about work, and it was going to be big. I was on my feet before she'd gotten the full sentence out.

"Newsbreak on television. LA-bound plane down in Chicago. Big one."

"On it. Baby, thank you."

I ran the whole way to my office and turned the television on.

"Letty," I said on the intercom broadcasting to the whole house. I didn't know what room she was in. "Come to my office."

She came at a run wearing an apron, and half-covered in flour, smelling of chocolate chip cookies.

"What is it?"

"Tell Pixie to come over. This is a big one."

We both turned to the television. Local newscasters were making small talk, then the screen shifted to pictures of the crash in Chicago. It was a night scene. The newscaster was standing in front of a taped-off area buzzing with official vehicles. Not much could be seen now, but earlier shots of smoke and flames, and plane wreckage were mixed into the feed. US news was always sanitized. They never show plane crash remains on live TV, at least not that I'd ever witnessed. European TV doesn't sanitize. The gore is all there.

Letty saw the images. Her hand rose to cover her mouth, leaving a smudge of white powder on her cheek.

"Where is this?"

"Chicago."

We stood silently watching one shot after another of destruction, of the fire, of the plane crumbling. It was US TV so there was the occasional glimpse of a gurney, but no bodies. European television was much more graphic, but I didn't miss the gore. The sound was off, but the images spoke louder than anything a newscaster could come up with.

Letty tore her attention from the footage, and said, "I'll call."

"Wait up," I said. I rubbed my thumb against her cheek, wiping off the flour. She flushed and looked down at the white powder on my thumb, then picked up the phone and dialed. Before it rang, she said softly, "Cookies. Some chocolate chip. Some peanut butter."

I gave her a thumbs up, and parked myself in a comfortable chair in my office for the inevitable phone calls. Everyone who knows me contacts me when they hear about a crash. They call in. I call out, too. In preparation for the trip to the airline's hotel, a stream of calls pave the way. This case was no different. I started off with a call to my aunt, letting her know I would be off to Chicago soon.

An hour after Jo called, Jason told me, "I don't have the manifest yet, but I can get it for you pretty fast. My bet is that most of the passengers lived in Los Angeles."

"Jason, Thanks. I appreciate you doing what you can. US rules are strict. We can't do anything right away, but I want to be ready."

Camila called when she heard about the crash.

"Let me know where you will be. I'll come to Chicago."

"Be great to see you."

Olga called from Germany as soon as she heard. "Please stay in touch with me. I know you will be headed to Chicago."

"Three or four days from now we'll leave. Count on me being in touch. I'll let you know where we're staying soon as I know."

"Amor, I'll try to do a landing in Chicago if you have time. You'll come and spend a few hours at the airport, yes?"

"Never too busy for you, Olga."

"*Me encanta cuando me llamas por mi nombre.*" [56]

"*Mi Olga preciosa.*" [57]

The news on television provided great coverage, but it was the inside information from Jason that was the foundation of the work. Pan Am's courier service delivered Jason's package. In what was only a few days after the crash, I was holding the manifest in my hand, along with contact information of the next of kin.

I told the girls, "The families of the victims who lived in Los Angeles or surrounding areas will be asked if they want to travel to Chicago and be put up in a hotel. You know the drill. In the next two days, the families will be in Chicago."

I called Puerto Rico. Juan was available.

"In the next couple days, you need to get to Chicago," I said. "Can you get away?"

"Anything you want, Boss. Yes, of course."

"You haven't met Tricia yet. She will be along on this trip."

Jo and Niley called from the management office. "We can go with you if you need us." Jo said.

"Got it covered, Babies," I said. I told them to stay put, but I wasn't kidding. I was ready to call them if we needed them.

Before we left for Chicago, Tom Jones called to give me advice. The cases would be going to Gonor in Chicago but Tom was still around for me.

---

[56] I love it when you call me by my name.

[57] My precious, Olga.

"Be careful. You know the rules in the US are different from those outside the country."

Tom was referring to soliciting the families of victims, a big no no. This was not the first US aviation case we'd handled. Thanks to Tom and Jason, I knew the rules and I could talk like an aviation expert though I had a long way to go. Tom Jones and Jason were my guardian angels. I wished that the cases could come to Oscar's former firm, but Tom was just beginning to dig out of the pit that Oscar had left them in. I really didn't know if Tom was digging out or not. I hoped he was.

Before leaving, I talked to Les Gonor, the senior partner of the firm. Gonor's office, where the cases were going, was in Chicago, convenient for getting retainers and anything else we might need from them. I had given them a number of small plane crashes across the country, but this was our first big commercial crash with them.

"It will be a big change for us since it's right in your backyard. Most of the passengers are from Los Angeles and a number of other cities." He didn't ask where I'd gotten my facts, and I didn't tell him that Jason had sent me the manifest, which details information the passenger had given the airline like departure, residence, next of kin, phone numbers, etc.

I was taking Tricia with me, leaving the house unguarded. Melina didn't gloat at all when I asked her to get me two guards to work twelve hour shifts sitting near the front entrance of the house. I wanted the house and, of course, the cash in the safes to be safe. She had stopped asking me about the cash. I believe her concern really had been for the danger she thought I was exposing myself to by holding on to house money, but now that I was working with LAI, she knew that Pepe Camacho and his family were a part of my life. We just avoided that topic.

Pixie arranged for our meeting reservations at the hotel. She enjoyed having charge of what Jo usually did for the team. "It's too soon to arrange for conference rooms," Pixie said. "But I already checked and they have a great selection of rooms and plenty of optional packages for catering."

By the time Pixie, Letty, Tricia and I took off for O'Hare airport, Juan was already in Chicago poking around the hotel where the families of victims were arriving. He was not to make contact with anyone unless he saw a Hispanic, preferably a Puerto Rican that looked lost and needed his help.

We got to our rooms. Their rooms were all connected to my suite. We used my den as a home base, went to bed early, and in the morning I briefed the girls. They'd all heard it before, but it felt good to get back to the familiar routine. The living arrangements were new to Tricia, though she'd assisted on a case or two.

"We get into the hotel where the families are. We get familiar. We don't hide our identities. We don't lie that we're a family member of someone that died in the crash. After a couple days, we will feel comfortable to befriend whoever needs comfort. After the funerals, we will know a lot of family members. We'll know better what to do. We may wait to see the families when they get back to their homes, especially those from LA. From the manifest, it appears that there are a hundred and ten decedents from Los Angeles proper. And remember this. We can never get used to the sadness of dealing with families of victims. Being sensitive to the families is the only way to handle it. The reward of the work is helping the families. That is the part of the job that we can love. Remember the family needs to hire a lawyer because the airline operator has powerful lawyers. Days and weeks from now, when it is finally time, when you've made a connection, tell them the lawyer they hire does not have to be the lawyer I am recommending, as long as their lawyer is an aviation specialist."

"Got it, Boss," Pixie said.

I gave them a thousand dollars each in cash.

As she put the money in her purse, Letty said, "We don't buy cases but if we feel someone needs financial help, we give them some green."

"Good girl," I kissed the tops of their heads as we walked out the door.

"Took the words right out of my mouth."

Tricia had worked the Las Vegas case with me so she wasn't quite a newbie. I'd had her investigate several local cases, so she knew the US rules concerning what we can and can't do with families of victims.

"Hang with Pixie and Letty," I said.

"Will do."

We entered the elevator. Standard hotel elevator. One floor down, an elderly couple joined us, riding down to breakfast.

"Good morning," I said.

She was in a housecoat, and he was wearing what Pixie called a wife-beater and jeans. They were both in slippers. "Good morning," the man said. "I hope there are waffles. Do you think they have waffles?"

"I don't know. It's our first morning here."

"They heat the syrup," the man said.

Pixie eyed the couple, and in a loud voice, told Tricia, "I'll teach you everything honey, but you may have to go down on me in installments."

Tricia was used to Pixie by now. "You got it."

We got out on the ground floor. The couple were gasping in shock, mumbling to each other. They hurried away to the free breakfast in one of the hotel restaurants.

"She's putting you on," Letty said with a laugh.

"If she is, I'll kick her ass."

"No you won't," Tricia said. "I think it's time I check your pussy out."

"I just came," Pixie announced.

"Fucking drama queen," Letty said.

We headed toward our hotel's exit to catch a cab. Letty and Tricia wanted to walk the two blocks to the other hotel, but Pixie was in heels. I kept my mouth shut. The heels usually go away after a few days without my having to say a word.

The girls got in the back. I got in front, and gave the cabbie our destination, then turned in my seat.

"Ladies, please. Don't scare the locals."

Pixie put on a pouting face. They all laughed, and everyone but Pixie agreed to try not to say anything too scandalous.

Pixie was running the team show now, and had her own mindset about dress. She preferred dressing casually. I wasn't sure that would be best overall, but in Chicago for this case, it was okay. It made the girls seem more approachable; and the passengers were largely used to LA casual style anyway. Pixie and Letty wore jeans and blouses that were tucked in, no belly buttons showing. Pixie insisted on designer shoes and bags, but I think that was a concession to her shopping addiction. None of the purses ever matched the magic of Jo's bottomless bags, however.   Tricia always wore a business suit, nice stuff, not designer, but with her military bearing, she wore what she wore very well. In California, her jacket concealed the gun that she carried on her left side. Neither Pixie or Tricia had permits to carry a concealed firearm in Chicago. Letty still did not have a gun permit in California, but she was still working on it.

I felt pretty casual in a two-piece suit and dress shirt. No tie.

The hotel where the families were staying was filled to capacity. Getting in the hotel was no problem, but areas where the families had their meetings with the airline's speakers were restricted to families who had credential badges. Those badges gave them carte blanche. Family members wearing them got them anything they wanted in whatever hotel restaurant they chose whenever they chose. And there were a lot of restaurants and bars to choose from.

Juan was staying without Valita, alone at a nearby hotel.

"I talked to a family that live in Chicago but are from Puerto Rico."

"Juan, you can't solicit."

"I didn't solicit. We are just talking. They know I'm a private investigator in Puerto Rico and that I work for a lawyer, nothing more. No discussion about nothing."

Juan had done well for me in the past using his own rules. Still, I was responsible that the lawyer I worked with never got hit with a solicitation slam from the state bar or from anyone.

While I was working, I would check myself in whatever mirror was convenient to make sure I was still looking professional. I wasn't the wrinkle-bomb Pixie could be on occasion, but I am a huge guy with biceps squeezed into the sleeves of an expensive suit. With the coat unbuttoned, the fine shirt hinted at the definition of my stomach and chest. I am a big dude and I found myself buttoning to look more professional, and unbuttoning to look less bulky.

The girls and I touched base frequently. When we got tired, needed a break or a strategy session, we'd find each other and walk back to our hotel for a little while, then return. That first day, I walked back with Pixie. She said her new heels had given her a blister and switched to flats.

One of the family members stared at me every time she saw me. I returned eye contact with eye contact, and smile with smile, not flirtatiously. On the third day, I introduced myself. She gave her name as Eleanor, and she was forty-five. Her hair was brown, styled in a beehive. She had brown glasses that hung around a chain when she wasn't wearing them. Her features looked careworn. We had coffee together.

"My husband died in the plane crash."

We didn't need badges to recognize the family members. They were the ones who were crying, or a wreck, or talking in low tones and wandering around in a stupor. Eleanor was one of the latter. She was slow and depressed, and probably lonely. I spent two hours talking with her about her three daughters at home, ages five, six and seven. She was from West Los Angeles, near Hollywood. Her husband had been forty-seven and worked for a company that made movie props. They owned their home. She wasn't sure how she would make the mortgage payment, and what the airline was going to pay her for the loss of her husband.

I just listened.

On our third chance meeting, Eleanor waved me over to the coffee shop. We had coffee and a slice of apple pie. Mine was à la mode with two scoops. Hers was straight up.

She sipped coffee. "I talked so much yesterday. I never asked you who you lost in this tragedy."

I told her the truth. "I didn't lose anyone, thank God. I work with lawyers who handle plane crash accidents and personal injury."

She had a few questions. She wondered again about her bills, and how the airline would pay.

"Are you here recruiting clients?" she asked.

"No. It is too soon. Maybe that will come later, but we're just having coffee and pie." I hate the word recruiting, but I didn't correct her.

I looked at her untouched slice of apple pie, and pushed it gently in her direction, and gave her a little encouraging pat on the hand. She started on her pie. I saw some tears.

On the fifth day of our acquaintance, Eleanor insisted that she wanted to go after the airline for taking away the father of her children. I handled this differently than ever before. Gonor's office was so close to the hotel that we walked over. I called in advance.

"I can sign her," I told Gonor. "But it would be nice if she met her attorney. Believe me, she pushed me. I encouraged her to wait until after the funeral."

Eleanor signed a retainer. Before long we were back at her hotel, and she called me over in the lobby to introduce family members of three decedents. Again, I explained it should wait. The family members lived in Chicago. The next day they walked over to Gonor's office and signed retainers.

Pixie and Letty started collecting contact information for family members that they talked to. They confided who they were, and how they helped families of victims. The way it works, you walk around, sit around, and eventually a man or a woman or a couple will approach you and ask who you are, if you lost someone on the plane. You get friendly. You never lie. Never.

Pixie sent Letty on her way alone and did the same with Tricia after several days. Tricia got buddy-buddy with two families that didn't want to wait.

"You did great, Tricia," I told her. "Good job for only being here a week."

"I feel like I know what I'm doing. I didn't do so bad in Vegas. Remember the tourist helicopter where I got the two families from across the country."

"You did, Baby. I know you're good at whatever you are given to do."

We were bundled up in coats and sweaters. November in Chicago gets pretty cold, but the walk wasn't far and got my blood moving. The first thing I noticed when we were in the warmth of our hotel lobby was turkey. The whole lobby smelled like Thanksgiving dinner. Sage and cinnamon. I felt a sudden nostalgia. I missed my aunt. I missed Melina. I missed home.

"Are you game for hotel sweet potatoes?" I asked Pixie. She had a persistent sweet tooth, and I know she loved sweet potato casserole with marshmallows roasted on top. Waiting for the elevator, I noticed that no one seemed to feel much like talking except Tricia, who was excited over a new client she thought she could sign.

"Not really," Pixie said, not even tempted. "We've got cold cuts and sandwich fixings in the room fridge. I'm not really interested."

We returned to the room in silence. Pixie brought the condiment packets to the table. Tricia brought the tray of meat and salad fixings, and the loaf of bread. Without a word, they formed an assembly line, putting together sandwiches and putting them in the center of the table. I pulled a six-pack of cola from the tiny refrigerator. We all took a seat. Then the phone rang.

"I'll get it," she said, with the first animation I'd seen in hours.

It was Lainey. Pixie curled up on the couch beside the phone, paper plate on her lap, laughing and talking for half an hour. The television was on, and Letty got up to turn the sound off so Pixie could hear, or maybe because Letty wanted to listen in. I realized what the problem was. I pulled out my credit card, and handed it to Pixie. She put her hand over the phone.

"Boss?"

"Tell Lainey to set us places for dinner. When you hang up, get us round trip tickets. First flight you can get. Let's go home for Thanksgiving."

On Thanksgiving Day, we celebrated at my aunt's house. I gave the home staff a paid long weekend off to have their own shindig back in their quarters.

Johnson drove us in Melina's Mercedes limo. Pixie and Lainey were already at my aunt's when we arrived. We'd tried to talk her into coming with us, but Tricia had stayed in Chicago, planning on Thanksgiving dinner at the hotel with the husband of one of the decedents. He was a retired military man.

I waited as the girls walked up the steps, then invited Johnson in.

He smiled at me, embarrassed, and stood stiffly in his chauffeur's uniform.

"I can't impose on a family gathering, Boss."

"C'mon man. It's no imposition. You are family." Johnson was probably the first person who had started calling me Boss. We'd been friends ever since he'd held a security job at Bunker Hill Towers. I almost wanted to sit inside the car with him instead of going inside. He assured me he was fine. I had sympathy for him and went inside.

Melina saw me come in alone.

"Where's Johnson?"

"He doesn't want to come in."

Melina had been sitting down, but I could see she was displeased. She stood up.

"We'll see about that."

When she went outside, I felt a little sorry for Johnson, but I wanted him to come in too, so not too sorry.

"How many places to set?" Lainey asked, her hands full with one place setting she'd just removed from the table. Jo and Niley and their families were doing their own thing in their home.

"Everyone who is here plus one more," I said, pointing outside. There was a good bit of noise going on but everyone got quiet. Melina's voice carried.

"We have a place for you at the table, and you know damn well you are part of this family. Get your ass in there. The food is getting cold and everyone is waiting on you."

Lainey put the place setting back on the table. We all heard Melina go off on him. Johnson joined us after all. He loosened up, and ate heartily, laughed and seemed to enjoy our company. A question went around the table, everyone saying what they were most thankful for. When it got to me, I said I was thankful for the health, prosperity and companionship of everyone sitting at the table.

I looked down the table. Jo was having Thanksgiving with TJ. Niley and her kids were over there. I'd been the walking wounded lately, feeling deep anguish after dealing with the loss of Sami and Oscar, and the crash families we'd been meeting every day. *Everyone in this room* was my family. Somehow having everyone here was healing the ache. Lainey read something she and my aunt had conjured up, something hokey about gatherings, and families being about love rather than blood, and how our hearts were big enough to hold one more. The words made me tear up. Then we all held hands, bowed our heads, and said a private blessing. My eyes met Melina's, and she squeezed my hand. I knew what she was thankful for.

It was good to be home, even if we were flying back to Chicago in the morning.

Back in Chicago, we went straight to work. Tricia welcomed us with another retainer. She'd gotten to be friends with a widower who brought her more local families. She'd caught on quickly.

The bodies were so badly burned that identification was close to impossible, but eventually identifications were made. Many families went home early to accompany the remains of their loved ones for burials, but most stayed at the hotel for a month before going home. Pixie made three trips to Los Angeles to accompany families. Letty made four trips. Tricia stayed busy in Chicago and so did I. Every meeting was one on one. I never held a group meeting. In the thirty-four days since the tragedy, we signed sixty-five families, twenty-two from Chicago and forty-three from the Los Angeles area. Sixty days after the tragedy, our signed count was a hundred-forty-one families from across the United States.

Pixie and Letty took an emotional beating in that case. Tricia handled four cases on her own. She said she probably could have done better, but she didn't want to cross any lines. Pixie and Letty went to funerals, Letty to Montana, Arizona, Wyoming, and Missouri; Pixie to South Carolina, Florida, Louisiana and Texas. I was proud of Pixie for running the show, and of Letty who wasn't a greenhorn anymore. She handled herself like a pro. I was proud of Tricia for catching on so fast.

I don't know who was happiest with the new cases, Gonor, Jack Fino, or me. Pixie and Letty were too worn out to be happy, but ten days after we had returned home, I gave each a hefty check that sure perked them up.

"I had no idea how hard this job is," Tricia confided to me. "I didn't realize there was such emotional wear and tear. You get to know the families, and you really feel their losses. It's sad, and it's painful, and you wish you could do magic and give them their sister back. Or their brother. Or their children."

"Stay home a few days," I told her. "Relax. Get over the jet lag. Do what makes you happy. Don't come back to work until you feel better."

As I suggested, Tricia went home to her apartment to recuperate. I wasn't expecting her back for a week at the least. She was back working foreclosures on the third day.

I gave her a hefty check as well. She would be making more on aviation than I paid her to be my driver and everything else she did, if I could keep up the pace. I felt guilty that Jo and Niley were not sharing in the pot of gold, but their share of the management fees was substantial.

Jack Fino knew how many cases we'd signed, but wanted to hear in detail how it had gone in Chicago with Gonor. I'd been home for several days before we met for lunch and talked.

"Jack, as you know, getting the cases in the door is only part of the work. Gonor has his hands full with just this case. I hope he has the personnel. Clients will be calling, and there is a lot of client maintenance. I told him this, but you may want to make suggestions."

"Gonor is a doer. He'll get with it."

"Will he be able to handle another big one?"

"Don't worry about Gonor. I got his back."

A week later, we met again. Pretty soon, our meals were a thing. He was much older, but the age difference didn't affect our friendship. I had the feeling he had a whole lot of acquaintances and business associates, but not a whole lot of friends. No matter the subject, Fino could talk and talk. His expertise and experience covered a lot of ground, including some hair-raising stories about some of his criminal clients, without naming names, of course. After a while, I felt I could level with him about some issues that bugged me. This thing with Pepe caused me some sleepless nights, wondering if I might be doing something that could get me into criminal trouble.

We were at The Tower for lunch, both of us sitting behind huge shrimp on shaved ice. Fino was dipping his in cocktail sauce. I had requested salsa instead. We were waiting for steaks, and I brought up what was for me a forbidden subject. I probably would have hinted around and never gotten to details, but he knew before I said.

"I'm not sure you know exactly what I do for LAI. And if you don't know, I'm not going to tell you."

"You buy buildings for LAI, and when you can, you use cash to pay the seller."

"You're a criminal lawyer. Am I doing anything illegal?"

There was a short pause, but it was not hesitation. He was eating. He wasn't as far along as I was. That's what happens when you go out to lunch, but you talk more than you eat. Usually he eats faster than I do, but while he was talking, I'd finished my shrimp.

"If there was an investigation, an aggressive prosecutor might make a big deal out of not using the internal revenue form that discloses transactions of ten thousand dollars or more. I wouldn't worry about it."

"I'm really not worried, but I have moments when I wonder."

"LAI has the source of the cash covered, should it ever come up." Fino's voice had changed.

I scrutinized his expression while trying to look nonchalant. He was confident in the LAI money stream. Olga had told me about withdrawals she made from banks in order to have receipts for large sums of cash on the plane in case it came up. I wondered how Fino was connected. It seemed obvious he would be, since he knew them through business. What kind of business though, I had no idea.

"Okay," I said. "I don't quite get it but I trust the Camachos."

"I'm here for you," Fino said. "I can't advise you, but if I had your opportunity, I'd go out and buy out everything I could. One day, those purchases will be more difficult, and the penalties will get stiffer. If a deal is real good and you need to wire funds, I'm certain LAI has no problem with that."

I nodded my understanding. Either Fino knew more about Camacho business than Oscar did, or his lips were just looser. Fino was straight forward and I didn't ask how he knew so much.

The waiter delivered our steaks, and I continued to eat. There was no more conversation about LAI, and the business I was doing for them.

"You are one of a kind," Fino said. "You have gift. People in need are drawn to you. Without you, lawyers would have no cases to handle. Some of these lawyers have no personality whatsoever, even if they can perform before a judge, and bring him to tears. In this business, you're a rare gem."

I laughed. "Come on Jack. I'm not the only source of new business. You're exaggerating."

"You may not be the only source, but you're the best. Gonor is so delighted with the cases you've turned over to him, there is nothing that man wouldn't do for you."

I had developed respect for Jack, and his compliments embarrassed me.

"I talk to him on the phone. He said he's hired two lawyers and three assistants to take the pressure off the staff he already had."

"That's right. I talk to him as well," Fino confirmed.

"I've been paid. He owes me nothing. I just hope he stays afloat. I hope he can afford those two lawyers and three assistants."

Fino laughed low, deep in his chest.

"That's no problem," Fino said. "The lawyers are established and bring a guaranteed following of clients with their own stream of revenue, and the three assistants are legal secretary interns studying to be lawyers at the University of Chicago School of Law."

I felt reassured by these details. I knew Oscar had never cut corners. He believed a good portion of his success meant that he had to look successful. Maybe he should have showed off less and budgeted more. But that had just been his way. My memories of Oscar were a pale shadow of the force he had been. Memories could not do justice to full impact of his big personality.

Jack finished chewing and gestured with his fork. "Personal injury attorneys run out of money. You'd be surprised how many of them start playing with the client trust account. You wouldn't believe how many come to me for help when they find themselves in deep shit. I suppose it's temptation. You have a bank account where you are depositing all the settlement money from cases. It grows and grows. If you slow down the distributions that need to be paid, the balance can be enormous depending on the size of the practice."

I believed him. I remembered my dear friend Jake whose death left his law firm buried in a mess.

I said, "Nothing about Oscar had ever revealed he'd been borrowing from Peter to pay Paul."

"Every lawyer knows if you fuck with a client trust account and get caught, you are out. Still, many do it," Fino said. "The smart ones pay their clients right away, and hold off paying doctors, hospitals, and other vendors. Companies are not likely to start inquiring about their money for a long time. Stupid lawyers don't pay their clients right away, and before they know it, the client complains to the state bar for not getting their settlement funds. Chaos strikes. Oscar paid his clients. I believe the money out of trust is mainly owed to doctors, hospitals and the like."

I knew Tom would have had to disclose everything in order to get that two million he borrowed.

Jack nudged me, and asked in a low voice, "Do you think our waitresses are sisters?"

To be honest, I hadn't been paying much attention to them. They were both light brunettes with tall beehive hair and identically dressed in the restaurant's short skirts. Their name tags had identical last names.

"Could be," I said when they came back to the table and refilled our water glasses together. The one by me filled Jack's glass, and Jack's waitress filled his. It seemed like sister schtick that probably got them good tips.

"Are you girls related?" I asked.

"Twins," one said, laughing.

I laughed back.

"What's so funny?" Jack asked when they left.

"Just thinking about twins," I said.

"Hmm," Jack said. "I guess with your looks, you get all the girls."

I don't think it's looks. I believe my attractiveness to the opposite sex has to do with being a big guy. It doesn't hurt that I have cash in my pocket, and I'm generous. That's what I think. But that's not what I said. All I said was, "Not my looks."

"Anything you care to tell?" Jack asked.

"There's nothing to tell," I said. Jack didn't push for more. His mind had already moved on. I didn't spill a word, because I don't talk to anybody but Melina about this kind of thing. I remembered the time I left Whisky A Go Go with twins. At the time, I hadn't been drunk, and was just feeling good. I made them a proposition that they accepted, and sat between them while Tricia drove us from the club to Pasadena. Nora and Laura handled me all the way home, and had an argument. What I remember most about the ride was how one of them said that I lived up to the tall dudes-huge cock myth, and the other said I was proof of big hands, big cock. I loved it, and wasn't complaining. I was hard under my boxers and slacks, and minded my manners. I didn't fondle them but thoroughly enjoyed their attention. They were tipsy, and dropped their jaws at the sight of the house. I sent Tricia home. As usual, Letty was nowhere in sight. If she heard me come home with someone, she would not surface.

They dropped their shoes and most of their clothes before we started the climb to my bedroom. At four, they called it a night. I found out they had office jobs that started at nine. After Tricia left to drive them home, Letty dropped into my bed. I nuzzled her ear and asked if she'd been watching. She'd said yes, but I think she said it just to get me excited. It worked.

"I love your breath when you breathe in my mouth like that," I said.

"Wrigley Spearmint," she said with a little laugh. Of course I knew it.

The twins at the restaurant brought dessert. I found their schtick tedious. They weren't half as sexy as Nora and Laura had been. But then they were working at the Tower as waitresses, not hanging out at Whisky A Go Go.

Jack had pie. I had ice cream. Our conversation shifted over to real estate investment, but I reflected later on one thing. My feelings about Jack had come a long way. I no longer felt he was connected with some insurance scam responsible for Oscar being killed.

Chapter 26
December 1980
Jet Set

I was at my desk reading the classified ads for the *NY Times*. Pixie was going through a stack of newspapers in search of small aircraft crashes. Jo and Niley were better at office stuff. Doing without them meant I had to work harder. I missed them. I was so accustomed to them, their absence felt like something major was missing. Some of the life had left the house.

Letty walked in, Miguel behind her with lunch.

"Homemade goodies," Letty said. "Nachos, soft beef tacos, soft chicken tacos, refried beans and four different salsas."

Miguel set it up at the opposite end of the conference table away from where Pixie was working.

"I'm so hungry," I said, taking a seat at the head of the table. "This is a snack?" I laughed, pleased as all heck. Letty sat down at my right, and Pixie at my left. We ate, and the three of us went back to scanning the news for plane crashes. Tricia had already been in to drop off some foreclosures, and she'd brought some papers from Randy on a small commercial building. It was small beans but interesting because the seller of the property was from Portugal.

In the afternoon, Pixie and Letty bundled up and went for a run. That was when I took a call from Camila.

"Amor, I'm in New York. Come over for a couple days."

"Great idea!"

"Amor, I'm in the Lear. I will send for you."

"No, I can hop a plane easy."

"I insist."

I thought about the millions in my safe. The Camachos spent money like it was water, so I didn't bother to remind her about the expense of sending a plane with a crew to fetch me to New York. Pepe and Camila had flown to London so I could visit with them in Brazil. They'd done it so often that it should be commonplace to me, but it wasn't. In my wildest flights of imagination, I'd never expected to be around anyone this wealthy.

I had nightmares about burying Oscar in debt. My conscience remembered. I often had dreams that started off with Oscar insisting I use his Learjet. In the dream, I would mention the expense, and he'd interrupt me and tell me not to worry about it. Then the dream twist would kick in, and I'd be in the coffin with him, except I was in bed and being covered with wheelbarrows full of bills, dumped on me till I woke up gasping. Sometimes I thought I woke up, but I'd be in Oscar's coffin with him and his bills. Sometimes Tom would be there, trying to pull me out using rope he got from Jack, only it was never enough. Until we met with Tom and Denise, I had no idea that Oscar was buried in debt. Much of it was due to his generosity. I seriously doubted that Camacho had a hidden secret about being on the edge of bankruptcy like Oscar. Whatever secrets Pepe had, they could not possibly involve a cash shortage.

After Pixie went home, I told Letty and Tricia I was taking off for a couple of days, and asked Tricia to hang around on security duty. Later, when I told Pixie on the phone, she pretended rage at being left behind, and wanted to go with me.

"I need to get away, Baby."

She backed off.

Letty and Tricia dropped me off at the airport.

The Lear was gorgeous. I had never been in this plane. The carpet was leopard, too big to be real but so well-made it was impossible to tell it wasn't genuine. The seats were suede but I didn't use them. I slept in the onboard bed which was far too short for me, but it was fitted with the cotton sheets I preferred, and covered with a mink blanket. I managed by curling up. I shut my eyes in California, and opened them in New York.

A car was waiting for me at the airport. Minutes after I was off the plane, I was in Camila's limousine asking the driver where we were headed.

"What hotel?" I asked.

"No hotel, Mr. Luna. She is waiting for you at the apartment on Fifth Avenue."

That was Camila. Full of surprises.

Olga opened the door. Her hug and kisses were enough to drive a saint up the wall, and I'm no saint.

Camila appeared in my line of sight. From the doorway I could see through the foyer to the living room. The view from the floor to ceiling windows was spectacular. Fifth Avenue.

"Some place!" I said, walking in, Olga on one side. Camila swept up to me on the opposite side.

"You like? Thank you for coming, Amor. I wanted you to see my new apartment."

"Very impressive. Thank you for inviting me. The plane. The limo," I gestured to indicate the penthouse. "This."

"Let me show you our little treasure chest."

Olga took my left hand, Camila my right, and we walked through the apartment. The kitchen was modern, sleek and spotless. Two large master bedrooms had bathrooms attached. The guest bathroom off the den looked like a work of art, faced in museum quality veined green marble. A small third bed and bath room suite off the kitchen was designated for the help. The living room had a statuesque view from the floor to ceiling windows overlooking Fifth Avenue. The dining room was small but easily accommodated a table with ten chairs.

"It's beautiful. Congratulations." I said. "Did you say you just bought it?"

"I bought it as is. Isn't it wonderful?"

I agreed heartily.

Camila ordered take-out, which was delivered and shared on a balcony terrace. Because it was a terrace, maybe I should have been reminded of Sami. But the whole ambiance of New York is so different from London. I did not make the comparison until I was flying home. Sami's terrace made us feel that we were somehow secluded. Maybe it was the London fog that did it. New York felt like we were out in the open. The traffic was louder, the weather sharper, the light brighter. It was just...different.

After checking out the terrace, Camila and I landed in bed. We got caught up in slow motion lovemaking. Olga was in my mind, but not in the bed; she left us alone, at least until we took a break. She appeared with two glasses of red wine. Her plain white robe reached from her neck to her wrists to the floor. The pure silk clung to her nipples, and the points of her hips, even the dip of her flat stomach. Her cloud of straight, nearly black hair was caught back in a ponytail. It was three in the morning, and Camila and I were naked under the sheets.

"Can Olga join us?" Camila asked with fake meekness.

"Of course." I lifted the comforter.

Olga handed over our wine. She undid something at her neck, and the robe melted to the floor, revealing only a thong beneath. I could not help but admire her, reached to touch her collar bone, and dragged my fingers down the slim line of her body to tug the thong free.

Olga straddled one of my legs. I could feel her warmth and wetness as she slid against me. I had one hand on her thigh as her arms clung. Her lips brushed my chest. On my other side, Camila's breasts pressed against me. She turned my face to hers, and pushed her lips to mine. I shut my eyes, and left the room. In the bed with two beautiful women, working to satisfy them both, but in my head, I was caught in the parade of women I have had before, and who have had me. I could see and feel and hear and taste them all—Letty, Pixie, Jo, Niley, Melina. All the girls I'd known in Europe. My senses were full to bursting. It took some real discipline to keep from exploding.

It was noon when we woke up. Back home it was nine. By now, I should have finished my workout, and breakfast, and should be in my office with a cup of Miguel's coffee and the classifieds spread across my desk. My mouth was dry, my head still foggy with marijuana and rolling with wine. I looked down and saw Olga's head at the foot of the bed, her long hair loose, gleaming like silk in a hundred subtle shades of brown and light. It had not been a dream. Olga stretched, reminding me of a cat, sleek and limber. I thought she'd cut her hair, but here it was long again. Some of what Pixie called beauty parlor magic.

"Coffee anyone?" Olga asked.

Camila was sitting up next to me in the bed. Her skin was moist and glistening, her hair flat against her head, and showing the lines of a comb. While I'd been asleep, she must have sneaked in a shower. She smelled fresh.

"Do you even need to ask?" Camila said.

Olga flashed a smile, and rolled off the bed. She retrieved her robe from the floor, but carried it from the room, naked, the robe hooked on her finger. I watched her leave. Camila tapped a button on her nightstand. The curtain moved about two feet, revealing a cloudy day with no direct sun.

How many people have electric curtains? I thought immediately that I should have a button like that installed as soon as I got home.

"Amor, am I right in thinking you enjoyed last night?"

"How could I not?"

Olga brought us breakfast. It was freezing outside, but Olga wore shorts and a top that looked painted on. It was not the breakfast of my choice: croissants, jam and coffee. It was delicious but I had been spoiled by Miguel who fed me all the protein I wanted, and tried to limit the pastries, except to please the girls' palates. Olga left a decanter on the end table for coffee refills.

It was noon, and I was fully caffeinated, but I pushed aside my uneaten croissant, and checked out for another four hours and so did Camila. I woke with Camila and Olga wrapped around me, in a cloud of sex and marijuana smoke. I made it to the shower. I'm sure I was in there for half an hour. The water pressure and very tall showerhead were almost as good as what I left at home, and I was so wrapped up in it and the memories of last night that I almost didn't notice Olga come in. She was setting out a razor and blades for me, plus three different kinds of aftershave lotion and two men's fragrances.

"Deodorant?"

"Right here." She handed me an Old Spice stick.

I was standing there dripping wet and naked, halfway in the shower. Olga had a towel wrapped around her, her skin glistening. She smelled like ripe fruit.

"Is Camila up?"

"She's in the other shower."

Our eyes met. Olga walked without a word to the bedroom. I followed her.

"I want you. Do you want to?" she asked.

We crashed on the messed up bed.

"*Quisiera que fueras mio, solamente mio,*"[58] Olga whispered.

It was five when we gathered around the table to have something to eat. New York is an international smorgasbord for anyone with a phone. They'd been here long enough or often enough to know who to call, and had a feast of

---

[58] I wish you were mine, just mine

Italian food delivered.

Camila's bare and beautiful kitchen counter was bare no longer. It looked like an Italian restaurant had opened up. There was spaghetti, lasagna, meatballs, rigatoni, containers of three different kinds of sauce, spinach and egg, Italian salad with pepperoncini peppers, two full loaves of garlic bread. I saw other cartons with something parmigiana, something beefy, something chickeny. Everything was swimming in tomatoes and Romano cheese.

"I'm so hungry. I could eat a 727 whole, boiled, fried or sautéed, without salt."

"That makes three of us," Olga said.

We filled our plates from the ersatz buffet, and sat at the table in the den, overlooking the New York view.

Camila was putting a dent in a pile of ravioli and pasta. She pointed to Olga with her fork.

"You always know exactly what to order, Amor."

"What to drink?" Olga asked between bites of garlic bread. "Wine or soda?"

"Sparkling water," I said.

"Wine," Camila said.

Olga returned with a bottle of red wine, a glass with ice, lime and a bottle of Pellegrino.

"Amor, you like my apartment?"

"I love your apartment," I replied. "Did you really just buy it?"

"I closed escrow two days ago. The seller wasn't living here so move-in was easy."

"These things are expensive in New York."

"1.5 including everything you see."

"Ouch," I said. "That is what I paid for my three acres."

"Someday this will be worth many millions," Olga predicted.

"It is hard to buy anything with cash."

Now that made me laugh. "I am finding that out. I'm getting better at it."

"You sure are," they both echoed.

"How did you approach the seller?" I asked.

"I told the broker I needed to talk privately with the seller, or there was no deal."

"I do that, too."

"You are doing wonderful work," Camila said.

"So, you handed him a suitcase with the cash?" I looked up from my rigatoni to her eyes.

"I didn't hand him anything. Olga did."

Olga had told me she was like the bank. Camila buys and Olga pays. So that was how it worked with the apartment, too.

"He was so happy you would not believe," Olga said in Spanish. I remembered when that mouth of hers was between Camila's legs. I was glad to know they weren't really sisters.

I got hold of the girls at my house.

"Melina wants you to leave a phone number where she can call you. She was pissed that you didn't tell her you were leaving."

"I did call her, I couldn't locate her."

"I didn't know that, but that's what I told her," Letty said.

I put my hand over the receiver and asked Camila, "Is it okay if I give out your phone number here?"

"Amor, why you ask?"

I could think of a bunch of reasons, but I kept quiet. I smiled and thanked her as she wrote the phone number down that I read aloud to Letty.

"When are you coming back?" Pixie asked.

"As soon as Camila throws me out."

Camila heard and laughed. "He's staying for long time," she said loud enough for Pixie to hear.

"Bitch," Pixie said.

"She called you a bitch," I said.

Camila laughed. "I am a bitch. That's not news to me."

Olga laughed at the exchange. She was so fucking sexy.

It was cold and looked like rain, but an hour later, the three of us were on Fifth Avenue walking off the meal. I was in the middle, a fox on each side, and feeling on top of the world. They wore full length minks with matching hats and designer scarfs. They looked like money. Camila had a mink muff, but every so often one hand emerged, flashing the diamond pear shaped ring she always wore. My guess was that it was half the size of the fifteen carats in my safe. Tonight I couldn't tell because she wore gloves, but Olga usually wore rings on all her fingers except her thumb..

When we got back to the apartment, Camila wanted to know what I wanted to do.

"Amor, we go out tonight or we relax here?"

"Here," I said. I saw a big smile on Olga, a mirror of Camila's.

When we started for the bedroom, the phone rang. Olga answered it. She talked so low I could barely hear her, but I knew it was Pepe. Camila took the phone and exchanged some small talk with her brother. Apparently, he already knew I was there because she never mentioned me. She handed me the phone.

"Amigo, my sister tells me you went to New York to have sex with Olga." He was laughing.

I matched his laugh, "I had an invitation," I replied. "And they took me by surprise."

"Amigo, you will have to marry both of them. Understand me?" Pepe said.

"I'm in," I said. "Of course, there's also my team, and Melina."

"Good. I will arrange the wedding, brother in law."

I hoped he was kidding.

I hung up. Moments later, it rang again. Olga handed it to me.

"Baby, how are you?"

"Don't 'Baby' me, Cuz. What the fuck are you doing in New York?"

"I came to visit Camila and Olga."

"You mean you went to New York to fuck Camila and Olga."

I knew Melina wasn't pissed, much less jealous.

"You are right. I came to New York to fuck Camila and Olga."

From across the room, Camila smiled and gave me a thumbs up.

Olga only smiled, but it was a bullseye right at me.

"Asshole!" Melina growled, then laughed.

I laughed. I avoided looking at Camila and Olga, and looked out the window at the skyline.

"Miss you."

"Prick. You don't miss me," Melina laughed softly. "Stay safe."

"You too," I said, then added, "I do miss you. Talk soon."

I hung up and joined Camila and Olga. I was in the middle. They put their arms around my waist.

"How can you miss her when you have two wild Colombian women like us?" They did their best to make me forget anyone else, but at least three times, I shouted out Melina's name. I wouldn't tell them whether or not it was a mistake. But I knew Melina would love the story when I told her about it.

After three days and three nights of insatiable Colombians, I was worn out when I boarded the Learjet. I often wondered where my sexual drive came from. Was it something I ate? Peanut butter? I knew that wasn't it. And I wasn't all that crazy about raw oysters.

Camila and Olga would be headed home to Colombia in about a week. They still had business in New York to conduct. It was not like I had been the purpose of their trip; I was just the entertainment, at least as far as Camila was concerned. It was up in the air whether they would spend Christmas in Bogota or with Pepe in Milan.

Tricia, Pixie and Letty picked me up at the Van Nuys Airport less than twenty minutes from home. I felt like driving, and chauffeured the girls home. Pixie sat beside me. Letty was in the back seat with Tricia.

"I called Janice Cooke from New York. She says the detectives are in touch with her but they have found nothing so far."

"Janice is too old for you," Pixie said.

"Hey, she's Oscar's widow, watch your mouth." I wasn't upset. Janice was older than me but she was a fine lady. In many ways, she reminded me of Melina and Sami—their style rather than their appearance.

"Didn't mean anything by it, Boss. Just thought it strange that you actually took the time to call her from New York when you were over there with Camila and Olga who I'm sure had you occupied."

Letty chimed in. "Did they have you occupied, Boss?"

"That's personal." My eyes were on the road. I don't know if they saw me smile.

"Well pardon me," Pixie whacked my shoulder. I felt her hand search between my legs, then a love-squeeze. That's what she called grabbing me there.

"It's always great to return home," I said, "to my favorite girls." Tricia never said a word. She was either asleep or ignoring us.

December was well under way when Pixie suggested, "Boss, let's go find a tree. A big fucker."

"Dig that, yeah," Letty said.

I took the wheel, and drove past all the stands of cut trees. Everybody and his brother had trees for sale, but Pixie wanted something big. On the corner of Foothill & Rosemead, we saw a tree lot with some monster trees. We found an eighteen-foot Noble, a jewel of a tree.

Later that afternoon, it was delivered with a solid wood base attached to the big trunk. Pixie directed the delivery people to put the tree next to the winding staircase where the ceiling was high and where it fit with plenty of space between the top of the tree and second floor ceiling. My gardener and handyman brought in two indoor ladders normally used to dust or clean the chandeliers. The girls went shopping for ornaments and lights and came back with bags filled. It was the first tree of my adult life, a grand tree. I was so happy I did a back flip, something I normally confine to workouts.

"Go daddy," Letty said, applauding.

"Let's decorate it."

Two hours into the decorating, I left everyone busy with ornaments, and lights, and strands of tinsel. I had an appointment with Betty for a massage.

"You'll miss the fun," Letty said as I followed Betty to the spa on the lower level.

"Is that true?" I asked Betty. "Am I going to miss the fun?"

"I can make it as fun as you want, Boss."

"Cool."

The temperature was perfect in the spa. It was a cold night outside.

The spa is located on the first floor, the level I call the basement. Although the area has no outdoor access, the opposite side of this lower level has French doors to the outside. I was relaxed, and listening to distant Christmas music that was playing somewhere in the house. If something is going on outside, you aren't going to hear it in the spa. All I heard was a door slam. It was faint. I think that was all it was, but I had a sense that made me jump off the table. I am not sure if it was something I heard, or a change in air pressure, something subliminal, or what. The hair on my arms stood up, and I got goosebumps.

It was 9:00 pm when I turned off the volume and listened.

"Something is wrong." I reached for one of many robes on hangers.

"I heard nothing. What's wrong?"

I couldn't tell her, but I was going to see for myself.

"Stay here, Betty."

I scrambled into a pair of workout shorts, exited the spa, crossed the gym in double time, and ran the stairs two at a time.

Suddenly, chaos. Rapid gunfire. Yelling in Spanish. I rounded the corner and saw the tree. Pixie and Letty were face down on the floor. Tricia was sheltering them with her body. The gardener and handyman were also face down.

I assessed the situation immediately. Saw two fools in my house with firearms. Their rifles were pointed toward the ceiling. The intruders had their backs to me. I didn't wait for them to turn around. I didn't think. Instinct kicked in. I ran. Leaped. Kicked one in the head. Heard the snap and crack of his skull. The second intruder turned. He was slow to act, and I was quick to attack. I jerked the rifle from his grasp, threw it across the room, and gave him a quick and brutal pounding. The motherfucker dropped, his face shattered, bleeding.

The gardener and handyman were up before I could say anything. Chete shoved his wife in the direction of the phone, then took off. Memo dashed off, probably looking for his wife, Yoli. Tricia got up like it was nothing, dusted herself off, and pulled the girls to their feet. The girls ran to me. Tricia headed for the intruders, her gun drawn. Caro was on the phone, hands and voice shaking, calling the police. She collapsed on a chair, head in her hands.

"Tricia, check those two assholes," I said unnecessarily, since she was already there. "Caro, you're not done. Call an ambulance, then you can sit down and drink a glass of wine."

"Guns in our purses. A lot of fucking good that was," Pixie barked, anger steaming off of her in waves.

"There was no chance to do anything. We were on a ladder when they came in. Surprised Tricia, too," Letty jabbered. "All the practice every week, and we were on a ladder and didn't do anything but lie down on the ground.

Standing on the ladder like a fucking idiot, and they say get down and what do I do? Get down, like a dog in obedience training."

I held Pixie and Letty, hugged them tight and kissed the tops of their heads. Letty was still babbling. I was shaking with anger and a sense of violation that this had happened in my own house.

"They are out. I think this one is dead," Tricia said.

"These two assholes were in the Sears parking lot where we parked earlier," Pixie said.

"Wait. You mean you know these two?" I asked.

"We don't know them," Letty said. "They were flirting with us. Pixie gave them the finger. They got pissed and tried to block us from getting in the car. I kicked one of them between the legs, and Pixie went wild on the other one."

Pixie took up the story. "When we went back the second time to get more decorations, the fuckers came at us again. This time I drew my gun and warned them to stay away."

"They just wouldn't quit," Letty said, shivering.

"Why didn't you say anything?" I asked.

"Boss, it was nothing. It was over. We handled it," Pixie said. "We thought we handled it. Didn't think they'd come back for more. No clue they'd follow us home."

"They were pissed off. They tried to get physical," Letty said.

"Boss, I kicked both mothers hard, the first time. The second time, I was ready to shove my gun in the big one's mouth, but I didn't."

"They're down now," Letty said. "They must have followed us home, but we didn't see them."

One of the intruders moved. Tricia kicked him in the ribs. He groaned.

"Be still fucker. Your ride isn't here yet," Tricia said.

"I heard gunshots. Was anyone hit?"

Pixie answered, "They ordered us to hit the floor and fired. You got a hole in the ceiling, Boss."

She pointed toward it.

"Ceilings can be fixed," I said.

"I was on a ladder," Tricia said. "Pixie and Letty were on ladders. Caro and Yoli were handing us ornaments. The doorbell rang, and Caro answered the door. These guys knocked her down, and stormed in waving their rifles."

I looked at the grandfather clock near the front door. It was nine ten. I took a second to call my aunt and tell her we'd caught some intruders, but we were all okay. I knew as soon as there was anything on the news, her gossipy friends would start calling and get her antsy. The door swung open. It was Chete, out of breath after running around the house to see if there were any more than two intruders. He hadn't seen anyone else.

The cops were there in ten minutes flat, at nine twenty. My foyer filled with cops, firemen and medical attendants. The Christmas tree, grandly patient in its spot under the vaulted ceiling, awaited the finishing touches, but that wasn't going to happen tonight.

The one we thought was dead wasn't dead. He was taken away with the other by ambulance, unconscious and handcuffed to the gurney.

My housekeepers, their husbands, Miguel and Tricia were standing around ready for orders. Our movements were restricted. The area was a crime scene.

"Miguel, please go to the kitchen and get some coffee going and anything else you can put together."

"Of course, Boss."

Two detectives arrived. We sat in the dining room close to the crime scene. Pixie and Letty sat next to me, across from the two detectives. About twenty minutes later, two more detectives arrived, the ones that had visited me after Oscar's death.

"What the fuck happened here?" Solé asked. He was the one who had taken the lead the last time he'd been here. He looked like a body builder, and wore thick glasses. His companion Ramos was still taking notes.

Betty joined us. "I was in the spa with Mario," she told the detectives, "I didn't see anything that can help you."

They took her statement and sent her home.

Chapter 27
December 1980
Shooters and Smoke

Melina joined us in the dining room in a gray felt suit and tie straight out of *Annie Hall.* She was in lawyer mode, and didn't wait for introductions.

Ramos looked from his notepad. At her entry, he and the other detectives stood.

"Gentlemen, time out. Give us ten minutes," Melina told the detectives. "I'm Melina Marron, Mario's attorney," she said, shaking their hands sequentially. She hooked her arm over mine, and as we stepped outside the dining room, she said, "We will be right back. We'll get you something refreshing."

Melina marched me sharply into the kitchen and rolled her eyes when she saw what Miguel was fixing. Something fragrant was baking in the oven. A pretty china teapot with nothing in it but a tea ball was waiting for boiling water. The kitchen table held pastries and empty teacups, bowls brimming with steamy soup, a bread basket and covered tortilla dish. My household staff was sitting around the table, looking ravaged, but Miguel was nurturing them with food, and buzzing around in his element.

Melina told Miguel, "Soft drinks, water, and coffee along with whatever you have planned."

Caro stood, but Miguel put a hand on her shoulder and pushed her back down into the chair.

"I'll manage just fine," Miguel said. "You just sit there till I get back."

"You're off duty until tomorrow," Melina told the staff, glancing at me for confirmation. "I am sure Mario agrees. I can send my people over."

Miguel stiffened. "No need. I can manage just fine."

"We can too," Memo said, glancing around. He spoke for them all.

I nodded. "As you wish."

I followed Melina into the butler's pantry where there were two tall stools. She turned on the light, and shut the door. We sat for a moment.

She took my hands and held them.

"Are you okay? You look like shit," she said.

"Thanks Cuz," I said, trying to make light of it. "Death follows me around. I'm sure one of those dudes is dead or about to kick the bucket."

"Anyone threatens my life, I'll take this gun I pack and shoot to kill without a second thought. You did what you had to do. Fuck it."

She might talk like a gunslinger, but the words were at odds with the puppyish vulnerability of her appearance. As far as I knew, she'd never actually shot anyone but the robbers who'd killed her father. She made me smile. "You a tough cookie, Baby."

"Fucking-A," she said. She reached up and smoothed my hair, and ran her palm over my bare abdomen. "What the fuck are you wearing?"

I looked down at my work out shorts. I'm pretty comfortable in my own skin and hadn't had my mind on how I was dressed. "I was having a massage when this thing started."

"Is there anything you need to tell your lawyer?"

"These jerks followed the girls home from shopping. No connection to anything else."

"From what Pixie said on the phone, I agree." She nodded, with one palm still resting on my stomach. "Why don't you get some clothes on, and I'll go talk to them."

We parted company. When I returned, dressed, to the dining room,

Melina was playing hostess. The detectives were looking calm and relaxed, and deep in conversation that had nothing to do with policing. I saw vestiges of Miguel's sense of humor in the room. Savory and sweet. Pigs in blankets, and doughnuts. Coffee, Pellegrino, soft drinks, ice, and a bowl of limes were in a cart. The detectives were looking fed.

Melina opened a Pellegrino, and handed it to me with a glass of ice with a couple of limes.

All four detectives were discomfited at being caught so relaxed. Melina looked me over, and as they turned toward me she gave me a thumbs up, and a wink. I took the thumb as being approval for the mandarin collared half-zippered shirt and jeans, and the wink for the balance of power in my direction, but it might have been meant another way.

"Mr. Luna, too soon to be sure, but it appears like a follow home robbery," Solé said.

"I think so," Melina said, before I could agree. "Sounds to me that the girls became targets of revenge or opportunity when they fought off their attackers. You fellows are the doctors. I'm sure you will get the facts and evidence together, and figure it out."

I was just sitting there, but ever since it happened, I'd been quietly simmering with anger at the violation of my household. I'd been keeping a lid on it earlier for the girls, and now because of Melina's presence. I don't know if it was the detective's usual routine, but Melina and I remained in the room as everyone came in one at a time and submitted to the detectives' questions. Several uniformed officers were working the case, and came in and out, and had short conversations with the detectives about evidence being collected. I could tell my staff was heartened by our supportive presence. Melina was working the detectives like a puppeteer with an iron hand and a cashmere glove. I could see it, but didn't know if the detectives knew it.

One of them got a radio call. We were still in the dining room, and heard along with him that one of the shooters had died as they prepared him for surgery. The detectives were silent.

"Self-defense," Melina said.

"Better him than any of us," I said without hesitation. It took a minute or so before I felt the impact that I had killed another human being, but it left as fast as it had come.

Melina put her hand up, signaling for me to hold my tongue.

Solé had done his homework on me. "How many does this make?" he asked me. "By my count this makes four and if the other one doesn't make it, five." He raised his hand and wiggled his fingers.

"Detective, you should know that each case was in self-defense. By the tone of your question, I'm not certain what game you want to play," Melina said. "There is no question that these intruders violated this household."

I had no remorse for the dead man. I didn't care if the other one died either. They had come inside my house with rifles. They had every intention of doing harm. Not talking made acid spill inside my gut. I kept my mouth shut and tried to look passive. On the other hand, I did have confidence in Melina.

"No game at all. A man is dead, and the other one may die, both at the hands of your client."

"If it was your house, what would you have done, detective?" Melina asked the right question at the right time.

There was a pause. I could tell she had scored a hit.

Letty poked her head in from the entrance. Melina nodded her in, and aimed her in my direction.

Letty sat beside me and whispered in my ear. "Jo and Niley just got here. They didn't want to interrupt, but they're sitting in the kitchen with Pixie and the house staff."

It was the first good news I'd had all day.

Solé grinned. "I would have shot both their asses." His attitude had changed, and I could tell that I was no longer on the chopping block. "There may be an inquest. Depends on the district attorney's office. Questions will come up about the history of the individuals your client has killed."

"I know you and everyone here are professionals. I trust your report will answer all the questions that will come up. My client was in the spa enjoying a massage. Everyone else was decorating a Christmas tree. These intruders stormed in and fired their weapons without provocation."

The detectives exchanged looks.

Solé agreed. "The evidence we have collected so far supports exactly what you just said."

"One of them had keys to a car parked across the street," said one of the uniformed officers working the case and who was standing at Ramos's shoulder. His tag said Harrigan. He'd just handed over a carbon copy of his evidence report on the car parked across the street. Letty got up from beside me, and offered him the tray of pastries. He took one. She walked the tray around to the standing officers, and got them drinks from the cart. She replenished the ice.

Harrigan said, "They followed the girls from the store, and probably made a run for the gate before it closed."

"When do you have lunch on the night shift?" I asked.

"We squeeze it in," Harrigan said.

Miguel replenished the beverage cart and looked at me. I saw doughnuts and pigs in blankets in his eyes, and shook my head. Not that.

"Lunch for the officers. Something warm. It's cold out there," I said.

"Yes Boss," Miguel said. He brought out a huge vat of chili, a stack of the disposable bowls we use by the pool, and a box of plastic spoons. Beside the paper cups were condiments, milk and sugar. The silver coffee urn was steaming.

By two, the cops wrapped up their crime scene record-keeping. Miguel moved the food station outdoors so all the officers working the scene could eat. After they and the detectives left, Miguel brought out filets for everyone still here and up, and they were happily consumed in spite of the hour.

"I hope the other guy makes it," I said. Taking a life is an ugly business, a big ugly gash in your soul to live with. I already have enough death on my conscience.

"I guess we embarrassed them," Pixie said, her appetite unaffected.

"Badly," Letty said. She put down her fork, looking uncertain.

"Shamed them enough they took steps to get even," Melina said. "You'll never know if they only intended to scare you."

I shook my head at Melina. Maybe she thought the karate had turned my girls into bullies. I don't know what she was getting at. The girls had enough to deal with without Melina making them feel guilty for defending themselves. She was the one who had gotten them into guns.

Pixie and Letty looked up from their plates. I guess they'd never really thought about the intruders' intentions.

"I didn't want to ask while the detectives were here, but where were your guns?" Melina asked.

"In our purses."

Melina said, "Don't feel bad. I carry my gun in my purse, too. When my purse is not with me I have no gun."

It was too late for regret. I hoped the one intruder still breathing made it. I didn't want the girls to have anything on their consciences.

"You have a right to defend yourselves," I said to them.

"For sure, Boss." Letty nodded.

"We've had years of karate learning to defend ourselves. Fucking-A we can use it." Pixie said.

"You did the right thing," I said.

Melina nodded in agreement. I saw her looking at her watch, and glanced at the clock. It was three. The cops had been gone for an hour, and Melina would usually be at work by seven at the latest.

I walked Melina to the door, and we kissed.

"Promise me you'll sneak in a cat-nap at work today."

"Perhaps," she said vaguely, fighting a yawn. "Goodnight. I'll be on my way," she said. "You have your hands full with the team all here."

I opened the door and stepped outside with her.

"I don't know what you mean by my hands being full."

She laughed, and leaned on me.

I put my arm over her shoulder and walked her home.

When I got back, Tricia met me at the door. I took her hand to lead her to where everyone was gathered, but she planted her feet, and wanted to talk in the foyer. I could see she was upset. Her face was pale, her lips set in a straight line. She stood with her usual military bearing, but her hands were at the small of her back, her chin raised.

"Boss, I should have drilled those bastards. I'm sorry I failed."

I put my arm around her. I could see she felt bad. "Trish, don't even think about it. Shit happens. You were here to decorate a tree. All I saw was you protecting Letty and Pixie."

"Thank you," she said, squaring her shoulders and putting her chin up even higher.

I gave her a tap on the chin with one finger.

"Don't lead with your chin, Baby. Surefire knockout."

Her stance didn't falter. Her lips wobbled a little, maybe.

"I'll walk away if you want me to."

She had demonstrated herself to be tough.

"You're family. You ain't going nowhere."

"Thank you, Mario. I love working for you."

I hugged her until she pulled away.

"Milk and cookies? Jam and bread?" I asked.

"I think I'm going home." She rattled her keys and put her hand on the doorknob.

I saw a glimmer in her eye, though no tears had fallen. I dabbed at her face with a handkerchief, and handed it to her. "Not tonight. It's after three in the morning. You have an appointment in your room here. Hot bath, then bed. We talk security tomorrow. Understand?" I pointed upstairs, and she marched up without another word.

The girls were still wide awake, and still here. I put Miguel to work again. Two varieties of hot chocolate, biscuits with butter, and two kinds of jam. It did my heart good to see my sweethearts, Jo, Pixie, Niley, and Letty sitting around the table munching in the wee hours, like old times.

"Take a guest room. I don't want you driving this late. This early," I said.

"We have no plans to leave, but I don't know about that guest room," Jo said through a mouthful of biscuit. "I already told Angie she's running point tomorrow, and TJ told me not to come home tonight. I cleared it before I left."

"He's a saint," I said.

"No saint, Boss, just no secrets. We talked about it before I left. I told him we'd probably end up in bed, all of us. He'll probably want a blow by blow account."

"We're swingers." Pixie said it like a declaration.

"I'm cool with that," Niley said.

The girls did their high five.

I went to bed, and Jo, Niley, Pixie, and Letty joined me. The girls hugged each other, and I hugged them.

"When that cocksucker ordered us to the floor waving around that rifle then shooting the ceiling, fuck, I really thought I was dead," Pixie said. "Fucking fool."

Letty nodded. "And the other *pendejo* tells me I have two seconds to hit the floor. I should have jumped him, and disarmed him."

"If I'd just been closer..." Pixie said.

"If any of us had been closer, we'd have taken them down in a heartbeat," Letty said.

"Honey, I would die if anything happened to you," Jo said to Pixie, kissing her hand. "If I'd been here, I'd have kicked his ass, gun or no gun. Hell, I'd have shot him with my forty-five."

"I don't want to be away anymore," Niley sobbed. "I need to be here. I don't want to manage apartments anymore."

"All that shooting practice. All that damn karate practice, and we were too far away to use any of it," Pixie said. "What I wouldn't give to have a leg twenty feet long. I'd have kicked that rifle out of his hands, and given him a raising elbow strike, rising punch, straight punch, straight punch, straight punch." She tested out a side kick toward the ceiling, then rolled on her back and did the other five strikes straight up. "And the fucking guns in our purses."

"I'm not even supposed to be packing," Letty said, "I don't have that permit yet."

"The permit wouldn't have done us any good today," Pixie said. "You were packing but it was in your purse just like me."

"We should use a holster like Tricia, wear it 24/7."

"Bitch, quit fucking with me. We're not supposed to do that with the Boss around."

Niley laughed.

"I killed a guy. I have sent four souls to the cemetery. We shouldn't be laughing."

"Yeah we should," they chimed.

"We're all breathing," Letty said. "Let's celebrate breathing."

"Let's laugh. Let's do everything." Pixie flung her arms around everyone she could reach, and hugged.

"Boss, he deserved it," Jo said.

"Does his family deserve it?" I thought of the shooter's parents, his family, and felt bad for them. His people would hurt over the loss of their son.

The girls were silent for a moment, then Pixie roused.

"Are you really going to quit management?" She egged Niley on. "A minute ago you were crying to quit."

"How can I quit? Boss depends on Jo and me. I just I miss us." Niley sniffed.

"Aw honey, I miss us too," Pixie said. Suddenly the girls were all hugging, and tearing up.

"Were you scared in the parking lot?" I asked. They'd both handled the situation but had never opened up on how they felt when it happened.

"I felt no fear," Letty said. "I kicked his ass. Period."

"I was surprised, but not frightened. The second time, I was super pissed off. I just ripped into them and so did Letty."

They were still mumbling back and forth with each other when I dropped off to sleep. An hour later at five, I woke. Workout time, according to my body alarm. I crawled to the bathroom and relieved myself of seventeen cups of coffee, took a ten second shower and gargle, then told the workout to fuck itself. In a towel, I stood from the vantage point of the bathroom doorway and looked over at the tangle of girls on my bed. I could just make them out in the dim night light. Letty and Pixie were on the outside, having given the middle to Jo and Niley. The opening where I had been had been wedged had disappeared. I dropped my towel at the foot of the bed, and had a wonderful, nostalgic sense of déjà vu as I slithered my way back between Jo and Niley. Niley didn't quite wake, but said, "Mmm," and shaped herself to fit against me. Jo sat up with her 'instant on' and said in a clear voice, "Boss!" in surprise. She realized where she was, smiled, threw an arm around me and Niley, and was out in seconds. It took me a while to join them in sleep because my body was too aware. I had realized by now that this thing that we had was not commonplace, so I was savoring all of us in bed together, linked by a hand or a leg or an arm. We dragged out of bed much later for a very late shower and even later breakfast. Miguel was all smiles. Hell, we were all, all smiles, grinning like fools because we were all so happy to be together in that moment.

The first morning the papers had nothing.

Jack Fino called. As always, he spoke in a low voice as if he were afraid someone was going to hear him. I don't know if he lived on the paranoid side, or if someone else was in the room, sleeping. I was getting to know him.

"Melina told me about the break in. I am so sorry this happened. Thank God you came out ahead without anyone getting hurt."

"Thank you for the concern. So far, one is dead, and the other is critical."

"Fuck them. They deserve it."

Last night, I'd still been full of adrenaline. Beyond a passing thought, I hadn't cared about the dead guy and didn't care if the other one kicked the bucket as well. This morning, my confidence was rattled. I didn't feel good about what had gone down.

"I didn't realize Melina had called you."

"You should have called me. I know Melina was with you and the cops, but I am here for you too. Remember that."

I could hear the concern in his voice. His reaction made me realize the break in could have had a different conclusion. I was almost choked up.

"Love you, Jack. Thanks for calling."

When I talked with Tricia, it was all about foreclosures, and nothing about break-ins. She's a tough chick. She left early, and went to work.

Jo talked to TJ a number of times in the morning. There were only so many times I could stand to see them check their watches, and calling in to check their trainee. In the afternoon, I talked Jo and Niley into leaving. Angie had called at least six times, and those were just the times I knew about. I know Jo called her mother at least four times to get straight the details about who got picked up from where, when, and Niley had called Nanny Delores twice that often. As much as they wanted to be here, it was hard on them to leave the management company. Their families were out of practice dealing with their being gone for an endless string of days, much less hours. Their lives now revolved around their children's schedules.

The house staff was still jumpy. I was ok. Letty was actually packing one of her guns tucked between her belt and jeans on her left side.

I told Letty, "Put that thing back in your purse before you shoot your ass off."

"I'm not a rookie," she said. She made a face at me, but got her purse, and stuck the gun in it. I couldn't help ribbing her, and double-checked it to make sure the safety was on. A little while later I noticed she was packing the gun between her belt and jeans only now, it was between the two rear pockets of her jeans.

I had called my aunt again. She'd seen the article and snapped at me for downplaying it.

Pixie took it in stride, like she was made of Teflon. Sometimes I forget how hard she had it growing up. In the late afternoon, she went home.

"Don't worry Boss." She pulled out her .45 revolver from her purse, pointing it toward the window as she showed it to me. "I'm fine."

"That's fucking huge. You think you're Dirty Harriet?"

She laughed at me.

I kissed my friend. "Don't shoot yourself with that big thing."

"Not in this lifetime, Boss." She glanced over at Letty, and pointed out the safety.

"Love you, Baby."

"I love you more," she said. "I'll stop by Aunt Carmen's. Reassure her a little bit."

She had a rapport with my aunt. Her appearance at my aunt's would go a long way to make her feel that everything was okay. I wanted my aunt to be ready when the *LA Times* and *Herald Examiner* came out with news of the break-in. When it hit the fan, I didn't need a crystal ball to know all the old neighborhood biddies would be coming out of the woodwork to voice their solicitude, but mostly to get their hooks into some meaty gossip. After Pixie left, Letty bumped into me for about the tenth time that hour. We were in my office, so I turned around and swooped her on top of the most convenient piece of furniture, which happened to be my desk. I noted her purse strap hanging over her shoulder. I put my hands on her shoulders.

"Are you okay, Baby?" I locked my eyes on hers.

"I'm totally cool, Boss."

"Totally?"

"Boss, I'm fine." Her lower lip was out and trembling. I know her well enough to see she was on the verge of waterworks, so I hung on tight until the storm passed.

"I could have shot both of them from where I was on the ladder. I should have."

"Baby, it's okay. Murder is not your deal. You don't want to kill anyone. It doesn't feel good."

"I should stopped them cold."

"They had automatics. You could have been killed. It worked out okay. No one got hurt but the bad guys."

The next morning, it started on the front of the *Herald Examiner.*
Robbery Suspect Killed by Pasadena Homeowner.
Mario Luna's Pasadena estate suffered a break-in the week before Christmas. One of the two robbery suspects was killed during the break-in. The second is in the hospital in critical condition. Detectives believe members of the household were followed home after a shopping trip. The police department recommends all shoppers stay alert to avoid being a victim of thieves this holiday season.

Melina came over with a copy of the *LA Times.* I poured her a coffee and sat down with her in my breakfast nook as she read aloud the article that the *LA Times* had on the front page. The reporter had supplemented it liberally with clips from old news. They quoted from the story they covered when Tanis was killed and I was wounded, resulting in the death of the shooter, and the two incidents when my apartment had been broke into at Bunker Towers.

"...both assailants dying after Luna kicked them out the window of his apartment." Melina read the last line of the article and put down the newspaper. "Fuck, Cuz, you're famous. You're going to get a rep as a vigilante," Melina said.

She took a careful sip of coffee so she didn't dribble any on her spectacularly ugly Christmas sweater.

After hearing the coverage, I wanted to punch the reporter in the face. Strike that. I wanted to use the reporter as my next workout dummy. "I don't need this shit. It's embarrassing. I don't even know my neighbors."

"You know me."

I saluted her with my mug hand, coffee splashing wildly.

"Live with it. Fuck it," Melina said. "Too bad you don't have some project brewing. It would be good publicity. I'm just thanking God it has nothing to do with those Venezuela hoods."

"Baby, join the club of believers that those hoods are dead."

"You believe that for real?" She had asked me that too many times to keep count.

"Yes." I wanted to believe it so bad that I believed it. If they'd been on the plantation property, there was no way the lawyers could have survived that fire.

I kissed her softly and sipped at my black coffee. "That's an unusual sweater you're wearing." It was a bright red coarse wool knit. The reindeer and sleigh looked like they'd been embroidered by a ten-year-old. Small lit bulbs were sewn on for Rudolph's and Santa's noses, and into a badly embroidered tree behind the sleigh.

"Yes, well, isn't it just the ugliest thing you've ever seen? Too bad the noses don't flash off and on," she sighed. "One of my marketing gurus had the brilliant idea to do a take off on the twelve days of Christmas. Twelve contests counting down to Christmas day. Winners of each contest in each store get a coupon for a free cooked turkey with all the trimmings. Today is UGLY CHRISTMAS SWEATER day."

"Surely you will win the grand prize," I said. "It does not feel like Christmas week."

"Come into one of my markets. We're fucking reeking with the Christmas Spirit. Fill in the blank with the one thing you want for Christmas, from anything we've got in the store. That's tomorrow's drawing. Or you can come the day after, and judge the best choral group. That should get you in the holiday mood."

"Thanks," I said, laughing at Melina's expression. She must be roped into judging some of those contests and obviously wasn't looking forward to it. "Can I fill in your name? Because you're the only thing I want for Christmas."

She flushed red with pleasure, and punched me in the shoulder. "Don't joke about that," she said.

"I need to call Pepe and let him in on all this."

"Make sure you call Cunt Camila, and Cunt Olga."

"Baby, why'd you say that?" I kissed her again.

"If I answer that, we'll end up in a fight. I'll plead the fifth and pretend I'm nice. You know I feel they hoodwinked you with sex into doing their shady shenanigans, but I'm saying nothing more."

"Try thinking the flip side, that I hoodwinked them into sex and a paycheck."

"That makes me feel so much better." She dripped with sarcasm, but at least I got a smile out of her. She stuck her tongue out at me and said, "I gotta go. Please try not to kill anybody today. I don't have the right clothes to visit you in prison."

I laughed.

She gave me a kiss that made me want to delay her arrival at work at least for twenty minutes. She came up for air, and said, "I mean this: stay safe today. Promise?"

"I promise."

"Can I send over some rent-a-cops?" Her smile was dazzling. A smile like that could win her prizes on television. A smile like that could get her out of drunk driving tickets. Hell, a smile like that could get her out of a manslaughter charge. But it wasn't getting me to let her hire guards.

"Out," I said, "No guards!"

"Asshole," she growled. "Oh, Felipe will be here at nine to assess the ceiling damage. He promised he'd handle repairs right away."

"I'd be lost without you, Cuz."

"Asshole. They would never have gotten in if you had the guards out there."

She could be right. "Babe, I don't want guards. It's bad enough with all the press as it is. All I need are pictures of this place crawling with rent-a-cops."

Ramos called to say that the second intruder was going to make it.

"I'm glad to hear that." I was tempted to say 'Better four down and not five' but thought better of it and held my tongue.

Letty was almost back to normal, but still glued to my side like old Señor Chapo's dog during an earthquake. "What's the deal, Letty? You're not that scared."

"It's you Boss. You need a bodyguard."

"And you've appointed yourself my bodyguard? Aw, Babies. I'm fine. I've been protecting my own ass for a long time."

I had her get Camila on the phone, then sent her into the kitchen to cook something comforting with Miguel as I sat at my desk and told the story.

"Amor, thank God you and the girls are fine. What do the police say?"

"So far they are calling it a follow home robbery."

Five minutes after we hung up, Pepe called.

"Mario, you should have killed both of them."

"That's how I felt when it was happening, and right after it happened, but now I'm glad the other dude didn't kick the bucket. I'm going to get some heat over this. It's all over the newspapers here. Two television channels have been showing helicopter pictures of my house."

"I'll send a plane for you. Come to Milan."

"You are too kind. I can't leave right now. If I left the country, it wouldn't look good. Besides, I have several deals for you about to go down."

"Good. Do the deals or not. Come to Milan."

"Thanks, Pepe. I'll take a rain check."

Camila and Olga were in Colombia. Shortly after Pepe, Olga called. "Amor, come to Bogota and spend Christmas with us. Pepe is staying in Milan. It is beautiful here."

"Baby, as much as I want to, I have to stick around here. The girls won't admit it but they are shook up, and I have a couple of building deals that could happen in the next few days."

"Bring the girls. Please say yes. I want to be with you so bad."

"Baby, I'll let you know. Christmas is still more than a week away."

I went to my office to work as Pixie and Letty finished decorating the tree. Tricia helped with the ladders. The marble floor was pristine, as if there had never been a drop of blood anywhere. A few feet away, painters were doing patch repairs and touch-ups while balanced on two rolling scaffolds. By sundown, like magic, the scaffolds were gone, the men were gone, splintered wood and holes were gone, and the Christmas tree was splendid. Melina was a fantastic organizer. I had planned to use Jo's people working for the management company, but Melina had it done before I got a chance to make the call.

I shut off the dimmer and flicked on the tree. The room did not burst into light. Instead, the tree trickled to life. It was more than a centerpiece. It was the heart of the house now that each of the fifteen hundred bulbs was mirrored in reflective balls and shiny tinsel. I could hear Pixie and Letty in my head, arguing over the placement of each strand of tinsel. The green scent of the tree seemed stronger now that the electric twinkles were going off. It was impressive, but it was missing something. I was wrong about it being complete. It was missing the gifts beneath the tree, and the family to open them.

Now it seemed unreal that a few feet from the tree, I'd killed a man.

Okay, maybe he had not immediately died, but there was no denying I'd started his trip to death. If he had just thought twice before coming here to invade my sanctum, he could have saved himself.

The phone rang incessantly. Reporters. With Christmas shoppers out and about, a follow home robbery was news in Los Angeles; a home owner killing one of two robbers put it on the front page, and now everyone knew my name and history. The lines the reporters were calling were forwarded to the exchange. Only my hotline rang through to the house, and that number was known only to the team and very few friends.

The newspapers identified the decedent as Carlos Chavez, a thirty-two year old single Hispanic who lived in Altadena. The critically injured one was twenty-nine year old Tony Alvarado. He was also Hispanic and a resident of Altadena. He was married and had three kids.

"What a fucking shame. So young!" I told Jack.

"They deserve what they got," Jack insisted.

Ramos called to tell me that neither Carlos or Tony had a criminal record.

"Detective, what the fuck were they doing with rifles and pushing their way in to my house?"

Solé, the lead detective said, "Of course, they had no business doing what they did, but their fingerprints have no record. No service record either. No gang affiliation of any kind."

Melina was over early for her breakfast coffee, again wearing the ugly sweater. She had brought pastries from her chef. Miguel was a little offended until he tasted one, then he wanted the recipe. She told him to call and get it himself.

"Maybe the karate went to Pixie and Letty's heads. Maybe this wouldn't have happened if they hadn't beaten them up, a couple of guys who were just flirting with them. I don't have the right to turn them into bullies," I said. "They could have diffused the situation without beating those guys up. And that's my fault." I know how mixed up that sounded, but my feelings were all over the place.

"It's not your fault. Those guys were rapists in training, or maybe even worse. Let yourself off the hook. You're human. The girls were just defending themselves. Karate probably saved their lives," Melina said. "For their sake, it was better they used karate than the guns in their purses."

I took a deep breath, and told her that Ramos had said neither guy had a criminal record.

Melina shrugged. "So? They never got caught before. Let the cops figure out why they had firearms with them when they followed the girls."

"Good point," I said. "Solé said neither of them had any record. They barely had licenses to drive."

"How do you barely have a driver's license? They're grown men." Melina laughed.

"He said they don't have any record. No gang affiliations. Nothing."

"The newspaper said they're Hispanic, but what does the truth matter when speculation can sell papers?"

After Melina left, I paged Tricia. "I want you to locate the family of Carlos Chavez."

"The guy that didn't make it," she said, recognizing the name. "Sure, Boss. What exactly do I do when I locate them? I'm not an assassin. So that's out. I'm good with pretty much anything else."

"I won't ever need an executioner. Unfortunately, I do a pretty damn good job of that myself."

"Killing is never fun, Boss."

"Have you killed anyone?" I considered her, the cute freckles on her cheeks, the short military cut except for the long bangs. She had the kind of taut muscularity that I associated with professional athletes, even though she'd been out of the military since 1975. Her voice tended a little to hoarseness, which was sexy to me, and if we hadn't already been intimate, I might have been intimidated by her military bearing and lightning reflexes.

"Evacuating the embassy in Cyprus in '74. Evacuating Phnom Penn in '75," she replied. "Some other situations. All when I was in the service."

"I'm sorry to pry," I said.

She shrugged. "Public record."

"Keep it quiet, but I want to pick up the funeral tab, maybe give the family some money. The newspapers say he was single, but who the fuck knows. They didn't look too hard. He may have twenty kids and be shacking up with someone who depends on him. Do it quietly. I can't wipe my ass right now without the newspapers putting it on the front page."

The Times had even posted an interview of Betty. She hadn't said anything except that she was my masseuse, but I felt that bringing her into it was a huge intrusion into my privacy.

"The papers say he's from Altadena, but the cops couldn't find anything about him." I handed Tricia five thousand cash from the safe. "Grease whoever you have to for information. Once you get to them give them this or whatever is left after you pay out what you gotta pay to get the information. I'm willing to give them more."

Tricia wasn't a big talker. She didn't argue orders like everyone else in my life. She didn't give her opinion on everything. She just did the job.

"Got it, Boss."

Tricia returned about the time I was going to tell Miguel what I wanted for dinner. I motioned her toward a chair.

"Breakfast," I told Miguel over the intercom. "Three for dinner." He promised everything would be on the table in half an hour. I turned to face Tricia and Letty, both across from my desk.

"I hope that is okay with you."

Letty gave me a thumbs up.

"Go on," I told Tricia.

"So, I find the parents of Carlos Chavez. They live in Altadena. The house is packed with people. Relatives. Friends, whatever. Everybody's drunk. Doesn't seem like a Christmas party. Doesn't seem like a wake. Just seems like a bunch of drunks. I don't know what the fuck it is. There's a front porch up a few steps. I wait at the door. The mother answers. She introduces herself. I introduce myself. Offer condolences. She says to wait. Shuts the door. The father shows. I offer my condolences again. More introductions. I say I'm there on your behalf. That you'd like to help any way possible. He says to wait. Shuts the door. I'm getting tired of this, but I have this job to do. Still waiting at the door, and I look up to see a herd of drunks rounding the corner of the house. I back off the steps, fast. Next thing I know, I'm surrounded. Almost surrounded."

"I pull back. My gun is out, and I'm pointing it at this burly bastard who is making more threats than anyone else. The wind is blowing. It's cold, and this bastard is wearing a t-shirt that is wet with sweat. He stinks of beer and sweat. I think my gun makes him sweat all the more. The crowd moves away from me when they see the gun. The father tells me that the only thing they want you can't give them. And that's having their son alive. I back my way to the car. It is right on the street. I get in and some drunk jerk comes charging at me like a bull. I peel rubber and get the fuck out of there."

"Are you okay?"

"No one put a hand on me," she said.

"I'm sorry I sent you," I said, getting up and going around my desk. I spun her around, like there might be physical evidence of her ordeal.

"It was nothing Boss. I can handle a bunch of drunks," she said stiffly, pulling herself away. I let my hands drop. "I picked up a bottle that had the father's prints on it. Maybe it can shed some light. I already gave it to Ramos."

"You did handle it. You're here," Letty said.

A bell chimed.

"That's Miguel's dinner," Letty said.

"Let's not keep him waiting."

I had Belgian waffles, pancakes, and fruit. The girls had the same, but chased it with crispy bacon and chorizo.

Like Letty, Tricia was renting one of my apartments. Lately she'd been moonlighting after hours here as security, staying in Letty's old staff room.

"Baby, sleep in the main house tonight in a guest room."

"No, Boss, I love that little place back there."

"I insist."

"Thank you, Boss."

Letty said, "Tricia, when I grow up, I want to be just like you."

Tricia gave her a knowing smile.

"Betty's here, and she's waiting for you two."

"Boss, I'd totally dig that, thank you. And I can pay her."

"She's on the clock for my staff. My treat."

Letty and Tricia went down to see Betty. I planned to take a shower and go to bed, but I went to the den. I had just pried my shoes off and put my feet up. A fire was crackling in the fireplace, and the whole house was scented with pine. My comfortable chair with a good view of the tree, but I closed my eyes, trying to lose the tension of the day. I felt a hand on my foot. Two hands. Someone was massaging my feet. It wasn't Letty. Her touch was much softer. This hand cut straight through to the heart of things. This was...

Without opening my eyes, I said, "Melina?"

"Bingo, Cuz."

Melina straddled my lap and gave me a kiss on the lips. She tasted like tangerine lifesavers and smelled like Mango salsa and cinnamon cookies.

"Is Tricia okay?"

"She's a trooper. She had waffles with Letty and me."

"That was dinner?"

"I had pancakes, too."

"If you didn't work out, you'd weigh four hundred pounds."

"Would you still love me?"

"Yes, no matter what, I love you. Even if you go off and get married. You'll always be my Cuz, my love."

"Hey, what's that about? Trying to get rid of me?"

"Never," she said. "I don't think you'd take to a halter. So I won't put one on you. It's how I feel."

I put one hand on her hip.

"Ah, I can feel how glad you are to see me," she said.

I felt how glad I was to see her too. I knew if I said so much as a word, it would be the wrong one, and she'd disappear, like cotton candy at the first lick.

"If Letty wasn't waiting in the wings, I'd do something interesting. But it's eleven thirty, and a school night." Melina sighed in a way that made me wonder if she'd just come.

"Letty's not waiting. She and Tricia are down in the spa with Betty before Betty runs over to your house."

"You can take my slot tonight, Cuz."

"Are you sure?"

"I'm sure, but first things first."

She was perched over me like a cut peach, with nothing between us but my damn jeans, and both of us ticking up to an explosion. I put both hands on her hips and pulled her down to ride the hard ridge. I moved her roughly against me. She moaned.

Hours later, Betty came upstairs to where I was waiting, in bed. Usually I take massages down in the spa. I could not rest. I kept thinking how unsafe it was for the girls. I thought about the cash in the safes. Maybe it was time to smarten up and better protect the residence. I didn't feel like talking, but made an effort to sound normal.

"How is Tricia?" I asked.

"Asleep," Betty said, looking next to me where Letty was already asleep on one side of my bed. "Like Letty."

As fierce and thorough as Betty's massage was, it did nothing to disturb Letty's slumber.

"I'm a mental wreck," I told her. It was half true, though Melina's surprise visit had eliminated a hell of a lot of tension. "Please fix me."

"With pleasure," Betty said.

I too was asleep when Betty left.

Two messages from Jack Fino were on my machine. I called him back.

"Are you okay now? What have you been up to?"

"I'm okay," I assured him with an excess of enthusiasm. "Sorry I didn't get right back to you. Jack, do you know of a hungry private investigator that has nothing going on in life and is looking for full-time?"

"You still have that pretty girl you introduced me to, Tricia?"

"I do. She's my driver, does public records searches for LAI acquisitions, and she's licensed to pack a pistol so she's also a guard of sorts."

"What do you plan to use this PI for? What skills do you need?"

"I'm going to park him at the entrance to my house during the day, and maybe shift his hours around so he has eyes on the house at night. I need someone reliable, someone more than just a security guard. He needs to have a concealed gun permit or anything else he decides to pack while taking care of business for me. A cool head is also essential, preferably one with some brains, so he can adapt to any other jobs I send him on."

"Good idea. Your property is walled like mine. The vulnerable parts are the gates."

"If someone is out to do harm, the entire property is vulnerable."

Jack agreed.

"Tricia is a sharpshooter, ex-military and takes care of business, but Melina is constantly on my ass about having guards. Sometimes I hire them for when I'm out of town."

"I have a lead for you," Jack said. "Tough as they come. Name's Bruno. Bruno Bruno. The name's a family thing."

"Go on."

"It's someone I use. An ex-sheriff. Reliable. Connected. He's a drinker, but it doesn't get in the way. He's who I call when something difficult comes up. He does it all. He's good at crashing hotel doors to catch a cheater in the sack. Banks use him on tough repossession cases because no one gives this guy any shit when he comes for the car. He's licensed. Has a permit to carry a gun. Divorced. No family. Lives in a back room of his office on First Street in Tokyo Town."

I chuckled. "I guess he watched that movie *Chinatown* one time too many, or read one too many pulp novels. I like Bruno already."

"I'll have him get in touch," Jack said.

In under an hour, Bruno was parked in my office, filling up an easy chair. Caro had led him in while I was taking a call from Jack who was asking if he'd arrived yet. Bruno was a rugged guy, three hundred pounds if he was an ounce. Not a pretty man. He was inch or two shorter than me, and covered in angry muscle that bunched up under his polo shirt, strained his short sleeves, and chunked his thickset neck like a pit bull or Sherman tank turned Homo Sapiens. I could understand that if he went over to a house to repossess a car, the owner would hand him the keys after just one look. His body was stocky and took up a lot of space, but his presence was bigger and took up even more.

I walked around my desk so we could shake hands. His grip was gentle, but his hand was engineered like a car crusher.

"Should I call you Mario or Mr. Luna?"

"Mario is fine. Do I actually have to call you Bruno Bruno?"

"Just one Bruno will do. It's a family name they stick on all the firstborn sons. My old man died a long time ago, so I just go by Bruno. Mr. Fino said you had need of my services." Bruno's voice was deep, rusty, and rumbling like a gravel-filled fork-lift going down a dirt road.

"I need someone full time. I have a PI that is now my driver and runner on legal matters. I'm looking for someone that looks after the house here day and night, depending on what is going on in my life."

"No problem. You got a place for me to sleep?"

"We can work that out, yes."

"What else you need?"

"I want an all around person. When I need you on something, I'll pull you out of the house guard stuff, and you go do it. I'm a short notice kind of guy, but I'll treat you fair."

"What else?"

"I want to know when the funeral will be for the guy I killed. I sent Tricia out there, and they swarmed her like a hive of bees. I need a status report on the guy who lived."

The detective had not called to give me an update. I gave Bruno the few details I had, but the information was sketchy at best.

"Like bees, huh?"

"I sent her to the Chavez's house to offer them some help. She had to pull her pistol to get the fuck out of there because a mob of the dead guy's kin were going to take her down."

"I can do that without having to go back to the house unless you want something to happen there." He was looking right at me. "Fino said I can trust you. I can do anything, Mario."

I returned the stare with a grin. "I like you, Bruno. I think we're going to get along."

"I got a kick out of reading how you handled that guy who shot you and your friend, and how you threw two guys out your apartment window."

"Off the Bunker Towers. Long way down. It was self defense."

"It was intended as a compliment."

"Thanks. I caught that the first time around."

He went off to handle the job. The girls snuck in as soon as he left. They'd been eavesdropping.

"It's cool you have this Bruno now, but why are you interested in the funeral?" Pixie asked.

"It is not just the funeral. I want to dig into both families. I need to know my enemy."

"Enemy?" Pixie asked.

"I think you are reading too much in to this, Boss," Letty said.

"Cops say these two had no rap sheets and were clean with no gang affiliations, but look what happened when Tricia went over there. I'm not reading anything. I need to know where they stand."

"Gotcha," Pixie said, her arms up in surrender. "I don't think the guy that made it is going to be hitting the streets anytime soon."

"Pix, you know better. It's his family, his connections."

"I hope you are mistaken," Letty said. "I hope the family will bury their loved one, and let this pass. And I hope the dude that didn't die is grateful he's alive."

The next morning, the girls were in the office with me when the hotline rang.

"Amor, I'm checking on you." Camila's voice instantly lifted my spirits.

"I'm good. Where are you?"

"Olga and I decided to spend Christmas in Bogota and Pepe will stay in Milan. You are invited along with your team."

"Thank you, Baby, but the timing is off. Pepe invited me to Christmas in Milan and I turned him down, too."

"When he goes to Milan, it is hard to get him out of there, even on Christmas. How are the girls?"

"They're fine. Pixie and Letty are here with me now."

I held out the receiver.

"Hi, Camila," the girls said loud enough for Camila to hear.

"*Que lindas,*" Camila said. "Kiss them for me."

"I will, Babies."

I told the girls the side of conversation they didn't hear.

"Both bitches are highly disappointed you aren't going." Pixie giggled.

"Pixie, easy," I said.

"Okay. Thanks for not going Boss. Let them buy dildos."

Letty laughed. "We can courier them so they get them by Christmas."

"Enough," I said.

They didn't leave when Bruno returned, but introduced themselves, shook his hand, and maneuvered him between them on the sofa across from my desk. He certainly noticed the girls, but they didn't rattle him. He let me know that the funeral was set in two days at Altadena Cemetery. The other guy was out of the hospital, transferred to the jail ward at General Hospital in East Los Angeles. His bail was set at $100,000.[59]

"Good job."

Knowing about the funeral and the whereabouts of the other dude made me feel less vulnerable.

Letty asked, "Bruno, how would you dig sitting out front and keeping an eye on the house?"

"I already beat you to the punch, Babies. I hired Bruno to do just that and to run around when I need him on other stuff."

"Very cool," Pixie said, and Bruno got a high five from both girls.

"Easy shit," Bruno said. "You expecting more unwanted visitors? More shitheads with guns?"

"Could be," Pixie said.

"Bruno, like I told you earlier, I can always hire guards, but I don't want to draw attention. The fucking news vultures are watching the house from above, waiting for the next scoop."

---

[59] $100,000.00 in 1980 had the same buying power as $314,774.45 in 2017

"That will wear off in a day or two."

"Bruno, let's try it for a month. If it works out and you want to stay, I'll hire you full time."

"Deal." We shook hands.

"Letty, show Bruno the quarters in the back house where you used to stay. Tricia is upstairs putting her stuff in the room she uses when she sleeps in the big house."

"Follow me, dude." Letty walked ahead of the big guy. He was so big. I almost laughed. It was a Chihuahua leading a Great Dane.

"Good move," Pixie said.

I thought about the drinking problem that Fino had mentioned. I wouldn't care about the drinking. If it didn't get in the way of his work for Jack, it wouldn't get in the way of his work for me. A hundred[60] a day was reasonable to me for a burly scarecrow pit bull with a license to carry a gun. These days, I paid Tricia more than that. We had moved on from her occasional invoice to regular wages plus commissions.

A while later, Bruno and Letty were back.

"I gotta go home and get some guns. I'll be back in couple hours." Bruno said.

"When you get back, I'll introduce you to Tricia. She's my driver, and handles my security. What do I owe you for the information?"

"Is a hundred good for you?"

I pulled two hundred out. "It's worth more than a hundred," I said, and handed it over.

"Thanks, Mario."

"Call him, Boss," Pixie said.

It was the first we saw of Bruno's teeth. He smiled at Pixie. He had good teeth. With his jaw, he looked like he could bite through a steel pipe.

"Thanks, Boss. I'll be back."

---

[60] $100.00 in 1980 had the same buying power as $314.77 in 2017

While he was gone, I told Tricia about him.

"When we have a case, you can come with us and I won't have to hire a guard or guards to look after the house. When I leave town and you are here, you move in your room in the house like you have in the past and stay here till I get back."

"Boss, I dig it. I'll get him up to speed on the intercom system, the security system, and that alarm you had TJ put in the gate today."

I'd been worried about that. I didn't want her to think I was bringing in a male cop because I didn't think she could handle the job.

When Bruno returned, I introduced them. I left them walking toward the staff building where Bruno had a place to leave his gear, and discussing how this was going to work.

"You know, most big guys like that have tiny dicks," Pixie said. At least she'd waited till he was out of earshot.

"You'd know, bitch."

"Who you calling a bitch, bitch?"

"Girls, I'm not in the mood," I said getting back behind my desk.

"What *are* you in the mood for?" Letty asked.

"Yeah, Boss, what's the mood?"

I grinned. "Food. Wine. Pussy."

Pixie jumped up and down like this was something new. "I'm staying the night," she said.

A chorus of bells and buzzers blasted me from a deep sleep. My head was still foggy-full of wine, Pixie, and Letty, but I hit the bedside lamp and staggered out of bed. The dissonant clamor tore through my ears, and set my heart racing. Burglar alarms, smoke alarms, intercom alert, alarms going off, racket all over the house. Like me, Pixie and Letty had been shocked from sleep and were scrambling into their clothes.

"What the fuck?" Pixie swore, grabbing my arm.

"I smell smoke," Letty said, looking frightened. "The house is on fire."

I smelled it too. My heart was beating so hard that it hurt. I didn't dress with discretion, just grabbed everything I'd had on earlier. Jeans. I reached in my front left pocket. Cash was there. Right rear pocket, my wallet. T-shirt. Sweatshirt. I slipped my feet into loafers. The door to my bedroom swung open, and I saw Tricia silhouetted like a figure at the gates of hell, the sconces behind her backlighting a cloud of smoke that billowed just below the ceiling.

Her voice was sharp, urgent. "Boss, grab a jacket. Exit time. On the double. I'm running ahead. Follow me."

It took a second for her words to register. I grabbed an armful of jackets from my closet, and shoved two of them at the girls. I bundled the girls in front of me, but Pixie hung back a little, and glanced at me with a frightened expression, the jacket gripped in her hands. I jerked it over her hair, like a shawl. By the time I looked at her, Letty had followed suit.

I did the same. "Let's get out, now. Cover your faces."

Tricia was ahead of us, already disappeared down the stairs. The house was still screaming for us to leave. I saw no fire but in the moments we had delayed, smoke had accumulated enough that I had to duck to avoid being choked by it.

"Move!" I said sharply. By the time we got to the staircase, Tricia was halfway across the next room. I realized I had one more jacket, and pitched it to her, low, skittering across the floor. She caught it, and pulled it over her head. I caught a bird's eye view of my den looking like the darkly lit stage set of a horror movie. Aged timbers crackled and popped. One second the evergreen was fit for a *Home and Garden* centerfold, the next it was a torch from hell. The Christmas tree burst into a furious candle, a nightmarish red ghost of a tree, bright flames leaping to the ceiling, eating their way down the wall and across the front of the house.

Pixie reacted to the burning tree, and cringed back, not setting foot on the stairs.

"Trust me," I said. "We will get through this."

"You're the Boss," she said. I could see the terror in her, and also her absolute confidence in me. I only hoped that what I'd said was true.

We could feel the heat, and were separated from Tricia by a river of fire. At least Tricia's way to the front door was clear. The fire was a live thing, skipping across furniture and fabric until the room we overlooked was painted in shades of red and smoke. Safety was on the opposite side of that that fiery impassable no man's land. The front door burst open, and Bruno was there yelling, "Boss, we have a fire! Get out of the house! I'm at the front door!"

I don't know if he saw us, but he saw Tricia.

I yelled a response, shoving the girls ahead of me, at a run, ready to drag Pixie if I had to, but she was cooperating now. No actual flame had reached the stairs yet, and though the heat rolling up the staircase was off-putting, it was the only way out. From the landing, there had been a view of the vast room we would have to cross to get to the door, but the path of fire changed our route to safety from instant to instant. We made it to the ground floor, and I could see glimpses of Tricia, her back to Bruno, standing mere feet from him, looking like she was going to run through the gauntlet of flames to come back for us. Bruno grabbed her from behind. I saw those massive arms of his close around her waist, and her feet came off the ground. She was kicking and screaming and trying to reach something vulnerable. He pulled her outside. I saw her fighting him. Then suddenly, I couldn't. The path ahead filled with solid opaque smoke churning from the inferno, a barricade between us and safety. In front of me, Pixie and Letty were coughing.

"We're going to get through this. Cover your faces. Don't breathe in the smoke. Try to filter air through your sleeve."

I herded the girls in front of me, afraid for them to follow. I wasn't taking a chance on losing anybody.

I remembered the client we'd had in the hotel fire, the one who'd wrapped herself in wet sheets. I wish I'd had that much forethought. I felt a shower of cinders and shards, and the girls probably suffered the same. The heat was all around us. And something else.

"Boss," Pixie coughed without turning back. "Do you smell gasoline?"

I smelled it too. The fumes were unmistakable.

"Keep moving," I said, barely keeping my eyes from closing.

I felt tears seep from the corners of my eyes, squinted, forcing them open, trying to find the way. Fresh air was ahead, but only theoretically. We were stuck in the here and now, dodging flame and searing bits, coughing, lungs afire. Here the smoke hung heavy, with only inches of clear air hugging the floor. Glass shattered, erupting in burning splinters. Bulbs from the tree, windows, glass, splinters sprayed us in flaming shards. I protected the girls as much as I could. It felt like my back was on fire, the heat was so intense. I focused on moving forward. No path to the front door. That whole wall was on fire. We were dodging flaming chairs, tables, and carpeting.

Bruno's and Tricia's disappearance made me fear an ambush outside. We couldn't wait, couldn't hide here. We had to move forward, ambush or not. Through the haze, I glimpsed one of the cars in front, burning.

"There could be a trap out there," I yelled at the girls, propelling them forward. Certain burning death was behind and all around us. Ambush was only a possibility. I made my way toward a window I thought we could reach. We would be okay once we got past the last couch. We inched forward, the fire chasing us forward. We made it past what used to be an end table, then the couch. The way was clear until a wall of fire shot across the carpeting, cutting us off.

"Fuck this!" Pixie screamed.

I heard a crash to our right.

Bruno yelled, "Coast is clear out here." His voice was coming from another direction. From outside, Bruno kicked open the French door to a side yard. He was still yelling. No idea what it was, but it made tracking him easier. Another alarm joined the rest of them.

"Right turn!" I tried yelling back, but it came out more of a cough.

Letty was leading the way, holding Pixie's hand. Pixie reached for me, and I shoved her along.

"Cover your mouth so you can breathe." I refused her hand. "I'm right behind you."

We moved in a group toward the splintered door. No other way to go. Everything was burning. Blazes shot up around us. We were close, but sanctuary looked a million miles away through a sunroom full of smoke and fire. I had been holding my breath, but couldn't any longer. Reflexively sucked a deep lungful of bad air. Choked on smoke. Eyes streaming. Could only guess the girls' condition. Just ahead, most of the glass was gone from the French doors. Bruno plowed his way through, grabbed Pixie and Letty, and dragged them out just as accelerant on the wooden frames ignited. Flames licked across and caught up with me. My coat scraped something, caught on the glass as I stepped through the fire. I felt it tug, and heard the suede rip as I surged through flame into the outside air. Coughed, sucked in cold air. I still smelled smoke, and burning hair. I ran towards Bruno, stomping out flames as I went, not stopping till the December breeze hit my back. Bruno shoved us down to roll. I don't know if any of us were actually on fire, but the cold grass we rolled around on felt better than the flames inside. I surged up on one knee, got up. Saw Miguel coming, then pulled the girls up.

Miguel, dressed in jeans, tennis shoes, pajama shirt, and windbreaker, ran in a slow lope from the staff's quarters. He's a body builder, not a sprinter, and was breathing heavily. He lurched forward, grabbed Letty, looked her closely in the face, and gave her a fierce hug. He tucked her under his arm close to his side, like he was afraid she was going to disappear.

"The rest of the staff went out the back gate to the street but the quarters are safe, so far." Miguel said.

I was filthy, sooty, and hurt in a hundred different places. Glass and burns. The cold air felt good. I looked over at Pixie fisting red, teary eyes.

"Don't do that. It makes it worse."

She grabbed my hand, catching me unconsciously rubbing my own eyes. "I'll stop when you do."

Pixie was facing the house with a terrible expression on her face. "We made it out. I don't see how."

We all turned to face where Pixie was looking. With a dreadful piercing crack, the timbers around the front door broke. A shower of sparks shot out, and beams fell burning to the front porch. I was transfixed, watching my house burn. Everything I'd worked for, up in smoke. Hundreds of hours of Melina's work, all of her decorating, all of the one-of-a-kind furniture. My fabulous unique bed. I felt a horrible loss, and a sense of unreality, nausea twisting my stomach. The crackling fire was eating everything. A voracious animal, a red monster, insatiable. Embers floated in the air around us like burning hail. The girls' cars, my Rolls and the station wagon were in their usual spots on the circular driveway. Like in slow motion, I saw a timber fall across the Rolls. It began burning.

Tricia shoved at me.

"Wake up, Boss!"

"I wish I could."

Pixie grabbed my arm, pulled, and poked me in the side, and I finally looked away. I saw Letty's teeth were chattering, my jacket huge on her, and Miguel still attached to her like he was afraid she would blow away. Cinders floated down all around us, sparks of light. I brushed one off my sleeve.

"Okay, we're too close to the house. Let's get to the gate," I said. We took off at a run, a bedraggled mess, all in shades of gray and black, nothing but sooty rags. The girls had purses flapping over their arms, no doubt with weapons inside. It was absurd. The ruined clothing, and the purses. I'd helped plenty of desperate families, more than I could count, but nothing in my life had prepared me to be the one losing everything. I focused on the run, my lungs strained by smoke exposure. Behind us, something exploded. Once.

Twice. Then a series of smaller explosions. I figured it was the cars, but did not stop to look. We were all heaving and coughing. At least the girls fanatic attachment to their guns had retained for them not only their guns but also their wallets. My sense of time was skewed. It took hours and seconds to reach the end of the driveway. Pixie put her hand on the gate and rattled it, looking at me. I didn't know if electricity to the gate had been burned out. If so, I'd have to find the manual crank, but only Memo knew where that was. Lucky for me, when I pressed the button inside the property line, the gate slid open. We all went through.

"How did it start?" Letty asked. Her eyes were pink, her tears making rivulets through the soot on her face. Her face was flushed like a bad day at the beach. So was Pixie's.

"Arson." Bruno said. His eye was looking bruised where Tricia had made contact.

"Did you see the bastards that did this?" Pixie asked.

Bruno nodded. "Three of them."

"Where were you?" Pixie asked. Her fists were clenched, and she was screaming. "Where the hell were you?"

"At my post," Bruno said, flushing. "I was on the front porch next to the front door. I'm guessing they jumped the gate, ran up to the house and threw their Molotov cocktails. I got blinded, couldn't get a shot and that's all the time they needed."

"I heard the glass break, but I thought I was dreaming. Fuck, I should have been out here with Bruno." Tricia was in better shape than the girls and me. She turned to Bruno. "Sorry about your eye."

I stopped dead. I was furious at the fire, and at my so-called guard's incompetence. Right or wrong I tore into him. "From the front door. You were at the front door? From the front door, how could you not notice three men running up the driveway?"

"I didn't hear them, Boss. I didn't see them."

"It's a damn fucking shame," said Pixie, turning on Bruno.

"What is?" Bruno asked.

"That you are blind, deaf or drunk," Letty said.

"I haven't been drinking."

"I'm sure the cops will want to talk to you. I'll pay your for your time. But this is it. We're done."

"Boss, don't do this."

"Bruno, you failed me. Trial's over. We're done."

I was being generous. Pepe would have killed a guard for allowing anyone to get close enough to throw incendiaries and destroy the residence.

"Come back for your things when things calm down," Letty said. "I won't let anyone in your room back there."

"Good riddance to bad rubbish," Pixie said nastily.

"Tricia, go round up all of our help and bring them here.'

"I've got this. Back in a jiff."

She took off for the staff exit, following the street alongside my property at a ground-eating run. The jacket billowed around her, like a parachute, but didn't slow her down. The housekeepers and their husbands would be outside the back gate.

I stood facing the house, facing the direction of the night on fire. Behind the gate, behind a stand of trees behind which we could only make out flashes of red, I knew the house was entirely engulfed in flames. I could not see it, and night hid the smoke, but I could hear. Fire belched out a boisterous roar, cracking and whooshing. I never knew that heat could make a sound like that, but there it was, rumbling, and hungry, and insatiable. For an instant, the wind changed, blowing toward us the harsh odor of my life on fire. The girls started their third or fourth round of coughing. The smoke was harsh in my eyes and nose. The wind changed again, but I was full of smoke and misery. I heard the sirens of the arriving firemen, and left the gate open.

"Boss, your house," Pixie said, looking devastated. She was shivering, still wearing the coat like head gear. I pulled it off her, shook off the glass, and slipped it over her shoulders.

"Ease up," I said. "You're safe." I put my arm around her, my other arm around Letty.

Two fire trucks arrived together, and turned inside the gates disgorging their crews. It was like watching an opera or a ballet, with every note singing the song of another fireman, or another action. It looked like chaos, but they worked together like an oiled machine. They knew what they were doing. Water hoses, men, more men, more trucks, some of them parking outside the gates, running towards the house. A couple of medics separated from the organized chaos and came toward us. All of us were covered in soot and cinders, our clothing bearing varying degrees of damage.

"Is anyone hurt?"

Tricia replied, "No burns,.I'm good."

Letty and Pixie were coughing again.

"I can give you some oxygen and make that cough better," one of the medics offered.

"Pixie, Letty, go ahead."

"Nah, I'm cool. Thanks," Letty said.

"Do it."I commanded.

"Only if you do," Pixie coughed at me, being her usual self.

"Fine."

We sat on the back of the ambulance, breathing oxygen through masks for a couple of minutes. I suffered through their ministrations so the medics could check over the girls without an argument. My young medic Max barely looked old enough to be out of high school, but he was efficient.

I pulled off the mask. "Max, I'm good. I have five workers out here," I said, pointing out Miguel and the two couples that worked for me. "Please check them."

"As soon as I'm done with you," he said seriously.

"I'm fine," I said, handing over the mask.

As the medics brought my staff over, Tricia came over to us. "Boss," she said, "Go to Melina's with everyone. I got this." I had not noticed her return. I could hear sirens coming closer. More trucks, more fire fighters. A patrol car pulled up, then another one, lights flashing.

I managed a smile. "Trish, I like my jacket on you. Keep it."

I got a smile back. She was a little more muscular than Letty and Pixie, but not so big that my leather jacket fit.

"Miguel, when you guys are done here, come to Melina's. No rush. Have them check all of you."

"Boss, there was no fire or smoke back there."

"I'll see you at Melina's. Bring the others."

I crossed the street with Pixie and Letty. In my car, I kept a remote for Melina's gate; but we were on foot. I used the gate's intercom.

"Melina my house is on fire. Open the gate."

No one replied, but the gate immediately slid open. We had started up the driveway when my staff came through the gate behind us.

Melina came out at a run, her nightgown and slippers flapping, and reached us half way down the drive. "Fire? What do you mean fire?" Melina screamed. The girls converged on Melina, frightened, babbling explanations and desperation.

I pointed toward the house. From here it was all but invisible, but the smell was unmistakable.

"Baby, my house. It's burning."

I felt like crying.

"Everything will be okay," she said.

Melina took my hand.

Epilogue

Christmas that year I had less than I'd had for many years. I was down-hearted, but things could have been much worse. No one had been seriously injured in the fire. Life did not end with my house, though I was at odd ends without somewhere to hang my hat. For the rest of the year, I bounced between staying with my loved ones, and living in a hotel. Eventually I roughed it in a little 5000 square foot cottage while I got my life back on track.

I was plagued by unanswered questions. Who had gone after Jake and Oscar? Who had gone after my house? I still had to hunt out who was targeting me. But that's a whole other story.

About the Author

George Hatcher is an entrepreneur with a gift for business and storytelling. Whether he's traveling the globe as a consultant/strategist for lawyers in high profile wrongful death cases, running one of his many enterprises, or at home with Molly amid the birds and cats in California, he's always got his eye on the next project. He does a whole lot more than what is mentioned here.

A longer bio is on his website at: www.georgehatcher.com/bio/bio.html